WILD HORSES

A NOVEL

AMY PENDINO

ISBN 979-8-218-09078-4
Library of Congress Catalog Number 2022920529
Printed in the United States of America

Cover design and interior design by Claire Brown

Desire is a wild horse to be tamed.
Guy Davenport

Finally he said that among men there was no such
communion as among horses and the notion that men
can be understood at all was probably an illusion.
Cormac McCarthy

Blame it or praise it, there is no denying the wild horse in us.
Virginia Woolf

PROLOGUE

The asphalt unspooled like a flat metal gangplank.

Where it split, a decision would be made. One route, promising ease and independence, offered a way to bypass continuing struggle.

Chances were that the danger keeping pace could be avoided. As long as they honored timetables, kept communication to a minimum, used only trusted contacts and abandoned buildings, there was practically no way to get caught.

Scarlet traced a thready line across the horizon, red smudging the tar with dull reflection. Sunrise. A new morning, nineteen miles still to go.

What was that old saying, 'red sky in the morning, sailor take warning'?

By the time they'd hidden the trailer behind the vacant pole barn, the sun had slunk away too.

Most of the product stayed wrapped in plastic. Moisture would damage it as well as any future business. The bricks weren't heavy and stacked upon each other neatly, both behind the false door as well as under the barn's decaying floor.

Once the load was hauled in, arranged, and covered by a tarp, they reinserted the old floorboards over the hole. A shovelful of dust, artistically scattered, provided camouflage. No one would be able to tell, at a glance, what lay underneath.
Not that anyone would look: this place, out in the middle of farm country, was hidden by a square windblock of ancient trees and scrub brush and bordered by endless fields. It was just one of the county's many vacant structures, a collection of sheds and outbuildings and barns deserted to decay, empty and forgotten.

No one would ever know.

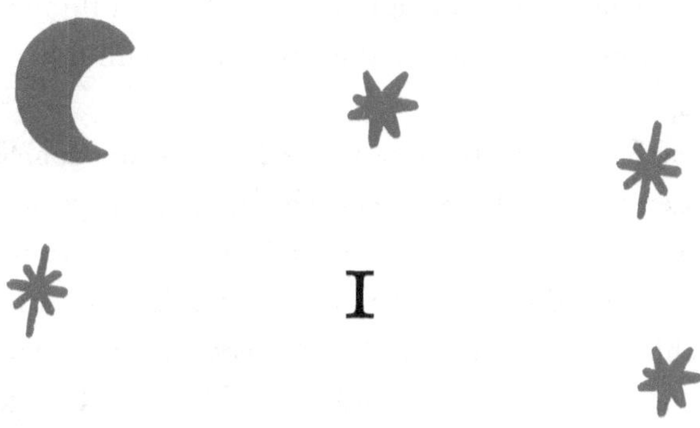

I

Summer, 2004

DANI NEEDED COFFEE. Susie's Café, the town's diner and central meeting place, provided it, as well as updates on the local news: who was planting what, who was getting married (and why), what the local eccentric was up to. The important stuff.

That morning, the café was so crowded there was only one vacant stool at the front counter. Dani squeezed in to wait for Donna, her friend since she first moved to Crestview. Donna managed the café: if the lights were on, Donna was inside.

Elsa Dorn perched on the stool to her left, complaining about rubber canning rings. A beefy guy whose T-shirt looked a size too small took up all the space to her right. He wiped a folded slice of toast around the yolk on his breakfast plate, scanned Dani up and down, then stuffed the bread into his mouth.

Disgust made her lip curl and her eyes narrow. Dani didn't need the coffee that badly. She stood to leave when a white ceramic mug with her name on it plopped down in front of her.

"You meet Jim yet?" Donna beamed at the man through fresh lipstick before moving along the counter to refill other diners' coffee cups.

Dani sat. She took a sip and considered Donna's reaction. She had to have seen the boorish look the man had given Dani, yet she hadn't uttered a peep. It wasn't like Donna to ignore such sexist behavior.

The man rotated his stool to face Dani, bracketing her between the V of his thick legs. "Haven't had the pleasure." He slid his open hand along the countertop toward her. A faint blue X marked the inside of his wrist. "Jim Kelly."

Coffee seeped back up into Dani's throat. She was pinned between the man's thighs. She spun herself the opposite direction, her knee pushing the man back toward the counter, to free herself from his crude confinement.

He chuckled and withdrew his hand.

Donna returned the carafe to its burner. "What'cha up to today, Dan?" She collected Jim's plate and dirty utensils. "Anything promising on the horizon?"

Again, Dani didn't know if Donna saw how Jim had trapped her: her expression gave nothing away. Dani felt paranoid, like she was the only one to sense danger, the sole witness to the rude behavior the man so casually exhibited.

"Thought I'd check the job board at the feed store," she choked out. "See if anyone's hiring."

"Hope you find something soon. Hate to see you have to give up and go back to the Cities." Donna's blunt assessment, delivered in her usual no-nonsense style, stung a bit, but Dani didn't want to get into it, not with the man next to her monitoring their conversation.

A bell rang from the kitchen. Donna left them to retrieve the order, toting the dirty dishes with her.

"So, ya looking for a job?" The man had found his in.

"Yep." Dani kept her reaction flat. Neutral.

"You ever drive a semi?" he asked.

"Um-hmm." Repelled by the way the guy persisted, she didn't elaborate.

He waited anyhow, one side of his mouth lifted in a cocky smile, for her to continue.

Dani closed her eyes, briefly, then sighed. "I help the guys in the fields sometimes; take a load or two out on the side roads for them. I can drive, but I don't really have the right license."

"Got a job for ya, if you're interested." The man leaned toward her. She could smell his strong cologne, a mixture like sharp spice and engine oil, slick and pervasive. "Need someone to drive a trailer for me. Short mileage, to Missouri. Once or twice is all."

"Don't think so, thanks." Donna hadn't come back yet, but Dani couldn't wait for her. She stood and dug in her pocket for change.

"First trip's not till next month." He lowered his voice. "Pays cash."

Despite her aversion to him, Dani found herself interested in the guy's offer. "What are you hauling?"

"Market stock."

Her clenched teeth muted her response. "Nope. I don't think I could do that." Dani shivered. "I'm used to grain. You know—dry product. Not stock." She crossed her arms over her chest. "And what if one got sick, or I had to pull over?" She didn't want to be the one to drag a bunch of living creatures to their deaths.

His chuckle sounded fake. Patronizing. His pupils were so large and black that Dani could see herself, pale and uncertain, in their reflection.

"They make the trip fine. Done it myself, plenty of times. It's just I got something else going when they're s'posed to come through."

He stood and hitched up his jeans, thumbs through the belt tabs, then placed a crisp bill on the counter. "Tell Donna, ya change your mind. It's easy money."

He left through the back door, the one that exited the kitchen. The one Donna used.

♦♦♦

When she first moved to Iowa after 9/11, Dani leased a small section of land and tried farming it. She enjoyed some success with field corn, but then she'd rolled her truck and injured her shoulder. Since she couldn't handle the farm work anymore, she was on the lookout for a new source of income.

Donna kept her ears open, too, but there weren't many paying positions this far out in rural Iowa.

In the meantime, Donna kept urging her to find something useful to do. She thought Dani should get a horse, that brushing and walking one would be good company and great therapy for her shoulder.

Donna had never had a horse before, herself. Dani hadn't either, but her grandpa did, and Dani spent many summer hours on and around his old gelding. While Donna's idea was good in theory, the extra work and money required to keep one kept Dani from consenting to the suggestion.

But when Dani got home and checked her old answering machine that afternoon, a message informed her that her friend's plan was still firmly on track. She and Donna were going to a horse auction the next day.

Barreling down Highway 8 through the bright morning sunshine, Dani figured it was as good a time as any, with just the two of them in the car together, to broach a subject that had captured her curiosity. She'd considered excuses for how Donna had disregarded the man's brutish behavior at the café, but none satisfied her. She knew asking her directly would probably result in hurt feelings or disagreement, so Dani approached the subject a different way. "So, Donna. How's your love life?"

Surprising them both, Donna laughed. "Not much in Crestview to choose from, is there?" She signaled, then turned off the highway onto a gritty side road.

"How about Jim? The guy you introduced to me yesterday? He seemed pretty into you."

Donna didn't have a quick reply. After a moment, though, she offered a hint. "He's okay. Different, you know, but he's got a good income and he's not a farmer, so that's a plus."

"He can make a living by trucking?"

"He does pretty good." Donna changed tactics. "But how about you? How's your love life, out here in the sticks?"

"I don't have one. Obviously." Dani looked out the passenger side window. The subject was usually a non-starter for her, but because she'd used this trip to get her question addressed, it was only fair for her to reciprocate. If she could figure out where to start.

Donna barged ahead. "Well you did, I know that. I know about that one guy, the one that died after you moved here. What was his name again?"

"Geoff."

"Geoff. Tell me again, why did you two break up?"

Dani shifted her hips on the worn seat, trying to find a spot with more padding. "He was an addict. Heroin." She remembered a timely detail. "And he called it 'horse'. The heroin, I mean."

"Yikes. I remember now." Donna slowed a bit as the road curved. "You must have dated other guys, though, right?"

The sun slanting into their faces from this direction was animated by tiny dust particles. Dani watched the dancing, twisting spirals and thought about her reply. She'd known Donna long enough now to consider her a good—if maybe her only—friend.

She spilled her secret. "Yea, there was another guy."

"You go out for a long time?"

"Not so long." She twisted her hands together before resting them on her lap. "He was really handsome—an older guy, someone from work—but it didn't work out." Dani added another thought. "Not in the way I wanted, at least."

"What happened? Was he married?"

"How'd you know that? Did I tell you about him already?"

Donna's chuckle was soft. "Nope. But when you talk about him like that, in that tone, or whatever… Well, you don't have to be from the big city to smell a rat."

"You're right. He was a rat." Dani tilted her head to her shoulder to release the tension there. "He was probably the biggest reason I had to move away, to tell the truth. Things between us were great, for a while: expensive dinners, and . . . you know . . . but it, we, never really progressed. We got to where you'd expect a relationship to go, but it—he—stopped. We stopped."

"What happened? How'd you find out?"

"A secretary from the office next door found out we were dating. I guess she knew the guy's wife." Dani, struck by the energy their conversation had stirred up, felt shocked that she was still bothered by what she thought she'd finished and put away. "I walked into the break room one day and all the girls stopped talking. They just sat there and looked at me until she, the wife's friend, spoke up. She made things pretty clear."

"You didn't have any idea he was married?"

"No, I really didn't. He didn't wear a wedding band, and he never left the office early like he had a reason to get home. He was good to me, and fun, and, well, I thought he loved me. He always answered when I'd call, but then again, I didn't call him that often."

The dancing dust motes, calmer now, had mostly sunk back down to the floor mats.

"Did your parents know, or your friends?" But Donna changed the subject midstream, before Dani could answer. "You know what, you never talk about your friends back home. Did you even have any?"

"Rude!" Dani sniffed. She was only half-joking. "I had friends. Sort of."

Donna nodded at a weathered sign ahead, advertising the proximity of the auction house, but kept her thoughts to herself.

"I guess my friends were the ones I worked next to, before I left, I mean. The girls I knew in high school all disappeared after graduation, and Richfield's so big, I didn't really run into any of them after that, you know?" She shrugged. "I think my mom used to wonder if I was lonely, but she didn't push it. They've never wanted to get too far into my private business."

"Huh," Donna's reaction was a feminine version of a grunt. "Wish my mom would've respected mine! She was always asking me about my friends or boyfriends, about my plans or what I'd be doing over the weekend." She sighed. "All the same, I miss her."

"I miss my parents, too. I thought they'd be upset when I said I wanted to move to Iowa and learn to farm, but they took the news like no big deal, just 'good luck, let us know how it works out', things like that."

"They were good about coming down after your accident, though, Dani. You know they love you, the way they moved your bed downstairs, doing the cooking and all…"

"You're right, I know they do." She thought she might as well go all-in, at this point. "But I don't mind being alone. And I'm not, really; I've got you. And the dog!"

Donna didn't laugh, as Dani expected her to, steering them from the gravel road toward the auction house parking lot.

♦♦♦

Every truck in the lot was American made, patriotic decals prominent on most back bumpers. There were hardly any places left. A sliver of space next to a handicapped spot up front looked too small, but Donna squeezed her Honda in, neatly arranging the two right-side tires precisely on top of the painted lines.

A woman with stringy hair slouched in an old hatchback on the other side. Her thin, blotchy face shot them a dirty glare.

Donna glared back. "I'm not over the line on your side, am I, Dani?" Her voice was loud on purpose. "Open your door and check."

Dani climbed out and peered down. "You're good."

"Thought so. Some people are so judgmental." Donna slammed her door and beeped the lock twice. An energetic, task-driven mode had replaced her earlier contemplative mood. "Let's go."

The woman in the hatchback raised her middle finger at them before sliding out of sight beneath the dash.

They joined the line of people threading out from the entrance. Spread low and dark like a dirty puddle, gray metal covered every surface of the squat building. Iron-piped corrals fanned out from the back. Miles of triple-stranded wire fencing hemmed the entire property.

"I didn't expect—" Dani struggled to gather her thoughts. "That lady? She was definitely on something."

Donna, checking her phone, didn't reply.

"I didn't think I'd ever see that here, like back in the Cities, I mean," Dani clarified, hoping for a response.

Donna didn't take the bait.

They were quiet as the line inched forward.

The metal entry was a passageway to loud country music, burnt popcorn, feed caps, and ponytails. Every backside was encased in denim, the female pockets embellished with rhinestones or fancy stitching.

Once inside the crowded building, Dani struggled to keep up with Donna. She watched from a distance as her friend's hair took a right and disappeared.

Dani turned at the same spot and entered the grandstand. The din inside smacked her like an open palm. The auctioneer, bantering with the audience, directed their attention to the stock below them. Boisterous responses and laughter goaded him on.

"Two-hunner-now-two-hunner-now-Larry-you-gonna-let-him-best-you-again? Two-ana- quarter- two-ana-quarter-don't-let-him-ride-Hank-he's-a-snake-ina-grass . . ."

In the arena, a group of eight to ten horses rushed around the pen like eddies of water swirled in a bucket. Their worried snorts and whinnies bounced against the building's dark edges.

"Dani! Yoo hoo! Up here!" Donna's shout cut through a break in the patter. She waved from the middle of the bleachers.

Turning to climb the cement staircase, Dani missed a step and lost her balance.

A strong grip steadied her, letting go the moment she could stand again. "Watch yourself."

Dani felt her cheeks glow.

"You hurt?"

"No, I'm alright. Thanks for the help."

The man's brown eyes squinted. "Shopping for anything in particular?"

"Not really. How about you?"

"Yep." His gaze swept across the lines of people packed into the bleachers.

"Hey, thanks again." She smiled as she turned for Donna's row. "Good luck today."

The man dipped his chin and returned her smile before climbing on to the upper level.

Dani had to bump past a number of hefty farmers to get to the narrow seat her friend had scavenged.

"What's the procedure?" Dani directed her question to Donna, but a skinny guy on the other side butted in to answer.

"The auctioneer's up to Hip 12," he said.

Each horse in the corral below wore a round white numbered sticker plastered onto its rump.

"Bunch of nags, you ask me. I'm Adam." The guy twitched. "And you are . . . ?"

Dani tried not to stare at the man's gray teeth. "I'm Connie."

"Who's your friend?"

Donna snorted. "You can call me Candy," she shot out. "And I'm engaged."

"That don't bother me none." He winked one bloodshot eye at Dani, turned back to the action, and continued his monologue.

Dani bent to Donna's ear. "Why the heck did you sit next to him?" she hissed.

"The space was open. Guess we know why."

"So why do I have to sit by him?"

"He's more your type." Donna smirked.

Dani rolled her eyes.

From her other side, Adam babbled on, oblivious to their private conversation. "What ya looking for?" he asked. "A worker or a rider?"

Donna ignored the question, so Dani fielded it. "A pet, I guess. Something gentle I can mess with."

"Ya see that little one, in the back? The one the others keep runnin' into?" He leaned into Dani. "That one'll be goin' with me. No one's gonna bid on that. That thing's bony and trips over itself. Good for nothin' but dog food."

His comment snared Dani's attention. "What do you mean, 'dog food'?"

"I take the leftovers, the ones that don't sell, bring 'em down to Texas. A plant across the border takes 'em. Don't matter the condition."

"They use these horses for dog food meat?"

"Any kinda meat. People in China love that stuff." He sniffed and ran a dirty hand under his nose. "Ain't my business. No one wants 'em. They ain't good for nothin'."

Dani's throat grew thick. "Donna, did you know about this? That they kill the ones that don't sell?"

"Hon, horses have to work to earn their keep. Just like cattle. People can't afford to feed stock that don't work. No one has that kind of money." She tsked. "Too many people think they're gonna breed the next Derby winner or the best cutting horse, but they end up with the second or fifth best or worse. No good. Some end up here, where there's a chance they'll find a new home. But if no one buys them…" She shrugged.

Tears clouded Dani's vision, her words stuck somewhere deep inside her.

"It's a better death than starving, Dani. You've seen those farms on TV, where the owner leaves and the animals just die?"

"But what a waste!" Dani finally found her voice. "That can't be right!"

"And that's why we're here, darlin'. This is where we find your new project."

In the arena, two cowboy types eased open one of the green metal panels, and the lot of horses they'd been watching streamed out of the corral through the gap.

"Where do they go now?" Dani wondered.

Donna, looking at her cellphone, didn't hear her.

Adam didn't respond.

A guy from the row in front answered her over his shoulder. "They go back to their pens and wait for the new owners to come around, pay, and pick 'em up."

"What about the ones that don't sell?"

"Your friend's right. They go to a kill pen."

"A kill pen?"

"Yep." He scratched the hair poking through the back opening of his cap. "It's better to let them go that way than to starve or misuse them."

Dani had no idea such a practice existed. She'd assumed animals had places to go when they didn't or couldn't work anymore, like the "going to the farm" phrase parents used when exasperated with a child's unruly puppy.

A new group of horses was prodded forward to the metal corral. Like the first lot, this frightened pack also moved in a group, individual members cutting inside to keep away from the grandstand of noise, color, and smell.

Dani sat up tall in her seat and watched, but her thoughts were on the horrible journey many of these animals had ahead of them, miles down a hot highway to a kind of death she didn't want to contemplate.

The auctioneer started up again, and people began bidding. Several of the stronger, fleshier horses—the ones Dani could see directing or reversing the flow—were the horses people wanted. The bid amounts grew by tiny increments, but the winning bids weren't high. Most went for less than $500.

It was still a better fate than what awaited the animals that trailed the pack, the ones that got jostled or run into, the ones that looked ribby, the ones with white-ringed eyes. Those, the crowd dismissed.

Dani knew then that these were the horses going to Mexico, the horses Adam would take when he headed South.

♦♦♦

More groups of horses were presented, examined, and dismissed. The stress of watching this process–witnessing the horses' fear, their bravery, their spirits as each animal's fate was determined–came to a head as the auctioneer announced the final lot.

"I'm ready to go." Dani stood and swiped off the seat of her jeans.

"Give me a minute." Donna hit a button on her phone with one manicured nail, snapped down the screen, and dropped the device into the cavern of her purse. "How 'bout we check out the backside?"

"What's that?"

"It's where they keep the horses."

Dani could only imagine what waited there. "Um, no thanks, I'd rather–"

Trying to waylay Dani's discomfort, Donna reframed her suggestion. "Most of them are probably gone already, but maybe we can find one that'll suit you."

"Maybe." Dani replied, but she was not convinced. "I'll follow you."

She'd seen how big the animals were as they circled the corral, how powerful and dangerous they could be. Despite the temptation to save one, she'd decided to give the whole project a pass.

She pushed the hair off her forehead and watched Donna descend the first set of steps as she planned how to tell her she'd changed her mind.

One level below them, the man who'd helped her earlier came through, trailing a few yards behind Adam like a shadow. They disappeared through the grandstand exit.

Donna turned and called for Dani to hurry and catch up.

◆◆◆

On the backside, lines of metal fence panels formed makeshift stalls that crisscrossed the enclosure. Maybe half of the pens were empty. A few horses called and squealed, twisting in their small enclosures to avoid capture; the rest stood quietly, waiting for whatever came next.

Those who'd purchased horses had their bills of sale in hand or in their back pockets. Through the windows and the open sides of the dim cavern, they could see the trailers lined up outside, waiting to load their new acquisitions.

We don't have a trailer, Dani realized. *If we don't have a way to get one home, maybe there's nothing to worry about.*

She stood taller and took a big breath, relieved.

"See that gal there?" Donna's voice nudged her attention to a stout woman working a horse inside one pen. "That's Roxie. I went to school with her. I always wondered where she ended up."

They drew closer to watch the pair. "S'okay, girl. You're a good girl," the woman chanted, her words a smooth cadence that matched the horse's strides around its pen.

The animal's wide nostrils heaved and flapped; dark patches of sweat appeared on its thin chest and ribs. The woman didn't give up: when the horse switched directions, the woman did too, placing herself at the animal's hip, out of kicking range.

The animal circled around and around the pen like a merry-go-round ride. Finally, it quit.

The woman stopped too, instantly; after a moment, she gently stepped toward the mare.

The horse backed away, bumped itself into the metal fencing, and reared on its hind legs.

Dani watched intently to see how the woman would respond.

She didn't, other than to raise her arm and track the horse around the pen once again. She didn't look upset or frustrated with the time it was taking to get the animal's halter on her.

Maybe I can do this, Dani thought. *Maybe it's a matter of patience, not force. I could–*

"You interested in a horse?"

The woman's question cracked Dani's contemplation, startling her. Dani looked to Donna, but she'd gone off somewhere, leaving Dani alone.

The woman inside the pen laughed, a light and sprightly sound completely at odds with the focused concentration she'd shown with the horse. She strode over and stuck her hand through the fence bars.

"Hey there." Her face was freckled and rosy. "I'm Roxanne. Roxie."

Dani met her handshake. "Dani." She pulled back, though, when the orange horse snorted.

Embarrassed by her reaction, she blurted, "I can't believe how great you are with this horse. It's like you have a special language with her."

Roxie leaned forward to be heard. "Not 'great,' really. Just stubborn." She grinned.

"Have you always had horses? Worked with them, I mean."

"Yep. Started training them when I moved to South Dakota with a fella who turned out to be worth less than the horse I brought with me. He left. I stayed."

The woman's forthright honesty surprised Dani. Maybe South Dakotans had a different set of small-town rules than Iowans. In Crestview, most didn't give information out directly, but while they waited to get it, they weren't above casting out a few nets.

"So, you here to buy?" Roxie nodded at the mare. "I thought I could find a home for this one, but no one's interested. Apart from the meat market, I mean." Her eyebrows came together.

"What's her story? Is she a beginner's horse?"

"I don't know much about her. She'd been kept out back behind some drug house. My neighbor found her after hearing her; seems she hadn't eaten for a while. The house was abandoned. Her, too, I guess." Roxie shook her head. "He fed her, but he couldn't keep her. When he heard I was bringing some stock here to sell, he asked me to bring this one, too." Roxie shrugged. "She needs lots of TLC, but she's got a sweet personality. Are you interested?"

"I don't have much money," Dani admitted. "And I've never had a horse before. But I'd hate to see her go to . . ." She grimaced. "I could give her a good home." Donna's words echoed through her thoughts. "I might not ever ride her, but I'd brush her and work with her. She'd be safe with me."

Roxie opened the stall gate. "C'mon in, then," she gestured. The sparkle in her eyes gave Dani confidence. "I'll show you what you'll need to know to get started. When can you bring her home?"

2

THE SHOULD HAVE BEEN A BETTER WAY to get the horse back to Crestview.

Donna was so pleased to volunteer Jim's help, though, that Dani caved. Next time, she told herself, she'd pay better attention to her instincts.

Tracing the same route back to the auction house that she and Donna had taken the day before, Dani observed the couple's interaction. Their conversation and the way they kept touching each other confirmed their relationship.

Dani looked out her window and tried to ignore their flirtation. She thought about what she'd learned about horses growing up, from her grandpa and from library books. Hopefully, it would be enough.

The miles passed in snapshots, like slides from an old projector. Each glimpse was a cousin to the last, featuring green fields, swooping power lines, and ditch grass, bent and dusty. Other trucks hauling trailers down the highway reminded Dani of updated wagon trains, lines of mechanical horsepower toting stock or produce or mail over the same track cut into the sod a century ago.

Reaching the auction house, they parked behind the building alongside the other trucks and trailers. Dani trailed the couple inside to the horse stalls on the arena's backside. Clangs, snorts, whinnies, and human voices swirled within clouds of dust pounded free by the many feet crossing the powdery surface. The musky scent of sweat, combined with the odors of grass hay and animal droppings, was sharpened by the day's rising temperatures.

Their goal was to get the horse home before the day grew too hot.

A white card affixed to one stall displayed Dani's information, marking the horse inside as hers. The mare stood close to the aisle and kept a watchful eye on the humans and horses that went by. When Dani reached through the metal panel to pet her, though, she spun away, stomping a hind foot. She didn't seem impressed that Dani had come to save her from the kill pen.

"Don't take that the wrong way, miss." A young man, the heels on his boots elevating him to a six foot height, clomped past. "She's kickin' flies, not you. She likes you—I can tell." His words were as creased and showy as his tight, ironed blue jeans.

Dani didn't believe him, that the mare liked her. She wondered if that line worked on "girls" of other ages. She followed him to a card table marked "Sales" and took out her ID to show the auction steward.

The horse's name was recorded as "For The Long Haul" on the paperwork. She was an old Thoroughbred racehorse.

Dani's heart rate accelerated.

She remembered reading that the breed was high strung and nervous, not the typical trail horse or backyard pet.

Instead of returning to the animal she now officially owned, Dani detoured to a rust-stained water fountain. Several gulps of lukewarm water didn't help. It was too late to do anything about the fact that a racehorse was coming home with her. She told herself she'd better figure out a way to make it work.

Donna and Jim, engrossed by a flashy blond horse a few sections away, didn't see her return. Dani figured it was her best chance to properly introduce herself to her horse, alone, without their advice or scrutiny. She opened the gate to her horse's stall and crossed toward the mare in what she hoped was a quiet and nonthreatening manner.

"Hi, girl. How are you today?"

The mare's ears flicked back as if to hear Dani's voice better. Or maybe she was getting ready to kick–wasn't that what her grandpa once said, that horses flattened their ears when they were mad?

Dani pivoted to the gate. She'd inadvertently left it open.

Chastising herself, she slapped it closed. Peering out from the corral to the aisleway, Dani didn't see the others; she hoped they hadn't noticed her gaffe.

She reminded herself that the horse was just a horse, like Grandpa's old Steve, like other horses people all over the world owned and enjoyed and interacted with every day. No big deal. She sent up a quick prayer, took a deep breath, then counted three steps toward the animal.

This time, the mare showed Dani both eyes. Big dark eyes fringed with long black lashes stared at her as if weighing her value. The horse inhaled, ribs moving like thin snakes under her skin. She swished her tail.

The mare was judging her, trying to determine if Dani was safe.

Dani swallowed the lump in her throat and found herself taking another step, holding her hand out so the mare could see it. She kept her voice quiet.

"I'll be your friend, girl. I'll be kind to you."

The mare blinked and sighed, a whoosh of air released like a heavy burden put down. She lowered her head and edged one front foot toward Dani, stretching her nose to sniff Dani's outstretched hand.

Dani wished she'd have thought to bring a treat—a carrot or a piece of sugar. Something she could give to the horse to show her she was a good person.

She had nothing but her open hand.

The mare took a full step her way. Then, as softly as a drape of silk, she whispered her lips across Dani's palm like a kiss.

A warm glow spread across Dani's chest like a soothing balm. She was no longer afraid.

"What's your name, girl? What should we call you? '107' doesn't really suit you, I don't think. Long Haul? Holly?"

Dani told her horse about her new home and Cody, the dog. She described her barn and explained how she'd have to tote water because she didn't have a trough. Dani asked in advance for the forgiveness she knew she'd need because she'd never had a horse before.

"But it looks like you won't mind too much," she added. "At least you won't be dead. And anything I mess up has to be better than that."

Jim's voice, thrown like a concrete block through their thin veil of privacy, interrupted their conversation. "Well, looks like you two ladies is getting along good!" He hoisted his bulk onto the lowest rung of a fence panel, causing the metal connection chains to rattle and shake.

Dani's mare reacted with a harsh sound through her nose like a collapsing bellows. She twirled on her thin ankles to show her lean backside to the intruder. She pinned her ears flat against her head. This time, Dani clearly understood that she should get out and away before something bad happened.

"Jim! Get down offa there!" Donna's brightly embroidered cowgirl heels thumped up next to his grease-spattered work boots. She tugged the back of his belt and he plopped down, clanging the fence like a bell again. "It's almost our turn to load." She smiled at Dani. "You stay here, hon. I'll come back and get you when we're ready."

Dani nodded. The mare edged out from her corner to stand quietly behind her. Together, they tracked the couple's exit, Dani's nausea rising when she saw Jim's thick hand cupping Donna's rear pocket.

Before they could move the big horse into the trailer, though, Dani had to figure out how to harness it. With her problem shoulder, Dani couldn't reach up high enough to get the strap over the horse's ears. She kept trying, feeling rushed, until the mare finally lowered her head, giving Dani the right angle to wrap the halter over the animal's mane, buckle it, and attach the lead rope.

Next, she coaxed the mare from her pen. They moved down the aisle to the huge sliding door on the far side of the barn. The mare's eyes shifted from side to side as other horses called out, but she kept pace with Dani until they reached the big door to the parking lot, where the borrowed trailer waited.

The mare balked. She didn't want to go into the dark, boxlike cavity. She wrenched away, jumping from her front feet to dance on her hinds, snorting and snapping the lead rope.

Dani persisted, urging her to step onto the trailer's floor, but the horse wasn't having it. She refused, again and again.

The back of Dani's shirt grew wet. Her eyes stung from perspiration. Her arm ached. She tried to ignore the looks and suggestions that swelled out from those waiting behind them.

Jim barged over from whatever he'd been doing and snatched the line from Dani's hands. He didn't ask.

Discarded to one side in his wake, Dani searched the drawn faces around her, seeking Donna's help. She couldn't locate her in the group nor in the line of those still waiting to load.

Meanwhile, Jim pulled on the rope with both hands, trying to muscle the horse into the trailer, but the horse planted her feet and leaned back from his pressure.

He cussed and swatted at her with the loose end of the rope. The animal circled from side to side but wouldn't go forward.

He swore at her and swung again.

Turning her own circle, Dani knew what Jim was doing was wrong, but she didn't know how to fix it. She continued looking for Donna, horrified and nervous, completely certain that owning a horse was a terrible idea.

The mare's darting eyes showed wide, white rings. She yanked Jim off-balance as he aimed a kick at her belly. She called out, a shrill shriek of desperation.

Then, a woman stepped out of the crowd and quietly moved to stand next to the horse's shoulder. She placed one hand on the horse's sweaty neck and crooned to the frightened animal, gibberish Dani couldn't decipher.

Dani squeezed her eyes shut. She couldn't bear to watch, couldn't make herself a party to what might happen if the horse freaked out or hurt the gentle woman.

Suddenly, all the noise and activity quieted. Others around her murmured; someone tossed out a compliment. Squinting one eye open, Dani saw the woman slide her hand back to take the rope from Jim. The woman didn't ask.

The atmosphere among those watching softened like the rope, now lank and swaying. The woman continued speaking soft nonsense. Her movements were slow, steady. She sweet-talked the mare into the trailer in minutes.

Dani inched out from under the stable's overhang. Observing the animal's response to both ends of the range of treatment—from Jim to the kind woman—changed her mind. Maybe she could handle a horse, if she could learn how to gain the mare's trust.

She went to the rear of the trailer, where the woman was locking the safety bar behind the horse's backside. "Thank you—" she started, but Jim muscled in.

"Hey, thanks a million!"

He positioned himself between Dani and the helper, so close that the fabric of his shirt brushed against Dani's bare arm. He reached out and reclaimed the lead rope from the woman.

His expression was calm now, his angry mask smoothed and serene. He generated a belly laugh and attempted an explanation. "What a bitch, huh?"

The woman who loaded the horse melted back into the crowd without saying a word.

But Dani did. "Wait a minute." She admonished Jim's comment and his cruelty to her horse, but as she considered the right words to confront him, she realized that the man next to her wasn't even paying attention.

Donna had reappeared, and Jim's focus fixed on her. "Ya see me get her in there? She's a tough one to handle, I'd say. Had my hands full!"

Her sunglasses hid her expression, mostly, but she offered a muted compliment before hoisting herself into the truck's passenger seat. "Oh Jimmy, I never doubted you for a minute!"

Moving to secure the trailer's rear gate, Dani found herself wondering, again, how much Donna had seen. Donna held her cards very close to her chest.

She rejoined the couple inside the truck, and their drive back to Crestview passed uneventfully. Dani looked back at the horse trailer from time to time, but there wasn't any way to hear or see what was happening inside it. She hoped the mare was doing okay.

Jim joked and teased Donna, as before, but on this return trip, her responses sounded a bit sedate, even forced.

What's going on with her?

Dani considered her friend's reactions, but when they reached her farm, she focused solely on getting the horse out of the trailer and into her new lodgings.

She rejoined Donna and Jim back on the driveway to offer her thanks.

Lingering in the unlit entryway to watch the rig drive away, its amber side lights and rear red signals soft and fuzzy through the dust it stirred up, an ugly realization dawned.

She now owed a debt to the man.

3

THE NEXT MORNING brought low growls of thunder from the gray, sleepy west. Dani rolled over, untangled the sheet from her legs, and looked at the nightstand. Not even 7:00 a.m. She turned away from the window, flipped her pillow to the cold side, and tried to go back to sleep.

The thunder outside returned, more intense. A hiccup of space, a breath, and the grumbling drew closer. The windowpanes rattled. It wasn't thunder but a semi out on the road.

Dani had been living at this address long enough to know that it wasn't the right season for a truck to be hauling. Not only that, but most drivers used the smoother, tarred roads to preserve their rigs and loads. She wondered why the driver chose to take the bumpy gravel road past her house, off the beaten path.

She squished her eyes shut, but her curiosity got the best of her. Swinging her feet off the bed, Dani crossed to the window in time to see the back of a stock trailer, the morning's angled sunrays causing the dark holes on its silver side to glint like hollow, evil grins. In its wake, a curtain of dust swept up her driveway, shredded into ghostly ribbons by the pine trees' outstretched fingers.

As she stood there, she remembered: somewhere down below her window was a horse, her horse, though there was no sign of it in the green paneled pen. She twirled around and snagged her sweatpants and a hoodie from the floor.

Cody met her downstairs at the front door, taking the lead as they rushed to the barn. He remembered that a new member had joined their herd.

The mare was backed into an inside corner of the barn, the safest place from which to defend herself. Her breath burst out in puffs as if she was trying to sniff and snort at once, some combination of curiosity and fear toward her guests.

"Hey girl, it's just us—me and Cody," Dani murmured. She ticked through the list of things she was not supposed to do: Don't speak sharply or loudly. Don't make sudden movements. Never pat her directly between the eyes.

The two large squares of grassy hay Dani had put in the corner the night before were gone, and a few piles of dark droppings dotted the enclosure. The water bucket was empty too.

"I'll be right back with your breakfast," Dani addressed the horse. "Don't go anywhere, 'k?" she added, amused at her own humor, thrilled that the mare had made it safely through their first night together.

The mare kept her place in the corner, but her eyes darted and tracked Dani as she retreated and returned with hay and fresh water. Only when Dani had backed out and refastened the gate did the horse shuffle over to the hay, biting and shaking a few wisps at a time to break the tightly woven thatch into a loose pile.

"We should find a new name for you, too," Dani decided. "How do you like Sandy?"

Dani wasn't sure what to call her, but she wanted to pick something that marked a change in the horse's life. A symbol for her second chance.

Trodding back to the kitchen, Dani thought about the strange appearance of the truck and animal trailer on her isolated road. There were some empty barns and buildings around, where neighbors had given up or had been bought out, but no one out her way had stock, as far as she knew. The farmers out this way grew crops.

She took her coffee to the porch, sat, and savored the first sip. She looked up past the porch's overhang: clouds eddied and swirled behind full, green leaves laced together like latticework over her rooftop. A passel of little birds scolded the barn cat out from under the biggest pine along her driveway. Dani's neighbor had cut his hay the day before, leaving it to dry in long, lush lines in the next field. Its sweet perfume mingled with the coffee's peaty aroma.

Cody barked, interrupting her musings. A blue Ford filled her driveway, the model with the big engine and dual sets of wheels at the back.

Jim.

Dani held her mouthful of coffee and waited, alert.

He swung out from the truck's cab, reaching behind his seat for a big paper sack with "Oats" printed on one side. Striding up to the house, he dropped the bag on her sidewalk. "How's about a cup of coffee?" His voice oozed charm. Confidence. Arrogance.

Dani could smell his aftershave all the way up on the porch.

"Just had the last cup. Sorry." She didn't get up, but Cody did, edging to the porch steps. "Is that for the mare?"

"You can eat it too, I s'pose," he joked. "But I brought it for the mare, yah." He didn't come any closer, but he didn't move away, either.

Jim's intrusive hovering made Dani recall the uncertainty between her and her horse. She wondered if the animal felt as uncomfortable with Dani as Dani did now, with Jim so near. She was aware that she and Jim were alone on this isolated farm, with no one to help her out, if she needed it.

"How'd she do last night?" His graveled voice broke into her thoughts.

"Fine."

Dani contemplated what to say in the silence that followed. She wanted to tell the man that he couldn't just come to her place whenever he wanted, but she didn't want him to interpret that to mean that she was uncomfortable or frightened, either.

She tried a sideways move. "How about you? Was Donna impressed with how you loaded the horse?"

He didn't answer. He left the house and aimed his way to her barn.

Dani followed, straining to bring the feed bag with her. It was heavier than she expected, but she didn't want Jim to think she couldn't handle it. She wrestled it to the barn on her own.

"Those feet sure need work." He pointed one meaty finger at the mare.

At the sound of Jim's voice, the horse stopped eating and retreated to her safe corner.

Resting a boot on a bottom rung, Jim stacked his meaty forearms atop one metal panel. "You should restring that wire there, back by the shed. Not that she's ready yet, but she should be out there soon, gettin' that good grass and sunshine."

"Jim, I want to thank you again for moving the horse for me." Dani's heart beat triple- time, but she made herself continue. "But I heard what you said yesterday. And another thing, you can't—"

"You heard it wrong," he interrupted. "I wasn't talkin' about the lady. I was pissed about the horse. No big deal."

He got down from the fence, landing close to where she stood.

Dani moved away. "You made Donna think you were the one who loaded the horse." She swallowed, but went on. "Why?"

"So what? She knows me. Even if she saw, she wouldn't make nothin' of it." He spit a big glob onto the grass. "Donna ain't like that. She don't care."

Dani frowned at him, but she didn't move off again. She wasn't going to let him get to her. Moreover, following a different train of thought, she found it curious that a man who'd known Donna for such a short while felt entitled to tell Dani, a close friend of over a year, what Donna was like.

The Donna she knew would have cared—before Jim came into the picture, that is, before her outspoken friend adopted her current unusual reticence.

Jim changed the subject. "So, you gonna help me out with that route to Missouri?"

"When's it scheduled?" she asked, to buy time.

His pocket jingled. "Not for another week or two." He pulled out his phone. "Depends on when we get a full load. You'll do it, right?" He glanced at the phone, then dropped it back into his pocket again without answering it.

Her heart sank. The money would have been more than welcome. But when Dani looked at him, she saw the startled faces of the people back at the auction house, the kind folks who'd stepped up to help load the horse. She remembered the fear she'd felt there as her intuition warned her to move away from the anger that boiled through Jim's uncontained frustration.

Dani recognized the tug of that intuition once again and felt compelled to obey that higher principle.

"Thanks for the offer, but I don't think so." She held her breath, waiting to see which Jim would respond: the jovial salesman, or the impatient egoist.

"I drove down and picked up that nag for ya." The corner of Jim's upper lip started to curl, but he was able to arrange the rest of his mouth into a smile. He tried again, like a shark attempting to convince a minnow he was trustworthy. "Borrowed a trailer, took the whole day off." He nodded. "Thought I was helpin' a friend."

But when his protests didn't produce the desired effect, Jim's face turned dark, his brows wrinkling into a caveman crease. "Ah, screw it." He cursed under his breath and strode back to the driveway.

Dani scowled at the back of his wide head.

He added one last retort as he reversed his truck: "That grain was $8.50. You can pay Donna."

When the dust from his six wheels cleared, Dani returned to the house. She slapped together a sandwich, stabbing a hole through the bread before admonishing herself to relax.

She called for Cody, gave him the sandwich, and they both got into her truck. They took the back roads into town. It seemed like a good time to check the job board.

♦♦♦

Dani's truck, the replacement to the one she'd wrecked, rolled to a stop in front of the Farm & Feed. Its radiator leaked, and there was rust in the rear wheel wells, but her insurance didn't allow her much choice.

At least finding a place to park wasn't an issue: the farmers who weren't sitting at Susie's Café were out in the fields or in their sheds, tuning up their machines. She passed a man at the entry wearing faded Wranglers and a plaid button-up, maybe thirty years old or so. He didn't wear a seed cap, and his steel-toed boots were so clean they almost shone. He held the door for her and dipped his chin like any other guy, but kept his eyes on hers for a beat too long.

Definitely not a local.

The store smelled like the dusty rope hanging in back and pungent oil spills from the car service area. Dani headed for the notice board, a cork panel on the wall by the restrooms. On her way, she waved at two red-aproned cashiers chatting between empty checkout lanes.

One of the new fliers advertised for an in-home babysitter. Nope. A second ad, posted by a septic company, provided training, but that was another no. Too much heavy lifting.

She turned from the notice board and bumped right into a shorter woman who'd come up behind her.

"Sorry!" The young woman's face glowed pink. "I'm trying to find the ladies room."

"Not a big deal." Dani couldn't tell if the woman was embarrassed or in a hurry.

"I just moved here," she continued. "I'm picking up a few things for the apartment I'm renting. This is the only place in town to get household stuff, right?"

"Yep." Dani found herself in the unique position of being thought of as a Crestview native. She liked it. "And welcome. Where are you from?"

"St. Paul. I took a teaching job at St. Nick's, but it doesn't start until August. Workshop, I mean."

"Good for you." Dani meant it, too, remembering how she'd felt as a newcomer to Crestview, when she didn't know anyone and was ignorant of the local customs. But boy, Dani thought, she hardly looked old enough to be in college, let alone a licensed teacher.

"I moved here myself almost two years ago," she added, padding the time span. "I'm Dani, by the way. Dani Holden."

"Jessica Peterson." The woman held out her hand, then looked at it. "Do you shake hands here?" The color returned to her cheeks.

"Sure, we do." The teacher's hand was soft, making Dani conscious of the calluses on her own palm and fingers. "Where are you living?"

The woman pointed to the south. "I think. . . that way? I'm renting the basement from Mrs. Dorn. Barbara." Her canvas sneaker tapped the linoleum.

"I didn't know she had space to rent," Dani replied. "It's good that you found her. I've been worried that she might be lonely, since—"

Dani stopped. She didn't know what Jessica knew about Barbara's recent widowhood, and it wasn't the local practice to volunteer too much.

"Anyhow," she plowed on, "are you settled in?"

"I've made a good start. I don't have all my things set up yet, but I know I need an electric fry pan and an extension cord. I think I do, anyway." Jessica's mouth twitched like she was trying to remember if there was anything else. "Barbara said she'd take me out to dinner tonight, to give me a little more time before I burn the house down."

Dani hoped she was joking. "I'll bet she's taking you to Susie's."

"That sounds right. She said it's the local favorite."

"It is. You'll meet almost everyone there, at some point. Anyway, it's good to meet you. And if I don't see you before, good luck with your new job."

"Thanks! See you!"

Jessica gave a little wave before disappearing into the women's restroom. Dani heard her voice from beyond the door and wondered if the woman was talking to herself or to another customer. Not knowing didn't bother Dani. The new woman seemed kind and open. Natural.

Driving back to her farm, Dani reflected upon the lack of suitable jobs on the job board. She thought about the drive she'd turned down and hoped she'd made the right decision. Her imagination conjured a dreary picture of pigs or cows, cramped and crushed into a steamy, dirty trailer, their snouts pressed to the air holes.

But that was part of the process, she reminded herself as she pulled up to her house. She enjoyed a good steak and counted bacon as one of her favorite foods. It was ignorant to disregard the sources her meals came from. If she was a true farmer, she told herself, the production cycle of market animals shouldn't bother her. She was no longer that suburbanite whose closest interaction with meat was at the supermarket.

But to be part of the journey that stopped their beating hearts?

She was doing the right thing, she decided as she opened the door for Cody to hop out. She'd just have to find another source of income. One that didn't involve an ass like Jim.

Cicadas buzzed from the untrimmed grass next to the house, harmonizing an overlapping summer symphony as afternoon shadows draped their hiding places.

After checking the horse's water bucket, Dani called in the dog and settled herself in the front room.

The day's hard thoughts eased away under the rounded, hypnotizing arcs the filmy curtains made in the breeze that teased them through her front windows. Eyes drooping, she stretched out on the sofa and fell into that space where she thought she was still cognizant of the gentle sweep of warm air and the bugs' soothing drone yet was paralyzed and unable, or unwilling, to pull herself out of her torpor. It was a satisfying way to spend a summer afternoon.

Her phone rang into the evening silence, as shocking as the snap of a wet washcloth on hot skin. She scrambled up, knocking her knee on the metal trunk she used as both a table and footstool.

"Shit! I'm coming, I'm coming!"

Hopping on one foot down the hall, Dani located the handset. "Hello?"

"Hey." Donna sounded ticked. "Jim called. He says you're not drivin' for him."

The comment woke Dani to full awareness. "I just can't, Donna."

"It's not that big a deal." She stressed the word not. "Look at it this way: they end up at the same place, whether you or someone else takes 'em there. You been scouting around for weeks for a way to make money. This is a no-brainer."

As much as she hated the idea of driving animals to market, what Dani hated even more was the thought of being in debt to Jim. This "favor" might be the only way to free herself from it.

Why was Donna even interested in a man like Jim? The unbidden question popped into Dani's mind. What did she see in him?

Donna coughed, interrupting her thoughts. "You need this, Dan. It beats hangin' around the feed store, lookin' for a job that won't pay you nothing anyways." When she didn't get a response, she tsked and changed the subject. "Least you got that horse. How's she doing?" Her voice was softer now, her anger tempered.

"Good, I think. Oh, and I owe Jim for those oats too, I guess."

"Oats?"

Dani was confused by Donna's confusion. *If she knew I turned down Jim's offer, why didn't she know he dropped off the feed? Maybe he didn't tell her he'd driven out to my place.*

What a jerk.

But before Dani could share this observation, a sharp sound from Donna's side hijacked her attention.

Dani could have sworn the sound was a match strike. "Donna, are you smoking again?"

"No." After a beat or two, during which Dani thought she could hear Donna fanning the air, Donna shifted to a different topic: a mutual friend. "Hey, you heard from Lilly lately?"

"I haven't talked to her for a while. She's been busy."

"What does an eighty-year-old do to stay busy?"

"You'll find out, when you're that age," Dani answered. "You two are a lot alike—full of energy."

"I'll be lucky to make it to eighty. Should've taken better care of myself."

Dani kept her agreement to herself.

After they disconnected, Dani padded back to the darkened kitchen to pour herself a shot of Jack Daniels. She carried it to the porch, sank into her chair, then lifted the glass for the first sip, breathing deeply to enjoy the vapors.

Leaning to one side, she stroked Cody's broad head. "I don't know what to say to her, buddy. I hope she can figure it out for herself." Dani took another sip. "That man is no good."

She nudged the pine floor with one foot and rocked slowly through the next hour, mulling over the recent changes and observations she'd encountered. The wooden chair cradled her; her shoulders settled into the smooth place along its curved back. She tried to match her breaths to the rocker's movement.

Eventually, even though there was still a swallow left in her glass, Dani decided it was time for the day to be over.

4

DANI AND CODY TOOK THE LONG WAY into town the next day. With the rush of fresh air through their windows, they wound through tree-spliced sunshine past the Lutheran cemetery and over the shallow Beaver Creek. Regardless of her current status as unemployed and nearly broke, Crestview felt like home, and Dani didn't want to leave. She was happy here.

She sat at the diner's counter and looked for Donna. Last night, she figured out a way to share her intuition about Jim and was hopeful for a quiet moment to spring it on her.

But Donna wasn't anywhere in the café, nor could Dani hear her voice ringing out from the kitchen.

Donna's brother, Pete, was there, though. He hurried up from the lower dining section, wearing an apron and a frown.

"Where's Donna?"

"That's what I'd like to know." Pete leaned over the counter to a line of mugs hanging on the wall there, locals' names embossed on their fronts.

"I can get it." Dani reached for her mug. "Looks like you have more important things to do."

Pete snorted. "Not exactly what I'd planned for today."

His tone stopped her. She looked across the diner: there were a few open seats, but only a few patrons were actually eating.

"Need help?" She directed her question to Pete's back.

From the kitchen doorway, his reply was muffled. "No, I'll be okay. It's not your problem."

"Wait." Dani ducked behind the counter. "I can take orders; you can move plates." She tied on an apron and grabbed a memo pad. "Where should I start?"

Pete held the swinging door open with one foot. "Thanks, Dani." He shot her a quick half-nod. "Would you see what Mrs. Dorn and her group wants? They're—"

"—sitting at the middle table," she broke in. "I got 'em."

The assembly seated at the middle table in the lower dining level differed from the gang who gathered there a year ago. Lloyd and Chuck and Bud—in their seed caps, plaid sleeves crossed over their chests—were still grouped around the edges, as they'd always been. But now, Barbara Dorn; Bud's wife, Missy; and Lloyd's wife, Marilyn, joined them. The women's presence added decorum, new points of view, and an expanded topic list no longer limited to crop prices, field conditions, and sports scores.

Each member of the assembly spun Dani's way as she approached with her white pad and a smile. "Morning! What can I get for everyone?"

"Well, nice to see you, Dani!" Lloyd's voice was graveled with dust and last night's beer. "Ya taking over for Donna?"

"She's busy today, so I'm stepping in." Dani stood next to his chair, pen ready.

"Yah, 'busy,' I'll bet!" Chuck snickered. He lifted one elbow to poke Lloyd but stopped when he got a look at Barbara's face.

She was not amused.

He reached under his arm and scratched himself instead.

"Is Donna sick?" Barbara asked Dani, but she didn't wait for an answer before turning to the others. "I knew something was the matter when we got here and she didn't have our food on the table."

Marilyn agreed. "She always has it waiting for us."

"That's 'cause you girls always get the same thing!" Bud teased. "I mix it up a little, keep her on her toes."

"She'll be here in a bit." Dani wasn't sure, but arranged her expression to reflect what she hoped would pass for composure. "Now, what can I get for you?"

Dani jotted down the women's selections first, then suffered through the myriad directions that accompanied Lloyd's order.

"I want the eggs firm, you know—but not hard," he started, winking at Chuck. "And just two pieces of toast—does she have any of that sourdough? I'll take that, but no butter. Use that oleo she keeps back there."

Dani struggled to keep up. She wrote longhand because she didn't know how else to keep the items straight. Plus, she didn't know who was on duty back at the griddle. If Ginny was working, she'd be fine, but that new cook was hit-or-miss.

"Okay, I think I've got everything." She started for the kitchen but remembered one more thing. "Oh, anyone need refills?"

"I've got it, Dani." Donna glided over to the big square table with a full pot of coffee. "Here you are, folks," she purred. Her face was flushed and puffy like she'd just woken up. "Sorry about the delay this morning, but we'll have your food out in a jiffy!"

She didn't meet Dani's glance as she sailed past to top off other patrons' beverages.

Dani brought her order pad to the kitchen. Back by the griddle—and thank goodness it was Ginny holding the flipper—she handed the list to Pete, standing between her and the cook.

"Did you see Donna?" Pete's face was tight like he was holding back words he probably shouldn't let loose.

"Yep, she's here." Dani waited for him to continue. He didn't.

She prodded him. "Did she say why she was late? Where she was?"

He lifted his eyes from her as he heard the kitchen door swing open. His face glowered as Donna's laugh rang through. Ripping off his apron, he threw it toward the coat hooks by the back door.

"I've got to get to the library." Pete's voice was low and edgy. "Tell my sister I'll talk to her later."

The back door snapped shut behind him.

"Hell's bells, what's his problem?" Donna rolled her eyes like a teenager. Then, she addressed the cook. "You keeping up?"

Ginny nodded, her hands a blur as they darted from a bowl of shredded cheese to a container of diced potatoes to a huge open carton of brown eggs.

Dani removed her apron and handed it to Donna before reaching down to snag Pete's discarded cover. "Where've you been?"

"Ha! A girl sleeps in one day, and the world stops spinning." Donna looked over the apron for spots before wrapping it on. "It's not like I don't help Pete out once in a while. Seriously."

She seemed like she was about to say more, but a request from the front diverted her attention. "Thanks for pitching in." She winked at Dani. "Call you later."

Head held high, Donna sashayed back into the dining area, the grand entrance of a queen reclaiming her domain.

Ginny's reaction to the exchange came out like something between a cough and a laugh.

Before Dani made her own exit, she peeked back through the prep window. She wanted to gauge the locals' further reactions to Donna's late arrival, but her attention was sidetracked to the two-spot by the front door. Jim was sitting there with another man, a guy even bigger than he was, both of them leaning in over their table for a private conversation.

The other man got up, taking his phone outside. When he returned just moments later, he didn't sit. Instead, he bent down and muttered something to Jim. Dani wasn't in earshot to hear his exact words, but the edges of his syllables sounded sharp and pointed.

Listening to the man, Jim's face fell. "Are you sure?"

The big guy's scowl transposed to a snigger. "What the hell you think? That I'm making it up?" He pulled a different phone from his coat pocket, slapped it onto the tabletop, and took off again, this time leaving the front door wide open after he'd swaggered through.

Dani backed away from the pass-through window. She'd seen enough. Snagging a leftover piece of bacon from the dish bin for Cody, she followed Pete's trail and left through the kitchen door at the rear, crunching over grit and pebbles to her truck around front.

A black pickup with shaded windows and a fancy chrome package idled in the lot's far corner.

Between the tinting and the sun's bright glare, she couldn't see through its windshield.

The truck's engine revved as she crossed to her vehicle. She picked up her pace. She hated not knowing who was hiding there in secret, messing with her.

Cody was standing on her driver's seat when she got there. The fur around his neck bristled; a low, raspy growl sounded a warning. Dani tucked her chin and kept her face averted as she reversed and exited the lot.

◆◆◆

She wasn't planning to, but she stopped at the Crestview Library on the way home. She wanted to learn what Pete knew about Donna's late arrival.

The library, cool and solemn and predictable, was an old friend. Back home, growing up, she'd bike to her local library at least twice a week to keep her reading inventory stocked. She preferred mysteries and anything about horses, though as she endured the junior high years, she also checked out a number of paperback romances.

Dani still loved to read, more so since her accident left her with little else to do. Working with the new horse would cut into her reading time, she realized, but at least she'd get some exercise.

She trudged up the stone steps, careful to avoid the slight dip in the center of each tread, the result of the many readers who'd come before her. As she climbed, she noticed that the huge hanging light that usually warmed the cavernous entry was unlit. Perhaps Pete kept it off to avoid adding to the day's rising heat. Maybe it just needed a new bulb.

At the landing, Dani peeked through the glass door as she pushed against it. Pete was behind the checkout counter, the "circulation desk," he called it, talking to a woman wearing shorts, a pink tank top, and flip-flops. His wide smile caught Dani off-guard: she'd expected he'd still be holding the same scowl from the café, twenty minutes before.

Pete noticed her when she came through and swept his gaze from the woman to include Dani in its glow. "Hey, Dan! You're not the newbie, anymore! Have you met—"

The woman rotated to see who had captured Pete's attention. It was Jessica, the one who'd run into Dani in the feed store. Her smile widened. "I know you!"

"We've met already." Dani grinned as she drew up to the desk. "Was your shopping a success? Did you find an electric fry pan?"

"I guess," Jessica laughed. "But when I got the thing back home, I thought, 'I don't even know how to use this.'" She raised her eyebrows and made a funny smirk.

The natural way the young woman made fun of herself charmed Dani. Despite their age difference, she wondered if they'd become friends.

Dani wasn't the only one to find the newcomer charming. "Jessica's going to teach at St. Nick's this fall," Pete put in. His teeth shone brightly next to his rosy skin. He projected this sunshine directly onto the young woman in front of him.

"She told me." Dani was amused by the librarian's need to comment. "And she also got to eat at Susie's last night, so she probably met your sister."

Pete's smile dimmed, and his eyes narrowed. "Yah. Right." He picked up a stack of books and placed them onto the rolling cart next to him. "That must've been a treat."

Jessica interrupted. "Sorry, guys, but I should get to work." She lifted a big cloth sack from the floor to one shoulder; it looked to be full of books and workbooks. "Where's the best place to sit?"

She directed her question at Pete, but Dani answered. "I sometimes use one of the conference rooms. You can spread out your work, and when you close the door, no one bothers you."

Pete nodded. "That'll be fine. I'll add you to the sign-up. Next time, let me know when you're coming by, and I'll be sure to reserve a room for you. If you like it, I mean."

Dani butted in. "He's kidding. No one's in here during the summer. It's hard to imagine what even keeps this guy busy." She'd never seen this side of Pete, this softer, agreeable gentleman. She couldn't wait for his response.

Behind a large atlas he held between himself and the young teacher, Pete scowled at Dani: without a word spoken, he warned her to keep still.

He lowered the atlas and pointed down the hallway toward the conference rooms. "Take the first one. I'll be right here, if you need anything."

Jessica thanked them both and carried her bag down the hall.

Dani scrutinized the librarian. "Don't you think you're a little old for her, Mr. Lund?"

He bent to the lower shelf so that Dani couldn't see his face, though the silver strands at his temples gave testament to the age difference between him and the new teacher. "What are you on about?"

"The new girl. Woman." Dani didn't form her thoughts, she just let them roll. "Your mood is a lot better since you left the café."

"Didn't you come here to bug me about my sister?" Pete hoisted out more books and let the armful fall onto the cart with more noise than one might expect from a more traditional librarian. "So, what do you know? She tells you everything."

Dani shook her head. "Not this time. Not about this."

He glanced at her. "Not about . . . what?"

Dani hesitated. She didn't know if Pete would be open to hearing her opinion about Donna's new beau, so she decided to test the water rather than diving right in. "I think she might have a boyfriend."

Pete barked out a laugh. "Right . . . who? It's no one in town. We went to school with the same people we still see every day, and none of them measured up for her." He started wheeling the book cart back to the stacks.

"But lots of new folks from out of town have started coming to her theme nights. You know—you work there Friday nights. And some of those folks come back during the week now, too."

"Yah, but if she was seeing someone—like dating, I mean—I'd like to think I'd be smart enough to notice. I live with the woman."

Dani watched him disappear between two tall shelves. *Maybe you'd notice,* she thought. *Maybe not.*

◆◆◆

That night, Dani tried to get into the new Dan Brown novel Pete recommended. Her windows were pushed all the way open to catch the fresher evening air and the sounds of bugs and frogs and the occasional coyote, which Dani preferred over music or TV. Her phone rang.

"Dani? Am I waking you?" The caller's voice sounded elderly and cultured, but winded. Or ill.

"Lilly?" Dani struggled to fit the call into an understandable frame. "Are you okay?"

"I'm fine. In fact, better than fine." Lilly sniffed quickly, twice, the way someone did after a long cry. Her exhalation burst out: "I may have found him! My son!"

"What? Are you serious?" Dani tried to imagine the joy radiating from her older friend's sweet face.

Many years ago, as a young unmarried woman, Lilly Bradstreet gave up her baby for adoption.

She'd lived each day since not knowing what had happened to the infant she'd borne but never seen, never held nor kissed; the child she tried to forget but yearned to remember. When that old witness tree came down last year, Lilly finally gathered courage to try to find him, to learn the story of his life, to work out if he'd ever wondered about her or his father.

"Where is he? How did you find him?" Dani bombarded her friend. "Tell me more!"

"Well, I haven't technically found him, but the next best thing."

The night creatures resumed their chorus as Lilly described this latest event in the years-long journey she'd traveled. Lilly explained that she contacted the religious charity that operated the adoption agency back in 1939. She somehow convinced them to root out the initial adoption report, though the organization refused to provide anything more than the adoptive couple's names and last known address.

"The couple can help me contact the boy—my son," Lilly exclaimed. "Or at least I hope so," she added quietly.

Dani recognized Lilly's elation but couldn't begin to imagine the fear and the conflicting turmoil she must also have been experiencing.

"Do you have a phone number?" Dani asked. "Have you called them?"

"Oh no," Lilly replied. "This isn't something for a phone call."

"Well, have you looked online, then?" Dani pressed. "In fact, if you have the parents' names and address, I bet you can find the son's—"

"No," Lilly replied again, more firmly this time. "No phone calls. There were no online searches. I want to meet the people who raised my son." She paused. "Only I can't. Something's come up." Another pause. "I wasn't going to tell you, Dani. Not yet. But . . ."

Dani rose from the sofa. "What?" The lower corners of the room held dark shadows, sharply angled from the lamp she'd turned on to keep reading. She snapped the light off. "Why can't you go?"

Despite Lilly's attempt to muffle it, Dani could still hear her crying.

To give her time, Dani moved out to the porch. Cody, splayed out on his side on the worn entry floor, flopped his tail as she passed, but he didn't get up. Opening her front door was like opening a hot oven; the air outside had grown oppressive and seemed ready to throw a tantrum. Dani eased herself into her rocker and waited for an answer.

"Lilly? You there?"

"Yes. Only I wish I wasn't, because I don't know how—or what—to tell you."

Though the air was swollen and hot, letting the rocker hold her gave Dani some security. She welcomed it, sensing that Lilly's second announcement would hold none of the joy that accompanied the first.

"I'm eighty-two years old, you know," Lilly started. "Lately I haven't been feeling right, sort of off-balance."

"Are you sick?"

"Um-hmm. More than that, actually." The older woman's voice broke again, but this time, she didn't bother hiding it. "I don't have a lot of time. Right when I'm so close to finding my boy . . ."

A hollow pang carved a hole inside Dani's chest, an echo of the impact of Lilly's two colliding events.

"I want to help," Dani said. "Please."

Cody whined and scratched the screen door. Hearing Dani's tone, he was driven to join her outside, where he could more easily protect her.

"What can I do?" Dani asked. "Can I come stay with you?" Her heart ached for her friend.

Lilly sniffed, then gently blew her nose. "I want you to go talk to the parents for me," Lilly said. "I want you to go to Missouri."

5

Dani couldn't rest after talking with Lilly. The older woman's news was hard to take in. Despite the short duration of their relationship, Dani had grown to love the woman she'd first met through a collection of old letters. She admired Lilly's independence, her bravery, and her strength. Her grit.

It was all so unfair, Dani told herself, tossing in bed through the damp, pressing darkness. It was a cheat that Fate or God or Karma had brought Lilly so tantalizingly close to finding her lost child, only for disease to snatch away any possible future happiness with its sharp, grasping claws.

Dani hauled the bed cover downstairs but didn't find sleep on the sofa, either.

She compared the timing of Lilly's request to Jim's offer—the synchronicity, the shared destination. The overlap wasn't random. She didn't like being forced to say yes to Jim so that she could say yes to Lilly; she wished there was another option. But no matter how many times she shook her head or how many alternative scenarios she imagined, each excuse distilled itself back to the same single fact: she was meant to go to Missouri.

She heard her horse nicker from the pen outside. Time for morning chores. Dani folded the blanket, started a pot of coffee, then grabbed her cellphone on her way outside to tell Donna about Lilly's news.

Donna didn't answer.

Dani tamped down the unease that bloomed when Donna's voicemail took over. Something was going on with her. Somehow, she seemed different.

As Dani crossed the yard to the barn, the serene coos of the mourning doves gathered by the roadside softly bracketed each step she took. She focused on their calm, unhurried melody, allowing it to chase the misgivings from her mind.

"How's it going today, Rusty?" Dani greeted the mare with a new option.

That name didn't quite do it. Whatever she was to be called, the animal's attitude hadn't improved much from the morning before. She still didn't know Dani well enough to trust her, tucking herself into the inside corner of her pen again.

Dani separated two flakes of hay from an open bale and shoved them just inside the nearest fence panel. She hoped the horse would be tempted enough to come closer for them—and to Dani waiting nearby.

The mare evidently knew that trick and opted to keep her distance. She fixed both eyes on Dani, though, and from Dani's location, the fearful white rims weren't noticeable this morning.

Dani gave her two more minutes to reconsider. Realizing the horse's resolve was firm, she poured more water into the animal's bucket and backed away to give her more space.

The mare wasn't much to look at. The bones in her ribs jutted out like ladder rungs. A person could hang a coat on her shoulder bones or her bony hips. Her poor tail just hung there, limp and thin, between her spindly haunches. Her fur—Dani reminded herself to call it "hair"—had spots where the orange or ginger had rubbed off, leaving her skin bare. Dani didn't know the correct anatomy terms for these places, but she knew other horses didn't have such a patchwork of textures.

In particular, Dani noticed the scrapes and scratches across her flank and down both back legs.

She didn't know whether the animal had run through sticks or sharp grasses or whether she'd been whipped. Roxie wouldn't have beaten her. Maybe the mare had been abused before she came to Roxie's barn.

Dani wrenched her attention from the broken body to the horse's face. The mare's dark eyes, fringed with long, angled lashes, were separated by a wide, white stripe from under her thin bangs down to her top lip. There was dust in her large nostrils, but they moved and squeezed and sniffed at Dani despite her reluctance to move closer.

Dani thought about everything those eyes had seen.

The rasping engine of a four-wheeler out on the road distracted her. The guy flying past wore an oversized bright-colored T-shirt, the type favored by local high schoolers. It flapped like a warning flag in the wind stream behind him. He was going too fast for her to see who it was.

On the heels of the four-wheeler, a truck and trailer trundled by, creating another sheet of dust to mingle with the first one. It took a good minute for that powder to settle.

Dani considered the variety of things a person could hide in a closed container, a trailer. Her thoughts shifted to the farmhouse in front of her. She examined its layout. This property had been uninhabited for at least three years before she'd moved in, and while she thought she'd explored it all, she figured there were still things she hadn't yet uncovered.

There were countless other abandoned buildings around Howard County, empty barns and silos, vacant homes and outbuildings. She monitored a few of Mr. Randolph's properties for him, in exchange for her rent, but she knew it was virtually impossible for anyone to patrol or secure every unoccupied place.

If she had something to hide, Dani would choose an abandoned farm to secrete it.

The mare blew her nose again, the sound like a burbling trumpet. Dani opened the metal gate, but when the hinges screeched, the mare stiffened. She focused on Dani like a laser.

Following some instinct, Dani sank to the dirt, the back of her jeans coming to rest on her heels. She didn't move.

Her drop to that level, below the horse's topline, caused a change: the mare lowered her head, curious about why this human was suddenly subservient in posture to her, the weakest of the pack. The creature's eyes softened; her ears pricked forward. She took a step toward Dani, sniffing much like a dog following a scent. Her curiosity about this smaller version of Dani overcame her fear.

Dani held her breath and reached out, inch by inch, and rested her hand on the wide, warm cheek.

The mare's gaze didn't waver from her own. She'd quit chewing when Dani first entered the pen, but now, five or twenty or a hundred minutes later, she started up again. Her great curved jaw moved like a small wavy sea under Dani's palm.

With that huge, lowered head still so close to her own, Dani realized how big the animal really was. She scooted back a foot or so. Like the mare, she didn't want to get hurt. Not now.

The mare edged toward her to fill the gap. She wanted to be with Dani.

Dani's eyes flooded so full she couldn't see her own hand, lifted to caress the mare's cheek one last time. She was more than content with their progress.

♦ ♦ ♦

The simple beauty of the morning soon melted away. Dani was supposed to get groceries yesterday, after morning coffee, but with Donna's late arrival and Dani's decision to check in with Pete at the library, she'd forgotten. She left Cody asleep under the dining room table before sneaking out the back door to her truck.

Tall grasses between the road and the fields were dull and starting to fade. The hardwoods' leaves, curled and muted, clung to their branches in crepey bunches. The fields looked dry and tired by the roadsides.

She was about to exit onto County Road 8 when an older truck came up behind her, fast, practically riding her back bumper. Her first inclination was to speed up, but then she recognized the driver through her rearview mirror. It was Tot, Bud and Missy's son. His music was so loud, she could feel the bass notes through her spine. Gray smoke streamed out his open window.

She slowed and pulled over to the shoulder, reaching out to wave a hello, but he blew past, not even stopping at the four-way ahead. Dani's adrenalin pulsed in tempo with his fading bass. She turned away from the dusty fallout that trailed behind him.

Tot's brother had been killed on this road. There was even a special sign ahead with his brother's name on it, erected in his memory.

It wasn't like him, the Tot she met last year, to drive in such a careless way. Dani would have to ask around to learn if anyone had heard anything about Tot or what he was into lately. Despite folks' protests that they didn't engage in gossip, Dani was getting the hang of how the small-town newswire functioned: if a person talked *around* a question long enough, she'd be able to figure out what was really going on in the middle, the place people liked to keep hidden.

A short time later, Dani left the grocery store with two dollars in her pocket and one paper bag of food. She took the short way home so she could swing by the café. Hopefully, she'd be able to catch Donna. Her talking points now included probing Donna for any news about what Tot was up to, besides asking her friend about Jim, and telling her about Lilly and her son.

The place was empty, the room rearranged for Donna's Friday night special menu event. A red-checked tablecloth draped each table; empty wine bottles with tall candles served as centerpieces.

Dani picked up a Xeroxed menu that read "Night of Italy." Ancient stereo speakers crackled overhead, and a high-volume rendition of "Volare" flooded the room.

"I'll be right there!" A muffled voice sounded out from the diner's utility closet.

Donna popped out a moment later, a huge grin on her outrageously red lips. She wore a tight black sleeveless blouse that showed off her shoulders, a slim patterned skirt, and sky-high heels. She'd even added a little beauty mark to her right cheekbone.

"Mangia! Mangia!" she exclaimed, waving her arms in the air. She teetered over to Dani and pretended to kiss each cheek.

Dani laughed, waving one hand in front of her. "Whew! You sure look… Italian!"

"Too much perfume?" Donna grabbed a white napkin from the closest table and dabbed behind her ears and over her cleavage. "I don't want to interfere with the food!"

"Add more garlic," Dani teased. "Really, it looks great in here. Is there anything I can do to help?"

Donna crossed to a serving cart near the kitchen and exchanged her perfumed napkin for a clean one. "Maybe you could help me figure out where to put everything. I'm going to try a buffet this time."

She pointed to the long counter in front, also covered by a checked tablecloth and various stainless steel trays. The Sterno warmers were set to one side.

"I don't know where I should put the pasta—first, because they eat it first in Italy?" She raised one bare shoulder.

"Where does the salad go, then?"

"Well, what I read is that Italians eat that last." Donna moved the large plastic salad bowl to the far end of the counter. "Do you think people will figure it out, or should I make a sign?"

"Maybe you should stand at the door"—Dani gestured to the left—"and welcome people. When you walk them to their table, tell them the order."

Donna agreed that it was a good idea. She shuffled two stacks of white plates to fill the open spot at the front of the buffet line.

"How many are you expecting?" Dani lifted a breadbasket from where it leaned against the counter and handed it to Donna.

"I'm full up—at least a hundred, I think."

"You don't have room for that many! Where are they all supposed to sit?"

"I'm doing two seatings: one at five for the early birds, and the next at seven."

Dani stared at her friend. "That's amazing! Wow! I didn't think there were that many people around here! I'm so, so proud of you. I don't know how you manage…"

But Donna was fiddling with a round tin burner, trying to wedge it into its warming tray, and didn't respond.

Dani shot a quick look to the ceiling, like a prayer. *It's now or never,* she thought. "So. Donna. I need to ask you something."

"What's up?"

Dani tried to sound casual. "What's going on with you and Jim?"

"Jim?"

Dani gave her time to come up with an honest answer.

"He's a friend," Donna finally managed.

Not so honest, Dani decided. "So you're not dating, then?"

Donna continued to insert the burners into their holders. She didn't look at Dani. "I can't see myself with a long-distance trucker like Jim. Think of all the girls he must have on his route, just waiting on him in their cozy bedrooms. I'm not one of those women. Never will be."

When she finally finished with the burners and turned, her face was unreadable.

"He acts like he really likes you, though. Seems he's been here almost every time I've stopped at the café this summer."

Donna's silence betrayed her. Though Donna had often declared her independence and determination to rely on herself, Dani sensed it was a screen to hide her friend's softer feelings.

This intuition was rewarded when Donna made a last comment.

"Well, maybe so. There might not be too many more chances for me." While her manner was neutral, her tone was serious. "Jim may be my last best bet."

Her confession hung in the air.

Dani felt compelled to tell Donna that she didn't think Jim was the right guy for her, but the wistful way Donna admitted her sentiment about last chances made Dani pause.

As if seizing the moment of hesitation, Donna placed her red manicured fingertips on Dani's shoulders and marched her to the front door. "Thanks for stopping, hon, but I got so much left to do. We'll visit later, 'kay?"

"No problem."

There was no opportunity this time for Dani to tell Donna about Lilly's news or ask about Tot. At least she'd been able to get a general idea of Donna's regard for Jim.

Dani swept her arm to take in the room, then gave her friend a quick hug. "It's going to be an epic night, Donna. Enjoy it!"

Dean Martin's voice serenaded her all the way back to her truck.

♦♦♦

After an overnight rainstorm, the next morning's sky looked swept by a watercolorist's velvet brush, robin's egg blue from one horizon's edge to the other. A gentle wind brought smells of earth and growing things. Skittery leaves on the poplar out front wiggled like kindergartners set free in the warm sunshine. Pasture hay in the next section poked up new green shoots through the shorn remnants of its last cutting.

Today, she called the horse Scout, but the name was not officially settled. One of Dani's favorite books was "To Kill a Mockingbird", and she'd always loved the little sister, Scout. She used to pretend to be Scout, rambling around the backyard and through her grandparents' acreage. The character seemed to have a hidden reserve of strength, and Dani hoped this mare would mirror her namesake and allow her curiosity to overcome her fear.

The mare ambled from her corner toward Dani and Cody, a huge step forward compared to how timid the animal had acted the day before. Cody wagged his tail and sniffed up at the mare, who lowered her head and sniffed back. When Dani came up to the fence, the mare pricked both ears toward her. Dani thought she looked more alert and confident than when she first arrived.

"You ready for another big day, Scout?"

The mare blinked as if considering the connection. Then she blew out a noisy gust and turned her attention to Cody, setting out to explore the new scents that had popped up since last night's perimeter check.

Dani moved from the bright daylight into the barn. She paused to let her sight adjust, then removed the plastic grain scoop from its nail on the far wall, lifted open the top of a dented white freezer underneath it, and took out a measure of oats. The freezer hadn't worked since Dani took over the farm, so she'd repurposed it as a grain bin, removing the interior wire shelving and the electric cord from the back. She hoped the thing was rodent-proof.

The mare waited at her feed bucket and began eating as soon as Dani poured the grain, nudging the bits with her nose and lips. Unlike the other feedings, she didn't wait this time for Dani to move away.

Because of those positive changes, Dani decided to try grooming her. She pulled out a soft brush from a bucket of tools Barbara Dorn had left on her porch and aligned herself next to the mare's shoulder. She took a deep breath, let it out slowly, then started smoothing the coat with firm, slow strokes, following the hair's natural direction.

The mare stopped chewing to consider the development. Then, as if satisfied with the sunshine and the breakfast and the attention, she returned to her bucket with a deep sigh that echoed her owner's.

Dani talked as she brushed the mare from her shoulder to her hip. This would be her therapy, hers and the horse's, Dani told herself. Twenty or so minutes together, every day.

Cody returned, pushed himself under the fence, and lifted his dirty front paws onto Dani's legs. "Everything okay, boy? Anything to report?" She tousled his fur before he plopped down to attend to another errand.

Dani toted an old shovel into the pen to deal with the increasing amounts of droppings. She did her best to remove them, making a pile outside the corral, but she didn't have a wheelbarrow to move them anywhere further. Another small but unforeseen problem to tackle.

That job finished, she leaned the shovel against the barn wall and crossed the driveway to the back of the house. Out behind the kitchen was a dirt plot Dani called her garden. She poked through the vines, picked a few ripe cherry tomatoes, and tugged out some weeds. All the while, she calculated the miles on the route Jim asked her to drive and devised ways she could distract herself from the load she'd be trailering behind her. If she took the job, that was.

She picked up a soothing sound from the south, where a sprayer threaded its fertilizer onto swatches of growing crops. The sprayer slowed to reverse directions at the ends of each row before gearing up again, over and over in a leisurely rhythm. The repetitions reminded Dani of swimming laps back and forth through a quiet pool.

Her back and shoulders relaxed in the warm sun that seeped into her skin. She hummed, happy in that comfortable cushion where time doesn't matter—until Cody sprang up from his guard post near the driveway, barking and racing off.

Her hazy mood broken, Dani brought the plastic container of cherry tomatoes to the back step. She wiped her dirty hands on her jeans before making her way to the front to see what the dog had cornered.

From the side yard, she spotted Donna's Honda parked out front. Its engine clicked and tinged.

"I'm over here," Dani called, and pushed herself into a jog. Finally, she could tell Donna about Lilly's news.

But her mood deflated when she heard a male voice's response.

Dani stopped running. "Just a minute," she managed, bending down to shove her heels into the backs of her shoes, a maneuver to hide the discomfort that blossomed the instant she realized Donna hadn't come by herself.

Coming around the corner, she spotted Donna by the horse pen, looking into the barn.

She didn't see Jim, so she assumed he'd granted himself access to the barn's interior.

"Takin' a nap?" Donna was clad in a new pair of tight blue jeans with rhinestones and a sleeveless cotton shirt. A red bandanna wrapped along her hairline completed her look.

"Nope. Out back." Donna didn't need to know everything. Donna sure wasn't telling her everything anymore, that was for certain. "What brings you guys by?"

Jim exited the barn with the horse's halter and lead rope. "These the only ones ya got?" he asked, striding toward the corral's outer gate.

"Um, yea." Dani unclenched her teeth to continue. "Why don't you let me do that, Jim?"

"I don't mind." He reached out with his free hand to unclasp the gate latch.

"Hold on," Dani rushed forward to stop the gate from swinging open. "I've already worked with her today. Why don't you—"

He held the gate out of Dani's reach. "It won't hurt her none. In fact, it'd do her good. Get her used to all sorts of people." He wore that salesman-like grin, a "shit-eatin' grin," as the farmers said. "She's gotta learn you're the master, or she'll start doin' things you don't want, like turnin' her back on ya or runnin' away."

Her pulse ticked behind Dani's right eye, near her temple. She darted past Jim through the gate, placing herself between him and the horse. "Jim, I don't want her confused." She held out her hand, both to stop his progress and to take back the gear. "I want to do this my way."

Jim's eyes narrowed. He didn't enter the pen, but he didn't let go of the tack, either.

A sibilant tsk from outside the pen broke the impasse. Though her visual angle prevented her from seeing the anger on Jim's swarthy face, Donna could still gauge the tension. "What's going on, Dani?"

"You probably don't think I know what I'm doing"—Dani closed her hand over the rope and halter Jim gripped—"but I've got this."

He held on just long enough to show Dani that he could prevent her from taking them, then let go with a laugh that sounded forced and out of place.

"Why, sure! I was only trying to help—wasn't I, Donna darlin'?" He pivoted to Donna, switching his expression from irritation to good-natured as smoothly as a card shark flips an ace from the bottom of the deck. "We just wanted to be sure you're settlin' in okay." His boots clomped over the dry earth back to Donna. "Don't want you to think you're in over your head."

What is it with this guy? Dani was steaming. *Why does he have to control everything?*

She forced a smile for Donna and hoped it looked at least half-genuine. "I'm following this program I read about online, and I want to give her a chance to see if we can make it work."

Her excuse sounded lame, but she didn't care. "After all, this is supposed to be a way to get my shoulder better, too—right, Donna?"

Dani dragged Donna back into it. As far as Dani was concerned, Donna was the one who'd ignited things in the first place by pushing the idea of a "therapy horse", the one who'd added fuel to the flames by pushing Jim into the mixture. Let her deal with it for a while, Dani huffed to herself.

"That's right, Jimmy. She needs that exercise for her PT." Donna stroked the man's bulky arm. "But we know you don't need the workout, do you?"

Dani felt sick. What happened to the clear-thinking woman Dani used to be able to count on? "Why don't you guys head to the porch? I'll finish up here, then join you. I want to hear about Italian night."

"Well, make it quick!" This time, Donna's voice sounded real. "After I tell you about that, Jimmy's got some news for ya too."

Dear Lord, Dani sighed, what next?

By the time Dani got back to the house, the couple was sitting hip to hip, shoulder to shoulder. They peeled their foreheads apart at her approach, separating from a sloppy kiss.

"So! Tell me all about it!" She wanted Donna's focus to return to her own priorities, the things she used to talk about and wish for, like buying the diner and updating it to suit her own dreams. She doesn't want to stand by and watch Donna exchange her life for someone so undeserving.

Donna's excitement bubbled out. "It was amazing! More people came than had reservations, so I ended up serving them on the picnic table in back." She took off her sunglasses, and her eyes twinkled.

"That old wood one? The 'smoking section,' you mean?"

"Yes!" Donna could barely sit still. "I threw an old tablecloth on it, and six people squeezed in!"

"Thought the thing would collapse," Jim added, patting his stomach. "But the food was fantastic. Real Eye-talian! You did yourself proud, Donna babe."

She beamed at him. "I was thinking, next summer, I'm going to get myself a patio, a concrete one. Like an outdoor eating space, you know?" She directed this comment to Dani. "It's pretty out there, against those trees. We could hang some of them white lights, and—"

"Tell her about the reporter," Jim interrupted.

Donna was so enthusiastic, she was practically shooting sparks. "I got a call this morning from a reporter for the Sunday paper. He wants to come up from Des Moines to interview me about the theme nights! I can't even believe it!" Her hands flew out to try to encompass the enormity of this good news. "They want to do a story on me! I'm going to be famous!"

Jim shifted his attention back to his phone, a clear signal that he'd reached his limit of his enthusiasm for Donna's news.

Donna noticed, too; her shoulders sagged. "Anyhow, enough about that," she moved ahead. "Jim has an idea for you. How 'bout this? He'll take you on an earlier load down to Missouri. Show you firsthand how to shift and how to switch loads at the dock. Make sure you'd be comfortable . . . You know, for when you'd do the next one on your own."

Dani hesitated, realizing what the development meant. The terms of Jim's offer had changed. Instead of having her make just one trip to Missouri, he now had her on the hook for two—including one with him.

No. Hauling one trailer full of stock to market would be horrible enough. She simply couldn't haul two.

But then Dani remembered Lilly's voice, so frail yet so determined . . .

She considered how to make the most of the situation: maybe she could do the test run with Jim to learn the ropes, then make plans to locate Lilly's son's parents when she returned on the solo trip.

Still, there was no way she'd put herself that close to Jim for all those miles. Not alone.

"Could you come with us . . . ?" she asked Donna.

"Course I could! I haven't had a vacation in . . . I don't know how long. Hopefully Pete'll cover for me." She grew thoughtful. "Did you know he moved out?"

"Really?"

In truth, Dani wasn't surprised. When he got the librarian position last year, he said he'd start looking for his own place. That was way before Jim arrived on the scene.

"When did he move out?"

"Actually, just this morning." Donna shot a glance at Jim, still scowling at his phone.

"Where'd he go?"

She shifted her attention to her hands. "He took the right side of that duplex across from the Catholic church. You know, the one by that pond?" Donna lifted her chin and gave a little shake. "Anyhow. If he'll cover for me, I'll go. It'd be fun to get away." She poked the man next to her. "It only takes a day, back and forth, right?"

"Yep. With two drivers, we can be down and back in a day." He had been listening, after all. "I'll show you the ropes on the drive. And hauling stock is nothin'. You won't even know anything's back there."

The burbling unease inside Dani made her want to run away. Just because she was thinking about accepting his offer didn't mean she'd accepted the man.

She rerouted the conversation. "Did you come up with the idea of taking a trip with me after you stopped by the other morning?"

Suddenly, Jim wasn't interested in his phone. He closed it, put it away, and hefted himself to his feet. "Might've."

Donna popped up, too. "You didn't tell me you came by here." Her hands on her hips made parentheses that mirrored the lines around her frown.

Aha. I knew the asshole didn't tell her. Dani stood, watching to see what would come next.

Jim clapped one paw on Donna's shoulder to maneuver her away from Dani.

"Jim! Just wait a minute, now." Donna stayed put. She readjusted the bandanna in her hair. It was clear she had more questions.

But the trucker hustled down the steps to Donna's car. "Oh darlin'," he drawled, opening the passenger door. He wagged his finger for her to come. "I'm busy, you know? P'rolly just forgot to tell you . . ."

She sighed, but she followed him, sliding into the passenger seat before he closed her door with exaggerated politeness.

Neither looked back at Dani.

Jim arranged his bulk behind the steering wheel and started the engine, but Dani could hear her friend's voice over the motor's growl: she was pressing Jim about his earlier visit. She paused just long enough to roll down the window for a quick "I'll call you," her forehead creased. None of her high spirits remained.

Dani gave the Crestview Farmer's Salute—two raised fingers—at the departing car.

She congratulated herself for standing up to Jim. But before the glow of success could settle, her imagination hopscotched to a vision of a crowded trailer and the distress of the animals crammed inside.

If I do this, I won't owe him anything else.

Sighing, Dani returned to the back step to retrieve her tomatoes. She'd come in second place again.

She flopped down onto the concrete step. It was still warm from the sun that shied onto the overhang, now draping the stoop in shadow. Dani closed her eyes, dropped her chin to her chest, and allowed herself to pry open that sealed chamber she didn't want to admit she hid from even herself.

The pricking barbs of Jim's behavior toward Donna had cracked through the seal that guarded that vessel, allowing old memories to seep and swill into her mind again.

Geoff was her first love. Heroin was his. He got in too deep and stayed too long. Dani tried, but she couldn't stay around to watch. He eventually fell off that "horse", dying alone.

What almost no one knew—what Dani almost never acknowledged, even to herself—was that she allowed herself to fall in love a second time. When she learned Mark was married, though, her soul clamped shut. She moved from that point as if in a daze, hours and weeks passing without recognition. During the day, she made herself smile, if it was required; during the nighttime hours, she replayed their times together, examining each occasion with a critical eye, but found nothing that would have hinted at his dishonesty.

She tried not to blame herself for not seeing what couldn't have been seen.

Then, 9/11 happened.

A few long weeks later, she left for Crestview.

Dani opened her eyes and wiped her cheeks. She chased each image from her mind.

Geoff.

Mark.

Now Donna.

She was damn tired of coming in second.

6

THE COOLER TEMPERATURE DIDN'T LINGER. As was more typical for Midwestern summers, the next day dawned hazy, humid, and warm.

Dani had to coax the mare out of the barn to eat the hay she'd thrown for her. A cloud of flies by her water bucket plagued her when she went near it, buzzing and crawling from her spine to her ears and eyes and down her stamping legs. When Dani swatted them away, though, the mare became edgy, whirling back inside to avoid the biting pests.

She'd been to town more than usual the past week, but the fly situation made it imperative for her to return for something to help her horse endure the infestation. And as long as she was there, Dani planned to stop at Pete's new place to check in. Since Donna wasn't available, maybe she could talk to Pete about the topics that swarmed her thoughts like the pesky flies.

Leaving Cody inside the house, Dani drove first to the Farm & Feed. Some of the local high school girls worked there and knew a lot about horses. She'd rather talk to them about horse matters because they didn't tease her for asking questions, the way the guys at Susie's loved to do.

The equine section was located in the back corner of the store. Dani nodded to people she passed; most nodded back. The gal

65

stocking the horse-care shelves wore faded blue jeans with big rips across both legs. Her eyes were ringed with heavy black eyeliner. She acknowledged Dani with a quick chin bob.

"Hi there. What can you recommend for flies?"

The salesgirl went to a different aisle, gesturing for Dani to follow. She stopped in front of an array of spray cans and bottles.

"Try this," she suggested, handing a yellow-topped container to Dani. "It's supposed to last a week. It won't, but it'll help some. Just don't get it into their eyes."

"That's where the flies go, though," Dani responded.

"Put a little into your hand, like this." She took the can and demonstrated, spraying a shot into her palm. "Rub it around their eyes and nostrils."

"Thanks." Dani hoped it would work. "Do you have any spray for the barn?"

"Nothing really works super good, but you could try"—she two-stepped back to the previous aisle—"this tape. See, you open it and hang it from the ceiling. Just keep it away from where they could bite at it. It'd kill them." The girl's inflection was matter-of-fact. "Plus, it's cheap. You can get a bunch for, like, ten dollars."

"Sold!" Dani's attempt at humor was met with a tiny smile. "And thanks."

The girl piled Dani's things into a plastic water bucket, which Dani brought to the front register. She paid, leaving the bucket.

Before going to Pete's, she detoured to the Stop-N-Save for gas. The price per gallon was higher than at the co-op, but it was closer. She topped off the tank, then went inside to pay. Tot was in line ahead of her. It looked like he'd lost some weight, the way his jeans sagged down in the back.

"Hey, Tot." She queued up to the register next to him. "Saw you pass me the other afternoon. It looked like you were in a hurry."

His hair was neat, and his expression was calm. "Really?" His reply was noncommittal, but he didn't have any problem speaking or following the conversation. "Didn't see ya."

He took a roll of bills from his front pocket and tugged out a few. He handed the cash across to the clerk. A bright blue X was newly inked onto the inside of his wrist.

Dani had seen that tattoo before.

She barely registered the young man's goodbye. "Take care," she responded—too late. He was already back outside.

Her stomach churned. Why would he have that marking? After paying, Dani decided to follow him, to see if she could learn for herself what he was up to. If it turned out that he was hanging around Jim, maybe she could warn him off.

Over at the far end of the gas station property, Tot was talking to someone through the open window of an older-model sedan. She went forward, a few more steps. It wasn't Jim but another man slouched behind the steering wheel.

Tot leaned down and handed something to the man. He didn't seem to be trying to hide anything, but his movements were fast and efficient. Then he straightened up and tucked something into his back jeans pocket.

Slapping the sedan twice, he backed away, crossed the lot, and hopped up into his own pickup. Its motor was already running, and in no time he took off from the station. If he'd noticed Dani, hiding to one side of the fuel pumps, he didn't show it.

Driving to Pete's duplex next, Dani took her time.

She tried to convince herself not to read too much into the situation. It might've been totally innocent.

But Dani knew better.

She knew what she saw, but she wasn't ready yet to allow herself to reconcile it with the behavior she'd experienced with Geoff, back in the Cities.

What she recognized, seeing that stoned woman at the auction house.

She thought she'd escaped all that when she moved from the Cities. She felt heavy, inside.

At the duplex, Pete was trying to pry open the front door with his foot while balancing a cardboard box on top of a TV cart held in his arms.

Dani tapped her horn, parked, then hurried up the sidewalk to help.

With Dani holding the door open, he muscled the load inside. "You're my first guest, but I don't have anything to offer you." His eyes were bloodshot, and his T-shirt, smudged and dirty. "Wish I had some beer."

"I don't need anything. Do you? Can I help?"

He rubbed his lower back. "How'd you know I was here?"

"Your sister stopped by yesterday. With—"

"I know," he broke in. "With 'Jimmy.'" A harsh expletive slipped out. "Sorry, Dan." He returned to his truck for another load.

Dani gave him a minute. To the right was a tiny galley kitchen. It looked like the bedroom and bath were located to her left. It was a small square floor plan, economical and compact.

When Pete returned, he was toting a dishrack full of loose, unwrapped glasses and coffee mugs, clinking precariously. He also had a big plastic garbage bag squeezed under one arm.

"Here, let me take that," Dani suggested, reaching for the rack.

"Thanks. Can you put it in the kitchen? It's to your right, there," he added sincerely, as if the layout of the apartment wasn't obvious.

"Got it. And the bag? Where do you want me to bring that?" She placed the rack onto the only kitchen counter.

He released his elbow and let the bag slip to the floor. It landed with a thud. "I don't know. . . It's full of towels and other stuff for the bathroom—I think? Or sheets?" He sighed and shook his head. "I didn't take time to plan anything. I just . . ."

"Don't worry. Here, let me." Dani opened the bag and started separating linens. "Do you need any furniture? A bed?"

"I got the bed set up yesterday, and I have a chair and a TV. What else would I need?" "Huh. I don't know; maybe another seat, for guests?"

He didn't react to her sarcasm. "Not expecting any." He returned outside for another load.

A half-hour later, the linens were unpacked, the dishes shelved, and Dani was perched on the recliner as Pete attached wires and cables behind the TV.

"Pete, can I talk to you about something?"

"As long as it's not about my sister," he replied from behind the cabinet. "What's up?"

Scratching her plan to get Pete's take on Jim, instead she shared the news that Lilly had found her son's parents.

"You're kidding me!" Pete popped his head up over the shelf. "Is she going to meet them? And her son?"

"She can't. But that's where I come in."

Dani continued, telling him about Lilly's illness and then, gently, about Jim's offer and the test-run to Missouri with him and Donna.

"I don't know. I don't like it." Pete squeezed out around the TV to the center of the small living room. "She likes him, but there's something about the guy—"

"—that isn't right," Dani said, finishing his statement. "I know! He acts all sweet around her. But when she's not around, he acts—"

"—like a dick!" Pete erupted, snapping shut the metal toolbox.

Dani nodded. "Yeah, like a . . . dick." The word was a bit coarse, but she agreed with the sentiment. "I don't know why we can see it but she can't—or won't, maybe. I want to say something, but I don't want to hurt her. I think she really likes him."

"Now I know why she wants me to work for her next week." He added another expletive, softly. "I shouldn't have said yes."

They were both silent for a moment, then Dani tapped the arms of the recliner, a signal that it was time for her to head out.

"Let me know if something else comes up, okay? About Jim, or Lilly's son?" Pete tucked his dirty t-shirt into the waistband of his jeans. "I've got to get back to the library. My lunch break is over, and I'm late."

They left together, Pete closing the door behind them.

"Aren't you going to lock it?"

Pete laughed. "They can help themselves. I've never locked a door before—not going to start now."

During the rest of the drive home, Dani thought about Pete and his new place, Donna's selective behavior, and Tot's shady deal. Had everyone suddenly changed, in the space of a summer? Or were things around Crestview not what she'd assumed them to be?

Cody met the truck in the driveway, having freed himself somehow from inside the house. She asked him about this as she brought the fly killers and bug spray to the barn, but he gave nothing away.

Dani retrieved the halter and lead rope from their new hiding spot, behind the grain holder. She felt a bit foolish: a grown woman shouldn't need to secrete her belongings on her own property. But if the trickery prevented Jim from helping himself, then it was worth it.

She carried the tack out to her horse. "Okay, Scout," she began, testing the name again. "You know this part's hard for me." She lifted the halter. "Let's get this up there so I can put the fly spray on you."

Dani positioned the nosepiece in front of the horse. The horse looked at it, looked back at Dani, and sauntered away.

"No fair! Come on, now, girl—you've got to help me here."

Dani followed her, still holding the halter. This time, she waited until the horse stopped moving before reaching the leather circle up the horse's nose. She managed to snare her muzzle and, after three tries, secured the band behind her ears. The horse didn't spook or show signs of fear or anger, which gave Dani the confidence to try to apply the fly spray, just as the girl at the store demonstrated.

Holding the lead line with her left hand, Dani depressed the button on the fly can with her right.

With a loud, sibilant hiss, it shot out a strong mist two feet ahead.

It flew nowhere near her front legs, but the horse panicked. For the first time since she'd arrived, the mare reared up, pulling the lead line taut, and danced on her hind feet, trying to get away. She snorted and huffed, desperate for a way to escape.

Dani dropped both the can and the rope. "Sorry, girl, sorry!" She tried to keep still. "Not used to fly spray, huh? We'll have to work on that."

She didn't pick up the rope right away, choosing instead to let the horse settle first.

Many long minutes passed before the mare finally sighed, lowered her head, and began nosing around for errant hay.

"Let's call it a day then, should we?" Dani took the opportunity to inch forward and unclasp the mare's halter. She gently smoothed the animal's mane. "We'll keep trying, though. We just can't give up. Deal?"

The big horse quit chewing to look at her. Blinking her dark lashes, the mare blurbled a soft nicker, causing her to drop the grass she'd foraged.

I guess it's not a permanent scar, then, Dani decided. *It's so easy, for her to forgive.*

She latched the gate shut, then reentered the barn to hide the tack behind the old freezer once again. *Forgiveness comes harder for me.*

On her way to the kitchen to rustle up something for dinner, Dani paused to check her email. A message from Lilly popped up in her inbox.

Before pressing the icon to open it, Dani closed her eyes and breathed a silent prayer. She remembered Lilly's visit to her special tree last summer: how Lilly's composure had faltered, how she'd plunged her hands and heart and grief into the earth before it. Lilly's visit to that place had been a mission, a holy way for her broken heart to begin mending. It somehow satisfied and quieted the older woman's spirit.

Dani hoped that Lilly's quest to meet her son's parents—and then meet him, too—had a similar result.

She opened the message. Lilly described a water aerobics class she'd taken and a dinner with a woman she hadn't seen in ages. She shared nothing about her illness—which, in the days since their phone call, Dani had intuited was cancer.

At the end of the email, Lilly added a line about finding a time to talk on the phone so she could share the name and address of the adoptive parents.

Could Dani call her Sunday evening? Lilly would be waiting.

Dani tapped out a quick reply and suggested a time.

Before logging off, she sneaked a peek at her bank account balance. It was lower than she expected it to be, and she kicked herself for looking.

She wasn't hungry anymore.

Instead of going to the kitchen, she went out to the porch.

The empty field across the road had been tilled in the last two days while she was away. The fading light smoothed the harsh, parallel lines, yet Dani could see long shadows in the depths of the scratched furrows.

She called Cody from the backyard, and they watched the twilight together. Dani told him that she didn't really need a drink tonight, that she didn't want to rely on alcohol to relax.

He thumped his tail.

They listened to the night's music. A pair of ducks or geese flapped overhead, calling out to each other about which slough or ditch or field would be the best for their lodgings. A whoosh was carried on the soft evening breeze from the mare's corral—a contented acceptance, Dani decided, of her place in this new environment. Daytime insects were all abed, but the refrain of their sunshine chorus was echoed on the rounded coos of a mourning dove nesting in the driveway pine.

Fireflies sparked through the dark trees along the far side of the hay field. The tiny bright lights flirted with one another, flashing together and apart again like blinking Christmas lights.

Then she heard a low whine. As the sound expanded across the field, the fireflies' lights bloomed, flitting closer through thick trunks and low, bent branches.

That's when Dani realized that the lights didn't belong to fireflies after all.

They were headlights. A group of four-wheelers careened across the shorn pasture. The engines' volume, amplified and distorted, bounced off her metal barn.

When the group neared the road, the headlights snapped off. Dani heard the machines skid in big arcs across the surface, spraying gravel that pinged and popped off the tree trunks before they accelerated away.

There was a full minute of silence after their departure. Nature's night creatures waited, apprehensive that the disturbances might reappear.

They didn't.

Gradually, as if released from under a cover slowly peeled back, pips and calls and coos tentatively reasserted themselves. Five minutes later, it was like the symphony's intermission had never happened.

Dani called the dog from the porch's edge, and they went inside. She turned on the hall table lamp and caught her reflection in the mirror hanging above. Her cheeks were flushed and rosy, her hair sticking out from the cap she'd shoved onto her head when she was trying the fly spray, and there was hay on her shirt collar.

Dani smiled at her image. But the smile faded as she recalled the evening's strange ending.

The face in the reflection was frowning by the time Dani and Cody went upstairs to bed.

7

THE NEXT MORNING after feeding the animals, Dani shuffled piles of manure from the pen to a pile behind the barn and thought about how much easier the job would be with a wheelbarrow. She heard a vehicle coming up her driveway. Happy to take a break, she tossed down the shovel, wiped her hands along the backside of her jeans, and went to meet her visitor.

Pete grinned at her through the passenger window of his truck's cab. "Hey. I wanted to apologize for yesterday, when you came to help me and I was so . . ." He eyed her hasty attempt to hide her manure-soiled hands. "What, are you trying to hide a new manicure?"

"No, I was busy doing poop patrol."

Pete laughed. "That sounds more like you than a manicure does." He held out a small silver tool, bent at an angle at one end. "I brought you a gift. Good thing you don't care about girly things—this'll get you dirtier than what you were doing when I drove up."

"What is it?" She tried not to let his "girly" comment get to her. Compared to his sister and the new teacher, though, Dani was decidedly more a tomboy than the other two.

"A foot pick. Sort of like a manicure tool for horses. You have one already?"

"I couldn't even tell you," Dani replied. "Barbara dropped off a bunch of old stuff from when they had horses. But to be honest, I've only used the brush so far."

Both she and Pete turned to look at the mare, standing patiently in her corner. "Can you show me how to use it?"

Pete explained the process as they entered the corral. The first step was to get Scout haltered. Dani volunteered to get the tack; she didn't want to explain why it was hidden.

When she returned, she waited a moment to assess the situation. Should she halter Scout herself? A sharp-edged flash of Jim trying to force his way with the mare skipped across her memory.

But Pete was different. The mare wasn't afraid of him. In fact, she'd ambled up to the fence to sniff at his shirt through the metal bars. Dani handed the halter to Pete.

She watched him approach the mare, talking quietly as he kept himself in her view. He stroked her shoulder, then looped one arm over her neck and gripped the strap there, while his other hand held open the circle part below her head. The horse dropped her nose in, just like that, and he buckled it seconds later. Easy as pie.

Dani was relieved that she let Pete do it—and embarrassed about the struggles she'd had chasing the mare around, trying to push up the halter from underneath. Pete's way was infinitely more practical.

He loosely tied the lead rope to one fence panel and pulled the hoof pick from his back pocket. "Here we go," he said. "Let's start on her left side." He waved for her to join him by the mare's front leg.

"I'm afraid she'll kick at me," Dani admitted. She placed herself by the gate for an easy way out, if need be.

"Has she kicked at you before?"

Dani shook her head. "No. No, she's really easygoing." She added more. "She lets me brush her, but I don't really stand close for that either."

"Let me tell you a secret: if you're standing away from her, she'll have more force to kick at you with, if she's going to kick." He stressed the *if* before he continued. "Stand as close as you can to her, even when you're brushing her." He chuckled. "It'll hurt less."

Dani did not laugh. "That's why I'm afraid of doing her feet or brushing her legs. When I'm down there, she's up so high and tall, I think she could really cause some damage if I get in the way."

Pete's tone turned serious, but a hint of a smile still pulled at the corners of his eyes. "Yep, she could. But she hasn't. Has she?"

Dani answered with another no.

"And judging from the way she looks to you, I don't think she will." He paused. "Do you think she will?"

The words tumbled out before Dani could stop them: "No. No, I don't."

"Then you need to act that way. She needs you to be her leader. She needs you to have confidence and show that you trust her. Then she'll trust you." He bent down and took hold of the mare's front leg, just below her knee. "Do you believe me?"

"I guess so."

What Pete said made some sense once Dani considered the progress she and the mare had made. The time they'd spent together had shown Dani a pattern to the animal's behaviors, and she'd come to expect these as the norm, the benchmark to measure the horse's improving health. She wondered if the horse was learning the same, from her daily attentions. Darting away, snorting in fear, and hiding in the corner were behaviors the mare had moved beyond. The horse continued to look better too—at least to Dani's eyes. She seemed sturdier on her feet, and the concave places below each hip had become slightly rounded.

"The trust part I get," Dani said, continuing her inner thoughts out loud. "But being a 'leader'? How am I supposed to do that, be in charge of her? It's so, I don't know, patriarchal or whatever."

Pete's laughter spilled out. "She doesn't care what sex you are. She just wants to know that you'll come out and feed her every day and that you won't hit her if she doesn't understand."

He pinched her leg, somehow, making the horse raise her foot, which he grabbed and held off the ground. "She wants to respect you. She'll respond better, if she does."

The mare sighed and dropped her head. "See how she's relaxed, just now?"

He flipped the hook pick so the point faced down and started scraping along the inside of her hoof. The horse craned her thick neck around to look back at Pete and Dani, both bent over her upturned foot. Evidently, the mare decided to go along with the procedure. She accepted their ministrations, turning to watch Cody prance along the far barn wall, intent on a mission of his own. She didn't try to take her foot away.

Dani knelt to see the hoof wall more clearly. "How do you know so much?" she asked. "Like, are you supposed to scrape along that inside part, or leave it alone?"

"I wanted to have a horse when we were little, but Dad called them 'hay burners' and said he'd rather spend his money to make money." He finished scraping and released her foot, which signaled the horse to put her foot down again. "But I used my high school work-experience class to explore the career of equine reproduction." He wiggled his eyebrows at Dani as he edged back to the horse's rear leg.

She rolled her eyes.

"The old fart that ran the repro barn had me and Tony, the other kid, learn everything from the ground up. Old school. We spent the first few days learning the 'correct way' to muck out stalls." He pointed to the hind foot. "Here. Come closer."

Dani bent down, shoulder to shoulder with him, and he showed her how to pinch the little pad near the knee, encouraging the horse to lift her leg. She did, and he used the little tool to clear packed mud and little rocks from the back hoof.

"Get it, now?"

Dani nodded. "Yep."

"Let's go to the other side, then. Your turn." Pete rubbed against the mare's rear end as he moved around her, to her front. "See? Stay close and keep in touch. Let her know where you are."

Dani thought she understood. She followed and knelt next to the front leg, running her hand along the back to search for that pad. The horse's hair was soft, and the heat of her skin underneath was a surprise, coming from such a thin and exposed limb.

"Find it?" Pete asked. "Need help?"

"I think I got it."

And she must have, for the mare lifted her foot and waited patiently for Dani to clean it. Now that she was actually doing it, she felt pretty comfortable with the process.

"To be honest, I didn't necessarily agree with Donna when she said you should get a horse," Pete confessed. "You seem to be adjusting to her fast, but still . . . Is this too much for you?"

"I'd be lying if I said it's been easy." Dani patted the mare. "But really, I think we'll be okay."

Pete moved to the side. "Okay, let's see you do the back one. By yourself."

Dani finished the process easily, without any fuss.

"I think you picked a good one, Dan," he commented. "She really has a good head."

"What does that mean, exactly?"

Pete smiled. "She knows what you're trying to do, and she's overlooking your faults to let you do it."

"But how does she know what I want to do?" Dani's voice came out a little shaky. "I don't have a clue!"

"She trusts you. That's step one." He unclipped the lead rope from the halter but left the other end hanging from the fence. "In case you want to try again later, I'll leave this right here. Okay with you?"

Dani didn't respond right away. It amazed her, how relaxed she was after spending the last minutes underneath a horse. She was also touched that Pete had given up so much time to help her. She wondered what it might be like to have Pete as more than a friend.

"Thanks, Pete," she smiled. She gave him a quick one-armed hug. "Can I get you a cup of coffee? Something stronger?"

"No, I'm good. But hey, are you thinking about getting another horse?"

"What for?"

"They rest easier, when there's two together." He noticed her expression and went on. "But maybe you're right—start with one, then think about another."

That tight fist of anxiety poked Dani's sternum. She couldn't really afford to feed one horse, let alone two. And she wouldn't be in debt to Jim now, either, if—

"I should get going." Pete's voice interrupted her reverie of self-incrimination.

"Right. Sorry. You've really helped me—us—out today."

"No problem. Good to do something else for a change, especially with my sister—and moving." His smile faded. "Actually, I was wondering if you could do me a favor..."

His question caught her off guard.

"The next time you see Jessica...?" Pete didn't look at Dani. "Could you—will you ask her if she's seeing anyone?"

So much for those tiny thoughts of their ever having a future as a couple. Not that she actually expected Pete and her to get together. Still, she didn't expect the idea to get erased within minutes of sort of, kind of imagining it.

"Sure. I'm happy to be your spy," she replied, but she couldn't resist adding a little dig: "You think she's okay with dating someone her dad's age?"

"Funny." He nudged her with his elbow, but his laugh sounded forced. "Do you really think that? That I'm too old for her?"

"I'm just kidding. If you ask me, a person's heart goes where it wants to, and we just try to keep up."

"Thanks, Dani. You got a good head."

"Ha. Next, you'll be wanting to clean my hooves."

He laughed. They went together to his truck.

"Thanks again, for today." Dani slapped the hood of his truck for goodbye and moved off the driveway.

He tooted the horn and pulled away.

Dani stood on the lawn a few moments longer. Flecks of quartz in the driveway gravel sparkled in the sun. A single songbird warbled from up near the top of the evergreen by the mailbox. An old maple between the house and barn was just starting to show a tint of red.

Cody scampered up to her, panting.

"How do I get stuck in the middle of these things, huh?" she asked him. "Between Donna and her brother, we're going to be busy."

Dani looked over at her horse once again. She was surprised and amazed that the simple chore they'd just completed gained them so much ground forward, as partners.

She called to the mare. "What do you think, Scout?"

The name was more than a Scout Finch allusion now. This name was the most appropriate choice. It was also an apt description for the keenly observant mare. Every time Dani peeked out from the porch or the truck to check on the horse, the mare was looking back at her. She liked to monitor Dani and Cody's comings and goings. She kept an eye out for them.

Like a scout, Dani thought.

The animal seemed to have accepted being part of Dani and Cody's pack, their herd. They all played their parts. They'd keep watch over each other.

Dani returned to the corral and placed herself next to her mare's round flank. She breathed in her grassy, warm tang, a scent that had become a signal for her to relax and let go.

The horse—Scout—brushed her lips across the top of Dani's head and gently tugged at a few stray hairs as if she was teasing. Both ears pointed forward, and she relaxed one hip. She let out a big whoosh, then lowered her big head against Dani's shoulder. She rested it there, encircling her. Like a hug.

Moments later, Scout disengaged from her owner. Spying a wisp of hay, she ambled to the metal panel to graze. She took her warmth with her, leaving Dani aware of her growing affection for the mare. Her friend.

She'd also become keenly aware of the other signs her friend left behind, namely a big clot of brown ooze now adorning her right shoe. Dani laughed, luring Cody into the corral for a look-see.

Glancing back at the manure pile and the shovel, wishing again that she had a wheelbarrow, she remembered where she could find one: Mr. Randolph had an old one in an outbuilding on one of his properties.

"How's about a ride, buddy?" she asked Cody. "Should we go to Mr. Randolph's? It's almost time for our monthly property check, anyway. What do you think? Go for a ride?"

She bent to give his scruff a scratch; he gave her cheek a wet kiss.

In Iowa, the late-summer days were warm, but darkness crept in earlier each night, bringing cooler shadows and clearer skies. As Dani and her dog crossed the county on their errand, she noticed hints of more autumn color in the trees and wild shrubs along the route.

Their first stop was a little square house with a low-pitched tin roof. The bushes planted under the front window years ago had become bright red, their little hard berries a temptation for wild birds who'd soon start journeying south for the winter.

The driveway was two gravel tracks, the edges and the middle swath between them nearly reclaimed by long grass. Two barns squatted ahead, but only one was whole. The other, a skeleton, was stripped of its weathered exterior boards, scavenged before Dani started monitoring the property. Every month, her task was to check that no one had come back to try their luck with the little house or the other barn.

This property was the one farthest from Crestview, so a person looking for materials would have to be willing to drive across the whole county to do so. The distance obviously didn't deter the original barn-board thief, but with the new yellow No Trespassing signs and Dani stopping every three to four weeks, Mr. Randolph figured the holding should be fine.

When Dani exited the truck, Cody ran around to the rear of the property, sniffing the perimeter. Dani followed more slowly, glancing at every opening for evidence of tampering.

Everything looked closed and tight.

"One down, two to go," Dani announced to Cody. "C'mon. Let's head over to the next place."

Returning to the truck, Dani heard a jingling coming from her pocket. The caller ID on her cell showed Donna's number.

"Hi. What's up?" Dani answered, sliding into the driver's seat.

"Hey, Dan! I can't talk long. Jim's got things set up for our trip. We're leaving first thing Tuesday morning."

"Oh. Okay."

Only two days away, Dani determined. *I wish I would've known sooner. I could've asked Pete to stop by and check on—*

"Well, then, I gotta run," Donna interrupted.

"Wait!" Dani blurted before she could stop herself.

Even though time was limited, Dani realized this might be the only opportunity to tell Donna about Lilly's news, without Jim hovering nearby. She let the words fly.

"I've been meaning to tell you: Lilly thinks she's found her son! Well, his parents, anyways. After all these years! Isn't that incredible?"

She expected to hear an excited, happy response.

She heard nothing.

Dani stumbled a bit but pressed forward into the difficult part of the story. "Well, um, the thing is, she can't travel to see him herself. Not right now, anyway."

Still nothing.

"She's sick, Donna. Cancer, I think, though she hasn't used that word. And she's starting treatment. She's just . . . she's not well." Faced with this abrupt silence, Dani didn't know what else to add.

Donna's eventual reaction was reserved, cool, almost insulted: "How long have you known about this?"

Dani didn't have an answer ready.

"Well, I haven't seen you alone, you know, for a while—with Jim and the café and all? I thought you'd rather have privacy when you heard." Saying it out loud stripped the ambiguity and extra feelings away, but the excuse still sounded flat. It was making things worse.

"What? Like no one here has ever seen me get emotional?" Her sarcasm had sharp edges. "And what about Jim? What's he got to do with it?"

Dani didn't dare heap her true opinion of Jim on top of the pile Donna had thrown her way. She opted for what seemed like a neutral response.

"He's pretty forceful, you know. I don't want you—your feelings— to get trampled." Donna started to argue, but Dani kept going.

"He wasn't around when we learned about Lilly and Cisco and their baby, and he doesn't strike me as the kind of guy who's super sensitive about things like this."

"You don't know him like I do."

Dani's better judgment stifled her immediate response: *You don't know him that well, either.* "True," she admitted, instead. "I don't know him. But I know you, so I guess I'll have to trust your opinion of him."

She didn't believe this statement, but it was one she could live with. She hoped Donna wouldn't decipher her unease or detect the hidden truth.

The other line went silent again.

"Anyhow," Dani changed the subject, "it'll be good to ride down to Missouri together. We'll get all caught up, with all those hours on the road."

After a pause, Donna agreed. "Yeah. It'll be fun." Her voice was a bit softer. But she couldn't resist adding a little barb: "You know Jim'll be there too, right?"

"We'll make him sit in the back," Dani teased.

"Huh, like that'll work!" Finally, Donna's voice regained some of its good humor. "Speaking of work, I really do need to split. See ya Tuesday, hon."

After they disconnected, Dani sat in the truck for a while longer. Both hands gripped the steering wheel, a solid surface to grasp in contrast to the recent, shifting changes that seemed edgeless and unpredictable. *When did it become so hard to talk to her?* The answer followed as quickly as thunder followed a lightning strike: Jim.

She tried to throw off the uneasiness that settled across her shoulders and pretended she couldn't hear the little voice of her intuition. I'll deal with it later, she decided. *Once I'm out of his debt.*

After a quick ten-minute drive, Dani pulled into the second property on her monthly route. It featured a big metal outbuilding in which Mr. Randolph stored boats and other summer playthings. She and Cody climbed out of the truck and ambled for the door. She keyed open the padlock for access to the structure's dim, hollow shell. There were no windows on the ground level, but opaque fiberglass along the top edges of the building let a little light seep in, allowing Dani to gauge her footing and avoid banging into the machinery stored inside.

They passed plastic-covered vehicles and tarped RVs on their way to the back wall. She spotted the old wheelbarrow right where she remembered it, tucked under the wooden steps. She planned to grab it on her way out.

But first, she and Cody climbed the steps to the loft, where an enclosed room sat behind another padlocked door. Dani confirmed that this lock was secure, as well.

She'd never been inside the room. She wondered what Mr. Randolph stored there. Old tax forms? Family mementos? Anything could be hidden inside.

She created a list of possibilities as she retrieved the wheelbarrow and pushed it out to the truck. "We'll talk to Mr. Randolph about it, next time he calls," Dani assured Cody, tipping the wheelbarrow into the truck bed. "We're just borrowing it for now. Right?"

Cody wagged his tail politely.

The third property, featuring an old trailer house surrounded by a forest of pines, was about six more miles down the road. Turning into the driveway, Dani immediately saw that it didn't look the same as it had the previous month. Dozens of tire tracks—the top ones still fresh—covered the dirt driveway. She could see more crossings on what used to be the grass lawn.

Dani rolled down her window and listened, trying to detect activity. She scanned the building carefully, noticing further damage. Its aluminum skirting was torn off; only the section under the kitchen end remained. Empty cans and bottles and other litter were scattered around and underneath the raised structure. Maybe high schoolers were using the place as a party house?

She needed to investigate to see what else had been ruined, but she wasn't keen on entering the place by herself. Still perched on the driver's seat, she dialed the sheriff's office from inside her truck.

A grumpy male voice told her to sit tight, that "someone'll be there in an hour. Or so."

Dani couldn't wait an hour.

Cody accompanied her to the home's entrance. They were both alert as they crept up the metal steps.

Dani peered through the dangling front door. From what she could ascertain, the trailer was deserted. All was still inside except for a rhythmic flapping noise, like a curtain in an open window, swinging against a metal screen.

Dani and the dog stepped in. The pungent aroma of mildew, urine, and vinegar invaded her throat, making her gag. Plugging her nose with one hand, she breathed through her mouth. Brown and green bottles littered the kitchen's built-in dining table. A section of shelves had been pulled from the wall into a silty pile on the marred countertop. Empty boxes, napkins, and plastic bags, used and discarded, covered the floor.

In the living room to the left, there was a makeshift bed in one corner—a stained mattress with an afghan crocheted in gaudy, cheap yarn tossed on top. The window in this room was shattered; only the flimsy curtains, pulled shut to cover the opening, were left as a makeshift deterrent against foraging animals. Muddy human footprints covered the carpeting.

Before taking another step, Dani opened her phone and called Mr. Randolph. She described the scene, assuring him that the sheriff was on his way and that she was in no danger.

She promised to call him back with any news after the authorities had inspected his property.

He told her to stay safe.

Hanging up, Dani continued to the bedroom, at the end of the hall—and froze.

This room smelled even more acidic, like pure vinegar. Huge sheets of industrial plastic covered the walls from ceiling to floor. The carpet was gone, replaced by plywood spotted with black and yellow stains.

Two rectangular folding tables lined the longer walls. One table was covered with a bunch of cardboard boxes, several brown grocery bags, and a huge mixing bowl. Someone had shoved more boxes and bags under the table, and a broken kitchen stool lay on its side on the floor.

On the other table was a metal scale. Strewn next to it were a handful of tiny plastic bags, blue Xs smeared across their fronts.

Whatever breath Dani had left in her lungs was instantly sucked out.

Cody whined and crouched close to Dani, like he was hurt or in pain. She stooped to check on him, careful to balance herself so as not to touch the soiled floor. He whirled for the door but looked back, wanting her to follow.

She did. They exited the trailer as if something more than their fear or imagination chased behind them.

They were almost back to the truck when a brown-and-white vehicle met them in the driveway. The siren was off, but strobe lights winked blue and red against the pine trees' dark branches.

"Cody, sit," Dani commanded, stepping to the side so the officer could see them both clearly.

The patrol car blocked their exit. The man inside climbed out. "Stay where you are, ma'am. And take out your ID." He positioned his car door as a barrier between them.

"It's in my truck. Do you want me to—"

"Don't move." He sidestepped around his door, one hand at his hip holster. "Your dog—do you need to restrain him?"

"He won't charge you," she managed. "Th— the license is in my glovebox." Dani swallowed. "I'm the one who called, Officer. I'm here on behalf of the owner, Cecil Randolph?" She unconsciously raised both hands in front of her.

The officer nodded toward her truck. "Please get your ID for me."

Dani kept herself in the open as possible as she moved to the truck and located her ID card. "Where do you want me to put this?"

"I'll come and get it. Are you sure the dog's all right?"

"I think he'll be okay." Dani didn't quite understand the officer's concern about Cody. The dog wasn't showing any aggression. He hadn't moved from her side nor given any indication that he was about to do so. It was as if he sensed the seriousness in the air and wanted to be as obedient and nonthreatening as his owner was acting.

The officer's demeanor changed once he scanned her card. "Hey, I know you." The smile that suddenly bloomed appeared genuine.

"I saw you at the auction, a few weeks back. You and Donna, from the diner, right?"

What? Why isn't he more concerned about the call? Isn't that the reason he's here?

"I was at the auction, yes." Dani's reply sounded frosty; she wasn't as quick to share the remembrance, with his gun holster so close to his shooting hand. "Sorry. I guess I was more into the horses that day."

The officer took a step back. He removed his hat and sunglasses. "I don't think I introduced myself. I'm John Davies. Deputy sheriff, but you probably already figured that out."

Dani noticed that his brown eyes matched his uniform. Then a sudden recollection flooded her memory. "Oh, you helped me up the steps."

"So, were you successful?"

She scrunched her nose. She couldn't tell if he was asking about her fall or the auction. And what about this trailer?

He clarified. "Did you get yourself a horse?"

"Oh," she understood, finally. "I did. I'm not much of a rider, though. She's more like a pet. A project, I guess."

"I'm not a horse person, myself."

She had to ask: "Then isn't a horse auction a strange place to go?" *And why are we talking about horses, with what's right behind us?*

He lifted his gaze to look past her shoulder, like he'd also remembered the real reason he'd been called to the address. "Right." He returned her ID and placed his hat back on. "How about you show me what you found?"

They climbed the trailer steps together. Dani entered the ruin first, explaining how she'd been hired to monitor the property. She told him about the former condition of the home and the timing of her last visit.

"That room is the worst," she added, pointing to the back bedroom.

He moved past her, glanced inside, then whirled back to the hallway. "Dani? Let's get you back to your truck now. I've got this."

He reached for the memo pad in his uniform pocket even as he shepherded her to the door. "Should I get a hold of you or Mr. Randolph for follow-up?"

The air outside the trailer was a fresh relief. "Me, I think. You can call or stop by my place. Whatever's best."

He jotted down her address and phone number, thanked her, and they returned to their vehicles.

As she pulled away, Dani heard him talking over the radio with his dispatcher, but she couldn't determine exactly what was being said.

She left the property, wheelbarrow in back, and steered for home. She'd barely gone a quarter-mile, though, before meeting a shiny red Chevy truck coming her way. She was curious about its appearance on this desolate stretch, especially now, after finding the trashed trailer.

The driver, his brimmed hat shadowing his features, didn't salute, turn his head, or acknowledge her as their vehicles passed.

Dani watched him through her rearview mirror. She didn't know how the shiny truck was related to the trailer's condition, but she was certain they were connected. Sure enough, it slowed at the driveway to the trailer site, then it checked its turn and hit the gas to speed past.

She smirked, envisioning the driver's alarm as he realized that a sheriff's vehicle occupied the property's entrance. Her smirk melted into a tight wince, though, when it occurred to her that this truck could have pulled in while she was inside the trailer, alone.

Were things like this going on when Dani first moved to Crestview? If so, she never knew about them.

The drive home was a blur. Dani recalled the semis. The four-wheelers. Tot and his exchange at the Stop-n-Save. Now Mr. Randolph's trailer. The blue Xs.

Jim.

He was involved somehow. Was he using?

Did Donna know anything about this?

Perhaps driving with them on Tuesday would give her some answers. She might see something that would explain it all away. Or, she might see more than she bargained for.

Maybe she should just mind her own business. Maybe she should walk away right now. An urge to call Donna nearly overcame her.

But if she backed out on Jim's offer, then she wouldn't be able to fulfill her promise to Lilly.

That final thought was the one that brought stillness to the questions circling Dani's mind. She pulled into her own driveway and rolled to a gentle stop.

For one long moment, she closed her eyes and tried to identify every sound she could hear through the open window.

She relaxed; her jaw unclamped and her shoulders released.

Sliding down from the truck, Dani made herself count each step to the porch. She placed herself on its edge to watch the sunset.

The thinnest rim of the sun's brilliant globe gradually slipped below the dark etchings of trees silhouetted along the horizon. The cloud cover that ensued, deep and dense, felt impenetrable.

But then a sudden crack emitted an unexpected glimmer, a flash of one steely ray slicing through the thickening darkness.

Dani took this as a sign, a signal that she was doing the right thing

8

THE EARLY LIGHT THAT TUESDAY MORNING was flimsy and transparent. Fog rested in the low places, the ditches and furrows, and between the stalks of growing grains.

When Dani emerged from the house, Scout was waiting near her gate. She followed on her side of the fence as Dani and Cody entered the barn.

"I'll be back soon," Dani told her. "Cody will keep you company."

Hearing his name, the dog trotted over to Dani. She attached a long rope to his collar, filled his dish with his kibble, then set out a five-gallon bucket of water just for him. She tied his rope to the bottom rung of Scout's fence so he couldn't tip it over, then piled an old blanket into a shady corner for him to rest on.

He whined. Cody wasn't used to being tied.

"It's better than being locked in the house, boy," Dani assured him.

Cody didn't look convinced.

Dani wanted the dog secured so Pete wouldn't have to search for him. When Dani called Pete the night before, he'd agreed to check in on Cody and Scout—though he'd sounded cranky about it. She chalked it up to his chagrin about having to manage the diner in Donna's absence, too.

Dani reached through the fence and smoothed Scout's mane, releasing scents of grass and heat and musk. Cody laid down on the blanket pile and sighed.

They'll be all right for the day, she told herself.

As she heard the first sounds of the truck down-shifting at the crossroads, Dani remembered what Pete told her before hanging up: "Call me. On the trip. You know—if anything comes up."

Steeling herself, Dani jogged back to the porch for her things, called goodbye to her animals over her shoulder, then hurried to the end of her driveway so Jim wouldn't have to turn in.

The truck's high beams weren't really necessary in the rising dawn. They poked wispy tunnels through the dust that streamed like dry rivers over the huge silver trailer. The unit's back lights bathed the falling debris in a shroud of red.

Dani heard the animals inside the container and took a deep, deep breath.

The truck's lights blinked twice at her. The rig slowed and the brakes chattered, propelling rocks sideways like buckshot into the ditch.

The interior light came on, backlighting Donna's coiffed hair into a halo. Jim leered over his steering wheel like a manic jack-o'-lantern.

Dani waited by the ditch until the rig stopped, then jogged to the passenger's seat. The huge door swung open, and Donna bestowed a bright pink smile down upon her.

"Watch those steps, darlin'." She reached out for Dani's gear. "Whoops-a-daisy! Here you go!"

Dani lifted her backpack and Thermos, then used the silver handrail to pull herself up the two metal steps.

"Good mornin'!" Donna exclaimed. "You ready for an adventure?"

Donna's good mood, on the heels of their recent uneasy conversation, raised Dani's spirit. Even Donna's outfit was bright and cheery, an off-the-shoulder tunic over capri pants and heeled sandals, a vibrant contrast to the uniform she wore at the café.

Stepping into the cab, Dani discovered it was more than she expected. The two front seats were deep and plush, something she learned as she sank into the passenger's seat. The area behind the seats was tall enough for a person to stand. Along the back wall, a bed was made up with a patriotic bedcover and two pillows encased in American flags. Cupboards and cabinets were wedged into every space in between, including the spaces under the seats and the ceiling overhead.

"How'd ya like it?" Jim asked before returning his attention to the road. "Not so bad, eh?" He pushed the gearshift at his right knee and the truck grumbled forward.

"Great," Dani managed. She didn't elaborate.

Her reticence was due to the glimpse she caught of his tattoo as he shifted, pricking her to recall the little bags abandoned inside the trashed trailer house, their blue Xs bright against the white sheeting they rested upon. And Tot, too—the new mark scratched onto the inside of his wrist at the gas station.

She wasn't just uneasy about the animals trapped back in the trailer, heading to the stockyard; now she wrestled with Jim's involvement in the mystery surrounding those Xs.

If it weren't for her commitment to Lilly, Dani would sooner leap from the truck than to go another mile forward next to this man. But she had to make it work. She had to find a way to repay Jim for bringing Scout home and, way beyond that, to help Lilly find her son.

She made herself focus on something she could control. She aimed her question at Donna, behind her: "Is there a place for you to sit, back there?"

"Sure is!" Donna bounced on the little bed. "And look, Dani, there's a TV, and a fridge. And see here—a cute little microwave!" One lacquered nail pointed out the various creature comforts. "And we got a little window that opens up. And here"—she pulled back a dark curtain—"there's even a little potty!"

"Got that for you girls," Jim stated, proud of the acquisition. "Don't need it myself, but I want you ladies to travel in comfort."

By that time, the rig was moving faster, but the jerks between gears had Donna grabbing for the cabinets and shelving to keep her balance.

"You stay up front, so you can see how it all works," Donna suggested. "I'll get breakfast ready." She was as delighted as a little girl playing house.

Dani reached for the seatbelt and clicked herself in. Her seat could have been mistaken for a living-room recliner with its lumbar roll, heating and cooling options, and adjustable arm rests. She watched Jim maneuver from their county road out onto the bigger four-lane, bringing the rig to cruising speed.

What Dani noticed most was the lack of sound inside the big vehicle. Except for Conway Twitty and Donna's chatter, the enclosure was as quiet as a cocoon. It reminded Dani of being inside a soundproofed room, the kind a patient entered for a hearing test, where silence pushed into one's brain space like a heavy weight.

"So, what are we hauling?" she asked.

"Hogs." Jim's reply was matter-of-fact. "I pretty much take whatever needs takin'."

"Where do you pick them—the load—up?"

The aroma of eggs and cheese wafted to the front.

"Depends." Jim shrugged. "I gotta guy, tells me what needs to go where. Ain't worth goin', though, unless I get a full load."

Dani considered this for a minute. "Do you always haul animals, or—"

"Yep," Jim interrupted. "Stock's got the best rate on return. Higher pay for a quicker turnaround." He switched to the outside lane. "Just gotta get 'em to the stockyard alive."

"In other words, I'll be hauling slaughter animals, for sure." She said this more quietly, to herself, as she looked through the front windshield. The huge sheet of glass revealed a gradient wash, from dark denim on one horizon to the hint of a pale calm sea on the other.

Donna maneuvered up to the front with a steaming burrito on a plate for Jim, then disappeared again.

"Thanks, darlin'!" he called back to her. "Whoo-ee, I'm a lucky guy." He sounded grateful for the distraction.

Donna returned with another plate for Dani, then dragged up an empty garbage can, flipped it upside down, and sat between them to drink her coffee.

Dani found it funny that the rig offered luxe accommodations for two but left the third passenger to fend for herself.

"Whatcha visitin' about?" Donna asked.

By this time, Dani reckoned, they were almost to Cedar Rapids. "I was asking Jim about what I'll be taking, hauling, for him."

"Want to try driving today?" Jim spoke up. "I can coach ya." His tone sounded almost genuine.

Dani assumed it was because Donna was there.

"Maybe after you've unloaded the pigs—the hogs, I mean," Dani decided. "I'd feel better practicing when there aren't live creatures getting banged up or bruised just because I don't know how to shift."

Jim guffawed, but Donna nudged him with her knee. "That sounds great, Dan," she broke in over him.

Dani knew that injuring the cargo wasn't an issue for Jim. He drove as a business, and hauling animals was the same to him as hauling merchandise or refrigerated goods or those new solar panel grids everyone had started installing. He got his money as long as he dropped off the freight where it was supposed to be dropped, mostly alive.

Donna changed the subject. "What do you think about the sleeping arrangements? Pretty cozy, right? Jim doesn't ever have to get a room, unless he's going all the way down to the border—"

"Donna," Jim's good humor vanished. "You know I don't need her for that trip. I've got my other drivers for that, if I can't go."

He enunciated each word separately. "She'll be doing the run from Iowa to Missouri. That's all."

The seatbelt over Dani's hips prevented her from seeing Donna directly.

"What I meant was, she can pull over to sleep, if she needs to," Donna amended her comment, emphasizing the word meant. "With this little nest right behind the driver's seat, there's no need for her to spend money on a room or be nervous about sleeping in a strange place." Her reply pushed back at him, but lightly.

Dani had no desire to prolong the discomfort hanging over the cab. She introduced a different topic. "So why are we taking this route?" She pointed to an exit sign for the state highway. "Wouldn't the interstate be faster?"

"Yeah, you can move a helluva lot faster on the interstate," Jim admitted. "But this route has less restrictions, and there ain't no weigh stations. Less troopers, too. It's not much difference 'far as time, though. You'll still be down and back before you know it."

For the next hour, Dani listened and watched as Jim explained the procedures, which all essentially boiled down to "shift to keep the RPM pointer in the orange range on the gauge."

Dani agreed it would be helpful to try driving with him on board, to be sure she could do it.

In Hannibal, Missouri, they took a break to stretch their legs and pick up a quick lunch. They parked the rig along the far edge of the truck lot, on the other side of a rest stop. Jim said he'd wait in line at the Subway deli while Dani followed Donna to the women's restroom.

"I think it's going great, don't you?" Donna's voice pierced the space from the stall next to Dani's.

Dani flushed before answering. "Yeah. It's not too bad." It was the truth—if she could keep the animals out of her mind. She went to the sinks in front of the mirror to wash her hands.

Donna joined her. "So, think you can do it? The solo run?" She shook her hands rid of the water, then pulled a tube of lipstick from her bra.

Donna was asking about Dani's ability to shift and maneuver the huge rig, but Dani attached a deeper meaning. Could she do it? Could she handle the emotional weight of her cargo? Could she settle her debt to a man with a blue X tattoo and an artificial smile?

"I think so." Once again, she tried her best to be honest. "I can use the money, Lord knows."

And I really need to help Lilly, she added, to herself.

Dani slid out of the way as a woman and her child rushed past.

Smacking her lips together, Donna gave herself a wink in the mirror before she responded. "I'm so happy this is all working out!"

She's overemphasizing the positive, Dani decided as they return to the semi, still idling with the doors locked. *I wonder why.*

Jim hadn't yet returned. They waited in the shade on the passenger's side.

Dani found it a little curious that no one parked next to them, though the lot was busy and there was a line of trucks waiting to refuel. The mystery didn't take long to solve, however.

"Pee-yoo!" Donna gasped. "Don't tell me those animals don't stink!" She plugged her nose.

Dani agreed. The stench was pungent and gut-churning. It was warmer in Hannibal than it'd been in Crestview that morning. The hogs in both levels of the trailer pressed their snouts against the quarter-sized holes for more air.

To distract herself from their plight, Dani launched into an explanation of how she'd use the solo trip to find Lilly's son's parents. It was as good a time as any, she figured, as they wouldn't have many other moments alone, outside of Jim's orbit.

"I've been meaning to tell you," she began. "The couple who adopted Lilly's son? Turns out they're actually here in Missouri, so I'm planning to—"

But Donna wasn't listening. Something else clearly riveted her attention. She stared intently over Dani's head, her eyebrows drawn so low they'd disappeared behind her shades.

Dani followed her friend's focus to see what was going on. In the last parking space past the Subway, Jim was nose to nose with a skinny guy. His cropped black hair gleamed; his mirrored sunglasses swiveled as he monitored the parking area around and beyond him.

Jim was trying to explain something. Two Subway bags dangled from one of Jim's wrists; he punctuated his words by waving his free hand for emphasis.

But the other man wasn't having it. He poked Jim in the chest before dropping a ring of keys at his feet, then he spun away and glided off around the far corner.

Jim stayed put. His big shoulders heaved up and down before he bent to retrieve the keys. Straightening up, he spotted the women watching him.

Instantly, that salesman-like grin came back, and he hurried across the asphalt to rejoin them.

Interesting, Dani mused. *That's the first time I've seen Jim bested by someone.*

"Who was that?" Donna's tone was a combination of curiosity, anger, and fear. "Why did he poke you?"

A fake chuckle preceded his answer. "Just another driver. He wants me to pick up his trailer on our return trip."

"How rude, though!" Donna stewed. "There's no reason for him to act that way, 'specially when you're the one doing him a favor!" She rubbed her thumb against her forefinger as she put two and two together. "What did he ask you to take back for him?"

Dani was also curious, and glad that Donna was the one to share her query out loud.

Before he could reply, though, Donna went on. "He looks dangerous, Jimmy." She reached for him. "It's not worth it, to get into trouble for—"

"Sh-h, darlin'," her boyfriend interrupted. He tried to hug her shoulders with his free hand. To an outsider, it would seem he really loved her, that he was concerned that she was so upset. "It's fine. It's all good. I'm just bringin' an empty trailer back for him. No big deal." He unlocked the cab and clicked open the passenger's door.

Dani climbed in first, leaving the passenger's seat open for her friend.

Donna settled herself, then fished through their lunch bags as Jim entered the cab from the driver's side. "And another thing"—she took out their sandwiches and distributed them—"Dani can't be involved in anything like that, either."

Hearing her name, Dani spoke up from the back. "Look, I'm just trying to get to Missouri to meet Lilly's son's parents, but she'll pay me for that. I don't have to do this drive. I'll have enough to get through . . . through Christmas, at least." Her comment wasn't entirely true, but she wanted to give herself an out if she needed one.

Donna's chin tucked back in surprise as she processed Dani's comment, like she hadn't heard Dani's report on the topic just minutes earlier. Her hesitation was momentary, though, and she returned her focus to the man behind the wheel.

"No, no—it'll be all right," Jim insisted. "I told ya—it's an empty trailer. I owe him— owe the guy a favor."

He slipped the big diesel engine into gear, and they rolled toward the exit. He held his sandwich in one hand, steered and shifted with the other, and tried to soothe Donna's concerns as he chewed.

Dani kept her own lunch on her lap and looked out on yet another field. They turned down the highway's entry ramp. Through the passenger's side mirror, she noticed a silver Mercedes pulling into the same turn lane. The driver had short dark hair and mirrored sunglasses.

Jim kept tabs on the man, too. He checked the mirrors like his head was on a swivel. He didn't let on that they were being followed, though. In fact, he became downright chatty, telling them his plan to take them out for dinner, once they'd finished at the stockyard.

As Jim went on, Dani ate and continued tracking the sedan. It looked like the same man who'd accosted Jim at the Subway.

Many miles later, it was still positioned behind them as they approached their exit. When they turned onto the ramp, the sedan suddenly veered off and disappeared.

Jim sank down into his seat and took a deep breath. He finally stopped chattering.

Fifteen minutes further on, they were at a stoplight when Donna broke the silence. "Hey, you mind if I take a little detour to the mall here?" Their route to the stockyard passed a huge parking lot which edged an enormous shopping center. She released her seatbelt and snagged her purse from the floor. "I'd like to do a little early Christmas shopping."

Dani's heart dropped. She didn't want to be alone with this man, but she understood Donna's desire to avoid seeing the pens stuffed with market animals.

"Fine by me, sweetie," he cooed.

He grabbed for her backside as she scooted past his lap and out the driver's door. Oblivious to the honking behind them, he pulled out a few bills from a wad he extracted from his hip pocket. He handed them to Donna through the open window.

"Here," he smarmed. "Buy yourself a little somethin', too."

Donna giggled and tottered away.

They missed the signal sequence and had to stay in place until the light indicated green again.

The return to silence felt heavy. Donna was the buffer. Without her, they were thrust back into the uncomfortable dynamic that existed between them since their first meeting in the café.

Even Jim seemed uncharacteristically awkward. He cleared his throat as the light finally changed and they pulled ahead.

"You'll wanna have your paperwork ready," he advised her. "When you enter the stockyard, that is. And you wanna swing wide at the entrance so the trailer won't scrape the curb."

"Does someone come and unhook the trailer for you?" Dani clambered forward and belted herself into the passenger seat. She needed to be able to see what she'd need to do, when she drove the solo route.

"Nope, but don't worry—you can do it yourself. It's easy. Well, if you want, I s'pose you could ask the guy at your dock to help. Most ramp rats are happy to help women drivers. Think they'll get some extra thanks, maybe." He winked.

Dani shot him a withering look.

They said nothing else during the remaining minutes of the ride.

A sign on the right side shoulder indicated the property's entrance; they stopped behind another waiting trailer for their turn to pass through the stockyard gate.

Jim became all business. He located the paperwork from the visor above his head, and, coming abreast to the gate, passed the sheaf through his window to a dour man in the guardhouse.

The man received it, slid his window shut, and started paging through the pile. He picked up a walkie-talkie and called someone to check the trailer.

Once the second guy finished a quick circuit around the trailer and gave his okay, the guard reopened his window and returned most of Jim's papers, keeping one set for himself. He directed them back to dock 3, pen 17.

"There's a turnaround between 3 and 4 there, if you can't back in," the guard added. He glided his window shut, not bothering to say goodbye. The metal gate in front of them slid open.

"See?" Jim asked. He clutched and shifted. "Nothing to it."

Dani wasn't ready to agree with him, not yet.

They passed scores of trailers with animals either crammed inside them or disembarking from them.

Huge portable corrals were arranged to contain pens for each trailer's load; each gate was marked with the appropriate label for a range of pens. Every pen shared a common fence with the next.

From Dani's viewpoint, it looked like they were driving through huge mega-pens stuffed full of cattle, hogs, sheep, and horses, all snorting and running and causing commotion.

In a steer pen on one side, young bull calves pushed and dashed at one another, ecstatic to be able to move after miles of forced congregation.

Outside a pen on the other side, a horse lay on its side in the dirt, its front leg bent forward at an unnatural angle. No longer alive, its mane stuttered in the breeze they caused as they went past.

Jim was still talking, but Dani wasn't listening. She'd been holding it together until she saw the dead horse.

How would she be able to deal with a similar death?

The stockyard was nothing, nothing like she'd ever seen.

Certainly, she'd never dreamed the animals would be so crowded and frantic. She tried to locate hay or water troughs in each pen, but their speed through the aisleway prevented her confirmation of these necessities.

Suddenly, Jim swore, braking the truck to a shuddering stop. Just inches in front of their cab, a young bull had gotten loose and was running pell-mell away from two men, one with a long rope or whip and another with a long stick. It lunged, pivoted, and sprang away in another direction.

Jim downshifted to get the rig moving again. Their own pen 17 was two more lengths ahead.

They passed their gate. Jim went another forty to fifty yards, at Dani's estimate, before he maneuvered the engine into reverse and backed the rig neatly to the entrance.

A man in long sleeves and jeans waited at the gate to their pen. He could've been anywhere between fourteen and forty years old. His flat affect gave nothing away.

Jim opened his door and, stiffly, got down from the cab. Dani heard the pen's gate open. "C'mon with me," he said, tugging up the waistband of his jeans before sauntering to the rear to watch the hogs unload.

Dani willed herself to join him. As she passed alongside the trailer, squeals and grunts rang out from the inside. Rear-facing, slanted lines decorated the metal from both levels, higher and lower—the result of an artful collaboration of highway wind and animal waste.

Jim waved Dani over to stand by him. The air smelled like rotting meat and sour dairy, punctuated by the iron tang of spilled blood.

The dockhand wedged a wheeled ramp against the upper level, just outside the trailer's back doors, and climbed to the top of the ramp. In a careful sequence, he reached for the lever to open the latch, leaned back, pulled the handle, then quickly jumped off the ramp to get out of the way.

As if responding simultaneously to a command, the entire herd burst toward the trailer's opening. The terrified energy of the suddenly released pigs drove itself like a brick wall into Dani's heightened awareness.

The hogs who got there first heaved themselves down the ramp and bounced into the pen. Those behind them were made to wait, as the pen opening could handle only one or two animals at a time. A third wave then crashed into the previous animals from behind. Several fell and were trampled in the others' rush to escape.

When the action was suddenly past and no more animals emerged, the dockhand clambered back up the ramp to the door. He kicked down one unlucky animal that had fallen, then pushed the skid to the other side. He repeated the process with the left side door, which opened the lower level of animals.

These hogs were just as frenzied in their maneuverings to disembark. But because they were closer to the ground, the entire mass exited without any one animal stopping or getting stepped upon.

"That's it, then!" Jim exclaimed. He looked pleased. "Seventy bucks a hog, and I think we're at about 200 animals. That ain't too bad, after gas and all." He turned to Dani. "Nothing to it, right? Think you can do it yourself, then?"

Dani blinked. There was no way she'd be able to go through this again. But she had to. She'd decided to. She'd given herself no other choice.

"Yep."

Her answer fell flat.

She wanted to run, to get away from this place. Away from the stench of doomed animals and the sounds of their cries.

She couldn't, though, because Jim began showing her how to disconnect the empty trailer. He pulled on a set of leather gloves and started his explanation.

"First, ya pull the two black hoses—them are the truck's air brakes—off from the red ones. Then, the green one, for the electricals. And the yellow's the air brake for the rig."

He was growing a little flushed, but his demonstration did make sense to Dani. "Then ya just grab this crank here—"

Dani saw a metal tube like the one on her grandpa's boat trailer. "—and give it a spin like this. Easy!"

She nodded.

"Head back to the cab, now. I'll be there in a minute."

Dani couldn't wait to get away. She needed to collect her thoughts and settle her discomfort. She sped to the passenger's door, wrenched it open, climbed up and rested there, insulated in that quiet cell.

At least five minutes passed before the driver's door opened, and Dani was thankful for every one of them.

"Got any questions?" Jim's braying voice scattered her concentration.

She repeated the steps back to him, out loud. He ticked off a nod for each point. "Good girl," he replied. His compliment, though backhanded and out of date, sounded genuine.

Without buckling his seatbelt, the man shifted into first gear and drove them away from the dock.

Instead of going back to the main gate, Jim detoured into the area marked Dock 1.

"Where are we going now?"

He didn't answer at first, busy with the next gear.

"That guy I was talkin' to in Hannibal, remember? We gotta get his trailer, haul it back up for him."

In the chaos of the stockyard, Dani had forgotten about this arrangement. The man at Subway and his silver Mercedes came back into her mind. Something wasn't right about him, either.

She steadied her voice, hoping to sound casual. "What number are we looking for?"

"He said the trailer'll be waitin' between 22 and 23. I'll show ya how to hook it up, 'case ya need to know."

Dani watched for the location with him, calling out the numbers from her side.

The trailer they located looked different than the one they'd hauled down. It was solid metal, not pierced with air holes, and the side doors were padlocked. With all the dents and scratches, it looked like it'd been driven around the country for eons.

It was also way filthier than the one they'd left behind. It was coated in so much dirt that messages scrawled by would-be humorists were barely discernible through the mess.

"This is it?" she asked. "I thought we'd be getting another animal trailer."

"I thought so, too," Jim said, peering out his window.

Dani couldn't tell if he was lying or not.

He slowed the rig and stopped. "I hope he left the BOL where he said it'd be," he added, opening his door.

"The 'ball'?" Dani repeated, stepping down to the pavement from her side. "What's that?"

"No, the BOL—B-O-L," he spelled. "The bill of lading."

Dani joined him at the front of the trailer by the jack, where a silver cylinder hung from the V-shaped metal wedge jutting out of the container. If possible, this trailer reeked more strongly than the previous one.

Jim crouched under the wedge and pulled out an envelope. "A BOL lists what's in a trailer. Which, in this case"—he ripped open the envelope along one short side, blew into it, then pulled out a sheet—"is nothing."

Still crammed inside the envelope, a block of paper remained, dark green and dense. It looked to Dani like a clod of bills.

Jim turned away and stashed the envelope between his plaid button-up and his T-shirt.

"Stay here by the jack, will ya?" He hiked up his jeans. "Tell me when I'm close." He hurried back to the driver's seat.

Dani stayed put. She wondered how he could even think she didn't see him, stuffing that packet out of sight, but the stinking waves of sulphur and rot, practically visible, deterred her attention.

She covered her nose and mouth, convinced that the stench would take weeks to go away and months to forget.

She didn't know how she was supposed to notify Jim that he was "close" when she wasn't even tall enough to see where the pin met the V in the greasy, crescent-shaped clamp behind his cab. She did her best, though, holding her breath and moving her hands apart and together, like airport-control people did, as he reversed the rig into place.

When she stopped him, Jim bounced out and congratulated her. Then he jumped back in and backed up another inch so that the clamp pinched the top of the pin. Next, he popped out one last time to pull the red handle to lock everything into place. He finally attached the hoses between the trailer and his truck and pronounced the connection complete.

Dani couldn't help but notice the unusual zip in his movements. She also couldn't help but assume that it was the envelope–or its contents–that had energized him.

Both back in the rig again, Jim put the engine into first gear. He pulled forward only a few yards before stopping to set the brake.

"Give me a minute, 'k? I gotta take a leak."

Jim slipped out of his seat, but this time he closed the driver's door before skirting the trailer to its rear.

Dani couldn't see him in her side mirror, nor did she wish to, if he was really doing what he said he'd be doing. But she heard him open one of the large cargo doors at the back. She felt the springs sag as he hoisted himself into the container, then felt a slight skip when he jumped back to the ground again. Though he closed the door gently, she could feel it seal shut.

She assumed the back doors were padlocked like the side doors were, which she noticed when they first encountered the dirty trailer. She remembered the keys the man at Subway dropped at Jim's feet. Those must've been keys for this trailer, Dani determined. What was he doing back there? What was he looking for?

He jogged back to his seat with a red and perspiring face. "Let's go find Donna!"

"Everything okay back there?"

Jim didn't meet her glance. "Yep. Just had to use the 'facilities,'" he replied. "All good."

He was lying. She'd have to be stupid to believe him. All the same, Dani kept her retort to herself.

At the main gate, Jim handed the paperwork to the same guard who'd checked their entry.

"You okay with driving a sealed container?" the man asked, holding out a clipboard and a blue plastic pen.

"No worries," Jim answered. "I know the guy."

"All righty, then."

The guard called for another security check. The same helper made a gratuitous orbit around the trailer, but it was obvious from the look on his face that the smell offended him. Nonetheless, he gave his approval, and the guard stamped and signed the bottom page of the paperwork, ran it through a copier, and returned the original back to Jim.

"Safe travels." He opened the exit gate, then rotated to the opposite side of the guard- house to check in a new arrival.

"And that's all there is to it!" Jim's voice sounded more excited than Dani figured it needed to. "Ya ready to try driving?"

"I'd like to, before it gets dark. Should we get Donna first, though?"

"Sure thing." He turned wide and traced the same route back to the mall. "Ya know, if your solo trip goes well enough, I've got plenty of other jobs for ya. Could be a pretty little moneymaker. But if ya decide ya don't like it, at least we get that one load delivered. We part with no hard feelings. Deal?"

The salesman was back. Something about his voice's timbre or the way his eyes didn't blink hinted at a barrier, a boundary, between his words and the truth he was striving to hide.

Dani couldn't deny that greasy unease she got from being around Jim, nor could she tamp down the dread warning of silent caution hovering nearby.

Donna's "retail therapy" looked to be a success: she had two big bags from the anchor stores plus numerous small bags hanging from each wrist, and she was wearing a new pair of platform sandals when she clomped out to the mall's big parking lot to greet them. She packed her purchases in the back and around the bed.

Meanwhile, Dani adjusted the driver's seat for her height and tilted in the side mirrors, only half-listening to Jim as he reviewed the correct shifting protocol. Although she was looking out over the steering wheel now, Dani reminded herself that the view on their drive north wouldn't be much different than the view they saw travelling south: flat roads, endless green fields, and tiny, one-light towns. But, like Donna said, a trip always seemed faster on the way back home.

Dani hoped she was right.

"Ready?" Jim asked. Before Dani could answer, he called back to Donna: "Ya better settle yourself on that garbage can, darlin'!" He made a big show of bracing his hands on the front dash.

"That doesn't help her confidence!" Donna twittered, trying to hide a laugh.

Dani ignored them. She got the big engine revved and eased it forward, inch by inch. Her eyelids were plastered wide open, her pulse bouncing behind them. Her throat was dry, too. But she'd be darned if she'd let Jim see her hands shake, so she gripped the big wheel hard and shifted the rig into the next gear.

The transition was remarkably smooth.

Donna clapped and hooted, and Jim bragged about his teaching prowess.

Dani again ignored them, snatched a glance into her side mirror, and aimed for the parking lot's exit. She cut the corner a bit short, and the trailer's back wheel bumped onto the concrete curb, shuddering.

"S'okay!" Jim assured her. "'Least there's nothing back there. A little wider, next time," he added, as if she couldn't figure it out for herself.

She was determined to do better. They made the next corner without error.

Dani held her breath, steered onto the ramp, and aimed the big rig down onto the highway. Jim reminded her to watch the orange part of the dial to know when to shift. She did.

As the miles passed, Dani settled into the comfortable seat and allowed her shoulders to relax. *I can do this,* she thought. *And it looks like I'm going to.*

They pulled off the highway near Jefferson City for dinner. Dani needed a glass of wine and asked Jim to drive the rest of the trip.

Back in the cab after dinner, with Donna in the passenger's seat and Dani balanced on the garbage can, they'd barely pulled out of the parking lot when Jim launched into salesman mode—this time, a salesman trying to seal a deal.

"So, I'll pay ya 25 percent," he offered, point blank.

It seemed an awfully high percentage for one short trip. Dani wished she could see his eyes, but they were cloaked in the darkness. She decided to parry.

"Cash?" she responded. "You said it'd be cash back at the diner, when we first met."

He nodded, the silhouette of his head enlarged by a shadow caused by an oncoming vehicle's headlights. "Yep. I can do that." He sniffed. "But I can't pay ya 'till I get paid."

For a moment, Dani wondered about the cash—she thought it was cash, at least—in that envelope he'd retrieved from the second trailer. But again, she pushed forward. Especially since she had another part of the deal to negotiate.

"It doesn't have to be a one-day trip, right? Can I stay a night in Missouri?" she continued.

Jim let out a doubtful hrmm and shook his head. "I need that truck back on the road. Sittin' overnight somewhere don't earn anyone anything."

"But I don't need to bring a trailer back, do I?"

"Don't know yet, but I expect so."

Dani needed that overnight. "How about I drive for a flat rate, then? I'd really like to stay over one night. It's a favor to a friend."

Donna figured out what Dani was hinting at and chimed in on her behalf. "One night won't hurt, will it, Jimmy? A flat rate's better than a percentage, right?"

Jim grunted. "Lemme think on it," he managed.

Seconds later, he broke off into a husky laugh as Donna trailed her fingernails along one side of his thick neck.

"All right, all right," he said, reaching for her hand. Donna twittered back.

As pleased as Dani was about getting her overnight, she was in no mood to witness what might happen next between the couple.

"I think I'll take a cat nap," she announced, plopping onto the bed behind them. She positioned herself on her side, facing away from their interactions.

With the red wine at work, Dani drowsed off as Donna started describing the items she got at the mall.

Dani came to, though, sometime later. The volume up front was low. She was only slightly ashamed about listening in on their conversation.

"Ya know it'd be good for us to be together," Jim's gravelly voice purred. "I'll move some things over to your place, and we can try it out."

"I don't know." There was no coquetry in Donna's response. "It's kinda nice and quiet, now that Pete's moved out."

"You can still have that when I'm on the road. We'll be together a few days, I'll take a job, and then we'll be back together, like honeymooners, again."

Donna's voice rose a bit. "I gotta tell you, Jimmy, I don't like what they're having you do."

He started to plead his case, but Donna overrode him.

"Really, Jim. If I was to do this—let you move into my mama's house with me—I'd need some, I don't know, insurance, that you won't work for Carl no more."

"You got it, girl," he cooed. "C'mon over here, now. Sit on my lap a minute, and let's talk details."

"No thanks! I don't want an accident." Donna giggled. "Anyway, we'll figure it out when we get back home." She began to whisper. "But don't tell Dani, though, 'k? I don't think she'd approve."

Dani didn't know how best to breathe and hoped she still appeared to be sleeping. To be honest, sleep seemed welcoming. Her energy was drained—and not from the red wine this time.

The next thing Dani knew, the truck stopped. She awoke abruptly. Sitting up, she tried to rub away the memory of the overheard conversation.

Alighting from the cab, she thanked the couple and said goodbye, then started down the driveway before their dust started flying. The rig beeped and drove off. She counted the number of times Jim shifted before he reached the crossroads. Waiting until she couldn't hear the engine anymore, she looked up to be sure the stars were where they were supposed to be.

Scout nickered from her pen, making Cody bark. "It's me, guys," she assured them.

She gave her horse a quick pat, then slipped inside the barn to unleash her dog. Cody jumped and wiggled and tried to kiss her, then darted away to chase something in the yard.

Dani considered all she'd seen and learned in the past few weeks—what she'd seen and learned just today. She made a mental list of the people she knew she could count on and wondered if Donna was still on that list.

She couldn't figure out how Donna could believe any of Jim's sweet talk. But one thing was clear, now: not all the wool had been pulled over Donna's eyes. She knew enough to disapprove of something he was up to, something with someone named Carl.

Dani knew enough now, too.

Scout angled her head sideways, trying to poke her mouth through the top two bars to get closer to Dani. She wanted another pat or maybe a treat, moving her lips over Dani's palm to see if she might be hiding one.

"Sorry, girl. Just a hug for you tonight."

Scout's gentle curiosity reaffirmed what Dani had been trying all day to forget: animals weren't just merchandise or lawn ornaments or "meat on the hoof." They had a purpose. They ought to be respected for what they contributed, not mistreated or abused because of their purpose or where their lives ended.

This rejected horse from the auction pen had learned, through Dani's careful and calm interactions, that she could trust this particular human. Didn't it make sense, then, that other horses—or other animals, for that matter—might also have spirits of trust, redemption, fear, or hopelessness?

How could Dani agree to drive a similar group of spirits to a cruel and painful death? As a favor to a man like Jim?

Her choked sob pierced the night's tranquility. The bright, chilly stars, still above, beamed vacantly as an owl hooted from behind the barn, a delicate, haunting underscore.

9

Dawn emerged on the wings of mourning doves. In her hazy half-conscious state, their soft, rounded calls—one question, two gentle replies—balanced themselves on the rim of her dream. They slipped into her awareness and dissolved back out again, teasing Dani to join the new day.

An angry scolding, intruding upon the gentle repetitions, chastised the doves with a busy jabber. A flash of blue wove itself through the branches framing the view from Dani's window. A male blue jay was acting the dictator this morning, bossing the doves.

Something I can't seem to get away from, either, Dani mused.

The blue jay didn't stop. He zoomed back and forth, his harsh screeches accompanying his frantic aerial gymnastics.

Dani opened the window and told the bird exactly what she thought of his intrusive, selfish behavior. It was what she wished she had the guts to say to Jim directly, in truth. But another voice, a quiet echo of the shy doves, perhaps, cautioned her to wait until she knew she was seeing the whole picture.

On her way to the kitchen, Dani flicked on her computer, then brought a cup of coffee back to the dining table. She sat to review her emails, with Cody curled up right next to her, under the table.

Most of the mail was either jokes forwarded from her dad (which she didn't open) or advertisements from an online shop she used one time. Junk mail. As she deleted them, a new message arrived. Jessica invited Dani to a little get-together at her basement apartment, a week from next Friday night.

Once again, Dani clicked Delete. But then she second-guessed herself: Maybe she should go to the party, try to be more social. Meet some new people. Enlarge her circle of friends.

With Donna so busy with "Jimmy," there wasn't really anyone else to hang out with. Then again, would it be any better to hang out with Jessica if Pete was interested in dating her? Dani sighed. Maybe she should've stayed in bed.

She caught a muted glimpse of herself in the monitor's surface. It reflected a pale face, sad eyes, and messy hair. It frowned.

She poked the power button and went outside to feed her horse.

Copying the technique she'd seen Pete use, she was able to halter Scout easily, the first time. Confident to try the next step, she situated herself at the horse's shoulder, and they passed through the gate and left the barnyard.

They paused in the middle of the area she wanted to use as a pasture. Though the small field was mostly bare, left to grow wild, Scout didn't mind eating the tough stems. Tractors off to the west caused the mare's pointed ears to flex and bend as the sounds reached her, but she didn't bolt or run away.

Dani rested her right hand on the curve of Scout's back and told her what a good girl she was. The sun caused the top hairs on her coat shimmer like bright copper.

Just then, a barking Cody tore out from the trees and ran toward them. The mare yanked her head up, ready to flee in an instant.

Dani absorbed the brunt of the force through the lead rope, its reverberation coursing all the way up through her injured shoulder. She winced but was able to tug on it enough to get Scout's eyes back on her.

"It's just Cody," Dani assured the mare. She hissed her displeasure to the dog: "Cody! Be quiet, you idiot! Sh-h-h!"

Cody wagged his tail and looked for all the world like he smiled back at her. Scout shook her mane, blew out a snort, and then returned to grazing.

"You're both so dramatic." Dani's gripe was mild. "Hardly any room for me to get hysterical, is there, with you two around."

The dog touched noses with the horse before taking off again. Dani watched him cross back to the barn, disappearing inside through the big opening. Dani realized she'd need to narrow that down somehow before winter to keep the cold wind and snow out. She added this task to her mental to-do list.

After Scout shortened the grass stems in her range, Dani gave the lead rope a tug, a signal to the mare to join her. Shoulder to shoulder again, they walked to the far edge of the pasture. Cody joined them there, but this time he came toward them from the front. Since Scout could see his approach, there was no reason for her to react in a negative way. In fact, she sort of nickered at the dog, welcoming him back to their herd.

Dani and her animals traced the invisible line around the remaining two sides of the property. She told them about what she'd seen at the stockyard the day before. She apologized for the way humans used animals so savagely, so unkindly, without regard to their needs or their pain.

She also shared what she'd observed at the second dock, when Jim went back alone, and how she wondered exactly what Donna knew.

She didn't tell them that she'd be leaving again soon to drive a trailer of animals back to that lot.

By herself.

It took until the end of the week for Dani to regain some of her serenity. When she finally checked her voicemail, she learned that Donna had left a message back on Wednesday, the day after the trip. Dani needed more coffee, so she and Cody drove into Crestview for a small bag of French Roast. She decided to touch base with Donna in person, rather than over the phone.

But as she pulled into Susie's Café, she felt her newly regained serenity falter. The parking lot was full. In addition to the usual vehicles, she immediately spotted two long black SUVs, their windows dark and opaque, conspicuously tucked into the back row, facing out. Their license plates, white with black numbers, had US GOVERNMENT in block letters along their top edges.

Busy chatter and Willie Nelson's voice greeted her when she stepped inside. Every seat at the counter was taken, as were most of the chairs at the restaurant's tables.

Dani scanned the room for a place to slide in. She started toward Jessica, bent over a pile of papers at a table in the corner, but then she heard Barbara Dorn's voice. "Sit by us."

She waved Dani over to a table of four. Today, the women weren't sitting with Lloyd, Chuck, and Bud at their usual table. Even this detail added to the overarching sense that something was off.

Dani settled into the open chair. "Where's Donna?"

The three older women looked at one another. Dani always recalled a flock of little birds when she watched the three old friends twitter and peck at one another. But this morning, their expressions were tight and serious.

Missy was the one to speak first. "She's in the back. Talking to one of the—whatever you call them. FBI guys, I guess."

"We're trying to figure out what's going on," Barbara added.

Just then, the kitchen door burst open. Pete hustled out, both arms lined with plates of food.

Before the door can swing shut behind him again, almost every diner's head craned to catch a glimpse of what might be happening in the back. When the door closed, they huddled back to resume their whispered interpretations.

Dani rose and followed Pete to the diner's far corner, where Lloyd, Chuck, and Bud sat. She distributed plates with Pete's direction as the old timers speculated.

"It's about all that illegal fertilizer dumping," Chuck insisted to Lloyd.

Lloyd shook his head. "Nah. It's about what's-his-name—you know, from over past the cemetery. The one that's been baiting deer."

"Well, why don't we hear it from someone who knows?" Bud said, twisting to look up at Pete. Chuck and Lloyd looked, too.

"And here's your patty melt." Pete slid a plate in front of Bud, ignoring the awkward attempt to extricate information. He pivoted to check in with the next table but whispered to Dani before he rushed past. "Meet me up front."

Dani returned to the counter. As far as food distribution or cleanup went, things weren't any better at the front, but no one seemed upset. To a person, everyone in the diner was curious to learn why government agents were in Crestview.

Rushing to the counter, Pete ripped off the top two pages of his order pad. "Clip these up on the spinner for Ginny, okay?" He retraced his steps to the dining area, his face solemn.

Even though Dani could easily reach the silver spinner, she stood on her toes to clip up the orders, hoping the few extra inches would allow her to see what was happening in the back.

She spied Donna, perched on the edge of a stool by the back door. Her cheeks were two splotches of color smeared with mascara, like she'd been wiping her eyes.

A beefy guy in a sport coat, his back to Dani, had his hands on his hips. He was peering down at Donna and appeared to be the one asking questions.

His partner, facing Dani, was short and wiry. His dark brows furrowed as he jotted down notes on some sort of electric pad.

Evidently, he couldn't quite keep the pace. He raised his stylus like a wand to interrupt the interrogator.

The larger man lost his patience. His strident voice was loud enough to burst back through the window, causing everyone at the counter to fall silent—which, in turn, caused the rest of the diners to follow suit.

The chastening voice quieted, but the event itself increased the heat burning a circle around the room.

Heads came together again to dissect the development.

Pete reappeared at Dani's side, clipped another order to the spinner, and brought her by the elbow to a nearby corner.

"I don't know what's going on," he confided, his voice low.

His pale face was outlined with whiskers he hadn't removed and worry lines deep enough to have been etched by charcoal. His lips were drawn. His bloodshot eyes darted from corner to corner. He couldn't settle.

"I showed up for breakfast and those guys"—he jerked his head to his left—"were already here. Donna asked me to help out, and I've been running ever since." He glanced at his wrist, but he'd forgotten his watch.

"It's late. I'm supposed to be opening the library, but I—" He was completely frazzled. His eyes sought Dani's. "I don't want to leave."

She reached for his hand. "Then don't. Stay here and help." She realized she was grasping his forearm; she quickly let go. "I can open the library for you. Give me the keys."

"You can't." Pete shook his head. "It's all—it's a state job. You're supposed to be on file."

He rubbed his hand over his chin, a motion that seemed to better clear his thoughts. He started laying out the logic, mostly for himself.

"It'll be okay to open late. It's just one day—and no one ever shows up till ten. Hell, it looks like everyone's here anyway."

He chewed on his lower lip. "Stay, can you? Help me with the orders?"

"Sure, I—"

"And you should be here, for her, when they go."

The cook's bell tinged. Another set of plates rested on the pass-through shelf, steam rising from the food.

As he'd done before, Pete arranged dishes on each arm and brought these to the diners.

Chuck called Dani over for a refill; she topped off his mug and three others before starting another pot of coffee. She wiped both hands on a somewhat-clean towel before scooping up the order pad Pete left behind.

Before she could even take her first order, though, the door to the kitchen whipped open. Trying to keep a low profile, the two agents glided out from the kitchen toward the café's entrance.

Both agents' heads snapped up when a sudden silence soaked the room.

The larger agent's eyes swept the area from right to left. The other agent, busy with the transcribing machine, fumbled to shove it back into his pack like he was hiding the scribbled facts from the diners' acute observations.

The men clambered out of the diner and down the front steps, fast. The front door closed behind them with a whoosh.

As if their exit somehow propelled missing air back into the café, the patrons' voices immediately came back to life in a chaotic chorus.

"Did ya see that? He had two guns! One on each—"

"Where's Donna? What'd they do with Donna? You don't think she—"

"I'll bet it has somethin' to do with—"

Pete flashed back into the kitchen, Dani close behind.

Donna hadn't moved from her stool. Her chin was tucked close to her chest; her shoulders heaved up and down.

Pete knelt in front of his sister and squeezed her crossed arms. "Are you okay? What happened?"

Dani waited near the siblings. She didn't want to intrude but was also conscious of wanting to protect her friend. Both of them.

Donna's lipstick had worn off, her hair hung in strands by her tear-stained face, and her frame looked to have been folded into a smaller version of herself. Dani had never seen Donna like this. Her devastating condition unsettled Dani's core.

Ginny brought a glass of water to the tableau. She thrust it out to Donna, patted her boss's arm, then reached past her to lock the back door. "Assholes," she muttered before shuffling back to the fry pad. She snatched the last paper order from the spinner as if she were pulling someone's head off.

Donna drew in a halting, staccato breath. She raised her eyes to Pete, then glanced over him to Dani, tears falling.

"It's Jim . . ."

But she can't continue. Her eyes clamped shut, and she pressed her lips together, trying to keep herself from crying out.

Pete removed himself from his sister. "What?"

At the same moment, Dani bent forward. "Why?"

Donna shook her head from side to side. "I can't believe it . . ." Her words sounded distant, as though she was in some other conversation with herself.

"Donna, what?" Pete pressed, his voice rough. He tried again, softening it. "What did they say?"

She sighed, then nodded as if making a decision.

"They said he, he's . . ." She gathered her words, only for them to spill out in a rushed jumble. "They say he's moving drugs. That he's part of a—a network. Or something. Some group—some 'cartel,' they said—that moves stuff between Mexico and the States. They said he brings drugs back from Missouri for them. How could they think that? He—he only has a few trucks." She rocked herself back and forth.

Pete shot a look at Dani, his face pale.

Dani's head throbbed in a way she's only felt once before, as if it might splinter apart. On one side was the reality in front of her: a friend in utter despair and shock. On another, the reality of the recent changes she cannot ignore: the blue Xs, the man at Subway, the secret envelope, the overheard conversation. Permeating these, her memory of losing Geoff to heroin twisted through like a serpent. Reconciling these realities was like trying to divide by zero. Dani simply cannot do it.

"Where's Jim now?" Pete asked. "Did they arrest him?"

Donna shivered. "I don't know." She placed her hands on her knees. "I have to call him," she declared, abruptly pushing herself up. "See if he's still home—"

Pete held her steady. With the way he was biting his lips, it looked like he was struggling to keep his opinions to himself.

"Dani." Donna glanced at her friend, suddenly remembering. "I'm afraid they're going to look for you next."

Dani stepped back. "Why?" Her voice sounded strangled. "Why me?"

"They kept asking all these questions, so fast, and I sort of told them that you and I drove to Missouri with Jim, last Tuesday." Her tears coursed down her cheeks again. "I had to give them some answer, Dani. I'm sorry. I'm really sorry."

"Donna," Pete went forward slowly, trying his best to hold back his anger, "are you saying that when Jim took you and Dani to Missouri this week, he was hauling drugs?"

"No!" Donna shouted, like she couldn't help herself. She wavered, about to collapse.

Pete grabbed her, leaning her backward to help her sit back down.

Donna rocked on the stool for a few seconds, finding her balance. When she spoke again, her voice was a tick quieter.

"No. Dani, you know! We were with Jim the whole time. We didn't see drugs or anything like them. That's what I told the cops!"

Dani managed to nod, but conflicting realities still warred inside her. She reconstructed the precise steps she and Jim made at the stockyard, and Donna was mostly right: he was never alone, except for when he went back behind the first trailer, and then again when he sneaked inside the other trailer, the one they hauled back to Iowa.

Suddenly, Dani second-guessed everything she'd been rehashing, what she'd noticed on the Missouri trip, and everything she'd noticed since first meeting Jim: without solid proof, what she thought she witnessed cannot be taken as truth, not without solid evidence.

Despite what she overheard on the drive home, Donna seemed adamant that her boyfriend was not involved.

Donna wouldn't stand for that, she decided.

Maybe her own suspicions about Jim, sparked with her fears about the drug activity that seemed to be growing stronger in their small town, were only real in the sphere of her imagination. After all, her perceptions had been filtered through her own biases and experience.

The insight filled Dani with regret and shame. She looked directly into her friend's worried face.

Maybe I'm just jealous. Jealous that Donna's found someone to be happy with.

An urgent need to protect Donna surged inside her. Donna and Pete were Dani's pack, her herd. She wanted to circle around Donna and shield her from more hurt, regardless of its cause or her own predilections.

That's what friends did. They looked out for each other.

Dani moved close, folded a shaking Donna into her arms, and held her. "It's okay," she soothed. "You had to tell the truth, that I was with you guys on the trip. I know. You did the right thing. We'll figure it out. It'll be okay."

Her words comforted Donna, who rested on Dani's shoulder. Pete scowled.

But to Dani's surprise, her reassurances and good intentions did nothing to quell the acid that flooded into her throat

IO

WHEN DANI PULLED INTO HER DRIVEWAY some twenty minutes later, one of the large government vehicles was parked right next to her house. As she knew it'd be. She'd taken the most direct route back. Although she could have used some time to clear her head, she didn't want to be accused of trying to evade the agents.

From the spot next to her, Cody's furious barking alerted her to the stranger on her porch. But instead of trying to calm him, she opened her truck door and let him charge out ahead of her.

She was pissed that the man had probably been looking into her windows—or worse—in her absence. She was also pissed that it was the same beefy agent she'd seen badgering Donna and dressing down his colleague.

Dani strolled to the porch at a slow pace. "Can I help you?" Her voice held no warmth. She did not smile. She stopped at the foot of the steps.

The agent, backed against the siding, held both hands in front of him, palms out. He scrunched down, attempting to appear smaller and less intimidating to the growling dog. "Is this guy friendly?"

The scene reminded Dani of when Deputy Davies arrived at the trashed trailer house. He'd been concerned about Cody at first, but the agent in front of her had a more legitimate reason to be worried.

Nonetheless, Dani whistled Cody to her side. He came, reluctantly, but his intense focus continued to target the intruder. The hair along his spine rose in a rigid wave.

"You must be Danielle Holden," the agent tried again.

His smile showed his top teeth only, white and sharky. He kept his sunglasses on, though the porch was shaded and the day overcast.

She didn't fall for his cheery facade. "I am."

"I'd like to talk to you, Ms. Holden," he went on, taking a step toward her. Cody growled.

Dani waited.

"I understand you took a road trip on Tuesday down to Missouri with some friends of yours. Is that right?"

Dani noted the interesting choice of words: a road trip with some friends. She wondered if the feds knew about her arrangement to make the solo delivery trip. Perhaps not. Donna didn't mention that, only that she'd told them about Dani being on Tuesday's trip.

Behind them, the second black SUV pulled into her lane. It was the smaller, darker agent who'd bumbled with the transcribing machine.

As Cody ran off to confront the newcomer, Beefy Guy seized the chance to jump down from the porch.

Dani situated herself to keep both the first agent and the new arrival in view. "What's going on?" she asked. "And do you have some identification? I don't know who you are."

Beefy Guy strode toward her, holding out a leather wallet with his badge and a picture ID. Dani took it, then backed a distance away. The ID identified him as Sergeant Steven Wahlquist, Bureau of Criminal Apprehension, Midwest region.

His partner, meanwhile, was attempting to cajole Cody into letting him exit the vehicle. She handed the wallet to the first agent.

He tucked it into his suitcoat pocket and attempted another smile. "We have some questions about that trip. Is now a good time?" His voice, in opposition to his genial smile, had taken on an official tone.

Her inside senses prickled as if a chill passed over her. It was the same strange reaction she sometimes got when she went hiking by herself. She recognized it as a hint from her intuition. She paid attention now, leaning in to receive its message.

These guys want something from me.

"Okay." Dani gestured to the other officer. "Does he want to join us?"

She went to the other vehicle to grab Cody's collar. The smaller agent slid out of the SUV but didn't come closer.

Dani placed Cody at her feet, between her and the two men. "All right. What would you like to know?"

"What was the purpose of your trip?" Wahlquist asked.

The other agent prepared to take notes on a small pad of paper instead of the computer pad he'd fumbled with at the café. He found a pen in his pocket, clicked it open, and waited for Dani's response.

"I went with my friend and her boyfriend, a trucker, to deliver a load of hogs to a stockyard."

Dani tried to answer the question with the bare minimum of detail. She had an idea of what they were getting at, but she'd rather make the agents work for it than give her opinions away for free.

"What stops did you make?"

"One, for lunch. Then after we dropped the hogs, we stopped for dinner, halfway back." Cody pulled at his collar, anxious to get out from Dani's grasp.

"Did you meet anyone at either location?"

"No." A vision flashed past her--that man outside the Subway, the shifty one who poked Jim. But since she herself didn't actually meet him, Dani felt safe in her answer.

Stick to the bare minimum.

Wahlquist paused. Did he sense her hesitation?

"Did you meet anyone at the stockyard?" he finally asked.

"Not really," Dani said. "Just the basic 'hello' to the people working there."

"Where did you go after that?"

Wahlquist came closer. Cody's growl intensified; he pulled back his lips to show his teeth. The big man tried another tactic, taking off his sunglasses to look more friendly.

Dani didn't trust the way his eyebrows crowded his eyes. They didn't match the smile he plastered onto his face.

"We came back to Crestview."

The other officer butted in. "What time did you get back?"

"About midnight, maybe?" She pursed her mouth to one side and tried to remember. "I fell asleep on the way back. I don't really remember what time I got home, for sure."

"So, the driver might have stopped without you knowing, is that what you're saying?" Wahlquist's attempt to derail her didn't work.

She narrowed her eyes at him. "No. I would've known if we stopped again."

Wahlquist's stare intensified. "At any point of the trip, did you see any goods transferred? Moved from trailer to trailer? To Jim?"

Anger twined up Dani's spine, goading her to release Cody and let him chase away the pompous agent. But maybe her reaction wasn't entirely appropriate. Maybe this wasn't anger, but uncertainty.

Her thoughts swirled. She didn't know what or how much to say next. It wasn't about sticking to the bare minimum; it was about not being able to trust her own recollections.

Centering herself on her need to protect Donna, Dani searched for a firm piece of knowledge to stand on.

Once she found it, she carefully phrased her reply. "I didn't see any drugs, I promise you."

Both officers continued observing her. They knew she was wrestling with something, and it was obvious they wouldn't let her go until they had more answers. And until they had what they needed, as her intuition reminded her, they weren't going to leave.

Dani acquiesced. "Why don't we sit down inside and talk?"

For one thing, she hated having to swivel back and forth to keep both men in sight. And two, she hoped a new setting will help her regain control over the way she replied to their questions.

The agents exchanged a look, a sort of signal between partners. "Thanks," Wahlquist answered for them both. "That'd be great."

When neither man moved, though, Dani sighed. She dragged Cody up the porch steps, opened her door, and paused at the threshold, the dog's collar still firmly in her grip.

"C'mon in," she said. "I'll hold him till you're inside."

Wahlquist entered her home first. The other man came through next, careful to press against the opposite side of the door's casement, away from Cody.

"Sorry I didn't introduce myself," he said. "I'm Brookins. Sam Brookins." Safely inside the entryway, he began to extract his identification.

"It's okay," Dani answered. "I figured you're with him." She let Cody go, and the dog sprinted down the driveway to bark at their vehicles.

Brookins's face relaxed. "Is it just you out here?"

She wasn't sure if he was making conversation or gathering data. The latter, she presumed. "Yep. Just me, Cody, and Scout, my mare."

She passed Brookins and entered the living room. Wahlquist waited, standing next to his partner, inventorying her possessions, lifestyle, and decorating taste. At least, that's how it looked to Dani.

Dani chose the chair near the hall and placed herself in the center of its worn cushion. "Why don't you both sit down?"

Brookins waved for Wahlquist to enter the room first. He did, heading for the sofa to Dani's right. He angled himself to face her and lowered his frame. Once seated, he didn't lean back.

Brookins followed. He positioned himself near the big window.

Watching their calculated movements, Dani was struck again by that surreal sensation of an out-of-body experience, that condition of removed observation like she was outside herself, watching. In addition to noting the agents' actions, Dani observed the way she gripped the armrest. She forced herself to relax her fingers. Taking a deep breath, she tried to center herself and calm her scattered heartbeat.

"So, what else do you want to know?"

The sooner they got their answers, the sooner they'd go. She hoped.

"Why don't we start with you?" Wahlquist, again. "You're not from here, are you?"

Dani snorted. She wished that, by now, people from out of town would recognize her as a Crestview native. "What gives me away?"

His answer wasn't what she expected: "The café owner told us. She said you'd moved here from the Twin Cities about two years ago. Would that be right?"

"That's right." Dani heard Cody whining at the front door.

"This your place? A family farm?" the bigger agent asked.

She shook her head. "Nope. I'm renting."

"So, what—you farm, then?"

"You're a farmer?"

Both questions emitted simultaneously from the officers. Wahlquist glared at Brookins. "This is the acreage I lease and farmed, last year."

"Not this year?"

"Nope. I got injured in an accident, so I'm actually looking for a new job—" She quit explaining when she noticed the men exchange another glance.

Strike one.

She tried to ward off the follow-up question. "I do have a temporary job, of course. I check properties around here for a guy from the Cities to make ends meet."

"Is that why you've agreed to do an upcoming delivery run for Jim Kelly, too? To make ends meet?" Wahlquist asked.

So they did know about the solo trip. Dani assumed Donna was their source of this information. A question skittered across her mind about what other information Donna may have provided about her.

Dani swallowed. "Jim asked a while back if I wanted to make a delivery run for him. And yes, I do need the money." Her words, enunciated clearly, slipped out with reluctance. "I have to eat and feed my animals, but there's not a lot of open jobs to choose from around here."

Brookins couldn't keep still. "Why don't you move back to the Cities?"

The smaller agent didn't notice the larger agent's exasperation, but Dani did. She eyed Wahlquist before answering Brookins.

"Because I live here, in Crestview."

"Wouldn't it be easier to find a job in a bigger town?" Brookins didn't give up.

She laughed, surprising herself. "Probably," she admitted. The idea was less imposing, weaker, when she said it out loud. "But I like it here. I know it's small, but I feel safe. Like people are looking out for me."

Wahlquist resumed control. "So, that's why you went on this trip to Missouri on Tuesday —as a test run for your paid delivery run." It wasn't a question.

Dani nodded. "I was seeing if I could handle it."

"You got a license?"

"Permit."

Shit. Strike two.

"But you're planning to do this run for him?" Wahlquist pressed.

Dani placed her elbows on her knees. "I was. But given all this"— she mimicked holding a huge package with open arms—"I'm leaning toward no."

There was a small clock Dani liked to keep on the hall table. Its rhythmic ticking counted off the seconds between her confession and the officer's next question. With each passing tick, she thought less about Donna and Jim, and more about Lilly.

Wahlquist shifted himself on the sofa, trying to find a more comfortable seat. "When's the next trip set for?"

Dani shrugged. "I think it's sometime next week."

Wahlquist cleared his throat.

Brookins clicked his pen.

"Here's the thing, Dani . . ." Wahlquist began.

His voice reeked of earnestness; his scowl, vanished. His brown eyes now showed excitement, heightened interest. It was as if he'd been following a routine road that just swerved off to an alternate path, a more exciting route he was stoked to follow.

"We have a proposition for you."

"I'm not sure I'm the one to help." She began to get to her feet.

"Wait! Sit a minute, will you?" Wahlquist held out one hand, a mostly symbolic attempt to prevent her from getting up or going away. "Please?"

Dani got up anyway. She wanted to get out of this room, away from these questions, away from any propositions.

The men stood then, too, still scrutinizing her.

I was right. They do need something from me.

"I should go check on my mare. You can talk to me out there." She fled for the barn, not waiting for them to follow.

Scout whinnied from her corral as she spied her owner.

Cody charged over to guard her. He barked at the men to remind them of his presence, though not with the same intensity as before, seeming to sense that the dynamic had somehow changed. Nevertheless, he ran a course between her and the men, trying to herd them away from her. Dani let him.

From the edge of Scout's corral, Dani noticed a scrape on one of Scout's knees. "Hey girl, what's going on? What did you run into?" She climbed into the pen and crouched to examine the leg.

The men caught up and watched from outside the corral.

Dani palmed the swelling, then gently squeezed the joint. "Probably nothing, right?" she assured the mare.

She wasn't confident about the truth of that assertion, though. She exited the pen to retrieve a tube of liniment from the grooming bucket.

The officers met her at the gate. "Here's what we're thinking," Wahlquist took the lead. "We can't say too much, but we believe Jim is involved in a state-to-state transport of illegal drugs."

Dani didn't admit that she'd learned as much from Donna, at the café, but the lack of surprise on her face spoke for itself.

"But we don't think you're involved," Brookins interjected.

The bigger officer went on like his partner hadn't spoken. "We want you to go ahead and drive that route next week."

This was not what Dani expected. She straightened, medicine in hand, and tried to appear composed.

She didn't want them to see the reactions she was juggling, but the effort was as difficult as trying to sort crashing waves at a lakeshore: while one wave receded, bringing relief, the next smashed forward, overwhelming her with confusion and suffocating the oxygen from her lungs.

"Why?" She stepped back into the corral.

"We need to know what's happening at the stockyard, without them knowing we're there. You can get us into play, behind the scenes."

"We're not asking you to put yourself in danger," Brookins added. "There'll be officers driving down with you and just outside the stockyard, too."

Wahlquist made the last sell: "All you have to do is what Jim told you to do—drop off your load, pick up the new one. We'll take over after the transfer takes place. You'll be out and done."

Dani stopped rubbing the liniment onto the horse. "Wait. Are you talking about a sting?" She shook her head. "No. No way." She considered Donna's most recent state and wondered if her friend was okay. "Get one of Jim's other drivers to do it."

"But you're the one scheduled to take the route," Wahlquist explained. "They're expecting you. If we suddenly bring in someone else, it might throw up a red flag."

"We can pay you, if that helps the decision," Brookins interjected again. When Wahlquist shot him yet another withering look, the smaller agent quickly amended his statement.

"I mean, we can pay you for the costs of fuel, meals, and an overnight hotel stay."

Dani tried to avoid showing any reaction that might indicate a second-guess on her part, but Brookins noticed her flicker of interest. He turned to Wahlquist and nodded.

Wahlquist interpreted it as a positive sign. "We'd insist that you keep your involvement with us a secret. From Jim, of course. But also Donna or anyone else."

"Wait," Dani interrupted. "Hold on, here." She held out her palm. "This was already going to be hard enough because of the animals." She paused when she realized it would be impossible to explain that concern to two BCA agents. "But to get involved in a drug sting? I can't—"

"Like we said," Wahlquist butted in, "you won't be in any danger."

"You're not listening! Or realizing what you're asking me, anyway," she added, bending to snatch up the liniment at her feet. "Where there's drugs, there's danger." She stared directly at Wahlquist. "I know, okay? Don't tell me there's no danger."

The men didn't say anything more as she sealed the medicine tube.

"And I know what a deal looks like," she continued, taking advantage of the opening. "But as I keep telling you, I didn't see any drugs on that trip. There was never any exchange—"

She realized, suddenly, what they're trying to root out with the sting. "Wait—you think the drugs were already loaded in that second trailer?"

"Something like that," Wahlquist confessed. He set it up in a different way. "Let me ask you this: Was that trailer clean? The trailer you picked up?"

"No. Definitely not."

The memory of the stench made Dani wince involuntarily. The second trailer smelled worse than the hog trailer. Worse than the back bedroom in Mr. Randolph's trailer house.

Dani needed more space between her and the agents. She checked the mare's water bucket, then left the pen for another flake of hay.

Both officers watched, but neither volunteered to help.

In the silence, Dani felt something attempting to reconnect inside her head.

Maybe she could trust her senses—and their conclusions—after all.

Maybe she did know what she'd seen.

She reconsidered whether to share the details she'd withheld earlier: Jim's encounter with that man at Subway, the wad of cash, Jim's pit-stop inside the second trailer. But something told her that they already had plenty on Jim Kelly, with or without her additional insights.

The sting sounds like a calculated move, not a wild swing.

And Dani did want to know, for certain, whether Jim was knowingly involved in drug running or whether he was just an innocent guy getting used. She wanted to help Lilly connect with her son. She wanted a paycheck to buy herself more time on the farm and more feed for her animals.

And she wanted to find out what was going on with Donna. Dani heard it straight from Donna's lips, that night she'd overheard their whispered conversation: Donna knew Jim was up to something she didn't like. But from the way Donna reacted today, it sure didn't seem like she knew it involved drugs.

Or did she?

Dani became still, that single flake of hay still in her grip, and listened.

That little voice, freed to share what she'd been trying to tamp down, rushed out in bursts: Donna must know, she decided. Somehow, she'd gotten herself in way over her head.

But did she know she was putting me in deep water, too?

She tossed the hay to her horse, then turned to the agents again.

It's about more than Donna now. I need to protect myself.

"We really do need your help." Brookins made his request in a soft voice.

Scout let out a sigh so that Dani didn't have to. "What exactly do you want me to do?"

THREE MORNINGS LATER, Pete gripped Cody's collar to hold him back from chasing Dani's truck. She'd reviewed Scout's feeding routine for Pete, but he cut her off when she started giving him instructions for the dog.

He told Dani to quit worrying, to stay safe, and to keep in touch. "If you don't call me by midnight," he added, "I'll call you, to make sure you're okay."

Before pulling out of the driveway, Dani touched the duffel bag next to her, as if verifying its presence. Two changes of clothing and other incidentals were packed inside, and her temporary driving license sat in a plastic sandwich bag at the top. Pete brought her an audio book from the library, but she didn't know if the rig would have a CD player.

Really, she didn't know what to expect from any part of the trip ahead: driving the huge semi, navigating the route, exchanging the trailer, finding Lilly's son's parents. Each part had its unique concerns and possible pitfalls. She tried to breathe deeply and evenly. She told herself to take it step by step.

The lot Jim rented for his trucks wasn't too far from Donna's little place in town. Two rigs sat idle in its corner: the blue semi they drove to Missouri and a dark red Peterbilt, the silver dog missing from its hood. The red truck had an envelope shoved under a wiper blade.

Dani parked next to the Peterbilt and stepped onto its running board to swipe at the envelope, stretching as best she could to the middle of the huge windshield. It took her three times to snag the paperwork.

A handwritten message was attached to the top of the packet: "*Thanx for your help. Do the same route as before. Your a good friend.*" Jim's signature was a scribble below this.

A silver ring with two keys slid out when she unfolded the packet. She also found the BOL and the truck's registration papers. A map with the route highlighted in yellow completed the collection.

She counted to ten, letting the air she'd been holding escape. She coached herself to be brave, then she set her teeth and stepped up into the cab.

The layout of this truck looked like what she remembered from the other rig. The double gear was on the floor to her right, and the clutch for starting the engine was to her left. There was no living space or storage in the back of this cab, though. The unit's rear window was directly behind the driver's seat.

Dani found the headlights and the wipers, both knobs already set on Auto. Placing the key into its slot, Dani shut her eyes, said a silent prayer, and pressed the glow plug to allow the huge engine to warm.

The dashboard lights and a radio set to an a.m. station came to life.

She flicked a lever, thinking it might connect to the high beams. Instead, water shot out from beneath the massive metal hood, startling her as it pocked the windshield.

As the engine warmed, she stared out at the huge hood and hoped she'd be able to see over it while out on the road. She noticed the slim slot for the CD player but decided to wait a bit before starting the audio story.

Once Dani saw the glow signal switch off, meaning it was safe to start the engine, she depressed the clutch and turned the key. The big rig roared. She adjusted her seat and shoulder harness, tweaked the side mirrors, and slipped into first gear.

The truck stalled.

Dani slammed her other foot on the brake. Immediately, she scanned the lot, wondering if the BCA agents were hiding nearby, watching her and shaking their heads and thinking they'd made a mistake.

Maybe they had . . .

Suddenly, she recalled a fleeting image of herself as a young girl, her toes curled on the very edge of a wooden dock, staring down at the waving lake below. Her young self knew that the first jump into the cool water would chill the arteries and veins in her every limb. Her eyes would burst open from shock, but then reward her with a view of a golden-green world of clouds and plants and sand and sometimes even fish.

But she couldn't explore this underwater world without a little bravery and a little grit. There on the dock, she'd make herself count backwards from three and then jump.

Each time, she'd be elated with the decision she'd made.

Now behind the wheel of a giant rig, Dani tried the same routine again. She closed her eyes, counted backwards from three, pressed the starter, and slipped into first.

The big rig rolled.

But Dani had no time to celebrate. The second shift must come within moments of the first, and the third, seconds after.

For the first minutes, she glued her eyes to the dial on the dashboard, checking that it was still in the orange range. But after a few miles, she came to rely on her hearing to tell her when to move to the next gear. Shifting the big engine became the pulse she learned to sense.

Twenty minutes passed quickly. She was about to pull off to the co-op to get her trailer when her cell phone rang from somewhere in her duffel bag.

Dani didn't want to disrupt the momentum she'd achieved; she let the call go. A moment later, it rang again.

Muttering a soft curse, Dani rifled with her right hand for the zipper, pulling the bag onto her lap to open it.

The ring stopped.

Her composure cracked, Dani offered a more strident curse and dropped the bag to the floor.

When she reached the co-op, there were two other rigs ahead of her at the loading gate. It gave her the chance to find the phone and see what was going on. She rummaged for it and checked the voicemail.

She was surprised to learn that the message was from John Davies, the deputy who'd shown up at Mr. Randolph's ruined trailer. Davies had some follow-up information to share and asked her to call at her convenience.

She thought about his timing and wondered if he knew about her trip, too. She tapped her finger on the steering wheel, easing ahead bit by bit until it was her turn to pull in at the loading gate.

Dani lowered her window and was instantly assailed by the pungent stench of penned animals. She handed the BOL to a guy standing by the entrance. With his cap and short-sleeved golf shirt, he didn't look like a security guard.

He was surprised to see her behind the wheel. "This is Kelly's rig, isn't it?"

"I'm driving for him today," Dani answered.

"You are, huh?"

"He said you'd tell me which dock to go to, to pick up my load?"

He looked at her for a long moment before flicking his eyes back to the paperwork. "Go to pen 4. Your trailer's there. The guys'll hook it up for you. Just show 'em this."

He scribbled a note and signed off at the bottom of the form, then gave the papers to Dani. "You know what you're doing, then?"

"Yes, sir." Dani tried to smile. "Thanks for your help."

The man nodded, but he didn't look convinced. He gave her a quick two-finger salute, then pointed to his left before waving for the next driver.

Dani had no problem finding the trailer. The co-op property was much smaller than the stockyard in Missouri. It was a grouping of holding pens where stock from outstate was collected before the longer ride to their next destinations.

She hit a snag, though, when she tried to back the rig onto the trailer's pin. After witnessing her four failed tries, the younger of the two men waiting in the yard knocked on her door.

"Looks like you could use a hand." She had no embarrassment this time.

The young man waited for Dani to move into the passenger's seat before he got behind the wheel. His dark-blue jumpsuit was dirty at the knees, and his hands were lined with grease, but his face was open, and his eyes looked clear.

"Ya done a lot of driving?" he asked, slipping into reverse.

"Nope. Not a lot." Dani watched his hands, devising a way to escape the cab if he became a threat. She started to chide herself for her paranoia, but then she chided herself for second- guessing.

I have no idea who I'm dealing with. I'd rather be safe than dead.

The young man backed the big truck as smooth as can be, aligning the pin perfectly to the disc-like connector on his first attempt.

"Okay, then. This'll be quick."

He braked smoothly, allowing the engine's momentum to back the coupling under the trailer's gooseneck. From her side mirror, Dani watched the older guy start to attach the various hoses as the young guy popped back out.

"Thanks," Dani said, adding, "Is it okay if I roll the window up?"

"Sure. You get used to the smell, after a while." He shrugged, already on his way to the trailer where his partner jacked the pin onto its plate.

"Yep," she added out loud to herself. "You get used to it all, I guess."

She could hear the contained animals through the closed window. She just wanted to get loaded and on the road before she talked herself out of this mission. The reasons she'd used to convince herself to undertake the assignment now seemed unsubstantial and unwise.

She couldn't bear to hear the animals. She found the audiobook in her bag, shoved the first disc into the CD player, and dialed up the volume.

Before putting her cell phone into the cup holder next to her hip, she scrolled through her numbers and put Wahlquist's number onto her screen so it would be available at the touch of a finger. If all went well, though, she wouldn't have to call until she dropped off her load and was on her way to her hotel.

A double slap on the window behind her made her jump. "Ready to go, miss!" the voice called out. "Have a good trip!"

Dani shifted from neutral to first and pulled out with just a slight hiccup. She nodded at the younger man, then set her sights on the miles ahead, praying they'd fly by quickly and safely.

She hoped the officers had done what they'd promised and had cleared the road, so to speak, of any surprise traps or checks. She wasn't planning to stop again until she reached the dock, eight hours and almost five hundred miles away.

But she did stop, after all, in Hannibal, at the same rest area they'd visited on the previous trip. Dani needed a restroom in the worst way, despite only one cup of her usual morning beverage. Not to mention, her stomach had been growling since she left.

Thankfully, the lot was emptier today than it had been when they'd come through before. She drove into a long empty stretch right by the curb, not caring if it was a legal parking spot or not.

She kept the engine running, turned on the blinking hazard lights, then jumped down. The tight spasm in her lower back released as she hastened toward the ladies' room. She was already seated behind a stall door when she remembered she didn't lock the cab door; she assured herself that it would be okay.

On her way out of the travel center, she paid for a bag of chips, a diet soda, and a granola bar, hoping they'd stave off her hunger until she'd delivered the animals and had time to find a better meal.

The animals in back were quiet, when she returned to the truck, but she could tell by the way the trailer vibrated that some were wiggling in their tight enclosures, looking for more space. Dark streams flowed out from several of the lower ventilation holes. Dani hopped into the cab to get on her way before anyone noticed the mess and asked her clean it up.

As she passed bigger cities on the route, she observed more trash on the sides of the highway, in the concrete spillways, and next to the rivers. In contrast, the shoulders near the more-rural hamlets were practically pristine, all the exit mounds were grassy and mowed, and some concrete flower planters were even set out in one place, all testaments to local, small town pride.

She thought a lot about the animals she was hauling behind her. She worried about their final hours. What would happen to their souls? Did they know the end was near? What would their last moments be like?

A sharp tone suddenly emitted from the speakers, a cue that the audiobook disc she'd shoved in had come to its end.

At about that same moment, she reached the turnoff to the stockyard.

To further electrify her nerves, her cellphone rang next, just as she downshifted and was rumbling up the exit ramp. It was Wahlquist.

"How's it going?" His voice sounded reassuring, but his pace was hurried. "Are you doing okay?"

"I am, but I can't really talk now. I'm just getting ready to exit." She tried to keep the exasperation out of her voice. Her ragged exhalation bounced along with the truck's shuddering deceleration.

"Yup, I know," he said.

How? But her response was a fleeting interruption. She had to stay focused on her turnoff.

"You ready for the drop off?" The tension in his voice unnerved her.

"I will be—if I can focus on what I'm supposed to be doing." She downshifted again and added, "I'll try to call before I get the new trailer. If I can. If not"—she gently pressed the brake pad—"I'll call after that."

"Don't do anything wrong," he said. "But don't get into anything foolish, either." Dani laughed. Her nerves were stretched so thin that she felt almost two dimensional.

"We'll be just outside the fence. And keep your phone with you," he instructed. "Okay. Gotta go."

She dropped the phone into her lap. The stockyard gate was just ahead, and she had to concentrate.

As before, the guard avoided looking at her. She handed over her paperwork. The guard called his assistant to make the cursory inspection while he scanned, then signed, the papers. He thrusted back all but the first page before waving her through the open gate.

"Dock number?" Dani asked.

"Fourteen. Round back."

Dani thanked him and pulled into the yard. A rusted Bobcat scooted across her path with its bucket raised, trailing excrement and something bloated and leaking. She paused, glad she hadn't eaten much today. After that, she turned to her right and followed the signs to the assigned dock.

Instead of trying to back in directly, Dani passed the dock, making a large arc. This allowed her to properly aim the trailer to reverse it into place. Every other dock was empty, which she found interesting, but she was glad to have the extra space in which to maneuver her rig.

She needed just two attempts to get aligned with the dock. She was satisfied and even a bit proud of herself, though the guy who came out from the nearby shed had a sour look under his ball cap.

"Papers?" he growled.

He didn't resemble the other dockhands she'd encountered. This guy looked like he'd just come from a ballgame or the golf course. He wore regular jeans and a pocket T-shirt. His boots had no stains or debris.

His hands were clean, too, as he took her paperwork. He didn't look at it, though, as he was busy monitoring the dockyard. He opened his phone and disappeared around the corner, leaving her on her own.

"Wait," Dani called after him. "You want me to disconnect the trailer?"

The man didn't reappear to answer.

"Great," Dani said, aloud.

She eased down from her seat and looked around, but it appeared she was on her own. Pulling on a pair of cotton gloves she'd found stuffed into the door panel, she was still worried about what she was doing, but that scared feeling of dread hadn't come calling. Yet.

As she was back behind the rig, trying to determine how to move the steel ramp to release the hogs, two men in a small, rusted pickup passed by. They stared at her.

Dani didn't hold their gaze. She focused instead on unhooking the wire wrapped through the lower door's safety latch. She tried to ignore the animals' growing excitement as they sensed that their confinement in the hot trailer was nearly over. She held her breath so she didn't have to smell them.

Then, she heard slamming car doors. She heard footsteps drawing near.

She stepped away from the trailer and positioned herself into the open, where she hoped she'd be more likely to be seen by Wahlquist's observant officers. Despite his assurances that the federal authorities were nearby, she hadn't seen them, and that made her even more than nervous, now.

The first man came toward her, tall and thin, with dark hair and eyes and a pale, shaven. face. His partner was also thin, but he averted his head to avoid Dani's contact. They wore identical blue zip-ups, clean and unfaded. The leather loafers that stuck out beneath each set were completely at odds with the utilitarian coveralls.

"You are Jim's girl?" the first man asked. His r's were trembly; his voice sounded Russian.

Dani nodded.

"We do this. You stay here. Wait."

He joined the other man, who'd gone back to the ramp. Metal slammed, the door screeched open, and the frantic melee of the freed animals became raucous as they called and cried out. The container swayed and jittered as the first group of hogs rushed to their pen below.

The process repeated. Dani imagined the second level of animals escaping the trailer down to the pen, but she was hesitant to step around the corner to watch.

The men reappeared. The first guy said something Dani didn't understand. He motioned for her to stay put and disappeared to work the jack. She could hear their soft patter as they disengaged the hoses from the rig and prepared to set the trailer.

She still couldn't see anything. She wanted to get closer but didn't want to poke her nose into something she shouldn't. Wahlquist's earlier pearl of wisdom came to mind.

Dani couldn't help herself, though. She sneaked closer. The men were shoulder to shoulder, fishing for something under the cylinder by the jack.

Dani's toe dislodged a hunk of cement from the walkway, sending it clattering off the path toward the workers.

The second man whirled. Seeing Dani, he spit out rapid-fire words that sounded like Slavic curses, then hustled out of her sight.

The first guy tried to get her attention. "Miss? Miss?" He pointed from her to the rig. "Okay to go. Number two-two. You go now Two-two."

Dani climbed up to her cab, locking the door as she watched the other man return to the rusted pickup. He looked thicker somehow, heavier, like he'd added stuffing to his midsection.

She recalled that image of Jim, stashing his envelope under his shirt, and her heart gave an extra thump.

The second man settled himself low in the passenger's seat. He lit a cigarette as they drove away from the dock.

Dani couldn't tell where they were headed. She waited a quick moment, her nerves increasing their jangling. She fished out her cell phone.

Wahlquist answered before it had a chance to ring. "You okay?"

Tears misted her eyes. She nodded. "Yes. Yes, but there are different people here than before—the one who took my papers, and two others who opened the trailer. They're not the same men I saw before."

She could hear Wahlquist pull his mouth away from the phone to direct someone to move to a different location. Then his rushed voice returned. "You're doing great, Dani. We're right here. Can you find the next dock?"

Dani's heartbeat echoed in her head as if she'd just survived a high drop without a parachute.

Again, she nodded before finding her voice. "Yes." She couldn't swallow. "Can you see me?"

He didn't answer, directly. "We'll meet you at the hotel, okay? Just keep going. You're almost done." He disconnected.

So much for "protection," she grimaced.

She smoothed the legs of her jeans, gulped her soda, gone warm, and set her shoulders.

For Donna, she reminded herself. She was in deep—and might be dragging Dani down with her. *I need to do this for both of us.*

After the one task left, it would be over. She must find pen 22, somehow hook up the return trailer, and get the rig back through the gate. Then it was as simple as driving to the hotel, where she'd trade the trailer for a rental car.

She promised herself that if she pulled this off, she'd treat herself to a hot bath, room service, and a movie. Maybe even a bottle of wine, since Wahlquist would be paying the bill.

Pen 22 ended up being the same pickup spot she and Jim stopped at before. A different empty trailer was waiting there this time.

There was no one around to help her connect it.

Taking her cell phone with her again, Dani slid off the seat and out of the rig. Her still-healing shoulder ached up her collarbone and into her neck. She was tired of all the up and down and in and out.

This particular trailer, the fourth container she'd seen up close, looked surprisingly new. The metal siding was clean and unblemished, and the many tires were dark and shiny. Even the jack and the connectors looked like they'd spent more time on the sales floor than on the road. It looked completely innocent and unassuming.

Dani distrusted it, instinctively.

She turned to a collection of tools affixed to the back of the Jim's rig. She clambered up to pull a long-handled shovel off the rack, judging that she'd be able to use it as a sight guide. She grabbed a bungee cord to attach the shovel to the connector and affixed it to stand vertically, a target to aim for as she attempted to slide the back of her rig under the trailer's gooseneck.

Back in the cab, she drove forward and realigned the vehicle with the shovel's handle in a direct line of sight to the pin on the front of the trailer. She eased backward, slowly, checking her side mirrors and opening her door to close the distance and finish the connection.

After removing the shovel, she raised the jack, locked the clamp, and attached the hoses. She located the paperwork hidden under the jack, as before. With each successful action, she enjoyed a prick of elation, having solved each problem on her own.

Perhaps the next thirty minutes to the hotel would also pass well. Then she'd be done and rid of Wahlquist for good.

Dani navigated back to the gate, gave the new trailer's BOL to the guard, and endured the final inspection. Not surprisingly, the rig passed.

Dani sped away from the yard with her adrenaline running high, so giddy she almost passed the road for the hotel. The near miss refocused her, bringing her attention back to her task.

A billboard for the hotel directed her another mile to the east. Finally, she could see the building at the end of the block. She gave a silent thanks when she observed the big empty parking lot in front of it. She pulled in, yanked the gearshift to neutral, set the brake, and sank down into the driver's seat, exhausted.

A dark four-door immediately came up next to her. Wahlquist and another man Dani didn't recognize climbed out. Wahlquist came toward Dani as the other man moved to the back of her trailer.

"How'd you do?" Wahlquist asked, jumping onto the driver-side running board and leaning through the open window. "Everything go okay?"

He was so close that Dani could see the individual whiskers on his face. She noticed that he smelled good—like a forest, she thought. Or a clean meadow.

Then she mentally shook her head. Her ability to focus on her task had overloaded. She was done.

"Good," she finally answered. "I dropped the animals with no problem, but I had to hook-up the empty by myself. Do you have someone to look and see if I did it right?"

"Yep, and good work," he responded, reaching for the new trailer's paperwork. "Did anyone give you any problem?"

Dani unclipped her seatbelt. "No. But like I told you earlier, the men at the lot were all different. Except for the gate guard, I mean."

"How so?"

"The first guy, the one who took the papers? He looked like he just got off the golf course."

Wahlquist didn't show surprise. "Go on."

"And the ones who disconnected the trailer were different, too. They weren't wearing the right clothes, either."

He opened the rig's door for her to exit. "What were they wearing?"

She handed her bag out for Wahlquist to take. She reached for the hand he offered.

"You know how most dock guys wear those coveralls? Like jump-suits?" She hit the ground, groaned, and let go of his hand. "The two guys—Russians, maybe?—who disconnected the trailer were wearing their street shoes under their zip-ups. No boots."

Wahlquist motioned for her to continue.

"And oh, when they were unloading? They were searching under the jack for something, and one of the guys looked like he'd stuffed something into the front of his jumpsuit—"

Just then, Wahlquist's new partner came around the front of the rig from the other side. Dani lurched backwards. Wahlquist dropped her duffel and reached for his sidearm. He grimaced when he recognized the man.

"Shit, Hanson! Next time, let me know you're coming!" He snapped his holster shut, gestured to Dani, and collected her bag. "Sorry, Dani. This is Tom Hanson, from the Missouri side. We're working together."

"Sorry 'bout that." Hanson gave a little wave. "You ready for this day to be over?"

"I sure am." As the words left her mouth, Dani's vision wavered. She felt like she'd just finished running a thousand miles. She rubbed her eyes.

"Did you get any names?" Wahlquist was back, with his questions.

"No. As I said, I think they were Russian or something. I couldn't understand them. And they left as soon as the second guy stuffed whatever that was into his jumpsuit."

Wahlquist raised an eyebrow at Hanson, who opened his phone and walked away to make a call.

Dani had her own question. "Who takes the trailer from here?"

As he replied, Wahlquist watched the other agent on his phone. "We have a female officer who'll finish the route for you." He didn't add any more details.

"But when will we know if there were really drugs inside? And what about Jim Kelly? When will we know if he's involved in it? And Donna—my friend?"

Hanson closed his phone; the men exchanged a glance.

"You've done a good job here, Miss Holden," Hanson began. "But we can't tell you much more than what you've figured out for yourself." He nodded at Wahlquist, took Dani's duffel bag from him, then started for the hotel. "Let's get you checked in."

Dani didn't follow. "That's it?" She wheeled to glare at Wahlquist.

"Tell you what," he answered, his voice low. "I'll get in touch with you after this delivery's made. Maybe next week. But right now, my hands are tied."

She shot him another evil eye.

"It's the best I can do."

Her mouth a tight line, she stared at him a long moment. She couldn't help wanting to know more—about what they'd seen, what would come next, what they thought of what she'd done to help them.

Wahlquist kept himself quiet.

Dani turned back to the other officer, who'd backtracked to wait for her. "Where will I find my rental car? And what time do I check out tomorrow morning?"

"It'll be parked right next to the front door. And I got a late check-out," Hanson said. "Is eleven okay?"

"Perfect. And do you know if there's a computer or a map I can use? I want to get my route organized for tomorrow."

Finally, Dani could concentrate on Lilly and the mission to find the people who'd adopted her son.

Hanson shifted her bag to his other hand. He pointed to the hotel again. "There's a business office of sorts inside," he said. "We'll get that situated—if you'll come with me?"

Before starting for the front desk, though, Dani had a last request: "Do either of you know where I can get a cup of coffee?"

12

Dani watched the hotel clock's white digits flip themselves closer to morning. When she'd checked in the night before, she had assumed she'd sleep forever. But when 5:30 a.m. flashed, she officially gave up, grabbed her bag, and left her room.

As she signed out, Dani asked the desk clerk about getting breakfast to go.

"We don't have a kitchen," the shy woman answered.

She had a gap between her front two teeth and wiry dark hair. Her quiet words tumbled in circles before escaping, leading Dani to think the woman wasn't born in the United States. She didn't want to ask, though. What business was it of hers?

Instead, she thanked the clerk, located the rental car out front, and started north on I-44 toward St. Louis and the suburb of Fenton, the city in which Gene and Betty Walker, Lilly's son's parents, were supposed to live.

When she spotted the first billboard advertising Starbucks, she pulled off for a large coffee and a scone, then got right back on the road. She gulped a few mouthfuls of the dark blend before dialing Lilly's number. She punched the speaker button.

"Dani?" Lilly sounded out of breath and a bit sleepy.

Kicking herself for forgetting the time difference in California, Dani plunged ahead. "Sorry to wake you, Lil. But I just wanted to let you know I'm on my way to the address you gave me for the Walkers. I should be there in less than an hour."

"Goodness!" There was a catch in Lilly's voice. "I don't know what to say! After all these years . . . this is actually happening. I'm finally going to learn about my son!"

"Remember," Dani said gently, "this may be a lot for the Walkers to take in. It's been"—she tried to do the math in her head—"more than fifty years since the adoption. They're in their eighties, too, I imagine. Just like you. After so many years, they may not be ready to disclose anything about your son. Most likely, they'll just pass this information on to him so he can decide for himself. And even then, it may take some time for him to make the next step."

. . . which you don't have a lot of, Dani added to herself.

The same thought must have crossed Lilly's mind. "Well, I've been busy working, gathering my family information and my genealogy for him. For him to have. In case I don't get to meet him."

Dani had to focus on signaling and merging into the passing lane, thankful for the natural pause it allowed her. "What does your oncologist say?"

"Oh, shoosh, you know—all the regular 'You may have between this amount of time and that amount of time' stuff they tell every patient."

"Are you telling me the truth?" Dani asked outright.

"Of course I am!" Lilly's retort was spiced with indignation. "Anyway, I've decided that I'm not going to listen to them and their plans for me. I'll—"

"You have to listen!" Dani interjected. "They want the best for you! I do, too. You need to do what they say, Lil."

The older woman waited a beat, then went on as if she hadn't been interrupted. "I'll do what I think I can do. And when I can't, I'll take care of myself, like I always have." She blew her nose. "I want to be in charge."

"Absolutely, you should be in charge, but—oh, hold on a minute."

Dani recognized the name for her turnoff on an overhead sign. Stealing a glance at the map beside her, she confirmed that it was.

"I'm getting ready to exit, Lilly. I'm sorry—I'll have to call you back. Do you want me to call you before I go to the Walkers' house or . . . ?"

"Call me after, honey. And do me a favor, though I know you will: Do your best not to scare them, okay? I don't want them to think I'm going to barge in and take over after all these years."

Dani could sense Lilly's brave front weakening. In her friend's voice—and in the echo of her own heart—Dani identified with that wrenching block separating longing from fear and regret.

"I'll do my best, Lilly."

Lilly couldn't answer.

"Love you, Lil. I'll call as soon as I can."

Disconnecting, Dani wiped her eyes with a trembling hand. She was minutes away from knocking on the door of Gene and Betty Walker, minutes away from forever upending their lives and the life of their son. Lilly's son.

She sensed her own brave front crumbling, too.

Dani gave herself a pep talk. She reminded herself that she was knocking on the door only as a messenger, a liaison, without threat or demand. She was there to give information to the family, if they wanted to receive it. What they decided to do with the information would be up to them and their son.

The Walkers' neighborhood was older. The homes were one level and shaped like small boxes, their front doors right in the centers. Most of the houses had cement driveways leading from the street to single-car garages.

Post–World War II era, Dani decided, recalling a large suburb of Minneapolis, near where she grew up.

Though the homeowners in the Walkers' neighborhood were obviously not rich, they kept their yards mowed and their driveways swept and tidy. The properties were dotted with pots blooming with tawny mums and yellow and maroon asters.

The Pendleton Street address Lilly had given Dani matched up with a house with blue siding and white shutters. Round green bushes flanked the front door. A metal lamppost governed the small front yard; petunias circled its base in patriotic red, white and purple colors.

An additional garage space had been added to the original structure. In front of this, a large black motorcycle leaned on a stout kickstand.

Dani deliberately passed the home, slowly, then swung around at the intersection and came back from the opposite direction. From this angle, Dani could see into the backyard. It was enclosed by a silver mesh fence, complete with a curious large dog whose ears pricked as he followed the car rolling past his property.

Dani made another U-turn at the next intersection. But this time, she slowed to a stop at the curb, one house away. She told herself that she wanted to scout out if anyone is home.

In reality, her nerves were faltering again. Dani couldn't tell if the last twenty-four hours had taken more from her than she expected, or that her heart was so invested in a positive outcome for Lilly that she couldn't bear for her friend to be rejected. Whatever the reason was, Dani needed a moment to get herself together before she walked up the driveway to knock on the door.

Her cell phone rang. Startled, Dani fumbled for the phone, chastising herself for not placing the ringer on silent beforehand. She didn't want the neighbors calling the police, thinking she was an unknown stalker or nuisance.

The incoming call's label was marked "Restricted."

"This is Dani," she whispered into the mouthpiece. Her eyes scanned the empty street to her front and side.

"You're gone already."

It was Wahlquist, checking up on her. And apparently calling from his office or some other number than the one he'd given her.

"I thought you'd still be sleeping, after your long drive," he continued.

Dani closed her eyes, briefly, and shook her head. The trailer, the stockyard, Jim, Donna—none of it could be further from her mind.

"I can't talk now." Her response was terse. "Can we do this later?"

He lowered his volume to match hers. "Absolutely. We'd like to bring you here into the bureau office tonight to share your observations with us. Is that—"

"I'm heading home tonight," Dani broke in. "Will you be back in Crestview tomorrow?"

"Yep."

From her rearview mirror, Dani watched a small gray car turn onto Pendleton Street from the avenue. It picked up speed as it neared.

"Hey, can you call me later? I need to go."

She didn't wait for his answer. She disconnected and leaned forward as if she was looking for something under the dashboard. She didn't want the driver to see her face.

To Dani's chagrin, the gray car turned into the driveway of the home immediately across the street from the house Dani was watching. A high-school-aged girl got out, backpack over one shoulder, and slammed her door, twice, before it stayed closed.

Dani slunk down in her seat, then peered out from behind the curve of her steering wheel. The girl was staring straight at her.

Shit, Dani grimaced, sitting up. *I'm not good at this spy stuff.*

With her cover blown, Dani needed a different approach. She opened her own door, arranged a wide smile on her face, and got out of her car.

Still in her driveway, the girl had taken out her phone and was tapping in a number.

"Hey there," Dani said quickly, trying to delay what she assumed was the girl's call to the police. She crossed the street toward the girl at an angle. "I'm looking for someone. Could you maybe help me?"

Still wary, the girl quit tapping yet gave no sign of agreement. "Who're you looking for?"

Her grim face presented what Donna would have described as a "tough cookie."

"I think my friends live across from you," Dani answered indirectly. "The Walkers—Gene and Betty. Do you know if they still own that house?" She pointed at the blue bungalow.

"And you are . . . ?"

The girl was tough.

"Donna Lund," Dani lied, surprising herself.

"How do you know the Walkers?" The girl came toward Dani, her phone in her hand.

"Well, I don't. Not really." Perhaps some truth might unsnarl the lies. "Actually, I'm here for my friend. She's not well, though, so I'm here on her behalf."

"In other words, that's why you don't know that Betty passed a few years ago." The girl's long hair, blown by a gust, wrapped itself around her chin. She peeled it away. "It's just Gene now."

Dani tried to hide her shock about Betty's passing. She'd never considered that Betty—or Gene or both—could have passed away since the adoption agency had last updated their contact information. And now Dani suddenly realized that for all anyone knew, even the son, a middle-aged man, may not still be alive.

"Is Gene home?" Dani pushed past these disorienting intrusions.

The girl gave Dani the stink eye. "Did you knock?"

Dani laughed, but it sounded fake even to her own ears. She cleared her throat and gestured again toward the blue house. "No, but I was just about to," she said. "Thanks for your help."

"I think I'll come with you." The younger woman joined Dani on the driveway. "I haven't checked in with Gene for a few days. He likes it when I visit."

Dani figured that the girl's distrust was the main reason for accompanying her to the front door. Yet Dani could hear the honesty in the girl's voice as she spoke about her connection with Gene.

"Um, my friend—she's sick. Cancer."

"I'm sorry," Gene said. "I lost my wife to that bastard." A shadow crossed his features as sadness seeped into the corners of his eyes and the folds that bracketed his mouth. His whole countenance sagged.

"What does that have to do with us?" The girl interrupted. Definitely a hard sell.

"Well," Dani tried again, aware that she wanted to move closer to the door behind her in case she had to flee, "My friend had a baby she had to give up years ago. A son."

Gene's face instantly hardened. The sorrow he'd momentarily given in to vanished, replaced by nervous agitation.

April rose from the sofa to stand behind him.

"My friend, Lilly Bradford, is in her eighties. She had her baby in 1939."

It hadn't been even five minutes since Dani stepped through the door. In record time, she'd yanked off the cover that had hidden the family's secret for over six decades.

Gene's shield of anger melted. "What do you want from us?" His voice was soft.

"What the hell is going on?" This, from April. "Who the hell are you, to come in here with this story?" She began to push past the older man in Dani's direction.

Gene grabbed her waist. "April! That's enough!" He struggled to pull the girl back.

Dani retreated to the door and fumbled with the knob, but it opened to the inside. She was trapped until the pair backed up, giving her enough space to exit.

The elderly man rotated April and met her eye to eye. "This lady came a long way to talk to us. We should hear what she has to say, okay?" He released her when she relaxed a tiny bit. "It's fine. It will all be fine."

The girl nodded, but she didn't look happy.

Gene turned back to Dani. "Would you, please, join us for a visit, Donna?" He gestured toward the sofa and loveseat.

"Thank you. I'm sorry for causing trouble." She chose the seat closest to the door. "And I might as well tell you, my name is Dani, not Donna. I don't even know why I said that. Nerves, I guess."

"See!" April blurted from her spot on the couch. "She's been lying this whole time! She's trying to get something from you!"

Gene gave her a stern look. "She's probably got a reason." Then, to Dani, "Would you like anything, Dani—tea, coffee?"

"No, thank you," she declined.

Gene sat next to April.

No one spoke for a long moment.

Dani gathered her thoughts, considering what she could best say next to gain the information Lilly sought without disturbing the family more than was necessary.

In the silent space, Gene glanced up, then nodded, deciding something. He directed his response to the girl, first. "April, our Jamie came to us from a hospital in Iowa," he began.

Jamie. Lilly's son's name is Jamie.

"I didn't know you guys lived in Iowa," April butted in.

Gene smiled at her, patiently. Dani saw the love this man had for this girl etched in his every crease and furrow. She wondered what the girl was to him; clearly more than a neighbor. Dani could see how they looked to each other for affirmation and comfort.

"We didn't live there," Gene explained. "We went there to get him."

The realization broke through the shell of April's tough attitude. "Jamie's adopted?" She swiveled to the older man, placing a hand with black-polished fingertips gently on his shoulder.

He nodded.

"Huh. I always wondered why he didn't have any brothers or sisters." April turned to Dani then. "And your friend—that's his real mom?"

"No!" Dani was quick to reply. But when confusion clouded both April's and Gene's faces, she realized she must amend her answer.

"I mean, yes, my friend is his biological mother. But she'd never say she's his 'real' mother. That's not how she thinks about it. She never got to know him, before she . . . before he . . . left." She scrutinized Gene, who was digesting her every word. "She wasn't married when she had him."

April's face grew dark again. "So? What did not being married matter?"

"It was different back then," the older man intervened. "When unmarried girls found themselves 'in the family way,' as they said"—he cleared his throat—"they had to go away to have their babies. Most of them were given up for adoption. Then the girls went back home and continued with their lives."

April tucked her chin back into her chest, her eyes wide. She didn't blink. "What? They never saw their babies again?"

"No, not usually. Most adoption services sealed the papers to keep them confidential, forever." His eyes met Dani's. "At least, that's what I thought our adoption agency did."

Dani raised her shoulders in a shrug of uncertainty and apology. If Gene was to ask how Lilly managed to unlock their information, Dani wouldn't answer, anyway. It wasn't her place to do so.

"I realize this is a shock and a lot to think about," she confessed. "I'm sorry."

April, examining the threads in her sweater's sleeve, was quiet, but Gene was able to go on.

"It's nothing we, I, haven't wondered about. Betty and I always wondered if his parents would reach out, if they could. What made your friend wait so long?"

"I think Lilly didn't want to intrude on your family. She didn't think she had the right."

"She probably felt, feels, guilty, too," Gene added.

Dani was surprised by the man's insight and empathy. What a great person to have had as a father. She reminded herself to tell Lilly this detail.

Next to Gene, April let out a huge, long exhale. "So, Jamie's adopted." The realization clanged to the bottom of her understanding. "That means I'm the bastard of a bastard."

Dani just about fell from her chair, partly due to the language the young girl favored and partly due to the revelation.

"You're Jamie's daughter?" Dani asked, astounded.

April's eyes rolled. "You're quick on the uptake, Donna."

Gene squeezed the girl's knee. "Yes. Jamie and April live right across the street." He pointed out the picture window to where April's gray car was parked.

Dani's body tingled. "Is Jamie home right now . . .?"

This trip to Fenton, Missouri, was only meant to be a visit with the Walkers, only the first step in Lilly's quest of connecting with her son. Never did Dani—nor Lilly—dream that she'd be able to meet the son in person as well.

But Gene shook his head. "No, not now. He's at work."

Dani was almost afraid to ask her next question, but she felt had had to. For Lilly. "Do I think I could come back later to—"

"You should go now," April shot out, the toughness suddenly reappearing. "I'm pretty done." She got up. "When Jamie's back, we'll decide how to tell him all this."

Dani had no choice but to acquiesce.

Neither did Gene. Placing his hands on his knees, he gathered strength to stand. His thin hair, carefully combed, was as neat as his shaven face. His trousers looked more like old suit pants than everyday wear. The seams at the toes of his polished loafers had split, showing little gaps.

He followed Dani to the door.

"Thank you, Gene," Dani handed him a card with Lilly's name, email address, and phone number as she crossed the threshold once again.

Gene received it carefully, gazed at it, then looked up and nodded.

His response gave Dani hope.

The door closed firmly behind her.

Somehow Dani made it back to the rental car and out of their neighborhood before stopping, pulling to a curb, and dialing Lilly's number.

Lilly picked up even before Dani heard the connection go through. "Dani?" Her voice was shrill. "Dani?"

"It's me, Lil."

"Tell me what happened!" she demanded.

"I met Gene, Jamie's father," Dani began.

"Jamie!" Lilly repeated.

"His mother, Betty, actually died a few years ago." Dani almost included the word cancer but kept that fact back. "And you'll never believe this: Jamie lives with his daughter right across the street from his dad!"

"I'm a grandma?!" Lilly's voice was incredulous.

Dani laughed. "You are! And she's a spitfire, Lil."

She knew the moment Lilly grasped the other piece of information she'd just shared.

"Did you say he lives across the street? Oh, my word. Did you meet him?"

"No," Dani said gently. "But Lil, I have a good feeling about it."

"Tell me everything!" Lilly insisted.

So Dani did. She told Lilly about the neighborhood and the house, about the kind way her son's father spoke to his granddaughter, about the girl's spirit, and anything else she could think of.

"Lilly—there were pictures. He looks like you, but with dark hair."

Lilly sniffed.

"And he has blue eyes. Just like you said."

13

DANI STOPPED JUST ONCE on her route back to Crestview, to refuel and use the restroom. When she checked her phone at the rest stop, there was a voice message from Gene thanking her for visiting. He said he planned to speak with Jamie that night.

It was dark by the time she reentered Howard County. Having consumed only junk food, coffee, and adrenaline for the past thirty-some hours, she considered what she had in her kitchen, then opted to stop at Susie's Café instead of heading straight home.

Her approach to the diner's parking lot reminded her that it was another theme night. The lot was full, so she left the rental car in front of the library and walked back to the café, her bag growing heavier with each step.

The evening's air soothed her after the canned air and gas fumes and animal odors she'd been processing. Tall lights rimming the sidewalk highlighted insects that undulated and spasmed in stark, illuminated cones. Unable to pick out the stars that usually graced the night sky, she figured there must be clouds overhead.

Laughter and music pulled her along to the diner.

Inside, the length of the front counter was draped in a jade-green cloth. Oblong silver tubs held the remnants of rice; bright vegetables in a thick brown sauce; and long, thin yellow noodles. A cake stand offered one lonely fortune cookie, cracked in half. The air smelled of oil and onions and incense. Eastern music with lots of flutes and wave sounds was barely discernible, overpowered by the animated conversations at every table.

"Hey. Dani. Where ya been?"

Jim Kelly, tucked into the far corner by the coffeemaker, came out of the shadows.

"Jim? How—"

Dani's heart raced while she composed her expression.

All sorts of questions whirled through her mind: Did he suspect that she knew about his illegal transport activity? Could he know she was reporting back to the authorities, or that she just completed her part in a sting?

For that matter, what was Jim even doing here? Wasn't he supposed to be locked up somewhere?

It took Dani a moment to remind herself that this wasn't some half-hour TV show, where the story ended the moment the good guys slapped handcuffs on the bad guy. From what she'd gleaned, the BCA was still building its case against Jim. Thus, the sting.

She made a mental note to squeeze whatever she could from Wahlquist the next day.

Jim continued, tamping down his volume. "Don and I thought we'd see ya last night." He wiped one large paw down over his chin. A wave of his cologne wafted her way. "Ya spend the night there or somethin'?"

"I visited someone for a friend of mine, remember?"

"Oh, yeah," he said.

Dani could tell that he didn't remember.

"So, how'd it go? Ya get that trailer up here okay?"

Her pulse quickened. "Yup. Dropped it off where you said." She didn't elaborate. He wouldn't know about that part of the plan, that someone else drove the trailer from Missouri to Iowa; she also didn't want him to know that she was up-to-speed on the fact that he didn't even own the business anymore.

Dani hoped to block further questions: "I don't think it's for me, Jim. I didn't mind the driving—that part was actually pretty good. But—"

"I don't know how much longer I'll have that route, anyhow," he interrupted. "So don't count on it being one of those long-term things. Least ya get some rent money this time, right? And don't worry—I'll get it to ya," he added. "I'm just waitin' on payment myself."

Positioned like that, under the overhead light, his shark teeth practically glowed.

"Ya know you can trust me."

She hated how he thought he could manipulate her. She couldn't trust him; she had no firm footing for the parts of him that could or could not possibly be true. As far as Jim was concerned, her eyes were open, and her heart, firmly closed.

Still, she found it vaguely comforting that he was being his usual smarmy self. She figured he'd be acting quite differently if he had any inkling about her involvement with the feds.

Dani peered past him now, scanning for an empty seat to escape to. Instead, she saw Donna speeding by, balancing stacks of dirty dishes.

"Hey, Dani," she mustered before she glared at Jim. "Think you could help me out a bit, buddy? Where's that new pot of coffee?"

As Donna pushed into the kitchen, her head as high as she could hold it, Dani realized her friend's true balancing act: managing to deliver a theme night experience to a diner packed with people hungrily aware of the accusations against Jim.

"I can help her," Dani offered.

"Nah, go take a load off."

When he ducked under the counter for the coffee grounds, Dani allowed the smallest bit of air to release from her lungs—but then Jim popped back up.

"Hey. Did you talk with anyone? At the stockyard?" His voice was low again.

"What?"

"Did you talk to the guys with the second trailer?" He leaned forward in a confiding manner, his dark brows drawn like a shadowed scar.

She swallowed. "I'm sorry?" Suddenly, Dani couldn't say for certain whether he was ignorant about her role in the plot against him.

"Did you see anything?" he hissed. Spit snaked out from between his gritted lips.

Electric acid shot through her exhausted body, but Dani didn't have enough energy left to form any response without accidentally revealing her part in the scheme against him.

At that very moment, Missy's voice rang out like a foghorn through a storm. "Heya, Dani! Come sit with us—we saved a spot."

From across the diner, Missy beckoned to Dani with a ring-encrusted hand. Sitting next to her, Marilyn and Barbara broke into Avon-hued smiles and cleared their pocketbooks from the unclaimed fourth seat at their table.

Dani darted over to the women, thankful to be spared further interaction with Jim.

She'd barely reached her chair when Marilyn, who'd chosen not to wear her hearing aids, yelled out: "So Dani, do you know why we've been entertaining the government lately? Don't they have enough to do there in Warshington?" She pronounced the capitol's name with an r, as did many of the older locals.

Then Barbara broke in. "You look like you need something to eat, Dani. Let's get you fed, before"—she raised her voice for Marilyn's benefit—"before we ask any more questions."

Dani had no time to reply: Barbara shot off to the buffet on a mission.

A bottle of soy sauce landed in front of Dani, next, before a red napkin unfolded and fluttered near her lap. Red wine appeared in front of her, but Dani waved it off.

"No thanks, gals–I'm so tired, a glass of wine would slide me under," she explained.

Barbara slid a plate heaped with vegetables and rice onto their table. "So go ahead and slide under! We can drive you home."

"Could you?" Tears welled in Dani's eyes. "I'd really appreciate it. You all are so great to me."

Barbara rejoined the table. "Oh, you must be exhausted, honey. Did you make it through the trip okay?"

Missy had her own question. "Are you really going to keep driving those awful, smelly trucks? Isn't there a better way to earn some money?"

Dani wasn't surprised that they'd known about her trip. She aimed for a neutral yet honest reply. "It went fine. I don't think hauling stock is for me, though. It's too hard to drop them off."

"I remember when I was a girl, on the farm." These friends, the same circle she'd leaned on and confided in for many, many years, knew this already, but for Dani's benefit, Barbara continued. "We had stock. Beef, mostly. We learned young about what they call 'the cycle of life.' But I never did get to that place of comfort, watching those little ones get separated from their mamas, or trying not to think about what lay ahead for the cattle." She toyed with the stem of her wine glass. "When I married Jacob, I wasn't any bit sad to move to a crop farm instead."

Marilyn spoke up. "But didn't you have that hog shed? Up on the hill? How'd you deal with that?"

"That was Jacob's deal. I got rid of that—you know, right after he passed." She finished her wine. "It eases me, though, to think that animals are treated better these days."

"That's not necessarily true." This was Dani. "The stockyard in Missouri was pretty bad. At least I thought so. And we don't know what happens to them in Mexico, where lots of them end up."

A morose mood settled over the group. Their table was conspicuously subdued, compared to the camaraderie enjoyed by the other diners near them.

Missy changed the subject. "Did you get a chance to meet Lilly Bradstreet's son?"

Once again, Dani wasn't surprised that they also knew the second purpose for her trip. That was how a small town's "information line" worked: people eventually learned what they weren't supposed to know. No one asked directly, but during the long hours in the fields or the kitchens or on the two-lane country roads, most were able to put two and two together. "Um"—Dani decided she would take a healthy swallow of wine, after all—"no, actually. I didn't meet him. I found his neighborhood, but no, I didn't meet him." Her answer, mostly honest, strained behind the details she didn't think it was her business to let loose.

"Why not?" Missy pressed. She wasn't asking outright, exactly, but her meaning could not be misconstrued.

"Missy." The admonition came from Marilyn. "I'm sure we'll all learn, when it's time."

Missy sniffed her disapproval but kept the follow-up questions to herself.

Of the three, Marilyn was the most reticent, though it was hard to reconcile this with her loud voice. She was also the most religious. "If you ask me, the Lord makes His ways known in His time, not ours."

Dani didn't know how much more she'd need to endure before she could call the day officially over. She was sure she could fall asleep right here at the table, if the ladies would just keep still for a moment.

Marilyn rearranged the napkin on her lap. "Where do you suppose they're keeping the dessert?" This last sentence was loud, even for her.

Grateful for the change of direction, Dani whispered to Barbara. "I'm so sorry, but I'm tired all of a sudden. Could you—"

Barbara gathered her purse. "Of course. Let's get you home, Dani."

They said good night to Missy and Marilyn. Dani waited at the door, as Barbara looped around the café in order to give the rest of the diners an appropriate Midwestern goodbye.

Dani didn't see Donna or Jim in the main room. They were probably in back, preparing the desserts.

Finally outside, the two women crunched through the fallen leaves scattered between the lawn and the edge of the parking lot. Barbara held up a small plastic case from which dangled a crucifix and a plastic grocery store ValuCard. She pushed a button to unlock her car's doors; the sedan's headlights shone a path for them to follow.

They had to circle the block for the right direction to Dani's place. Most of the homes they passed in town were older bungalows, cosseted by large elms and big front yards. Streetlights shone from the main intersections; the town's only traffic light blinked yellow.

Barbara turned onto a county road that ran level until it reached the city-limit line, where it regained its true nature, climbing and flattening with the rolling fields on either side. There were no lights out in the country, no yellow or white lines on the tired asphalt. But the women had traveled the road enough to anticipate slowing at the crossroads, keeping their eyes open for the deer that dashed across the road like shot arrows.

Barbara placed her plump hand on Dani's arm. "You don't have to say anything," she began, "but do you at least think this story— between Lilly and her son, I mean—will have a good end?"

The woman's comfort warmed Dani. "I don't know, to be honest. Maybe? It's up to them, I guess. They'll have to forge their own way through it. I'm sad, though, that she's sick and doesn't have a lot of time." Then Dani remembered that Barbara didn't have time, either, to say goodbye to her own husband before he died. "I guess none of us do, really," she added.

Barbara gave Dani's arm a gentle squeeze.

They arrived at Dani's place moments later. As they pulled up her gravel drive, Dani noticed she'd forgotten to leave on the outdoor light. It helped, then, that the stars had emerged from the cloud cover. They were bright in the cooling air, allowing her to pick out the sidewalk edges through the thatch of overgrown lawn she needed to mow.

She reached over and gave Barbara a quick hug, then snagged her duffel, thanking Barbara for the ride.

Dani hesitated on the porch steps after Barbara pulled away. Her knees, stiff and sore, ached more than her shoulder. She had a pounding headache.

She couldn't take any time for herself, though, to relax or process what she'd endured, as Cody spotted her arrival from his lookout at the front window.

Dropping her bag first, she freed the dog. He jumped and yipped and licked her face, his brushy tail whipping back and forth.

They went together to the barn.

Through the pen's slats, Scout's large eyes shone in the dim light. She touched noses with Cody, then lifted her head to welcome Dani.

"How're you doing, old girl?"

Dani entered the enclosure, wanting nothing more than to hug the horse, to press herself against her and breathe in her warm scent.

The horse stood still, her head curved back toward Dani, and waited patiently for her human to gather her strength and courage and feet again.

Scout knows all about this, Dani thought. *This worn-down, I-give-up confusion.*

They breathed together under the dark sky.

Dani held out her palm to the horse as an offering or, maybe, a vessel for forgiveness.

The horse brushed her warm lips over Dani's skin. Finding no grain or other treat, she turned to see what the dog was up to.

In the barn, Dani located the horse tack, then returned to the pen to ease the halter over the mare's nose.

"So, I've been pretty busy," she shared, securing the buckle. "I found Lilly's son. I think. Well, his family, at least."

The two passed through the gate toward Scout's future pasture. Though it was night, the stars' scant light allowed her to see a few paces in front of her, the oblong silhouettes of the treelines marking the edges of her property. Inside this glowing space, Dani told Scout about the trip. She swallowed the details of the animals' cries and their confusion and the pain she'd witnessed. Instead, she described for her horse how she drove the big rig down those long, flat miles, the shady guys at the stockyard, and Lilly's granddaughter.

Dani's eyes filled again. She realized she'd been nervous, but her tears weren't infused with anxiety: these tears released the fear she'd had to tamp down, every mile, both ways.

The insight caused Dani to look up through the stars to utter a quiet thanks, grateful for the gifts of getting home safely and for the accomplishment of locating Lilly's son's family. The tears flowed, unimpeded, down her cheeks and across the mare's broad neck held close against her, cleansing her worry and stress away.

And at last, the fear subsided. Dani took a deep, deep breath and wiped a hand across her warm face.

Her comfort no longer needed, Scout eased away to pluck up delicate grass stems, her lips roving over bits of stone or hay like fingers sorting peas from a pod. She breathed out pleasant gusts that smelled primordial, basic, anchoring.

Dani filled herself with the crisp evening air, the starglow that governed her steps, and the pungent, dusty smells of the animals keeping watch over her. Peace enveloped her with its calming insulation. For this moment, it was enough for Dani to simply be.

Then a night bird swooped past, causing the air current's silky threads to hiccup; as the soft breeze smoothed out again, it pulled her thoughts toward home.

She gently collected Scout's lead rope. They retraced their path to the barn, where Cody sat waiting for them, centered in an illuminated circle thrown down by one overhead light.

Dani saw that Pete had tidied the barn in her absence, even raking the dropped hay. Slender furrows in the sand led from the pen to the service door. Cody's paw prints, like little beads, marred the lined surface like notes penciled onto sheet music.

So much had happened in these days and hours that being here, at the farm she called home, felt almost felt new again. She was a strange combination of tired, scattered, curious, and proud.

Dani paused, climbing the porch steps, and closed her eyes. She listened to Scout from across the yard. The horse chewed her hay in rhythmic mouthfuls, a soothing duet with the calm songs of the night bugs, hiding deep in the shadows.

14

DANI WAITED UNTIL THE KITCHEN CLOCK READ 8:00 A.M. the next morning before dialing Steven Wahlquist.

He picked up after four rings. "Dani?" There was an echo on his side, making it sound like he was in a tunnel.

"I know you said I should come into your office today to talk," she began. "But I'd rather meet here, at my house."

He didn't reply. Or if he did, because of the interference she couldn't hear what he said.

"It's just that I've been gone forever," Dani continued. She sounded crabby to her own ears, but she didn't care. "I've got tons of laundry to do, and the front lawn's turned into another pasture."

From the agent's side of the line, she heard a door shut. "Okay, let's see what I can do." Wahlquist's voice became clearer. "Does noon work? We can make it a lunch."

"That'd be great. But you'll have to bring it. Sorry, but I don't have anything to eat—grocery shopping is also on my to-do list."

"Sure. I can grab something from the café before I head over. Can I get you anything?"

"Whatever you're having is fine." Dani paused. "Thanks for understanding, by the way. I just want to stay at home for a while, at least until I feel like myself again."

"It's fine. And you can call me Steve. Or Wally, if that's easier."

Dani couldn't help it: she laughed. "A cop named Wally? Intimidating!"

He chuckled, too. "Well, some like it," he teased. "Whatever works for you." His voice tightened as he prepared to disconnect. "Noon then, right?"

Despite the lighthearted foray, Dani's smile faded a pulsebeat later when she remembered the reason for the agent's visit. She wanted this chapter closed so she didn't have to keep thinking about drugs and dead animals.

"Okay, see you then."

Because another human would be entering her living quarters—a detective, at that—Dani made a half-hearted attempt to wipe off the top layer of dust in the living room. She ran the dry mop around the main floor, then put away the dishes she'd left on the drain rack before her trip.

She dug a scented candle from the back of the hall closet—"Springtime" printed on the floral label–and lit it, hoping the essence would dispel the fusty odor the old house expelled whenever it was locked up.

Cody monitored her from the throw rug in front of the sofa.

"Don't think you're going to hop up there, mister," she warned him.

She knew his scheme: he jumped up on the cushions when she wasn't around to scold him. The proof was in the dog hair that decorated the backs of her clothes, a battle to remember to remove.

"C'mon. Let's go out and see what Scout's been up to."

He scampered to the front door, his tail aflutter. His glances alternated between the doorknob and Dani to be sure she was still behind him. She pushed open the screen for him, and the dog took off, sailing over the steps in one bound.

Dani scolded herself for forgetting to lock the door the night before. It wasn't her practice. She'd have to stick a note up as a reminder.

Scout nickered from her pen, her curved ears pricked forward. Just a few wisps remained of the hay Dani had thrown the night before. Dani reached between the metal fence to pat her.

"We can take a walk later," Dani told the animals. "I should get started on the lawn, before old Wally comes for lunch."

There wasn't a garage on the property, so she kept the little gas mower in the barn. She checked the tank for fuel, pushed the machine to the driveway's edge, and set the choke.

Four pulls later, the mower gasped to life, and she set off at an angle to the lawn's opposite corner. She pivoted the machine there and aimed for the driveway again. She kept the front tire in the track left from the previous strip to maintain that same sharp angle. At the drive, she turned yet again to parallel the first swipe.

Dani smiled. Creating patterns always satisfied and calmed her.

And so the rows and minutes passed, step by step, swath by swath, until the front section near her porch was finished.

As she shut off the engine, the pop of gravel shifting on her driveway reached her ears. She arched her back, stretching, and watched Steve Wahlquist park his black SUV in reverse, nosed out toward the road.

A quick glance at her watch revealed that it was only 11:45. But Dani was steadier now, stronger. She felt ready for the interview.

Holding a brown grocery sack, Wahlquist walked with her to her front door. "Too early?" "Nah. C'mon in," Dani said as they mounted the steps.

The moment she opened the front door, a scented wave of flowers blasted out from the living room.

Dani left the candle burning unattended. Not a crime, but perhaps a sign of reckless negligence to a federal agent. She quickly blew on the wick. A slender spiral of smoke followed the air current she created when she quickly passed into the dining room area.

"So, what did you bring?" She pulled out a chair for the agent, then arranged a chair for herself on the opposite side of the table.

"I ended up getting these at the grocery store." He produced two cellophane-wrapped sandwiches from the bag. "The café was closed when I drove by," he added, dipping back into the sack for a plastic container of salad.

The news filled Dani with immediate concern. Since she'd lived in Crestview, that café had been open every single day, every week.

"I wonder if Donna's sick?"

"Or on vacation," Steve suggested. He paused, standing next to his chair.

Despite her distraction, Dani noticed the old-fashioned gesture. She sat. "Well, I'd think Donna would've called me if she were on a vacation. We're pretty good friends."

Or at least, we used to be.

Steve sat, too, and pulled out his phone. "Mind if I record this?"

"I guess not." Dani unwrapped the sandwich—chicken salad— and had a bite. Dry. She opened and sipped from the diet soda he handed her. "First things first: Why did I see Jim Kelly at the café last night? Didn't you arrest him?"

The agent swallowed before answering. "It's not something I can get into," he said. "But trust me when I say it's all part of a long-term plan." He didn't elaborate.

"Okay." Dani reached for her sandwich again. His reply made only some sense to her, but apparently this "plan" was above her pay grade, so she let it go.

Steve turned on the phone's recorder, then pulled out a notebook.

Dani could see a checklist of discussion points from across the table. She felt like it was a chance to see the teacher's answer key before a test.

"What were you told about driving this route for Jim Kelly?" he began.

She considered her answer. "He asked if I could take the route because he had another one lined up for himself. He heard I was looking for work."

"Who first broached the idea: Donna or Jim?"

Good question, she thought. She wondered what was behind it. "Jim. But Donna was there, too."

"How was your pay decided?"

"He told me up front that it'd be cash. Then we talked numbers on the way home from that first trip," Dani explained. "He was going to pay me a percentage, but I offered to do it for a flat rate."

Steve jotted a note. "Were you paid?"

"Not yet."

He looked up from his notebook. He hadn't touched his sandwich. "How long have you known Donna Lund?"

The question hit Dani off-center. "What? Why? You don't think Donna has anything to do with it, do you?"

Steve didn't commit. Not one eyebrow hair moved. There was no telltale mouth twitch, no uneasy resettling in his chair.

A twinge of desperation poked a gnarled finger into Dani's chest. She wanted to shore up the sands that had begun eroding from under Donna's declarations. She wanted to rebuild the solid footing she and Donna shared before Jim and trucks and horses and theme nights.

"I've known Donna ever since I moved here." Dani wanted to sound confident, but a razor-thin slice of doubt inserted itself into her answer.

"Which was not that long ago," he countered.

"Still. We've spent enough time together for me to say I know her. Well. And she would never be involved with drugs."

Dani's answer was complete, but her need to redeem Donna overruled it. She added one more thing. "She knows that my boyfriend—my fiancé—OD'ed. Back in Minnesota, before I moved here."

Steve's eyes still gave nothing away.

"She's a small-town girl, honest and reliable." Dani knew she sounded desperate now, but she couldn't stop herself. "She has plans! She wants to buy Susie's Café, and—"

"If she wants to buy the restaurant, maybe she needs some cash," Steve interjected, watching her.

Dani pushed up from the table. "No. She's not like that. And I don't want to answer any more questions about her. When I said I'd help you, I didn't mean that I'd help you ruin my friend's life. She's a—a—bystander. Sucked in by Jim Kelly."

Steve didn't get up.

Dani didn't sit down.

"So, Jim Kelly, then." Steve tried a different tack. "When did he show up?"

Dani didn't remember. "A few months ago? Maybe when Donna started the theme nights? Lots of newcomers started showing up on Friday nights for that. I assume that's how she met him. He's not from around here, and—"

She stopped herself. *Let him figure it out. It's not my job.*

"You ever see him with anyone else? Another driver? Maybe someone on that first trip?"

"He's into Donna—though it hasn't stopped him from looking when another woman walks by." She didn't care that it wasn't the point.

"Um-hm." Wahlquist nodded, jotting another note.

The hall clock ticked slow seconds.

Steve's breath was steady, even, waiting for her real answer.

It wasn't that she wanted to hold back important details that could strengthen the case against Jim.

It was just that she suddenly realized that there was a tightrope between the case against Jim and the case against Donna, taut and whisker-thin. Dani didn't want to be the one to snap it.

The agent's phone vibrated. He tapped off his recorder and looked at Dani. "You mind if I take this? Shouldn't be more than a minute."

She mouthed her okay, and Steve brought his phone outside to the porch. As much as she yearned to tiptoe behind and eavesdrop, Dani didn't want to take the risk of getting caught.

Good thing, because he returned in a hurry to start packing his belongings. "Sorry, but I've been called out. Can I swing back in later?"

She shook her head. "Not today. I have to meet Jessica, the new teacher at St. Nick's. She wants some help with her classroom."

Dani didn't have any idea how she'd been able to concoct that fib so quickly, but it sounded plausible.

"I'll give you a call tomorrow, then. Okay? Just a few more things to clear up."

"I look forward to it." Another fib.

She closed the door behind him, resting her forehead against the cool wood frame. From the window next to it, she watched the agent fly down the driveway, barely pausing as he skimmed the corner and zoomed away.

The SUV's dust was still hanging in the air when yet another vehicle turned into her drive from the opposite direction. This one, a brown-and-white sheriff's sedan, stopped in front of the porch.

The driver seemed familiar: it was the deputy she met at the auction and then at Mr. Randolph's trailer. Recalling his face reminded her that he'd left her message while she was at the stockyard; she was supposed to have called him back. Although she remembered this point, she fumbled to recall his name. Hiding her fluster, she opened the door and stepped out onto her porch.

"How're you doing, Dani?" the deputy called.

Mike? Luke? She couldn't remember.

"Fine, I guess. Good. What's up?"

The deputy looked up from the bottom of the porch steps. "Just wanted to give you an update on the trailer."

"Oh?" To Dani, it felt like it'd been weeks, instead of days, since she discovered the disaster at the trailer house.

A pink glow washed over the man's stubbled cheeks. His brown eyes darted away. "Well, it's not much, but I figured you'd want to know, anyway. I sent that evidence we found to the state's forensic lab, some fingerprints, and those little plastic baggies, too—the ones with the writing on them. I also requested info on where the scale might have been purchased. Remember that big one? Not an ordinary kitchen scale, and nothing I could find to purchase online."

He scrutinized Dani like he was gauging her reaction to his efforts.

She attempted a smile. Frankly, she was still pretty wiped out, and the result felt more like an expected social reflex than an expression of genuine appreciation.

The deputy plowed on. "When I called to ask for the results, they said my request had been overridden, that the results were sent elsewhere. I guess the BCA guys took over. Apparently, it has some connection to something the feds are already working on." He shrugged.

Dani had already connected the dots between the makeshift lab in the trailer and the hidden loads Jim had been ferrying—not to mention the BCA's role in all of it—but it seemed that the deputy had not been apprised of the link.

"They did give me one piece of information, though. One set of fingerprints came back to someone in this county. A young man."

Dani instantly knew whose fingerprints they were. "Is it Tot's? I mean, Matthew White?"

The deputy pursed his lips. "I can't, um, confirm that."

Silence hovered for a moment, the silence of withheld information. By now, the infuriating response was familiar to Dani. Neither he nor Wahlquist was able or willing to tell her the details she was dying to know.

"Thanks for coming out to let me know. It was nice of you," she added, making a better effort to share a genuine smile before retreating back inside.

"Hold on!" The deputy raised one hand.

As Dani hesitated, he plucked a folded paper from his back pocket, climbed the steps, and handed it to her. "You said you were looking for work?"

Dani didn't remember telling him that. She didn't remember not telling him, though, either. She supposed she must have, but two days' worth of details and steps and gauges and mile markers had overloaded her memory retrieval system.

"Well, I do. Need a job, I mean . . ." Her voice trailed off. "At some point."

"Our dispatcher is going out on maternity leave, and we'll need a replacement till she comes back. I thought of you." His smile was bright, his brown eyes measuring her reaction in a friendly way.

Or maybe "friendly" wasn't quite accurate, Dani wondered, though she was too tired to probe any deeper. "Is this the application?"

"Yep." He nodded. "And put my name down as a reference, okay?"

"Thanks . . ."

What the heck is his name?! She panicked a bit before glancing down at the badge on his uniform. ". . . John."

She hoped he wouldn't notice the long pause. "I'll drop it off. Soon."

15

WAHLQUIST WAS TELLING THE TRUTH. Susie's Café was closed, locked up tight. No lights were on anywhere inside, not even in the kitchen in back.

Dani was mystified. What concerned her most was that there wasn't a note or poster—something explaining the situation—hanging from the door or front windows.

With her cell phone tucked against her ear, Dani backed out of the empty parking lot and turned toward Donna's place on the edge of town, a tiny bungalow she'd inherited from her parents.

Donna had painted and redecorated the interior, but the outside still looked as Dani assumed it had for decades: brick planters under the windows, a cracked concrete sidewalk, a big oak in front, and a wild morass of scrub backing up against the abandoned railroad tracks behind.

Dani's call to Donna's went to voicemail.

The detached single-car garage just yards from the home was filled with the furniture Donna had removed but couldn't give away, which meant she had to park her car outdoors all year round.

The driveway was empty. Dani left her truck running and hurried to the door. She wasn't hopeful; she just wanted to be certain. And sure enough, the doorbell went unanswered.

The front curtains were open, so Dani peeked in. She could see through the living room to the galley kitchen in back, where the sink was empty and the coffeepot back in place. A magazine was curled open on the couch, but otherwise the home looked like a movie set waiting for the next scene. Lifeless.

She called Pete from her truck.

He picked up, out of breath. "What's up?"

"Where's your sister?"

"Heck if I know. Is that why you called?" Dani heard a stack of books drop.

"She's not at Susie's," Dani continued, backing out from Donna's driveway. "It's closed." "What? It's never closed."

Dani let the comment go.

"Can you go by her—" he began.

"Just left," Dani interjected. "She's not there, and her car's gone."

At the stop sign, Dani signaled right and drove toward Jim's lot.

"Shit," Pete whispered. Then, more loudly, "I hope she hasn't done anything stupid."

Jim's lot was bare. Both rigs were gone.

"Pete?" Dani disrupted the uneasy silence. "Both of Jim's trucks are missing, too."

Pete thought a moment. "I can't leave the library. Well, I suppose I could, but—"

"No. You stay there," Dani decided. "She could just be somewhere else, around town still. Maybe she's just running late again."

Pete snickered. "Yah." His tone brimmed with disdain. "Maybe holed up somewhere with her boyfriend." A library visitor interrupted him, but he quietly added "Let me know if you find her, okay?" before he disconnected.

"I will," she replied, though her voice now echoed across an empty line.

She repeated it again, for herself: "I will."

Dani continued to the Stop-N-Save. Connie, the day cashier, was a walking fount of information. She was on her fourth husband, a guy from the next town who had a daily a.m. radio talk show.

She and Donna had graduated high school around the same time, though they'd never been amicable for some reason, probably having to do with them being more alike than was comfortable for either. Still, if there was any information about the closed café and Donna's whereabouts, Connie had likely picked up on it.

Inside, Dani got in line and waited for a woman to finish her transaction. Connie returned her change, then the woman placed each dollar precisely into her leatherette wallet before stepping out of the queue.

The extra time gave Dani the opportunity to think up a plausible reason for stopping.

"Hey, Connie—would you get me a two-dollar Powerball ticket?"

"That's not like you, Dani, playing with luck," she replied. "You must've scored big, doing that ride to Missouri."

Dear Lord, what doesn't she know?

Dani dredged through her pocket and found some wrinkled ones. "No, just feel like taking a chance, I guess." She held the bills out to the cashier, adding, "Just let the computer pick, okay?"

"Woo-hoo!" Connie teased. "Goin' all in, hey?"

She punched in a code, and the machine spit out a red-and-white ticket which she exchanged for Dani's bills.

"You're not the only one gettin' lucky . . ." Connie added.

Bingo. Dani's intuition was rewarded. *Here we go.*

Dani folded the ticket in half and shoved it into her back pocket, where it would probably stay until the washer ate it up. She threw a quick glance over her shoulder. No one was waiting behind her, which was good: she wasn't planning to leave until she could pump the cashier to find out what she knew. Of course, she'd have to feign some confusion to get the information flowing.

"What do you mean?" she asked, setting her head at a deliberate tilt.

"Your friend? Donna?" The cashier rested her elbows on the counter. Pale little freckles skimmed her pert nose and the tops of her plump cheeks. "She and that guy she's seein' were in here yesterday," she started. "Well, 'missy' didn't come in, but that Jim did—met another guy over there by the freezer. Guy gave him a wad of bills, then drove off in Jim's rig. Then Jim and Donna took off in her car, goin' the other way."

Connie stopped, inspecting Dani's face to gauge her words' impact.

"Really." Dani tried to sound noncommittal.

It wasn't too difficult because she honestly didn't know what to think of the information. All she knew was that she couldn't ignore the uncomfortable miasma that had been simmering inside her, growing more intense as time passed. She needed to talk to Donna and clear the air.

Dani thanked Connie for the ticket, then headed back to her farm.

She was almost to the crossroads when blue lights came up behind her, soaking the deepening night.

She pulled off to the shoulder near the dilapidated bar the locals called Jonesy's Tavern.

Dan heard their stories of sneaking out there as youngsters to buy beer, and how old Jonesy, the owner, supposedly slept nights on the pool table, leaving greasy streaks on the green felt where he laid his head.

Slowing to the shoulder, Dani noticed that someone had begun building a wood fence around the old saloon. A high fence. Was it legitimate—or yet another cover for illicit activity?

Though Dani had no reason to believe she was being pulled over, she was still oddly relieved when the sheriff's car passed her, swerved into Jonesy's, and stopped there instead.

Dani signalled and pulled back to the tar. Behind her, a big dark SUV turned into Jonesy's from the east side of the crossroads. And coming her way was yet another law enforcement vehicle, its blue lights twirling. Leaving the road, it tucked in close to the others.

Dani's head throbbed. Official vehicles and lights and meet-ups were commonplace in the Cities. But not so much in Crestview.

This was not the place it used to be.

Dani didn't need a note to remind herself to lock her doors. Not anymore.

She got up early the next day to hunt through the odds and ends in the back of her barn. Pete had gotten a used solar-powered charger for free online and said he'd be out to help her string some wire she'd found for a pasture fence. She'd also found some metal stakes. She needed to drag the lot of it out of the barn to the back of her truck, and transport the materials to the back of the property.

When her cell rang, it was Pete.

"Good morning!" she said as she continued her work. "What's the news?"

"Well, Donna's doing well . . . and so's her husband."

Dani dropped the metal stake she'd been holding. "What did you say?"

"You heard me. Her husband."

Dani stumbled out of the barn into the bright sunshine. "You mean, Jim?"

"Listen," Pete replied, "I'm on my way over. We'll talk when I get there." He hung up without a goodbye.

"Donna got married? To Jim?" Dani repeated out loud. "What the heck is she thinking?"

Cody came into the barn to see who Dani was talking to.

"Donna married Jim!" she told him. The dog gave her a quizzical look. "I know! I can't believe it either!"

Cody trotted off, leaving her to her task. Gathering metal stakes, though, was suddenly not the most important item on her mind.

The pit in Dani's stomach sank even lower when Pete's truck fish-tailed into her driveway. He climbed out of the cab with a six-pack of Michelob in one hand and a mallet for pounding the stakes in his other. He didn't greet her.

"Where are we starting?"

"Back there." Dani gestured. "I'll drive the truck so we don't have to carry the poles. Want a ride?"

He put his head down and strode away in the direction she'd pointed, the glass bottles clinking with each pounding step.

Dani was thankful that the process of setting poles and fastening wires consumed almost their entire collective focus.

They worked in silence.

By midafternoon, one line of poles was up, spanning one side of the eventual pasture square. Both Dani and Pete were perspiring, though it was the first week of September, the official start to harvest season. They decided to take a break before tackling the first corner.

As they reclined in a shady spot under one of her neighbor's oaks, Dani finally broached the subject. "So, Donna and Jim . . ."

As soon as the words left her mouth, she swallowed a big swig of her beer.

When several moments passed without a response to her open-ended conversation starter, Dani opted for a yes-or-no question: "Did you know they were going to elope?"

"Nope."

"I found out late last night. Out of nowhere, Donna suddenly calls me—after no word from her whatsoever that first day. Before I can even say anything, she launches into some story about how they're out in Vegas, how they got married by some 'minister' named Elvis at one of those chapels, how they won all this money at the Golden Nugget."

Dani put down her bottle. The absurdity of Donna's behavior was getting harder to digest.

"Then she goes on and on about how Jim's sold his trucking company and how they're gonna use the money to buy the diner."

She didn't know what to feel. Donna's longtime dream of buying the diner had come true . . . but at what cost?

"And get this," Pete went on, "she had the gall to ask me to open the café, though she still won't be home for a few more days." He cursed. "I told her what I thought about that."

Now Pete sat up. His eyes were angry slits.

"I don't care if she is my sister, I don't care how much that café means to her—this is not the right way to do things." He got to his feet. "And if I see that asshole, Jim—" He drained the remaining liquid from his bottle. "I hope I don't see him, is all."

He grabbed the mallet and stalked off down the fence line. Dani gave him time to himself before she followed, dragging another length of wire behind her.

That night, Dani sat in her darkened front room with a notepad and sorted the information she'd gained into two categories: "What I Know" and "What Doesn't Make Sense."

She knew Jim was no good. Not for Crestview, not for Donna. But then why in the world did she marry him? She placed this observation into the first column of her chart.

Dani wondered about Donna's true loyalties and motivations. Had she been playing Jim all along? And now that she'd gotten her café, would she revert to the Donna Dani knew, the Donna who would never put up with a jerk like Jim? Could Donna even find her way free now, or was she too enmeshed with Jim and his issues? She added these thoughts to the second column.

Maybe this was what Donna wanted. Maybe she didn't care that Jim's money was dirty, so long as it bought her the diner. Maybe this version was closer to the "true Donna" than the woman Dani once counted as her friend. More items for the second column.

And either way, what was Dani supposed to do, stuck in the middle of the investigation against Jim? She reconsidered Wahlquist's questions and insinuations.

Dani's notepad showed lines and lines of messy questions and problems in the "What I Don't Know" column, just one item on the "What I Know" side, but no clearer plan emerged from the exercise.

She tossed the pad to the floor. Dani refused to spend another minute on what she couldn't control. She decided to work on what she could: helping Lilly reunite with her son. She located the notepad, ripped off the chart and settled back with a clean page, noting ideas and questions for Lilly Bradstreet and for Jamie Walker.

Time passed. The cornered shadows softened, and a bird called outside her window, teasing forth the new day. Cody, asleep at her feet until now, yawned and stumbled upright, stretching with a little squeal. He strolled out of the front room toward the kitchen, knowing that his breakfast would arrive about the time the coffeepot finished perking.

Dani waited until 8:00 a.m. to place her first phone call. Hopefully Gene had talked to Jamie by now about the opportunity to connect with his birth mother.

To Dani's surprise, a female voice answered with a cheery and energetic "Hello?"

"Oh! Hi," Dani began. "Um, I was hoping to talk to Gene?"

"He's not here. Who's calling?"

"This is Dani, from Iowa."

The other voice waited.

"Will he be home later today?" Dani asked, still unsure.

"Dani. This is April." The voice giggled.

Dani struggled to reconcile the cheerful voice on the line with the spiky, protective girl she'd met in person.

"April? Hi."

Dani fumbled for what to say next, but she remembered how April had had no trouble putting the pieces together about her dad and his birth mother. It gave her the nerve to plunge ahead.

"I'm calling to see how things are going—if your grandpa has talked to your dad. About meeting his mom." She paused. "If he wants to, that is."

"Yeah, I heard them talking about it," April answered. "I don't think Jamie was totally into it at first. But then I told him that I'd like to meet her, so he said yes. We'll do it together. And I told him we gotta meet her right away, 'cuz I don't want her to die before I get a chance to see her."

For a moment, the girl's blunt comments put Dani off, but she sensed that April's heart and intentions were good. It was obvious that she cared about her dad and her grandfather. And perhaps, it seemed, her grandmother, too.

"Thanks for helping. I know Lilly would love to meet you, too—she was excited to learn she's a grandma."

"Can we maybe all meet at your place? You said you're from the town where Jamie was born, right? He should see where he came from."

Dani's mind raced. How in the world could she host Gene, Jamie, and April plus Lilly? For that matter, could Lilly, sick as she was, even make it? Maybe with the help of a nurse— though that would add yet another head to the count.

Nevertheless, Dani heard herself say, "Sure. If that's what Lilly wants."

"Cool!" April's voice sounded even cheerier. "Let us know what Lilly says and when it's all gonna happen!"

Dani barely got out a goodbye before the girl disconnected.

Instantly, Dani tried Lilly's number next. When the call rang through to the answering machine, she realized that, with the different time zones, her friend was probably still in bed.

Grabbing a mug of coffee, Dani headed outside, pondering the delightful surprise of her conversation with April. Though the young woman was still a bit spicy, her open and friendly manner was a great improvement over her brusque defensiveness from their first meeting.

Dani liked her. She suspected that her family raised her with a lot of love—and probably a good dose of patience, too.

At midday, Dani drove to the diner for lunch. According to Pete, Donna would be back by then, and Dani was curious to see for herself how the soap opera was playing out. She couldn't help but admire the new sign, with "Donna's" lettered in elegant script, in place of the old one.

They sure didn't waste any time, she tsked. *They just got home—how long have they had this plan in motion?* But then, she admonished herself for falling into that judgment before even checking in with Donna.

Lunch service was in full swing. Dani waited about twenty minutes before Donna finally stopped at her table, the "Dani" coffee mug in her hand.

The moment Dani saw Donna, something inside her melted. She set her suspicions and assumptions aside so that she could properly congratulate her friend. "You're married!" Dani rose to hug her.

Donna's returned embrace felt shaky. She looked like she hadn't been getting much sleep. "How does it feel?" Dani asked.

"So far, so 'kay. He's back on the road, though, drivin' for someone else." She didn't elaborate.

Dani wasn't sure how to smooth away the awkwardness. She'd never felt awkward with Donna before. "And the café! How's it feel to finally be the owner?"

At this, Donna's expression came alive as she explained several changes she planned to make in a future remodel, including a new seating area out back, under the big tree. Her eyes sparkled with every word; her grand gestures swept from here to there, pointing out all the details.

Donna's enthusiasm spread to Dani. "I've got some good news as well," she said. "Lilly's son and granddaughter want to meet her—and it may all happen here at my farm! Can you believe it?"

"Mm."

And just like that, the joy in Donna's eyes dampened as she glanced around the diner that now bore her name.

Her attention, her heart, was somewhere else.

Dani reached over to squeeze her friend's hand. "Hey—this has all been a big change for you. You doing okay with everything?"

Donna nodded. "Yup. It's what I always wanted."

She glanced once at Dani, quickly, then turned for the kitchen. "Hey, excuse me a sec, I gotta do something while I'm thinking about it . . ."

Dani left the table once she realized Donna wasn't coming back. She left a bill under her mug, and was almost to the door when a voice from behind interrupted her departure.

"Dani, is that you?"

At a four-seat in the corner, Jessica was almost hidden by towers of paper workbooks stacked around her.

"Don't you have school today?" Dani asked, reversing her exit.

"It's a workshop day," the young teacher explained. "And"—she pulled in a deep breath—"and I just had to get away from there, you know?"

Dani waited for Jessica to explain.

"Can you sit a minute?" Jessica asked. "I want to run something by you."

Dani slid onto a chair, making the tallest tower teeter. "Whoa, sorry!"

Jessica squared the tower into place, then tapped the table like her fingers were playing imaginary piano keys. "OK, here's the thing: I don't think I'm doing anything wrong, but the other teachers are acting weird toward me."

Dani arranged herself so as not to upset the paperwork again. "What do you mean?"

"Well, for one thing, they're all two-faced. They smile and make small talk with me in the hallways, but then they suddenly act busy whenever I stop by their classroom with a question about a student or their home life or something."

Jessica leaned forward. "You're not from here, right? Maybe you can tell me what's going on. Is there some sort of code here, some sort of initiation I don't know about?"

Dani was trying to construct a truthful reply when Pete came through the door. Dani saw two opportunities: one, she could enlist some help with this delicate subject; and two, she could score Pete some time with Jessica.

"Pete!" Dani called. "Hi! Can you come over here for a minute?"

She detected a slight blush behind Pete's whiskers. "Sure—though I've got to get back to the library in fifteen. I'm just grabbing lunch."

"We won't keep you," Dani explained. "Jessica was just asking me about 'Crestview courtesy.' You'd be a good sounding board."

"Yes!" Jessica blurted. "I'd love to get your opinion, too. Lord knows, you've been around here long enough to know how things work." She began clearing the paper towers into two big canvas bags on the floor.

Meanwhile, Dani raised her eyebrows at Pete, noting his discomfort.

"She means you've lived here your whole life," Dani whispered to him. "She doesn't mean you're old. Really." But she didn't hide her grin.

"Funny." His smile was forced.

With the table clear, Jessica shared again how she'd been receiving the cold shoulder from the other teachers.

"I just want to know what I'm up against," she concluded. "So what is it? Some sort of invisible barrier keeping newcomers out?"

Pete wrinkled his face. "Well . . . yeah. Sort of."

"But that's ridiculous!" Jessica exclaimed. "I'm trying to ask them important questions about my students—students they know better than I do. I'd like to know more about their families, what kind of support they have at home. Or maybe what kind of struggles. So why won't the other teachers help me? Why won't they share their insight? I'm a professional, just like them!"

"But that's not how it works," Pete answered. "That's not how they see it. The thing is, they—we—don't know if you'll still be around next year. They're worried that they'll tell you all this personal information about folks, but then you'll decide to head back to the Cities, like lots of people do. They don't want to stir up secrets or bad blood if you're just passing through."

Jessica crossed her arms. "I'm not like that."

Dani suddenly wished she could have talked to Pete back when she herself was a newcomer. It would have been much easier to hear his explanation than to uncover it, piece by piece, on her own.

"It's not just that," Dani chimed in. She paused and considered how best to phrase it. "People here have grown up helping one another, depending on one another, yet they don't really talk about it. They just do it. For generations. And a newcomer tends to upset the balance sheet. It's nothing personal, I don't think. It's just their 'normal.'"

Jessica pressed her lips together.

"She's right," Pete added. "It's not a plot against you or anything. And besides, they will eventually get to know you. Just give them time. They'll love you—I promise." Pete's voice dripped sweet syrup.

To both Dani's and Pete's surprise, Jessica leaned over and tucked her head onto his shoulder. "Oh, thank you, Pete!"

With that, Dani got up from the table. She found it impossible to conceal her smirk. "Hey, I just realized I've got to head home. Scout still needs to eat." She winked at Pete.

Pete winked back. He knew that Dani would never have left Scout without feeding her first.

Jessica peeled herself up from Pete's shoulder. "Thanks for listening. It helps to know that I'm not sticking out. In a bad way."

"No, not at all," Pete reassured her.

He continued, but Dani didn't linger to hear it. She waved, then returned to her truck. Alone.

As the miles passed on the drive home, Dani pondered the spark of attraction she'd witnessed between Pete and Jessica.

It was hard to meet single people, out here in the farm belt.

But to be honest, Dani didn't mind being alone. She knew the difference between being alone and being lonely.

Loneliness wrapped itself around that hollow core of isolation. Rejection. It was what she felt when Geoff left her for his new "love", and how she'd felt when she found out that Mark was already married.

All things being equal, she'd rather be here in Crestview, alone but for a few good friends, than back in the Cities, surrounded by lies and fear.

Being alone wasn't all that bad. It was how she mostly preferred to spend her time.

16

Lilly's flight would leave San Francisco at noon. She'd travel with her nurse to Minneapolis, and from there they would take a special medical van to Dani's home in Crestview.

Dani cleaned and organized her home for the visit. She planned to bunk on the sofa to give Lilly and her nurse the bedrooms upstairs.

Jamie and April, driving from Missouri, would arrive later in the afternoon. They'd stay overnight at a local motel. Grandpa Gene decided to stay home, claiming he was too old to sit in the car that long. Dani suspected he was looking forward to being on his own for a few days.

It was impossible for Dani to sit and wait for Lilly's arrival, so she went outside to brush Scout. Even there, with Scout's warmth and nearness, her imagination continued to conjure a number of scenarios for their reunion. Years, days, and now hours would disappear, and Lilly would finally be face to face for the first time with her son.

Would she cry? Faint? Rush to him, or let him come to her?

Dani had no idea what she would do if she was in Lilly's position. All she knew was that she could barely stand waiting and watching from the sidelines.

When she finished brushing Scout and cleaning her hooves, Dani brought the mare to the gate and released her into her new pasture.

Dani then looped the lead rope on a post, for when she'd later call the horse back in. As she leaned on a metal panel to watch Scout, a car horn brought Dani back to the present.

A silver passenger van eased to a stop in front of her house. She ran to welcome her visitors, elated to recognize Lilly's light hair through a side window.

A round-faced woman unfastened Lilly's seatbelt, while the driver got out to open her door.

"Lilly! Hello!" Dani called. "Are you finally here?"

Her friend's face creased with laughter. Though she was pale and very thin, Lilly's regal elegance had not deserted her. One stylish loafer, then two, brought her to the edge of the van's door frame. The nurse and the driver grasped her under the sleeves of her smart wool jacket to balance her as she stepped down.

Lilly reached for Dani.

As they held each other, their warm tears trickled down their cheeks, mingling together.

"My darling Dani! I can't thank you—will never be able to thank you—enough for making this. . . this miracle come to be." She staggered a bit, stepping back, but her nurse was there to steady her. "And here is my dear Maya, another angel," she added, introducing her. "And this is—"

But the driver was already at the back of the van, taking out suitcases and bags and boxes.

Lilly laughed in delight. "Tomas! Thank you! You can put those— where should he put our things, Dani?"

Dani wrapped one arm around Lilly's waist. She was so thin. Her ribcage could be felt through the jacket and sweater she was wrapped in.

"Upstairs, please." Dani instructed Tomas. She turned to Maya, on Lilly's other side. "If she can make it up the steps, you two can have the bedrooms. But we'll all have to share the bathroom. Sorry."

Maya's smile was shy. "It's okay. We can put most of Miss Lilly's 'necessaries' in her room, and I can get what she needs. Some of her meds do require the refrigerator, though. Is the kitchen downstairs?"

"It is. I'll clear a space for her in the fridge. I got a bunch of groceries, but I don't know what everyone likes, so—"

"Anything will be just fine, dear," Lilly interjected. "I don't eat that much, anyway."

Over Lilly's head, Dani looked at Maya, who met Dani's glance, her lips drawn tight.

In the time it took the three women to mount the porch steps, Tomas had hefted and transferred all the luggage to the bedrooms on the second floor. He held the screen door open for Lilly and held her arm so that Maya and Dani wouldn't crowd her through the threshold. He walked her to the recliner in the living room.

Lilly sat, her face drawn, and shuddered. Reopening her eyes, she looked at Dani.

"It's not so bad, darling." Her voice trembled. "It's part of the process, they say. And I'm not in pain. Not really."

She reached out one hand to hold Dani's; it was icy cold but strong as she grasped on to her younger friend.

"I'm so, so happy!" Lilly smiled. "And it's thanks to you that we're all going to be together today."

Maya opened an orange vial and held out a tiny oblong pill for Lilly. "Hold this for me, Miss Lilly, while I get a drink for you."

Anticipating the request, Dani gently returned her friend's hand to precede Maya down the hall, to the kitchen.

"I have tea, too. And some fruit and cheese, if you think—"

"She needs to rest now," Maya said. "There are more hours ahead, and this might be her only time to get it. She runs on adrenaline now and gets very exhausted." She took the glass Dani held out and filled it from the kitchen tap. "If you would please, could you sit with her for a while? I'll pay the driver, and then I'll unpack what we'll need for her nap."

They went back to the front room, where Lilly was telling Tomas about her son.

Before they joined the others, Maya whispered to Dani, "And please, try not to visit too much . . . ? She is so happy to see you, but—"

"No, I understand," Dani insisted. "I'll do whatever you say. I want her to be rested for when Jamie and April are here."

Dani placed a cozy afghan over Lilly's knees before settling on the sofa across from her. "Lil, Gene said that Jamie will call me when they get to Crestview. Do you want to rest a bit until then?"

"Isn't that something—that Jamie's dad and my dad have the same name?" Lilly's eyes were bright. Her body had all but disappeared into the recliner, her slight legs indiscernible under the blanket.

"Um-hm," Dani agreed. She crossed her legs, tapping the air with one toe. "You know, we'll have loads of time to get caught up. But right now, you need to save your energy for later. Okay?"

"Dear girl . . ." Lilly murmured. Her eyes closed almost instantly.

But then they blinked open when Cody bounded into the room, Maya just behind him. Dani jumped up to intercede. "Cody! Here!" But the dog made straight for Lilly.

She held out one thin hand, and he skidded to a stop at her feet. "Such a sweetheart!" she cooed, patting his broad head and letting her hand rest there.

"Cody!" Dani hissed, but the dog didn't flinch.

He didn't jump up or paw at Lilly, either. Rather, he sat like a perfect gentleman, alert and respectful, as immobile as a stone garden statue, guarding her at her knee.

"Do you think she'll be okay to nap with him there?" Dani asked the nurse, who'd returned from the driveway.

"I don't think you'll be able to get him away!" The nurse smiled. "And don't worry—if you have things to do, please feel free. I'll oversee Miss Lilly and am used to her habits. You go, if you want." She turned for the stairs. "I will call for you, if needed. Okay?"

Dani admired Maya's single-minded devotion to her patient. The bond between Lilly and her caregiver was no mystery, though. People were simply drawn to Lilly's open heart, gracious hospitality, and giving nature. Dani recalled how their own friendship cemented almost instantly when Lilly visited Crestview a year ago.

Lilly valued friendship in a way most didn't. She'd learned how tenuous friendships could be. She told Dani that she would always regret not trying harder to mend the relationship with her friend Elaine, which had fractured years ago, when Elaine learned about the events of Jamie's birth. From that point on, Lilly said, she wanted to make sure that those in her circle knew that she loved them and cared for their lives.

Dani slipped outside, giving Lilly space to rest. Scout grazed in her new pasture, sampling some purple-tinged alfalfa blooms blown in with the wind. She wasn't interested in leaving the delicacy to join Dani at the fence, so Dani returned to the porch to wait for the next arrivals.

On the property to her right, a huge green combine advanced loudly through the first rows of corn, testing the grains to see if they were ready for harvest. The machine looked like a tank, but its green metal cones delicately whisked through the rows like nimble fingers parting strands of hair. A great cloud of chaff and stems billowed out behind, leaving the ground forlorn and denuded, stripped of movement and sound.

Less than an hour later, the screen door screeched open. It was Lilly who stepped out, tentatively, with Cody beside her. She didn't look any more rested.

"May I join you?" she asked. "I can't sleep. I'm too excited."

Dani tucked Lilly into the rocker, going back into the house for the afghan. Once Lilly was settled, Dani sat in the chair at her side.

"Are you nervous or happy?" Dani asked.

"Both, I think," the woman's answer was honest. "I just want him to know, after all this time, that I gave him up because I loved him.

And that it was the same, with his father."The rocking chair stilled. She glanced at Dani.

"Things were so different then. I could no more have married Cisco than, I don't know, become president. 'Good girls' didn't have many choices." She twisted one silver ring, trapped between swollen knuckles. "Most of my choices were made for me. And that's why I decided to make my own decisions, from then on." She clapped her hands in rhythm, to emphasize her declaration.

"You were brave," Dani replied. "And I think your son will know that. When he meets you," she added.

They continued visiting as the minutes dragged by. Even the combine next door moved in slow motion.

Lilly complimented Dani on the changes around her farm. She especially admired the new horse and praised Dani for taking on such a project.

"That's brave too, you know," Lilly added. "You're showing good faith by putting your trust into something others may think of as risky."

"I never thought of it that way," Dani responded. "The way I see it, Scout and Cody needed homes, and I have one. Right now, at least."

"Will you try farming another field again next year?"

"I'd like to. But we'll see. Mr. Randolph has this place up for sale, though no one around here wants it. It's only a quarter-section, and they're all looking for bigger acreage." She rubbed a smudge of dirt from her jeans. "I suppose if someone from out of town wants it, he'd sell. But there are lots of empty houses and barns around— more holdings than buyers. Not too many want to move to small properties anymore, so I think I'll be safe."

And there was always that dispatch job… I should find where I stashed that application and fill it out, in case this place isn't available next year . . .

Lilly moved on. "How about Donna? I figured she'd be over to visit by now."

"Hmm."

Lilly waited.

"She's got a . . . she's married now. Sort of surprised us all. She met a guy, a trucker who started coming into the café."

"That is a surprise!"

Dani made a face but didn't offer a verbal opinion.

"You don't like him."

"Nope. I don't. But I don't have to deal with him."

Dani didn't want to say much more, so she maneuvered them to safer topics.

Soon, Maya came out with a small plate with a half-sandwich, some apple slices, and five or six colored pills.

"Miss Lilly, I made something for you to eat with your meds. Would you like to eat out here? Or perhaps inside would be more comfortable?"

"Let's head in," Lilly decided.

Each taking a delicate hand, the two younger women gently eased Lilly from the rocker and accompanied her to the dining table. Dani couldn't imagine how such a frail person could summon the strength to sit and move and visit pleasantly. But Lilly's mind, still so strong, continued to command her entire being.

All three were arranged around the table, Dani trying not to notice how little Lilly was eating, when a knock sounded from the door.

Cody rushed to get there first, but April was inside and on her way toward them before he could reach the entrance. He growled. She growled back, then laughed.

"Donna-Dani?" she called. "Are you home?"

"Hi! We're back here!" Dani rose but then moved away, to allow Lilly to have the first glimpse of her granddaughter.

And her son.

Lilly found her feet, keeping hold of the table in front of her.

"Grandma! You're cute!" the girl announced. She propelled herself forward like a spinning dervish and clasped the older woman, though very carefully. "Are you going to eat that sandwich?"

Lilly's laughter rang out. "You darling! Eat away! I was saving it for you," she added.

But her eyes were still searching, peering past the blue-haired girl to the shadow standing in the hall behind her, waiting.

Then he stepped toward her.

Lilly raised her arms to him, the first time that she'd actually touch and hold her baby.

She cried softly from inside his embrace.

Jamie's reaction was hidden beneath his stoic expression; his face gave no clue of the feelings he kept inside.

Each day of his life, Lilly had dreamed about this. Her muffled cries disintegrated into a thin howl, a piercing distillation of the anguish she'd borne so long. Her mother's soul, whittled down to a frail thread of sorrow, had been stretched and thinned to near extinction.

Her expression of longing and remorse and fear and wonder contained the one beating pulse of a love that would not die, that would not fade, that continued, beat after slow, measured beat, to bring them both to this moment.

Jamie looked like he didn't know what to do next with the wisp of this person in his arms. He didn't seem to want to release her, glancing around for direction like he was somehow afraid to hold her too tightly, fearful of breaking what remained.

Her tiny body, now dissembled and stripped to sinew and porcelain, carried him—carried this rugged and hefty man, angular with heavy bones; a thick thrash of hair; and hooded, careful eyes. Their two bodies were the physical containers for one soul that had given breath to the other. Though riven apart, their divided spirit finally found its home place again, wrapped in the comfort and company of the other.

Gently, Jamie loosened his embrace and peeled her from his chest.

With bright eyes and trembling, shallow breaths, she peered up at him from under his shoulder.

"Hello." His soft voice held a melody, rich and resonant. "I'm glad to meet you. Lilly." He released her a full minute later, revealing the joy beaming from her tear-stained face. Jamie then turned to his daughter.

"And this—this person eating your sandwich–is April."

Lilly turned her smile to include the girl, but she was drained. She stutter-stepped back to the table, with Maya creeping up to help place her into a chair.

Watching from the staircase, Dani wiped her own tears and breathed in a long, shuddering breath.

When she discovered the letters Lilly had written so many years ago, she'd never imagined that this meeting between the adventurous small-town girl and the unexpected baby she delivered would ever happen.

Nor did she ever imagine how deeply this meeting would affect her, herself. To witness this profound reunion in the midst of her own distress over Donna, Jim, and the whole drug situation—it felt surreal.

April gulped down the last bite. "Jamie, you're acting all weird again." She ran her tongue over her teeth, revealing a silvery stud. "Let's all relax and get to know one another, how about? And where can I get more to eat?"

The laughter that erupted brought them all back to an easier, more natural atmosphere.

Wanting to give mother and son some space, Dani enlisted April's help in the kitchen. As they assembled some lunch, Dani listened to April's rapid-fire monologue about their trip up (very long, bad music), her grandfather (Gene was happy, really, that Lilly got in touch), and their plans for the evening (she wanted to go to a music store she discovered during some internet research, but Jamie said it was too far away, considering the early darkness and how all the fields looked so similar).

By the time Dani and April emerged with red plastic trays carrying the lunch plates, Jamie and Lilly were in the front room, having a quiet conversation. Dani set her tray on the nearby trunk and nodded for April to do the same. They both each took a plate, then seated themselves quietly on the floor to hear the discussion in progress.

"And that's why," Lilly said, "you got to grow up with your mom and dad instead of with me."

Jamie tilted his head. "Did my fath—Cisco—did he know about me?"

"No. But I see him, in you. In your smile."

"Where did you meet?" He snagged a sandwich but didn't take a bite.

Lilly unraveled a story she'd knitted close to her heart, unwinding the strands of love and longing, of dreams and desires.

"We knew we'd most probably not be together again. His family had gone back to Mexico, and he didn't know where he'd be working, the following summer."

"He was Mexican?" Jamie chose that moment to begin eating. One hand held his sandwich, the other cupped under it to catch any errant crumbs.

"Half, I believe," she answered. "One parent came from there, and the other was from Texas. From a ranching family, I think." She shrugged. "I didn't think to ask him about his family until I knew I would have you, but then . . . I'd lost track of him."

She didn't need to say it, but she did: in the 1940s, a white woman and a migrant Mexican would never have been accepted as a couple.

Lilly folded her thin hands together. "I didn't know what happened to him—his death, I mean— until Dani came along and helped put the pieces together."

Jamie placed the remaining half of his meal onto the side table. "Can you tell me about it?"

Lilly did her best to steady her voice as she explained how Dani had located her after finding some letters Lilly sent to a friend after their high school graduation. And how, together, the two women were able to determine that Cisco had lost his life at the tree Dani had helped to cut down—the double-headed tree that was said to be cursed.

"It was a horrible, horrible tragedy," Lilly's mouth pursed. "One that still makes me so, so—just angry. Furious." Two bright-red splotches appeared on her powdered cheeks. "I'm sorry to tell you these things. But you have a right to know."

Her son carefully wiped his top lip with his forefinger, thinking. "I've wondered about so much, through the years. Things that didn't match up . . . like always being drawn to fights I can't win. Or, I don't know, losing my shit—sorry—when things don't go right, when things aren't balanced. Or unfair."

He looked at his daughter, then back at his mother. "Was he like that? Cisco?"

"He was the fairest man I've ever met, then and now." Lilly's voice was strong. "Before I left, we talked about where he was going next—to help organize some of the other workers who travelled from farm to farm. He spoke his mind, and not just to me." She nodded. "He'd speak up to anyone."

"But maybe that's what got him killed," Jamie replied, matter-of-fact. "Why wouldn't he have been more careful? Wasn't he afraid?"

Maya held out a small glass to Lilly, half-filled with water.

Lilly pushed it away. "He wasn't afraid of anyone. He was a wonderful man, Jamie. Truly wonderful." She shrugged again. "But I don't know, really, if he was meant to have a family."

A pause settled over the group, but it was a safe place in which to digest the news and its impact on the two who remained to honor it.

Dani waited to acknowledge the moment, then got up to collect the lunch plates. The mood lightened a bit, though even April was subdued as she observed the scene in front of them.

"How about you?" Jamie asked Lilly. "Tell me about your life."

Lilly sketched the outline of the life she'd lived in California. She described how she found satisfaction working as a secretary and then an administrator for the Boeing aerospace company. She detailed how she also volunteered each week to help migrant farmworkers trying to avoid being sent back to Mexico. She helped them find new occupations or sponsors who could help until they could secure incomes again.

Dani loitered with the tray of dirty plates in the hallway, listening intently as Lilly spoke about her partner, Paul—a part of the woman's life that Dani did not know.

The couple met in California in the '60s, at a meeting with the newly formed United Farm Workers union. Paul felt as strongly as Lilly did about fighting against the horrific working and living conditions the migrants continued to endure.

"Paul and I never married—I didn't think we needed to," Lilly said. "But we lived together for nineteen years, until he passed." Lilly smiled. "I've missed him every day since."

"I guess it's in honor of Paul, and of Cisco, too, that I kept working for the farmers. I consider it my best work." Lilly's voice grew softer, as though she was talking to herself. "I kept going to demonstrations, writing letters to the newspapers—anything I could think of to tell my neighbors the truth about the people who bring us our food."

She grew silent, her eyes fixed on something far, far away.

"I never would have known what the workers had to endure—no bathrooms, dirty water, unfair wages—had I not met Cisco." She raised her chin and turned to her son. "Your father opened my eyes. And my Paul—he moved my feet."

Hearing of Lilly's amazing work made Dani think about her own farming community. In the past, locals would often hire migrant farmworkers as seasonal help. But there weren't any migrant workers in Crestview these days.

That was mostly because the small family farms had evolved into larger corporate holdings with thousands of acres, thousands of animals, and machinery that could handle in an hour what human hands took a day or more to accomplish. In addition, new chemicals and fertilizers practically guaranteed growth and yield—that was, if Dani could believe what Lloyd and Chuck said.

She'd also heard the old timers' quiet conversations about their farms' futures. Neither man's children wanted to continue farming. They'd discussed pooling their properties under one umbrella to keep them going a while longer, but they didn't have the capital necessary for such a huge change.

Even if they did, Dani suspected the men wouldn't do it, anyway. Neither man would give up his own family farm until he was interred under the sod at the Catholic cemetery.

The story could come full circle, though, Dani noted. She thought of her grandpa's farm, back in Windom. A Mexican American family owned it now, and it was the same for the sections to either side. The fields thrived, the cattle grew and were hauled to market, and the local church held as many brown faces as white ones on Sunday mornings. The people who, decades ago, were hired help were now the future of the community.

Dani wondered when, or if, a similar transformation would come to Crestview.

"Like Jamie, I was a surprise, too," April suddenly broke into the conversation.

Her admission tugged Dani back to the present and made Lilly laugh. Jamie rolled his eyes, but there was a hint of a smile where tension had been pulling at his features.

"And I bet you're still surprising him!" Lilly added. Her laughter continued—until it dissolved into a coughing jag.

Maya swiftly retrieved a canister of oxygen from behind the sofa. She held the plastic mask over her patient's mouth and nose. Slowly, Lilly's color returned, but the nurse decided to draw a line.

"This will be a good time for Miss Lilly to rest, just for a bit," she said. Her tone was gentle.

Those in Dani's living room could see for themselves what the past hour had cost Lilly.

Jamie helped Maya coax Lilly to her feet. With her son's arm to guide her, Lilly crept upstairs.

"Can I see your horse?" April asked Dani. "I saw her when we pulled in, but Jamie said I should go in and meet Lilly first."

"Sure," Dani replied, grateful to have something to occupy their time.

The two drifted out to the barn with Cody running ahead. Dani asked a question she'd been holding since she'd first met the young woman back in Fenton.

"Why do you call your dad Jamie and not, you know, Dad?"

The girl's smile was snarky, but her eyes lit up. "'Cuz he hates it. And 'cuz my mom called him Jamie, I've always called him that, too."

Scout crossed the metal corral toward them. Her new pasture was now bridged with an open gate, which allowed her to graze and then return for water or shade under the barn's overhang, one of the reasons why the horse's weight had increased since she'd come to Dani's. Her coat was now a glossy burnt orange.

April reached through the bars toward Scout. To Dani's surprise, the mare didn't pull away.

"And before you ask: no, my mom isn't in the picture anymore," April added. "I guess they met at a weird time in life. And she's way younger than my dad." The girl grew thoughtful, stroking the horse through the fence. "She's a singer. That's how they met—at some club. Jamie loves music, jazz. Mom is on tour now."

Dani was curious about the girl's mother but didn't press. She figured April would probably just spill out what she wanted Dani to know, when she wanted her to know it.

April turned to Dani. "Can we go in with her?"

"I don't know why not."

As Dani went toward the gate, she anticipated the young woman's next question. "I don't ride her. Not yet, anyhow." She hoped offering this admission would keep April from probing deeper.

It didn't.

"Really?" April raised one skeptical eyebrow. "How come?"

"Well, when I got her"—Dani pushed open the gate—"she was really thin. Misused, I think. It's taken us a lot of this summer to get her to relax and know she's safe."

And for me to relax and figure out what the heck I'm doing with her, she added to herself.

It was apparent that April had had some experience with animals. She inched steadily and calmly toward the horse, her hand out, palm up, for Scout to take the long grasses she offered.

"Are you ever going to ride her? I mean, I suppose you don't have to. But wouldn't it be fun?"

Dani couldn't help but to like and enjoy the girl's energy. She was passionate about everything, her opinions splashing out without reserve.

"Yeah, it would be fun. But I think she's just as happy being a pet."

"I wouldn't be." April sniffed. "I'd get bored in this same small pasture without any friends. You could ride her around and meet some, maybe." She scratched the horse's neck, just under her mane. "That's what I'd do."

"We'll see." Dani didn't commit. "If you want, we could take her for a walk. Do you know how to halter her?"

"Great!"

The girl's exuberance caused Scout to back up a step, but she regained her nerve and followed the humans into the barn.

Dani didn't even think twice as she scrounged behind the old freezer to gather the rope and halter. But the young girl noticed the oddity.

"Dani—what the heck? Why do you keep that stuff back there?"

Flushing a bit, Dani didn't want to admit that she'd hidden these items from Jim. That was a long story, and any condensed version would sound strange. She fashioned a different excuse.

"Huh," Dani grunted. "They probably fell."

April shot her a strange look. With some obvious effort, she managed to keep her comment to herself.

Dani positioned the halter under the horse as they'd practiced, and Scout lowered her nose into it. Though it was such a simple act, the feeling of accomplishment made Dani beam.

Next, April attached the lead rope, and the two moved to the outer gate.

Dani watched April move close to Scout's head to whisper something she couldn't keep in any longer: "How'd she know the rope and halter were back there, then, if they'd 'fallen'? We're not so stupid, are we?"

Dani laughed out loud. *That girl doesn't miss too much!* She latched the pen gate behind her before running to catch up.

The earthy aroma of brewed coffee enticed Dani to the kitchen early the next morning.

Maya stood at the stove, poaching an egg.

"I have a toaster, somewhere," Dani offered. "Should I get it out?"

"That would be great. Miss Lilly won't have any, but I would." Maya's brown eyes were the same color as the coffee she'd poured for Dani. "Do you have cream?"

Dani located a small carton hidden in the fridge and put it on the table, next to the sugar bowl Maya had unearthed.

"Did you sleep okay?" Dani asked.

"I did, though I spent most of the night in a chair by Miss Lilly's bed. She was unsettled."

"Is she all right . . . ?" Dani searched the nurse's face for clues, but the woman was careful about letting her emotions show.

A scuffling sound preceded Lilly's entrance. She looked paler this morning; her skin was almost translucent above her brightly colored cardigan.

"I can't get this buttoned." Her voice wavered. "Can you help?"

Dani wasn't sure whether Lilly was asking for her assistance or Maya's, but she moved forward, ahead of Maya, to fasten the garment for her friend.

"Here," Dani added, pulling out a chair. "Why don't you take a seat, and we'll eat breakfast in here?"

Dani opened and spread a napkin on the woman's lap as Maya brought the egg on a plate to the table.

"I have coffee, too," Maya said. "I've already added your cream."

The nurse set a cup in front of Lilly. The liquid looked pearly. Dani couldn't tell if there was any coffee in the cup or just milk and sugar.

"Thank you," Lilly's hand trembled as she brought the cup to her lips.

Dani noticed that Lilly had applied lipstick before coming to breakfast; the color spread past the outline of her lips.

It's okay—she'll wipe it all off when she uses her napkin. Dani didn't want to point out something that would have embarrassed her friend or undermined her independence.

Maya would probably take care of it in time, too.

The older woman set her cup back onto the table. "What's our plan for today?"

"How about a birthday party?" April's voice entered the kitchen before she did: clomping in with those heavy black boots, she yanked out a chair and flopped herself into the conversation.

"I was thinking about it last night: we've missed every birthday over the years. I think we should celebrate them all today."

Lilly looked startled. "But I haven't brought any presents!"

"No presents, Grandma!" April smiled. "Just the celebration! Me and Dani can make a cake, and we'll have candles for everyone!"

Dani's eyes grew wide. She looked at the girl. "I'm not that good at baking, April. I don't know if anyone would want to eat what I'm capable of making."

"I can do it, then." Determined, April got up and began a search through the cupboards. "Crap. Don't you have anything to bake with?" she complained. "What do you even eat?"

"April." Jamie's quiet voice stole attention from the girl's loud inventory. "I'll drive you to the grocery store for what you need." His demeanor with April was more reflective of an uncle's patient amusement than a father's direct authority.

Jamie addressed his follow-up to Dani as the shadow of a dimple betrayed his slight smile. "There is a grocery store here, right?"

"Yes. And why don't I take her?" Dani suggested. "I can show her the town. And you can stay here and get caught up with your—with Lilly."

"Good idea, my dear," Lilly placed both arms onto the table and tried to stand. Jamie gently slid her chair back so that Maya had room to assist her effort. With the added help, Lilly was able to rise.

Maya, Jamie, and Dani shared a look. April, now searching for a cake pan and a mixing bowl, didn't notice the others' concern.

Together, the team got Lilly situated in the living room chair she liked, by the door. Then Dani retrieved the afghan for her legs, Maya headed upstairs for some medication, and Jamie took a seat on the sofa.

April joined Dani, a paper list in her hand. "Are we going now?"

Dani shook her head. "Not yet. First, we have to feed Scout. Want to help?"

"Absolutely!"

April shoved the list in her pocket, then gave Lilly a peck on her forehead before waving to her dad. "See ya!"

Her enthusiasm was like a shot of vitamin energy.

As April ran outside, Lilly beamed at her son. "She's an absolute gem! I wonder if you were like that, when you were a little boy."

Dani used the segue as a good opportunity to exit. She let herself onto the porch, gently closing the screen door behind her.

April was perched on one of the green fencing panels with her arm stretched through, patting and talking to Scout. Cody, at the girl's feet, anxiously waited for her to show him some attention, too.

Dani sat on the step to put on her boots. "Go ahead and get started, April. I'll be there in a minute. You know where the grain is, right?"

The girl hopped off the fence and jogged into the barn. Cody followed her.

Dani picked up voices and laughter, warm and gentle, from the room behind her. Her heart swelled, and she lingered a minute to listen in on their conversation.

"I must say," Lilly began, "I'm excited for this birthday celebration. What a lovely idea!"

"Yes," Jamie agreed. Then there's a pause. "But we'll probably head back to the hotel shortly after that. We need to get on the road early tomorrow morning." It was hard to tell if he was sad or just being practical.

Lilly didn't hide her reaction. "I want to spend as much time with you as you'll let me." She paused. "It's going to go so quickly."

The conversation turned silent.

From the other side of the door, Dani struggled to keep her own sorrow contained.

"Maybe we could come to California for Christmas," Jamie proposed. "Would that be okay?"

Dani waited for Lilly's answer. "Of course." Lilly's volume was subdued. "If it works out. And I'd like Dani to come, too."

Just then, April popped out of the barn. "Are you coming, or what?" she yelled at Dani.

Dani bent down like she was tying the lace on her boot. She needed to hide her face. She didn't want April to see that she'd been listening in on the conversation.

"My—my boot string's snapped," she managed to reply. "I'll be there as quick as I can. Can you throw a flake of hay to Scout for me?"

"Yah, you betcha!" April loaded her answer with an exaggeration of Midwest twang before disappearing back into the barn.

Dani refocused on the conversation inside. Now the two were talking about Jamie's childhood. He explained to Lilly how he grew up as an only child but that his parents made sure there were plenty of other kids and cousins around to play with.

"Not that I needed it," he added. "I was always happy being by myself. I liked tinkering around with stuff, playing in the woods down the block, listening to music. Stuff like that."

Lilly's voice was too low for Dani to hear the next question, but Jamie's reply was clear.

"No, not until I was drafted. Some of the guys in my unit played the guitar, and one guy had a harmonica. That's when I started getting into it."

Dani figured now that Lilly asked whether he sang or played any instruments. She once again missed Lilly's next question, but Jamie's answer seemed to confirm Dani's hunch.

"I tried when I got back from 'Nam, though my parents didn't like it. They thought I should have a more solid career, something like my dad did, you know? But I'd just spent a tour doing what other people told me to do, so I went my own way instead."

There was a scraping noise, someone adjusting a chair across her wood floor, it sounded like, before Jamie continued.

"To be honest, the band didn't pay very well. But music was more an escape for me than a job anyway." He coughed, awkwardly. "About the only thing a music career got me was April."

Dani moved closer to the window. She didn't want to miss any more of the conversation.

"Tell me about Vietnam, Jamie." Lilly's voice was hushed. Reverent.

"Not much to say." He sighed. "It was nothing different than what any other guy went through over there."

Silence followed. Dani knew, though, that wasn't an empty silence. In this quiet moment, Lilly was gracing her child with the gifts of patience, acceptance, and respect.

And Dani knew what Jamie was leaving unspoken. She imagined a steamy jungle. Scared Americans crouched behind and between giant trees and overhanging vines. Staccato bullets pinging off bark and bones. Clouds of smothering gases above and around. And terror asphyxiating the soldiers like invisible demons from every direction.

Jamie's voice intruded into her dark musings. "I don't talk about it much," he admitted to Lilly. "I never wanted to burden my parents with the details. And I don't want them to interfere with my time together with you, now."

"Let's talk about something else, then," Lilly suggested. "April's mother. Were you in love?"

Jamie's laugh was gentle. "I thought I loved her."

"Did she love you?"

"I don't know. Even now, I'm unsure," he added. "She was, is, so much younger, you know? And she wasn't into having a family. It was a bit of a shock to suddenly find ourselves having a baby."

Lilly's sharp inhalation made her cough. Someone, Jamie or Maya, brought a drink to her, as she was able then to clear her throat and continue.

"I have to tell you, Jamie—it's so very strange to me that the child I had out of wedlock had a child of his own, the same way."

This time, Jamie took his time to respond. "Did you love my father . . . ?"

Her response was immediate. "With all my heart!"

"And so it was, Lilly, with me. I loved April's mother with all my heart as well. But when she decided she didn't want that kind of life, I couldn't lose my little girl just because of what I couldn't have with her mother."

Dani sniffled. She could hear that Lilly's reaction was similar.

"I'm proud of you, Jamie," Lilly managed to continue. "What a hard road you must have taken."

"I had my parents," he said. "The three of us together are, were, April's family."

A sudden metallic shriek from the barn area hijacked Dani's attention. The metal gate to the paddock hung open. Scout was gone.

Dani scrambled to her feet. "April?" she yelled.

The girl wasn't in the paddock either.

Dani pounded down the steps and ran to the barn. "April!" Her shout was no longer a question.

From inside the barn, rasping hooves raced across the dusty floor in a hurried tempo. Scout burst from the enclosure, her head stretched out and low, April clinging to her back. They broke into a lope where the paddock opened to the pasture. April pressed herself down onto the horse's neck to avoid tangling herself on the metal uprights that spanned the open gate.

"April!" Dani screamed, rushing to the wire fencing. "Wait!"

But she was too late.

Dani skidded still to take in the sight before her: April rode Scout in graceful, fluid circles around the inside perimeter of the enclosure. With every rhythmic plunge, her hair and the horse's mane blew out like twirling ballerina skirts.

April had fashioned reins from the lead rope attached to the halter. There was no saddle; she gripped the mare's ribs with her long legs, her seat centered perfectly behind the animal's long neck.

It was like watching a painting come to life.

The two make more circuits around the pasture, effortlessly cantering back, at last, to the opening where Dani waited, with Jamie right behind her.

April signaled the horse to stop, then slid down from the rump to make an exaggerated bow to her audience.

Dani had no words.

She had no idea of what she should say.

She waited for Jamie to discipline his daughter. To rebuke her for her carelessness. Or at least to request that she apologize to Dani for her behavior.

But Jamie went to his daughter, enveloping her in a bear hug. He clapped her twice on the back before stepping away.

"Where did you learn to ride like that?"

"Oh, Jamie," she replied, a gleam in her eye, "there are many things I've learned that you do not know about."

Dani couldn't find her breath. As April related some intricate tale of horse training and flying souls and freeing yourself from within, Dani backed away.

She tried to pinpoint her truest reaction to what she'd witnessed. She distilled her responses down to two emotions: one, amazement—that April was safe, that Scout was okay, and that the pair performed so beautifully. And two, longing—for even a quarter of the girl's confidence to ride so bravely and live so beautifully.

However the girl was raised, Dani was astonished at who she was and who she was becoming.

And then, a third emotion pushed its way forward, striking Dani the way a mallet hits a chime. Genuine sadness—that such a child would not have the encouragement, the support, the love of a grandmother so like her in spirit and bravery.

Lilly would be gone too soon to fully experience the gift of April.

17

Their echoes lingered, though: their laughter during the impromptu birthday party; quiet sobs after Jamie and Lilly shared their stories; April's promise that they'd see her soon in California, even if they had to ask Santa to come earlier this Christmas.

Dani parked herself on the bottom step, leaned against the wood risers behind her, and clasped her hands. She prayed Lilly would stay alive and be alert enough to welcome her son and granddaughter to her West Coast home.

But Dani knew the odds were slight. From Lilly's progressively gray countenance, to her bowed shoulders, to Maya's decision to have Lilly transferred to the airport via ambulance—it was obvious how much this trip to Crestview had cost Dani's friend.

"Enough." She pushed herself up and gave herself a talking-to. "I've done what I can. I can't predict the future." Dani didn't care that there was no one to hear her. Just hearing her words out loud made her feel stronger.

Cody didn't trust that she was her own audience, though. He scrambled to his feet, jogged to the front door, and peered out through the side glass for a glimpse of his owner's visitor. Seeing no one outside, he returned to his spot under the dining table, a disgusted look on his furry face.

"Sorry!" Dani laughed, surprising herself. "But what I can do—and actually should do—now is figure out what I should do next."

She joined him in the dining room. Next to her computer, she dug through a pile of ads and a few bills, searching for the application John Davies had dropped off.

"I think this could be a good change for us," Dani continued. She located a blue pen and sat at the table. "Howard County Dispatcher," she read. "Why not?"

Her application was complete in a matter of minutes.

Reviewing her answers, she was especially proud of the answer she'd written about wanting to help others. She then folded the application in thirds, found an envelope, and stuffed the papers inside.

"Let's go drop this off at the government center," she told the dog. "I know it's a drive, but we don't have anything better to do."

At the word drive, Cody's ears pricked up.

It took a little over thirty minutes to travel from Crestview to Decorah. They drove with both windows down and listened to the local country music station. It was a bright day, windy—good for drying hay.

In Decorah, Dani turned onto a street lined with homes newer than those in Crestview. These were the split-level homes so popular in her own hometown of Richfield, Minnesota. Most were 1960s two-stories with a window in each corner and a front door placed right into its center. The trees weren't as large, either.

Dani sat through three red lights before spying the tall brick building straight ahead. The downtown area was arranged around four square blocks of businesses and restaurants and shops in a tidy cluster.

At the Howard County Government Center, Dani pulled into the line for the closest parking lot—only to learn, to her dismay, that she had to pay to enter. She didn't have her credit card with her, so she had to reverse out of the line, forcing those behind her to back up as well. Though each of the drivers gave her a pointed look as she backed past their vehicles, no one honked.

She found a shady spot two blocks away. She left the windows down, telling Cody to stay put, then followed the sidewalk back to the government center.

Meat was grilling at one of the restaurants ahead. Pop music pumped out from an older low-slung sedan at the curb, the two occupants inside slouched down in intimate conversation. A woman on the sidewalk ahead of Dani wore heels that clicked rhythmically as her shoulder bag bumped from hip to hip.

A placard inside the brick government building listed various offices, including parks and rec, driver and vehicle licensing, real estate filing, and burning permits. The instructions at the top of her application indicated she must return her paperwork to the human resources department, though she couldn't find anything remotely close to it on the placard.

Dani pivoted from the sign at the same time the elevator to her left opened; a number of brown-uniformed male officers disembarked, noisy and teasing.

"Dani?" one of them called out to her. "What are you doing here?" It was John.

"Hey—glad to see you!" she answered. "I'm dropping off that application you gave me, and—" She cut off her explanation when she noticed that the other deputies had stopped as well, eying John and Dani's exchange with curious expressions.

John was aware of them, too. "Guys, go ahead," he coaxed.

They bid him an exaggerated goodbye with a few whistles and teasing comments.

"I guess they haven't had the sexual harassment seminar yet." Once she said it, Dani instantly hoped John understood that it was meant as a joke.

He didn't react to it, though. Instead, he moved ahead to a completely different topic.

"Hey, I'm glad I ran into you like this. I want to"—he stopped and looked around—"um, actually, let's step over here for a minute."

He indicated a more private corner outside an office marked "Hunting & Fishing." Dani shuffled over with him, weaving through another elevator load of workers headed out for lunch. She tried to keep her confusion from taking over her expression.

"So," John's voice was low, "have you heard anything about Jim Kelly lately?"

Dani nodded. "He and my friend Donna got married. And they bought—"

"No," he interrupted. "Sorry. I mean, about the . . . trailers?"

He scanned the people around them, but everyone rushing past was intent on their own agenda; no one paid any attention to the couple in the corner. He lifted one hand to casually cover the lower part of his face, but Dani could still hear his voice from behind his fingers.

"Jim's in jail."

Her task forgotten, Dani's carefully composed expression also flew away. "What?" she whispered. "When did this happen?"

"I heard about it at the morning meeting, before my shift started. The feds finally had enough on him to bring him in. They picked him up today, early. Told us as a courtesy. Like I thought, they've taken over the case."

Dani nodded. She tried to digest this development, but she had a question. "What's he being charged with?"

"Transporting illegal drugs. Heroin. But you knew, didn't you?"

"I . . . I had my suspicions," she admitted, not knowing what John knew or what more she could say.

"Yeah. And heroin is schedule 1, a felony."

Dani's next question followed quickly: "What about Donna?"

The deputy shrugged. "I don't know. Captain didn't say anything about her." He looked closely at Dani. "How are you holding up?"

Dani managed a smile, but she felt weak. To tell the truth, she expected this day would come. She knew it would. But with Lilly and Jamie and April and the emotion of their reunion, she'd allowed herself to take a mental vacation from the drugs and the trucks and the animals and the foreboding suspicions surrounding Jim Kelly and, by association, her friend Donna. Jim Kelly's wife.

Hearing this news now was like returning from vacation and finding your front door kicked in.

"Yeah, I'm okay." She tried to sound assertive, but her voice wavered. "Well, I think so. But I— before I go home, I need to find human resources. I need to drop off this . . ." Her voice faded.

John reached for it. "Here, let me," he suggested. "I'll take care of it." When he took the envelope from Dani, he placed his other hand on top of hers. "Are you really okay?"

She allowed the contact to continue. "I will be. I think."

She welcomed the weight of his connection, the feel of his calloused palm on her skin. He made her feel safe.

Eventually, though, Dani recognized that tinge of embarrassment that can come when one's honesty is too quickly or thoroughly exposed. She gently withdrew her hand. Her next smile was genuine.

"Thank you, John. Deputy Davies, I mean."

"John is good."

He smiled back, but his brown eyes didn't crinkle at the corners as they had when he'd first spotted her. "I'll let you know if I hear anything else. About the application, I mean." Concern shaded his tone. "And if anyone asks you about Jim Kelly or what you know, don't say anything right away, if you can hold off." He shook his head. "People'll know soon enough—they always do."

Dani nodded.

She needed to get back to the truck and Cody. She needed to think about this develop- ment and what it would mean for her, going forward.

She knew that his arrest was just the beginning. A trial would come next, unless he did the unthinkable and pleaded guilty. And if there was a trial, she'd be expected to testify because of her involvement with the route to Missouri. No one had told her this, yet, but she knew.

The deputy's question interrupted her train of thought. "Are you good to get home? Do you need a ride?"

"No, I'm fine. And thanks, for taking that for me." She gestured to the application. "And for . . . and for the information about Jim."

They returned to the hallway, where officers and deputies and men in suits and women in high heels continued to rush both ways, talking and arguing and pushing ahead to their own tight schedules. Dani suddenly felt conspicuous in her jeans and T-shirt. She quickly slipped herself into the flow to the exit.

She forgot to say goodbye.

The miles between the government building and her home passed without regard as Dani replayed the activities and conversations and thoughts she'd put aside during Lilly's visit. By the time she pulled into her driveway, she felt the effects of all those miles as well as the last dregs of a large coffee. Her priority was to get to the bathroom.

But when she snatched open the screen door, something wedged against the front door thumped down onto her sneaker. It was a dense package wrapped in brown grocery bag paper. The package was heavy, like a brick.

There were no identifying marks, but she knew what was inside.

She wouldn't open it, though, until she was indoors with the door locked behind her.

The moment she unfolded the wrapping, Jim's trademark cologne wafted up from the package. It was a big clod of cash.

Dani scrunched her nose and riffled through the stack. A blue X marked the upper right corner of every fifth bill.

She didn't want it, but she didn't know what to do with it, either.

After attending to her personal needs, she repackaged the currency, wrapped it inside a big bath towel, and headed outside for her hiding spot: the makeshift grain box. She dug out most of the oats, placed the package inside the freezer, down at the bottom, and replaced the grain over the package to disguise it.

Outside again, Dani studied the yard and pasture, searching for anything that looked remarkable or out of place.

Everything appeared the same as it had before she left to deliver her application. The colored leaves danced in the breeze, innocent and cheerful; two glossy crows argued from the fenceposts, but it didn't seem serious. The sun shone with genuine glee, blithely unaware of the storm rising inside her.

She tossed a flake of hay to Scout, called for Cody, and headed back for the house.

She locked the door.

18

Bow hunting season started October first. Dani didn't
have to look at a calendar to know this, though. Everyone in town
had started wearing blaze orange, from caps to vests to jackets also
dotted with camo print. Though the hunters themselves donned
forest camo, those who worked or walked in the woods chose the
bright colors to distinguish themselves from the deer.

Dani would need to take care if she wanted to continue hiking.

She'd started hiking back when Donna got married. It was a way
to give herself some breathing room as well as give her horse some
better exercise. She, Cody, and Scout logged miles on the nearby
country roads, passing fields that emptied day by day. They watched
the last greens give way to hues of gold and ochre. They witnessed
the dancing foliage age to arthritic stiffness, stripped to branches
that rustled like bones.

The hikes offered her time and space to digest what she'd been
asked to do.

As predicted, she'd been called to testify. The prosecutors in Jim
Kelly's trial would attempt to connect him to the drug traffickers
and determine whether he knew what he was really hauling.

Dani's testimony was key.

During each hike, Dani ran through what she knew, what she suspected, and what she feared.

Dani knew that the angry man in the Mercedes, the one who'd stopped Jim outside the Subway, had something to do with the pipeline. She knew that Jim had stashed that envelope under his shirt.

She suspected that Tot was not only using but somehow involved with the distribution, given his new tattoo and the wad of cash he flashed at the Stop-N-Save.

And she feared the role Donna had played in the drama. She feared what her friend really knew, why she really married Jim, and how she really came to own the local diner.

Dani hadn't seen Donna for at least six weeks—since that day she'd stopped by the café after the newlyweds returned from Vegas. Dani figured it would be best if she kept to herself, what with Jim's trial coming up.

And Donna hadn't called.

Actually, Dani hadn't seen anyone for weeks.

That was because her intuition hadn't stopped whispering, just under the surface of all these facts and fears. Over and over, this sense hinted that she should keep herself at home, that she should try to stay out of view and speaking range of those who populated her hometown and the fields around it.

The only person she regularly saw was Denise, the assistant district attorney's paralegal. She'd been preparing Dani for her upcoming testimony. They didn't go over her answers, but they discussed delivery, how she should sit in the witness box, and where she should look when she was being questioned. It seemed there was more concern about portraying her as a credible source than about reviewing what she'd seen and heard.

Dani hoped the sacrifice of telling her truth would smooth itself out in the long run. But when she considered and weighed the loose ends, her serenity flew off with the autumn winds.

On the second-to-last Saturday before the trial, Dani woke to pressing silence. The clamor and frenzy that accompanied harvesting was mostly absent, leaving room for the softer, subtler sounds of falling leaves and burrowing animals.

She tied an orange scarf over Cody's collar and donned her fuzzy orange sweatshirt with the broken zipper before they crossed through Scout's fenced pasture to hike behind her quarter section. Scout had to stay near the barn, as her color could be so easily mistaken for a deer hide.

Today's clouds were heavy and low, like they'd been drawn in pencil by a toddler's uncoordinated hand, oblong objects with drooping edges and holes where an eager eraser had smudged the sky.

A pine-scented breeze from the north sang between the taut electrical wires above. Dani leaned into it, the wind, as she and Cody trod forward through empty charcoal-hued fields. Round wheels of ditch hay slumbered along their shorn edges.

They crossed a trickling stream clotted with colored leaves, then made for the trees near Beaver Creek. Dani tried to match her breath to the tempo of her steps.

When she first moved to Crestview, Donna became the sister Dani had never had. If Jim Kelly had stayed on the highway, probably nothing would have changed.

But if Jim hadn't come to town, would Donna have ever earned enough on her own to buy the café and fulfill her dream?

Maybe her choice was her sacrifice, Dani thought. She hoped it was worth it.

A red squirrel chattered at them from the path. Cody bolted toward it, though his playful bark for the squirrel quickly shifted to a warning about something up ahead.

Around the bend, Dani spied what looked like a colorful piñata dangling from a high, thick branch.

Its unexpected appearance caught Dani off guard. The piñata-object was tepee shaped, pink and tan. The object became more grotesque as she neared and discerned its true form. It was a dead deer, hanging by one leg, its hide skinned and half of its meat harvested.

Standing before it were two shirtless men wearing black face paint. One attempted to bear the weight as the other sliced through the fascia and sinew with a sharp, shiny blade. Bright crimson was smeared across their chests and forearms. As the man cut, the animal jerked and shuddered as though it was still alive.

Dani couldn't help it: she gagged, startling the men.

They stopped scraping to scrutinize her approach. Sweat had smeared their face paint, making each man appear hollow-eyed and gaunt.

One turned his head and muttered to the other; the second guy nodded. They stopped whispering, stared at her, and waited to see what she would do.

Dani raised a hand in what she hoped looked like a friendly wave, then she called out over her shoulder to a "friend" who didn't exist.

"Hey, Steve—don't bring the dogs this way, okay?" she yelled. "They're gutting a deer here. Let's go back toward the road instead."

She retreated, Cody on her heels.

Dani's breathing was shallow. She could barely bend her knees as she stiffly moved away, attempting to create more space between herself and the hunters.

A few minutes later, the dog, who'd been trotting next to her, froze. He pivoted and growled, but no one was behind them.

Dani felt an icy chill prick the back of her neck: she needed to hide.

She detoured from the path, spotting a deer trail leading down into a ravine. She stepped gingerly on fallen grasses and mossy patches to hide her footprints.

Cody kept himself right behind her, quiet now.

They kept to the center of the trail, skirting the ravine around its edges. But before they could take off toward home, Dani picked up the growl and hiss of men's voices.

They were quickly advancing her way.

She grabbed Cody's collar, and they hunched down, curling themselves behind a granite boulder.

Sticks snapped. Someone spit.

"Where the heck she go?" a voice blurted out with no attempt at stealth.

"Don't ask me, lardass. If you could keep up, we'd be on her by now."

When Dani recalled the knives they were using to gut and clean the carcass, black spots orbited into view and her ears rang. She rested her hands on her knees so she wouldn't pass out. Cody pressed against her, though his alert ears tracked the clumsy route the men used to access the ravine.

She wished she would've brought her cellphone with her, but as usual, she'd left the thing on the table at home, deciding that the coverage was so patchy that it wouldn't do her any good.

If she had it with her now, though, at least she could have attempted a call for some help. The point was moot.

"She go down here, ya think?"

"Who knows." The reply, followed by a grunt and a curse, had less volume than their previous exchange. The men were moving farther away.

Dani had read books and seen movies like this, where the hero ticked through a list of options as the bad guys hunted her down. But experiencing it as she was, right now, was eerier and more monstrous and dreamlike than words or pictures could describe.

"Why we chasin' after her, anyhow?" one of them asked.

"Shit, Carl—she's that girl who lives by herself, the one Jimbo had drive to the yard for him. She's testifyin' at the trial."

A curse followed a muffled thump. "She's the one what shut us down!"

Dani was at once gratified and dismayed that her intuition had proved to be right. She was at the root of the townspeople's conjectures. And the traffickers, those others Jim alluded to who also drive the trailers, had their own theories about her as well.

The hunters' undisguised racket faded as they moved deeper into the ravine. It brought Dani only slight relief.

These men knew who she was, what she'd done, where she lived. Out in the woods, by herself, was not the best place to be.

Dani shook herself from her dark thoughts, patted Cody, then shifted around to the boulder's front side. From there, she lunged for home, keeping her speed until she and Cody burst through the edge of Scout's pasture. They banged into the house; Dani locked the door behind them.

Once she'd regained her breath and her composure, she grabbed her phone from the table and dialed the sheriff's office. She asked to be patched through to Deputy Davies.

As they waited to connect, Dani and Cody tiptoed up to her bedroom. She felt safer behind a second locked door.

John's strong voice came through the line. "Davies, here."

"John!" Dani didn't know how to start. "I was out walking, with the dog, and these guys—hunters—knew me. Knew I'll be testifying. They were skinning a deer with these knives. And they, they followed me, and we hid, and—"

"Where are you now?"

Dani peeked out onto the front lawn from behind her bedroom curtain. "We're good, now. We're at home. The door's—"

"Lock the door," the deputy commanded. "Did you recognize them?"

"No," she replied, "but I remember what they look like."

Through the phone, she could hear a car door slam and voices over a radio or walkie- talkie. John was in his squad.

"Where were you walking, exactly?" he asked.

Dani did her best to convey the landmarks and crossroads to the deputy. "I think it's been, I don't know, twenty minutes since I was there?"

"Sit tight. I'll be by as soon as I can. Don't answer the door until you hear my voice." She heard his vehicle siren start, its pitch a high scream.

"Are you sure you're okay?" He raised his voice to be heard.

"I'm—we're—fine."

No. Not really, she admits to herself. *Not fine at all. Not good. Not okay. I haven't been good, haven't been myself, since summer.*

She reached down to hug Cody, choking back her terror. If she gave way to her fear, Dani didn't think she'd be able to find her strength again.

Just a little longer, she repeated to herself, sitting on the bedroom floor, rocking the dog in her lap.

Just a little longer.

They stayed like that until the squad pulled up. From behind her closed curtain, Dani spotted the driveway and an idling brown patrol car through the falling dusk. She unlocked the bedroom door and rushed downstairs to meet him.

The knock on the front door roused Cody's protective instinct. He growled, low; the hair on his spine was upright and rigid. She gripped his collar with one hand, just in case, and slid open the lock with the other.

"You hanging in there?" John removed his felt hat; his face was set and serious.

Dani nodded.

Cody stopped growling, but he continued to regard the visitor with distrust. He didn't sit.

"I went where you said to look, but the men are gone," he began. "They took the carcass, too, but I saw blood under the tree you described, by the path."

They went to the table, where the deputy recorded Dani's recollections into a small notebook, including the exchange she overheard about her being "the one what shut us down."

John turned his pen in his hands.

"I hate to think things have changed this much in Crestview, but I'd be stupid to say they haven't," he said. "We're so close to the interstate. I guess it was bound to happen."

The deputy went on to explain that they'd started searching through the pile of hunting applications for suspects, but it was hard going, without names. He told Dani that they'd monitor her property as often as they could through the night and the days leading up to the trial.

As he readied to leave, the deputy pressed his lips together like he was trying to hold something back. He took a deep breath, though, and continued.

"Do you have someplace you can stay for a while? A friend? Boyfriend, maybe?"

Dani shook her head.

After feeding Scout early, Dani locked herself and Cody back inside for the rest of the evening. She was still awake after midnight when her phone rang.

Alarmed, Dani plucked the phone from her bedside table without checking the caller ID. As everyone knew, a late-night call typically meant only one thing: something bad had happened to a loved one.

"Hello? Lilly?"

"Nope. Pete."

"Idiot!" Dani exhaled with force. "I thought you were Lilly! Why are you calling so late?"

"Can't sleep." His reply was simple.

"Me either." She exhaled again, more softly. "Pete . . . I have to tell you something. Today, when we were walking out toward the creek, me and Cody came up on a couple of hunters."

"Yeah?"

"Yes." She wasn't sure how much to reveal, but she plunged on, carefully. "Well, they scared me. So we took off. But—but they followed us."

"What? You okay?" His voice now held urgency and concern.

"We're fine. I think. I called the sheriff when we got home, but the deputy couldn't find them."

"Who were they? Anyone you knew?"

Dani shook her head, though Pete wasn't there to see her. "Nope. But . . . but I heard them talking." She paused. "Pete—they knew about me."

"What do you mean?"

"One of them recognized me from driving Jim's truck."

"Asshole!"

His interrupted assessment, however coarse, made Dani feel better. Understood. It also gave her the courage to continue. "They said that I'm the one who 'shut them down.'"

Dani still wanted to keep her role in the takedown quiet, especially with the trial still ahead. Like her, Pete had been called to testify, too. Dani reckoned that Pete had probably figured out her place in the investigation against Jim, but she wanted to let him be the one to bring it up.

She felt tense, then, as Pete waited an extra minute before responding. "Dani, how about I come over and sleep on your couch?"

"No, that's too much. I'm fine. I've got Cody here, and I locked the doors."

She didn't tell him that she'd also located a nice hunk of firewood, which now rested next to her bed. Or that she'd hidden a kitchen knife in her bathroom.

"Would you mind talking to me, though, for a while?" she asked. "Until I can get to sleep?"

He sighed. "Of course. I'd feel better about coming over, but it's up to you."

"Thanks."

Dani pulled her comforter tight and leaned into her pillow. The bathroom light was on, though she'd closed the door so only a tiny slit of brightness peeked out.

"What do you want to talk about?" he asked.

Dani tried to think about something other than her scare, but what came out of her mouth was only a degree or two removed: "Are you ready for the trial?"

"I guess so," he answered. "I hope they've got enough to put that jerk my sister married away for a long time. But I don't know." He waited a beat, then added, "How about you? What do you think his lawyer will ask us? They're gonna try to shoot holes in everything."

Dani shuffled her pillow for a cooler spot to rest on. "This isn't going to go well, is it?"

"I don't think so, Dani. And I don't mean that for me. I'm not the one who drove with them. I only know him from when he'd stay over, before I moved out."

He paused to form the next question.

"Have you decided what you're going to say if they ask if you knew what you were hauling?"

Even though she'd been expecting Pete to broach this topic, the knot in her stomach pressed upward and lodged itself in her throat. "No," she gasped out, then coughed to cover her reaction. "No, I haven't. What makes you ask that?" *I wish I wouldn't have promised Wahlquist I wouldn't tell anyone,* she fretted.

He didn't respond.

Dani pushed forward, carefully. "Did Donna say something?"

"Donna?"

"Well, who else could it be?" Her volume rose. "You wouldn't have brought it up, otherwise."

Again, her comment was met with silence.

"What would you do?" She tried to keep from sounding shrill. "If you were me, I mean. What would you say if they asked if you knew what they were hauling?"

"You can't win, either way. Either you answer that you didn't see anything, yourself, or you try to go a step further and tell them what you think you knew."

"The ADA said the defense can't ask me to interpret what I saw," Dani countered.

She crept out of bed to stand behind the curtain at her window, squinting down at the road in front of her property. The waxing moon made the dry, spindly grasses beside the empty field look like bony skeletons. There was no other movement; all looked quiet and still.

Pete's statement broke the silence. "You knew what he was doing, Dani. We both did."

Dani had nothing to say about this.

But what about his sister?

"Listen, call me again if you need anything, 'k?" Pete yawned. "Otherwise, see you tomorrow. I think."

She thanked him for calling, promised she'd let him know if she got scared or anything bad happened, and disconnected.

She didn't sleep until dawn started coloring the walls in her locked bedroom.

Dani slept a scant hour. She got out of bed around seven because Cody wouldn't stop whining. He was scratching her door, hellbent on getting downstairs. She grabbed her phone from her bed table, though, before releasing him. He bolted down the steps, panting.

She followed the dog to the entryway.

She opened the lock, turned the knob, and then pushed open the screen to let him out.

Cody burst from the house with his hair on end, barking and snarling.

Hanging from the tree in her front yard was a butchered deer carcass, a blue X spray-painted across its denuded backbone. It twisted on a rope attached to one hind leg like a demented upside-down ballerina. The grisly hole left when its entrails were gutted out grinned at her, an unending accusation.

Her own breath torn from her lungs, Dani had to make herself calm enough to scream out for her dog to return. With Cody inside, she slammed the door, locked it, and retreated to her bedroom to dial the sheriff's office.

But John was no longer on shift.

Rather than taking the time to replay everything to yet another deputy, Dani disconnected and called Wahlquist instead.

After a series of holds and reroutings, they connected. Her voice wavered as she told him what happened.

Though he was concerned, his solution was not very reassuring. Or practical.

"Here's what you'll do," he began. He sounded like someone giving directions to a lost motorist looking for the interstate. "Drive down here to Des Moines. We'll put you up in a hotel overnight. And through the course of the trial, maybe we could find a stipend to get you into a hotel that's closer."

The call didn't last long after that. Dani knew she wasn't safe at home, but the thought of being ensconced in a public hotel somewhere didn't settle her nerves. The wrong person seeing her there would place a big X on her body, too.

Plus, Dani knew that Wahlquist couldn't supply someone to take care of Scout and Cody. Usually Pete helped with that task—but he was also testifying at the trial. Another no go.

"I'll get back to you," she replied flatly.

She called Pete next. When he learned what happened and then heard Wahlquist's idea, he came up with a solution of his own.

"Stay with me," he suggested. "You can bring Cody, and I'll go back and take care of Scout."

Dani hesitated. "Are you sure . . . ?"

"Yeah. Forget staying in some hotel," he replied, more assured now. "You'll feel more comfortable close to home. And, well, I'll feel better keeping an eye out for you here."

It took fifteen minutes for Dani to pack some clothes, feed and water her horse, and get herself and her dog out of the house and down the road to Pete's apartment.

He greeted her at the open door and enfolded her in a hug. "You're shaking," he said, patting her back. "You're going to be okay, Dan. No one'll know you're here."

Dani wiped her eyes. "What about my truck? I don't want anyone to see it here—and not just because I'm hiding." She managed a weak smile. "There's enough talk floating around about me without adding this to the list."

They decided that Pete would park her truck behind the library, back near the dumpster. Dani would pick him up in his truck every evening after work. Hopefully it would be dark enough that she wouldn't be recognized behind his steering wheel.

Dani left a voice message for John about her "hideout." She also tried to call Wahlquist but only managed to reach his partner, Brookins.

That night, Pete asked her for a list of books to bring back from the library to help her pass the time. They watched an old movie. They didn't talk about the trial.

She felt bad about moving Pete from his bed. He claimed that it was a better position, combat-wise, to sleep on the couch.

She felt worse about being so near to him, about giving him the illusion that she was trustworthy, yet she'd been forbidden to share her part in the sting.

Dani just didn't know how Pete's sister figured in.

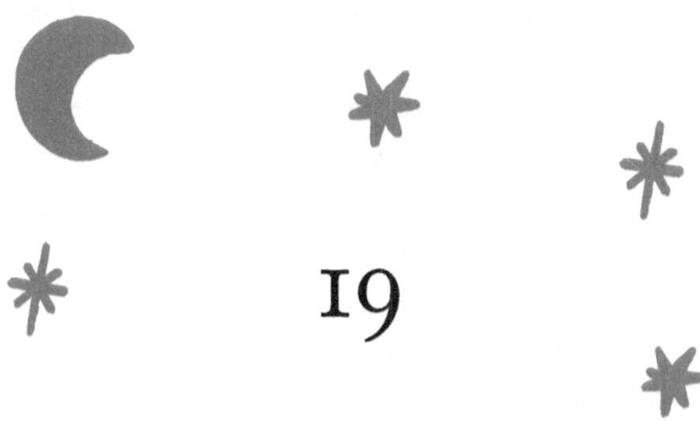

19

THEIR PLAN WORKED. Two days passed. Slowly.

Around ten o'clock the third morning, Pete called Dani from the library with a schedule change. Donna had asked him to close the restaurant that night for her; apparently, Jim's attorney wanted to go over some details with her for the trial. As the defendant's spouse, she wasn't required to testify, but there were some points he needed to clarify for her husband's defense.

"I gotta do it," Pete explained. "If I refuse to help out, she'll wonder what's up."

"I see your point," Dani agreed. "She's quick to spot anything that looks out of place."

"Donna will come get me from the library," Pete added. "I made up some story that I don't have the truck 'cuz I'm getting my oil changed. So, I'll come home over lunch to give you my truck—do you think you can get yourself out to feed Scout without getting noticed?"

"Of course, I can," Dani answered. "It'll be good. I'm bored to death here. No offense," she quickly amended. "I'll just go slow and duck down and stay out of everyone's way. It'll be great to see my girl."

"Okay. I'll call when I'm done at the café, then you can drive out to get me."

"No problem."

Out of nowhere, Dani came up with another question, though not necessarily how to ask it. It wasn't like she wanted to intrude, exactly. But after being tucked away in such close quarters with Pete for two days, her curiosity overtook her apprehension.

"Hey . . . has Jessica said anything? About me staying here, I mean?"

"Not to me. But she's busy with school." Pete cleared his throat. When he continued, his tone mirrored the curiosity Dani's tone had held. "It's not like we're dating or anything, so unless she asks outright, there's no reason for her to know what I've—we've—been up to."

His answer created a stir in Dani's stomach. She told herself it was nerves.

"Thanks, Pete. For making all this effort for me."

She could hear Pete's smile in the slight way his tone softened. "You're welcome. And just so you don't get all conceited, it's not just for you, you know. I'm hoping my sister will come to her senses, eventually, once we get this asshole put away."

Dani waited until the afternoon had almost faded before she slipped out of the apartment and sneaked into Pete's truck. She disguised herself with one of his old caps and his big sweatshirt, puffing it up around her face and neck.

Cody stayed behind in Pete's bathroom. Dani turned the radio's volume up high before leaving, to mask the sounds of his howls.

Driving back home relaxed and soothed her nerves. She paused at the last crossroads before her section, but there was no one else on either road. Every field in each direction was empty. Swept clean of their harvests, they were tucked in and waiting for winter.

As Dani eased the truck onto her property, she saw Pete had dragged her garbage bin to the edge of her driveway for pickup.

Excellent detail. She smiled. It looked like she'd been home this whole time.

Scout nickered when Dani parked next to her pen. It was probably because Scout had learned to connect Pete's vehicle with food, but Dani told herself that her horse was happy to see her.

Together, they moved under the barn-covered portion of the pen to the old freezer. "How you doing, girl? You holding up?" Dani nuzzled the horse after pouring grain into her green bucket. "You miss me?"

The outside gate screeched open.

Scout burst from her grasp as Dani whirled to face the interruption.

It was Tot.

The knife he grasped glinted like a snarl.

He charged toward her.

He misjudged the girth and size of the horse between them, though. In his hurry to get to Dani, the knife pierced Scout's upper shoulder. The horse screamed before bolting for the open gate, crashing Tot hard against the ground.

Tot scrambled up from his knees.

Dani flew at him without hesitation. Furious instead of fearful, she'd found the courage to act on her first instinct. She knocked him back to the dirt. He lost the knife.

As she wrestled with him, he flipped over and twisted her down flat. He sat on her stomach, holding her arms against the ground.

"I'm not gonna hurt you!" he gasped, trying to catch his breath. His face, pocked and mottled with red splotches, looked the way Geoff's did, toward the end.

Dani thrashed, trying to free herself, trying to find the knife, trying to locate her injured horse. "I—I don't care, you—you asshole! Get off me!"

"I'm sorry! I'm sorry!" He repeated the apology like a broken record, but he didn't allow her her freedom. "I just need the money!"

Dani flung herself upward from her heels to try to dislodge him. But even in his thin and unhealthy condition, Tot was too strong for her to overcome.

"I don't have any money, Tot," she tried. "Get off me! I can't breathe."

He leaned back a bit and loosened his grip on her arms, but didn't let her up. Something planted inside him, in his younger years, reappeared just long enough to make him look ashamed.

"I didn't think you'd be here. You haven't been here for days." He sniffed. "I just need—I need some—" He lost his thought for a second. "I need some money. I just need the cash Jimbo gave you. That's all."

"I don't have the money anymore," she insisted. "It's not here!"

Despite her repeated denials, Tot wrangled a twisting, spitting Dani to her feet. He recovered his knife and, holding her arm tight against her back, marched her back to her house.

"Tot." She tried to appeal to that glimmer of decency she'd glimpsed. "You know me. I wouldn't lie to you. I mean it when I say I—have— no—money." She paused between each word, hoping that, somehow, the message might sink in.

He kept pushing her ahead, but he slowed so she could climb the porch steps at her own speed.

Dani used the time she was given, but she stopped when she reached the door. "I don't have my key." This sounded like a stall tactic or a lie, so she quickly added, "I only came out to feed Scout. I wasn't planning on going into the house."

With one arm, Tot held her against the door frame, and with the other, he battered the butt of his knife through the slim pane of glass within the door. The pane shattered, spraying glass over his bare arm; blood streaks appeared, twining from his wrist to his bent elbow. He reached through the opening and unlocked the door from inside.

"Let's go," he said, his voice a monotone.

Still oblivious to her protests and excuses, he wrangled her to the dining room, where he noticed her computer. He snatched the cord from the monitor and yanked hard. The screen fell as the cord disconnected, but no one else was on the property to hear the crash.

He backed Dani onto a chair.

"Tot! Look at me!" she pleaded. "I'm Dani! You know me. I'd give you money if I had it! Why are you doing this?"

He didn't answer. Holding her down on the chair with his left hand, he used the other to wrap the computer cord around her midsection.

Dani writhed and kicked. She screamed. She pleaded, again.

But nothing stopped him. He was a robot, now holding her firm with one knee, weaving the cord twice, three times, around her and through the chair's back slats.

Tears and snot and perspiration ran down Dani's face. "Please, Tot. All I have is about $30 in cash in the kitchen, behind the coffee canister in the cupboard. But that's all. You can go and look—go ahead. There's nothing more. Tot!"

His pupils were huge. His unblinking eyes darted from side to side.

Abruptly, he left her to check out the kitchen. The cupboard doors opened, then slammed shut, one by one, until he located the coffee canister. He strode back into the dining room, holding a few bills.

"Is this it?" he asked.

"Yes! I told you! I don't have the money from Jim."

Dani recognized his hunger as he stared at the bills in his hand: Tot needed a fix. He was out of control, frantic for his next hit.

And that reality scared her even more than the violence she'd just endured. She knew from experience how single-minded an addict became as the minutes ticked by between one fix and the next.

Mumbling, Tot left her.

She heard him stumble down the porch steps.

His footsteps on her driveway dissipated.

He was gone.

The vacuum his departure created stifled Dani. Though his physical presence was gone, she couldn't allow herself to feel any relief or safety until she was certain that he wouldn't return. Or that he wouldn't return with someone else to help him.

Dani pictured Tot's young face, a ravaged sign of how his life had so dramatically changed.

She cursed the drug that led him down its sexy but sinister path.

Tot was a ticking time bomb about to detonate. Dani could only sit, tied to her chair, and pray and hope that his denouement would occur far away—and out of the sight of his parents.

Her arms growing numb behind her, Dani's focus turned to her horse. She worried about where Scout had run to hide. Dani couldn't stop her spiraling thoughts about the lonely roads and the darkening sky and the speeding drivers who wouldn't expect to see a horse in front of them.

She worried about the wound to Scout's shoulder and how she might find a vet at this time of night. Or whenever she got free.

Tears flowed down her face. She didn't know, didn't care, if they were for her horse or for the young man who had fallen so far so fast. Or if she shed some for the lost love that was taken from her so brutally.

She knew, though, as all who loved drug addicts did, that there wasn't a damn thing she could do about Tot's addiction. He was on his own, holding on until he hit that place where there wasn't enough powder to satisfy the craving that infiltrated every part, every cell, every atom, of his entire being.

She was sad, so very sad, but there was not one single thing that anyone but Tot could do to make it go away.

The rasp of a vehicle's tires on her driveway jolted her attention. She straightened her spine. It wasn't Tot, she concluded, as he'd taken off as he'd come, on foot. She still couldn't determine, though, whether the driver would be hostile or helpful.

Her first instinct was to hide, but she couldn't, not trussed up. Nor could she do one single thing to protect herself. The impotency of her entrapment stole the last wisps of hope she'd been praying to maintain.

She wondered if she should stay silent or if she should scream and yell to alert whomever had arrived, friend or foe, of her horrific situation.

She chose the latter.

She screamed. Gut-wrenching fear and dismay and exasperation and anger swelled from her depths.

She pounded her feet against her wood floor like she wanted to burst through it.

Every fiber of Dani exploded against the disregard she'd been shown, against the ugly truths she'd endured and the lies she ignored instead of confronting. She raged against Jim, against this new Tot, against the demon drug that stole souls and left empty husks behind.

Dani was done accomodating. She was done being complacent. Done trying to conform to others' expectations.

No more. Ever, she told herself. No more.

Gravel spewed across the frozen driveway. Car doors opened. She heard Pete's voice, along with another she didn't quite recognize, rushing her way.

Through her tears, Dani lifted her face as John burst through the front door, his firearm in front of him. She grinned at him. She grinned, too, at Pete, just behind, his features gripped by anxiety.

John rushed past her up the stairs.

Pete knelt behind her chair and fumbled with the cord. "Are you okay?"

John bounded down the steps from her bedroom. "Are you alone?"

Dani nodded.

After freeing her, Pete moved to Dani's front. "Who did this to you?" His hands rested gently on her forearms, scanning her as if to determine any injury or damage.

With his handgun holstered, the deputy stepped to one side to use his shoulder mic. He watched her and Pete intently.

"Tot was here," Dani began. "He—"

"He did this to you? Tot?" Pete flew to the front window.

"He was high. Is high." She swallowed. She hadn't yet gotten up from the chair. "He needed money. He said he didn't expect me to be here, but . . ."

"Did you see where he went—Tot?" John now filled the space in front of Dani.

She shook her head. "No. I wasn't watching." She raised her chin. "I was praying."

"Had you been in contact with Tot before he attacked you?" John's calm voice contra- dicted his intense stare.

"No. I saw him at the gas station a few weeks ago, but not since then." She rubbed her wrists.

"How did he seem then?"

It was hard for Dani to conjure the image of Tot at the Stop-N-Save without it morphing into the memory of him lunging at her with the knife that slashed Scout. She pinched the bridge of her nose.

"He looked . . . normal, I guess. Not tripping. Or at least not like how he looked today."

Pete whirled from the window. "Yeah, but didn't you also see him doing a "drug deal" in the gas station lot?"

Davies followed this detail. "What made you think it was a drug deal?"

"Guys, can't we do this tomorrow? I've got to find Scout."

"What do you mean? Where's Scout?" Pete's face paled.

"She bolted," Dani answered. "Tot . . . Tot hurt her. Stabbed her. She ran."

John frowned. "Okay, Dani. But where are you going to look?"

"She could be anywhere. I need a four-wheeler or something. You know anyone we can call?"

"Use mine," John volunteered. He turned to Pete. "Your truck's got a hitch, right? I'll lead you over to my place, and you can hook up the trailer." John returned his attention to Dani.

"Let me know if you see Tot. He's my priority. Don't confront him, though. Let me deal with him first. You just find your horse. And call me, if you need to."

There was a pause. Both men looked down at Dani, still sitting in the chair she'd been tied to. They had a plan, but they waited. Waited for her to put it in action.

Being tied, being immobilized, being unable to move—it reawakened the anger she'd long continued to put aside, to hide, to avoid confronting.

Anger over the path Donna chose. Anger for the addiction Tot battled.

Anger at the man who died and took a part of her with him.

She'd ignored her anger in lieu of an impotent wishfulness in her heart's side-pocket that things would somehow revert to the way they used to be. She'd allowed herself to stand back, to choose to give over her own power, to let others' decisions leave their impact upon her.

But the price for her willful disregard had been paid, and it shifted the way she'd live her future.

She wasn't who she used to be.

Her heartbeats, steady and slow, filled her with the rich gifts of confidence and assurance that she'd now do what she needed to do. Do what was right.

Dani got to her feet.

"I'm ready."

20

Once they'd picked up John's trailer and four-wheeler, Pete dropped Dani at the corner of County Road 8 and Highway 2, by the cemetery. Dani wanted to take the four-wheeler and drive through that section first.

Meanwhile, Pete planned to head back to Dani's place to search on foot around the barn and Scout's pasture.

It wasn't difficult for Dani to twine the ATV through the bare and scraggly tree line nearest the cemetery, but she quickly realized that Scout hadn't chosen that place to hide.

The next open portion was an empty hayfield, but it didn't provide enough cover for a hurt horse to conceal herself in either.

Just past that grew a thicker copse of trees, mostly oak. Dani drove slowly to avoid the ruts and roots threatening to tip her off the vehicle.

The labored pace meant she was able to hear her phone ring when Pete called to check in. He'd been able to follow Scout's blood track out of the paddock and into the pasture, but where the grass grew more thick, he'd lost the trail.

The next piece of Pete's news horrified Dani: in her rush to escape, Scout likely ran through the wires stringing the edge of her pasture.

Perhaps she'd jumped but failed to clear the wires, or perhaps she just pushed herself through the strands meant to enclose her.

"Keep looking, okay?" Dani pressed. "She's got to be somewhere."

"Yeah, but don't you think we'd have better luck in the daylight?"

"She might not last that long, Pete. He cut her, and if she's still bleeding—" Dani gave up trying to explain. "I've got to go. I'll check back in a half hour."

She didn't wait for his goodbye. She revved the engine as she approached the next section: the property owned by Tot White's family.

Dani crossed the gravel road and turned into the ditch paralleling the Whites' first pasture. As she sped along their service road, their barn road, and their house's driveway, the ATV's headlight bounded along with the swells.

Despite the late hour, the house lights, both upstairs and down, blazed out. A floodlight splashed the circular turnaround area with its bright beam.

Dani spied the rear gate of Tot's truck poking out from the barn's open door. The sight sparked a flash of anger. She was tempted to ride up, hunt Tot down, and challenge him.

Thinking that Tot might be close by steamed her, caused a sharp ache to rake the edges of each breath she gulped in.

Just underneath that courage, though, lay apprehension. Remembering that Scout was out in the dark, alone and hurt, helped her keep her focus.

Behind the Whites' barn, Dani felt more than noticed a shadow off to her left. She scrutinized the underbrush, but she couldn't discern any movement.

She turned off the machine. As the engine cooled and ticked, she scanned the darkness, listening for snapping branches or horse noises. But the night's stillness enveloped her, maintaining its false serenity.

Then, she heard a soft whinny.

Jumping from the four-wheeler, Dani rushed into a stand of trees. There was Scout, her big head hanging, the gash on her shoulder slick with blood.

"You're okay, girl," Dani crooned, but her spirit quailed inside. How did the horse make it so far, losing so much blood? Dani needed to find help, fast, before the mare's time completely ran out.

Dani was afraid to touch Scout, fearing that the horse might spook or that the pressure of a hand could further injure her. She tried instead to encourage the mare with a subtle gesture.

"Can you follow me, Scout? Hm? Can you walk?" But Scout was afraid. She didn't want to take another step. "I'll be back, girl; you just wait here, okay?"

Dani ran to the lights in Tot's house, scrambling for her phone as her feet pounded the ground and her knees and ankles absorbed the stones and hollows in the pasture ahead.

"Pete? I'm at Bud and Missy's. I've—"

"At Bud and Missy's? What the hell! Is Tot there?"

She didn't tell him about seeing Tot's truck in the barn. "Call John, then head over. Scout's here—I need a vet. If Bud and Missy are up, they'll help me get Scout out of the woods and into their barn."

"No! You can't!" Pete couldn't control himself. "What if Tot's there?"

Dani's stride faltered; she fell to one knee. Cursing, she got up and started running again.

Pete seized the moment to continue his protests, but she cut him off. "I'm doing this, Pete." She swallowed her thickening fear. "But hurry, okay?"

Dani disconnected. Her heart throbbed.

She purposely looked away from the barn, charging directly through the open garage to the utility door inside. She knocked, then instantly pushed the door in. "Bud? Missy?"

The middle-aged couple were sitting at their round wooden kitchen table, Missy in her robe and Bud in a white V-neck and jeans. Shocked, they stared at Dani like a storybook character come to life.

"D-Dani?" Bud's confusion was obvious. "What're you doin' here?"

Dani took a half second to register the Whites' reactions. They were concerned and puzzled, but they showed no sign of understanding the deeper meaning beyond her sudden presence. She used the other half second to register that there was no sign of their son in the kitchen.

"I need your help," she gasped. "My horse is hurt. She's back behind your barn, and she won't move. Can you come out?"

Missy directed her husband forward. "You go, Bud. I'll call Melissa Jensen. Hurry—see what's going on out there."

Bud snatched a tattered barn jacket from the peg by the door, shoved his bare feet into some dirty rubber boots, and followed Dani outside. He tried to keep up as she crossed through the bright light of the yard to edge the shadowed barn.

"Her shoulder is cut," Dani shouted to him over her shoulder. "She's really weak. Do you have anywhere we could move her till the vet can come?"

"Sure. But how'd it happen? She get away from you?"

Dani almost couldn't answer. "Yep—something like that."

As they neared Scout, Bud let out a whistle. "Woo, that is bad." He eased himself to Scout's side to assess the damage. "Must've cut herself on something sharp, huh? She break through her fence?"

Dani ignored this, also. "I should've asked—do you have a rope to bring her in?"

"In the barn. I'll get it." He retreated.

"You'll be good as new, girl." Dani smoothed the mare's jaw and blinked away her tears. "We'll get you fixed up and back home again. Soon. I promise."

Bud returned with a length of white rope. "Here ya go. You'd better do it. I'll help from the back. But you get up front—she knows and trusts you."

Now her tears fell. "Thanks, Bud." Dani adjusted the rope behind Scout's ears, twisted the ends together in a loop, and gently pulled. "C'mon, girl. You've got to help, too."

Before they eased her horse inside, Dani tried to peer past the darkness to search the barn's entryway, but Tot's truck was gone. Missy was outside, though. Now wearing jeans and a sweatshirt, she held a cellphone to one ear.

"Yes, that's right. We'll be in the barn." She saw them and covered the mouthpiece. "Can you get her inside? The vet's just turning in."

Under the barn's overhead lights, the damage to Scout's flesh looked even more horrific: a gaping slash ran under her neck, across her shoulder, and down her front leg. The skin hung off the injury, and while the edges still bled, the raw, pink meat underneath looked dull and pinched. The mare could barely move. Whether she was incapacitated or just out of energy, Scout appeared ready to fall over.

Dani and Bud positioned her so that her good side aligned with a wall and the injured side was open to the light. Dani held the rope, murmuring to Scout as they waited for the vet, while Bud rummaged through a dark pile of metal discards in the back. He dragged up a fence panel, placed it behind the horse, then retreated for another one to form a sort of stall.

Missy entered, trailed by a slight-figured younger woman toting a square plastic box. "This is Melissa—Dr. Jenson, I mean," Missy said. "She grew up just down the road. One time, when she was little—"

"Missy," Bud interjected. "You remember where that bucket is? We need some water."

As Missy set off for some water, the vet came forward, knelt, and took a quick peek at the shoulder. She pursed her lips. "Hi. Let's get some sedation and some pain relief on board," she said, turning briefly to Dani. "Are you good with holding her while I clean her and see what's what?"

"Absolutely."

Dani wouldn't be leaving her horse's side, not until she knew for sure that her mare would be okay.

An hour later, Scout had received an infusion of blood and another of electrolytes, and Dr. Jenson was suturing the long wound.

The vet recommended stall rest for the next few days. For now, the horse had to remain at the Whites', with Dani planning to come over every day to administer the antibiotic pills and wound ointment Dr. Jenson gave her.

After that, Dr. Jenson said, Dani could walk her back home—as long as Scout had no fever. Dr. Jenson would stop by Dani's later in the week to see how the injury was healing.

Pete arrived, then. Dani saw him take Bud outside the barn. She couldn't hear what they were saying, but she watched them as they talked. She saw Bud's face fall. He scrunched his eyes shut as if he couldn't bear to hear any more.

Deputy Davies pulled into the White Farm's driveway next. He parked his squad directly in front of the open barn door, where Tot's truck had most recently been.

"How you doing, Mr. White?" Dani could hear John ask from across the barnyard. Removing his hat, he didn't wait for the older man's answer. "Have you seen your son tonight?"

Missy popped out from the barn like she had antennae homed in. "What's that you're saying, John?" she called.

Dani couldn't bear to witness the moment she learned the truth about their son and his role in this event. She patted her horse goodbye carefully, gently, then broke into their conversation before John could continue.

"Bud, Missy—thank you both for your help tonight."

John gave her a quick nod of understanding, then turned to Missy. "You have any coffee, yet?"

"I'll get a fresh pot started."

Missy's ongoing commentary accompanied their trek to the house.

Bud didn't follow his wife and the deputy. He stayed behind, frozen, his stare fixed on something far, far away.

Dani knew that feeling. She reached out and gave him a quick hug.

Startled, he recovered and squeezed back, adding a quiet whisper before releasing her: "I'm sorry, Dani. Really am . . ."

He moved away from her, grabbed a balled-up hanky from his pocket, and wiped it across his face.

Dani nodded, then followed Pete to his truck. When she'd buckled herself in, he switched on his headlights. As they reversed from the barnyard, the headlights illuminated Tot's father, just inside his barn. He'd dropped his hands to his knees, crouching forward, and was sobbing openly, his big shoulders heaving with every heavy gasp.

"You need to stop anywhere before we head back to my place?" Pete asked once they'd passed the cemetery crossroads.

Dani's eyes were closed, her head propped up by the seatback cushion. She was thinking about nothing, absolutely nothing, but her own bed in her own room in her own house.

Home.

"Actually, can you take me back home?"

Pete paused a beat. "To grab some stuff?"

"No. To stay."

"Nah, don't think that's a good idea." Pete flicked off his turn signal. "Why don't you stay at my place again, at least till things clear up with Tot still out there? I mean, your front door's all busted up."

Though her eyes remained shut, Dani shook her head. "No, Pete. No. I need to be home now." She blinked and struggled to sit upright on the truck's worn seat. "I'm done."

Memories of being tied to the chair, of hearing her horse scream, of racing over rocks and past sharp branches that struck her in the night—they all coalesced in her mind and pushed a new flame of strength through her exhausted body.

"I can't be afraid, anymore." She turned to Pete. Her face was open. Clear. "I'm not that person anymore."

Pete didn't react to her announcement, at first. Turning onto Main Street, he made a suggestion. "Then let's stop and get Cody. And your things. I'll gp out there with you. I can—"

"No. Pete. Just . . . no."

He let the truck slow to a stop on its own. It was almost midnight, and the street was empty. He waited to hear her explanation.

"I haven't been able to sleep at your place, and—"

His body language shifted, the preamble to an attempt to redirect her thinking.

She cut it off. "No, I know. And thanks. But I need to be home. Now. I've got plywood for the door. I can get Cody and my stuff tomorrow. But right now, I need to be by myself."

She gathered the rest of her thoughts.

"Even with what happened there with Tot tonight, I'm no longer afraid. He did his worst, and I'm okay. I'm okay, and I got through it." Dani nodded. "And I'll get through this trial, too. And then, once Scout is better, maybe things will be good again."

A tear finally fell, released from a place of cleansing, a place of pride. "I'm not putting up with Jim Kelly—or anyone—anymore. Never again."

Pete reached out with his free hand and traced the tearstain, wiping it clean. "Good for you, Dan," he said. "Good for you."

21

AFTER OPENING STATEMENTS, Dani Holden was the first witness called to the stand.

She closed her eyes as she was sworn in, and she stumbled over the simple two-word response to the bailiff's request that she tell the truth: "I—I do." Her hand trembled on the black Bible he held out for her.

Charles "Chip" Harrington, the prosecuting attorney, was an assistant district attorney. He was a thin fiftyish man wearing a light-gray suit, silver-rimmed glasses, and a kind smile. He got right to it. "How do you know the defendant's wife, Donna Lund Kelly?"

"She's my—best friend," Dani replied.

She didn't look at Donna, watching from the gallery. She'd seen her on their way into the courtroom, but Donna was so preoccupied in locating her husband that she didn't notice Dani.

Or maybe Donna didn't want to see Dani, even though there was practically no one else there. To protect Dani, Pete, and the others who would testify, and because of the sensitive nature of information to be covered, the Honorable Harold Whitby, presiding, closed the trial to outsiders.

"How long have you known Donna?"

It was curious to Dani that Harrington didn't use a more formal name for Donna, but she didn't have time to ponder this more. His question was an easy one to answer.

"About two years—since I moved to Crestview."

His next jump was steeper: "Will you please describe Donna's social attachments, since"—he snagged a glance at his notes—"since June 2002?"

It was a question the paralegal, Denise, didn't prepare her to answer. She did her best.

"Donna works at the café in town. She's there a lot, so I'd say she knows pretty much everyone."

"Have you known Donna to be in a relationship with anyone since June 2002?"

Eric Anderson, Jim's public defender, struggled from his seat to interrupt. His dark suit wasn't as sharp or tailored as the ADA's is. Rather, his coat pulled tight beneath his arms and across his chest. Even though they'd just begun, his round face was shiny and pink.

"Objection," he managed. "That answer is open to interpretation."

Judge Whitby overruled the objection. "Please continue, Ms. Holden."

Like the prosecutor, the judge had lost most of his hair. His voluminous robe hung from his shoulders like it was draped over a hat rack.

"No," she finally replied.

All that work for a one-word answer.

"When did you meet James Kelly?"

"I believe it was the first week in July. This year." Dani nodded, certain of her reply.

Harrington continued in this lockstep manner, asking a series of questions that led them to the first trip the three made together to the stockyard.

"We have a phone record here"—he handed some papers to the judge—"which indicates a call made between a phone in Jim's possession and a number associated with a convicted drug dealer. Did you observe Jim making any phone calls during that first trip, the one you made with Mr. Kelly and his, er, wife?"

Dani shook her head. "I did not see him make any calls." She wondered if her answer would suffice or if she should explain herself further, but the prosecutor moved on.

"Did he receive any calls?"

"Not that I saw."

"Did you observe Jim interacting with anyone, other than Donna, during the trip to the Missouri stockyard?"

Now Dani looked at Donna, seated on the other side of the room, behind her husband. Donna stared right over the top of Dani's head, her eyes hard and unblinking. Her face was granite.

Jim, though, flashed a satisfied, sharky grin Dani's way.

This is it, Dani told herself. *This is where I jump off the ledge.*

"I did," she said.

Jim's grin morphed into a slitted grimace. He looked away.

Dani shot a quick glance to Donna to gauge her reaction: she too frowned, her mouth a sour pucker.

Harrington unbuttoned his suit coat. "Who else did Mr. Kelly talk to?"

"I don't know his name. I only saw his face. Part of his face, I mean. He was wearing sunglasses," Dani added.

The attorney walked Dani through the observations she'd made at that lunch stop, asking questions that Dani could answer simply.

"What did Mr. Kelly say to explain his interaction with the man outside the rest stop?"

"He said the man wanted him, Jim, to bring his trailer back to Iowa for him."

"Motion to withhold the statement, Your Honor?" Anderson couldn't keep the smile from edging onto his chubby face. "There's no way for Ms. Holden to know what was said, unless she was standing right there next to them."

The judge agreed, and Dani's statement was struck from the record. They moved on.

The prosecutor gave her a stapled collection of papers and asked her to look at the bottom of the first page. "Can you tell us what you see on the last two lines?"

"Well, there's a signature here—over a label that reads 'gate guard,'" Dani began. "And the address of that stockyard we went to."

"Will you recount any details you recall from that moment, when the guard allowed Jim Kelly's truck to come through?"

She started to explain but was interrupted again by the defense.

"Judge Whitby? Can I approach? I want to clarify something . . ." Jim's attorney got to his feet and aimed himself for the judge.

Harrington joined Anderson in front of the bench. Dani tried to keep her eyes and ears to herself, but she was tempted to lean into their private conversation.

As if reading her mind, the bailiff situated himself between her and the bench. "You're under oath, but I'd be glad to fetch some water for you, if needed," he offered.

Dani thanked him but declined. She concentrated on her animals and the sunny weather and happy things, and tried to make herself relax.

The attorneys reassumed their places, and the prosecutor finished Dani's interrogation.

Following a lunch break, Jim's attorney would begin his examination of Dani's account. Once the judge left the courtroom for the midday recess, Dani sagged back into her chair. She could have really used that water now, but the bailiff had disappeared with Judge Whitby.

Denise, the ADA's assistant who'd prepped Dani for her testimony, escorted her to a conference room. "You're doing great, Dani," she smiled. "Remember, you don't have to add anything—make your answers as short as you can, okay?"

Dani nodded. Despite her desire to be strong and unshakeable, she felt numb.

When Dani was recalled to the witness stand, Anderson, the public defender, gave her a smug look from behind his table.

Her mind raced despite the slow breaths she made herself take. She had a sudden, irrational notion that Anderson could somehow see into her mind, that he somehow knew what she planned to answer.

She was terrified.

"Ms. Holden. You're not a farmer by training, are you?"

Dani gulped and told herself to take it slowly. "No, I'm not, but—"

"And prior to your . . . sojourn, I guess I'd call it, into farm life, did you have prior experience in agriculture?"

"Well, no. My grand—"

He cut her off again. "Thank you. And before coming to Iowa, you were a secretary for"—he made a big show of holding up a paper to examine, but Dani knew he was milking it—"for a Mark Schmidt, of the Dorcas and Thilby firm in Minneapolis. Is that correct?"

Why is this jerk bringing Mark up? And how could he even know?

Quickly, anger replaced her fear. Obviously, Dani realized, the public defender wasn't as sloppy as his appearance suggested. Somehow he'd gotten details into her past, his investigation more thorough than she would have imagined.

Harrington spoke up. "Objection. What's the relevance here?"

As Dani waited for Judge Whitby's decision, a thought lit up: Maybe Donna told him.

Her shock at this betrayal was more subdued. It motivated her to regain her self- confidence. She would not let Donna's greedy quest and self-serving behaviors overwhelm her.

Finally, the judge overruled the objection.

Dani was obligated to answer Anderson's question about Mark: "Yes, I was."

"How did that 'professional' relationship come to an end?" The lawyer made air-quote marks with his fingers.

Moron.

"I decided to follow my dream, to farm—"

"In Iowa. Yes, we heard that. But what incident, specifically, brought you to that deci- sion?" He arranged himself into a posture of patience as he waited.

Dani knew he was trying to smear her as a credible witness. But she wouldn't allow it. She told herself that she had nothing to be ashamed of. Other women had been misguided, lied to, entangled in similar affairs.

Dani lifted her chin and looked straight at him. "We had an affair. He was married, but I didn't—"

"A married man?"

Dani immediately went on. "I didn't know he was married. As soon as I found out, I left and came here. And I never went back."

"Objection!" Harrington found his feet. His face was furious and tight. "Relevance? What are you trying to achieve here, Anderson?"

Judge Whitby's bass voice cut through the melee. "Mr. Anderson. Please. Try again."

The silence that followed felt thick and sticky. Jim's attorney stalled, a sly upturn to one corner of his mouth.

He wanted to make Dani uncomfortable, but she wasn't afraid of his tactic. She got courage from the smile she received from Harrington, then settled herself more firmly into the back of the wooden seat.

She wouldn't give in.

"Everyone lies." Anderson cast about to find his rhythm again. "Kids, parents, cops. Even lawyers. Witnesses, too."

He pasted on a new smile. Jim Kelly, behind him, mirrored the same smug look.

Anderson sauntered back to his table and sat behind it. "Do you have reason to lie about what you reported to have observed in Missouri?"

"Absolutely not." Dani wanted to spit at him. At them. The lawyer and Jim, both.

"How about the 'dock rats' that loaded the trailer for that return trip? Did you see Mr. Kelly interacting with them?"

Dani's pulse quickened with unexpected excitement. "You've made a mistake," she replied. "No one loaded that trailer. No one was even there. Jim connected it, all by himself."

Take that, she thought.

Anderson turned away from her. "All right, Ms. Holden. Did Mr. Kelly talk to—or take money or other material—from anyone at the first loading dock?"

She considered this for a minute. "Yes, actually," she confirmed.

Anderson whirled back, his expression startled. "Wh—? Wait a minute. Did you—"

This time, Dani interrupted him. "Jim was alone with two dockhands behind the first trailer for a few minutes after they unloaded the animals."

Jim's attorney looked pissed, like this was the first time he'd heard these details. "That's it." His decision to finish was a quick one. "No further questions."

But Dani continued. "And he took money, too."

This statement completely unnerved the public defender. Anderson slid his chair away from Jim, plopped himself into it, and lowered his chin toward his chest. The voice that emerged from that cramped and sweaty crevice was tight and restrained.

"What money, Ms. Holden?"

Dani clasped her hands together to keep her from pumping her fists. "From the second trailer, the locked one we picked up and drove back home to Iowa. There was an envelope hidden by the jack. Jim knew it was there—he went right to it and opened it. He tried to hide it from me."

Jim blew out a gust of air that sounded like a strangled laugh.

The judge shot him a look before redirecting Dani. "Go on, Ms. Holden."

Dani nodded. "He didn't want me to see what was in the envelope, so he held it close to his chest. But then he had to open it to get the BOL—a bill of lading. We needed it to get the trailer released and back on the road for the guy Jim met in Hannibal. And even though I didn't touch it, myself, I am ninety-nine percent certain that the paper wadded inside the envelope was cash."

She watched Jim to see how her revelation landed, but he was whispering with Anderson's intern. Still, Dani couldn't help it: she grinned. It felt so good to allow herself to share out loud what she'd had to keep inside for these past long months.

After that small victory, Dani was excused for the day. As she said goodbye to the prosecution team, the energy that had buoyed her performance quickly faded.

Her drive home was uneventful.

Up in her bedroom, Dani shed her blouse. As the silky material slid over her head, it teased out the tears that she'd been holding inside. Round, hot droplets splattered her chest. She dropped her head into her hands.

The release through the back of her shoulders calmed her. After a while, she found a bit more energy to finish her day.

Cody romped to the barn at a quick pace when he was released from the house. But instead of continuing his rounds as usual, he returned to sit next to Dani as she fed and groomed Scout.

The scar over Scout's shoulder was healing. The naked skin pulled together in rippled puckers, but Dani believed it would all be hidden once Scout's new coat grew back over it.

"And it hasn't hurt your movement, has it?" Dani reminded the horse, who closed her long lashes and allowed herself to lean into the soft bristles of Dani's curry brush.

Dani told Cody and Scout about the trial, about how she'd had to tell herself to breathe and not cry, how hard it was not to anticipate her answers to the horrible questions before they'd hit her, how being face-to-face with Donna and Jim was so much harder than what she'd expected.

She told them that she was sad, so sad.

Both were extra responsive to her presence, keeping themselves near as she moved through her chores.

After filling Scout's water trough, Dani and the dog went back into the house. She locked the door, thankful for the new safety glass. It was supposed to be unbreakable.

She wasn't hungry. For the first time in many weeks, Dani went straight up the stairs to bed and slept until her alarm woke her the following morning.

The next day, Dani searched for Pete's truck in the parking lot, as it was his turn to testify.

She found him in the hallway outside the courtroom, wearing a suitcoat that looked a size too small over one of his "library shirts," a white Oxford with a buttoned collar. His jeans had been exchanged for khakis, but he wore his usual hiking boots.

"How're you feeling?" Dani's greeting came out crooked and scratchy. She coughed and tried again.

Pete closed his eyes. "Like I'm going to throw up."

"Hang in there, bud. It'll be over soon. And good luck." As she finished her pep talk, she noticed Harrington and Denise coming up the staircase to the courtroom. The ADA's assistant carried a large portfolio.

Dani sneaked into the courtroom behind the prosecution team. She didn't know if she'd be allowed inside, but figured she'd rather be asked to leave than ask if she could stay. She saw that Anderson was already seated and waiting. He was wearing yesterday's suit, but his attitude was refreshed and reenergized, evidenced by the sudden smile and nod he gave her as she entered.

Dani sat up front, as far away from his team as she could get. Searching the other side of the gallery, she located Donna sitting by herself in one of the back rows.

After Jim was brought in from behind the steel door and uncuffed, Judge Whitby reminded the attorneys about his expectations, then reviewed his instructions for the day's events. Then the bailiff called Pete.

Donna's brother stalked down the center aisle to the witness stand. To Dani, he looked pale and tense, his fists clenched at each side.

Once sworn in, he sat, but his upper body vibrated with the way he jostled his knee.

Observing that Pete's nerves wouldn't allow for a long testimony, Harrington started his line of questioning right in the middle of the events.

"Mr. Lund, we know your sister is the defendant's spouse. How long have you known your brother-in-law?"

"Huh." Pete's derision was acute. "Too long."

Oh crap, Dani thought. That wasn't going to go over well.

She was correct. The judge was unamused.

"Mr. Lund, you need to know that I don't tolerate nonsense. Answer the question, and don't elaborate."

Pete shuddered and tried again. "I've known him since the start of this summer. My sister, too," he added, his eyes popping open. "She's only known him for a few months."

Dani looked back for Donna's reaction to her brother's comment. Donna's head was down, like she was busy digging in her purse.

"What is his occupation?" The ADA didn't look very confident about the question. And in fact, Anderson objected.

But not before Pete started to answer. "He's a dru—"

Now Judge Whitby looked to be just moments away from losing his temper. "Mr. Lund? Do that again, and you'll be joining Mr. Kelly in a cell overnight. Got it?"

"Okay." Pete sighed. "He says he's a trucker."

Harrington continued. "What vehicle or vehicles do you know Jim Kelly to own, drive, or use?"

Pete had this answer ready. "He has two rigs used for moving cattle and hogs. But whether he drives them himself or has others drive for him, I don't know. And he has a pickup."

"Have you ridden in any of Mr. Kelly's vehicles?"

"I have. In the pickup."

"On what date, please?"

At the defense table, Anderson rifled through his papers, his mouth a grim line.

"Maybe five times, between the Fourth of July and the beginning of August. My sister used his truck sometimes to pick me up after work, before I moved out of her house."

"Anything unusual about any of those rides?"

Pete looked like a wildcat eager to pounce on a rabbit. "Yes! The last time I rode with her, I was digging through the glovebox for a napkin, and there was a bunch of cash in there, in an envelope, under some other stuff."

"Then what happened?"

"My sister saw it, right after I did. She seemed surprised. She—"

"Objection!" the defense called out. "Interpretation?"

"Sustained," the judge replied.

Harrington asked Pete to rephrase his answer.

"Um," Pete began, searching for the right words. "She said she didn't know what the envelope was and that she hadn't seen it before. She—her face—she looked upset. Sad. I asked her—"

Jim's attorney left his seat for this one. "Objection. Again, he can't interpret her emotional response."

This time, when she turned to gauge Donna's reaction, Dani couldn't locate her: her spot in the back was vacant.

Looking back to Pete, his frustration was apparent on his tense expression. He'd started bouncing his knee again, making the witness stand wiggle.

She thought about the wad of cash that showed up at her house, plus the cash she likely saw in that envelope Jim tried to hide, plus this money Pete saw in Jim's truck. Apparently, there were huge stacks of cash everywhere.

No wonder Donna could buy the café . . .

Judge Whitby's low voice returned Dani to the scene in front of her. "Mr. Lund—just facts, please. Not thoughts. Facts."

Pete flinched away from the judge. "I kept asking her about it, where it came from and all that. She stopped the truck, grabbed it from me, and put it into her purse. Then we went home."

"Did you ask her about the money after that?" Harrington asked.

Pete nodded. "I did. But she tried to convince me it wasn't money. She claimed it was a collection of receipts Jim was keeping for his business."

"Can you share your response to her claim?" Harrington continued.

A grin escaped before Pete could stop it. "Probably not. The judge already told me to keep things civil."

To Dani's surprise, someone on Jim's side laughed.

Judge Whitby was not amused, however. "Last warning, Mr. Lund."

Pete sighed again. "We never talked about it again. I moved out after that." He rubbed his chin. "But I know what I saw. It was money—that's a fact." This last statement seemed to bring him a momentary sense of vindication.

The prosecution's side, finished, turned the witness over to the defense. Pete sat up in his chair, his eyes sparkling like he was ready for the competition.

Dani straightened up, too, but her adjustment was to allow her to better see the area behind her. Donna was still absent from the courtroom.

Where is she?

She shook away her observation and resettled for the next phase.

Jim's attorney wanted to revisit one of Pete's previous answers. "You stated that you don't know if Mr. Kelly drives the rigs himself or has other drivers doing the routes for him. Is that correct?"

Pete confirmed this.

"Have you, personally, ever seen Jim Kelly behind the wheel of either rig you say he owns?"

Pete shook his head, his anger clear on his face. "No. I have not."

"No further questions, Judge. Thank you." Anderson tipped his pile of papers back into a manila folder and smiled to himself.

Dani's breath ceased. She realized, with this back-and-forth, that this was Jim's loophole, his escape. The defense was contending that, outside of the trip to Missouri with Dani and Donna, Jim never drove the rigs himself and therefore had no knowledge that they were being used to transport heroin. All the defense needed to do, then, was paint Jim as an unwitting patsy, rather than a willing accomplice, on that one trip.

Dani's jaw tightened. She hugged her arms against herself as if physically stopping her own objection from escaping out into the open courtroom.

Hugging herself also staved off the trembling that threatened to erupt. She even more deeply understood now that the entire case against Jim was on her shoulders. She was the only one who could prove that he knew exactly what he was hauling on that trip—as well as what she was hauling on the solo trip.

Harrington stood for his redirect. "Mr. Lund," he began. "Going back to your sister's relationship with the defendant—when did you learn that she planned to marry Mr. Kelly?"

Pete laughed. "I didn't. No one did. No one knew she was 'planning' to marry him—until she came back from Vegas with a ring."

Harrington asked his final question. "Before you moved out, did Jim Kelly spend nights in the house?"

Anderson started to object, but the judge waved Harrington on.

"Yes. He was with her every night except for the times he said he was 'on the road.'"

Dani smiled. Harrington closed the loophole about Jim driving. "Thank you, Mr. Lund," Harrington said. "You're excused."

Pete bounded down from the stand, stripping off his sport coat as he went. He didn't look at Dani.

The thick double door he thrust open thwacked shut after he stormed out.

Dani's crossed arms grew chilled. The air left behind Pete's exit seemed icy.

She knew he wouldn't return. He wouldn't in the courtroom, when she was recalled to the stand. When the prosecution would tease out the final pieces of her testimony.

She was alone now.

Dani was recalled after the morning break. She still hadn't seen Donna, but in a way, she was glad. The testimony yet to come would be grueling; not having to see Donna's face might make the task a tad easier.

Harrington walked her through the events of her first trip, getting her to confirm that, indeed, Jim drove the rig from Crestview to the stockyard, and then drove from around Hannibal back to Crestview again.

He then transitioned to the second trip, Dani's solo route.

"What arrangements were made for you to take the second trip on your own?"

"Mr. Kelly said he couldn't take the route himself. He asked me to do it instead."

"Did you talk about payment?"

"We did. He said it'd be cash. He offered a percentage, but I asked for a flat fee."

"How were you paid?"

"The money showed up on my porch. In an envelope." She tried not to elaborate.

Harrington removed his glasses. Anticipating what Anderson would likely ask on the redirect, Harrington cut through the cord himself.

"Do you know where the money came from?" He waited behind his table, patient and friendly.

Despite the attorney's calm demeanor, Dani couldn't look at him any longer. "No."

She knew what came next were questions about the packet that mysteriously showed up at her door while Jim was in the county jail, awaiting his trial.

"So, you didn't see anyone drop it off? Didn't recognize any handwriting, or . . . ?" Harrington tapped his silver frames against his free hand, but the smile he showed Dani was pleasant. Calm.

Nevertheless, the courtroom was silent. Paralyzed. Waiting, not one person moved. Not even Jim.

Dani's breath was ragged as she inhaled. "No." She swallowed to clear her throat. "There wasn't any writing on the envelope. No note inside it either."

The ADA slipped his glasses back on. "According to county records, Jim Kelly was in a cell when that money appeared at your home. Could it have come from someone in his stead?"

Dani hated this question, hated the truth it was ferreting out, hated being this close to needing to name Donna as the person who likely delivered the cash.

"It smelled strongly of his cologne. But yes, I guess he could've had it sent to me—" She was relieved when Anderson interrupted. He didn't bother to get up from his chair.

"Request to strike? Conjecture."

The judge nodded. "Accepted." He flicked a finger to the court stenographer. "Strike that last question, please."

Harrington tried again. "Did you see anyone deliver the money to your home?"

"No."

"Did you hear of anything in the community, perhaps from—"

This time, Anderson struggled to his feet. "Redirect?"

Judge Whitby recognized the redirect with a nod. "Go on," he added.

Harrington inhaled a quick breath. It was the first time he'd looked nervous, Dani noticed. Then he composed himself and asked again.

"Did you talk to Donna Lund Kelly about the money you received at your home while Jim Kelly was in jail?"

"I did not."

"Thank you." His relief was obvious. He connected Donna to the money the best way he could, short of an outright accusation.

Dani's relief was obvious, too. She exhaled, squared her shoulders, and prepared herself for the sequence that was about to come next.

"Why did you agree to take the trailer to Missouri by yourself, Ms. Holden?" Harrington asked.

"I needed the income, and I thought this was the best way to get it. But . . . but I didn't think Donna knew Jim was using his trailers for that purpose." Tears threatened, but she refused to blink.

Jim laughed, then shrugged. His humor seemed misplaced; his attorneys ignored him, as well.

Denise, Harrington's paralegal, got up from behind the table. She removed an enlarged color photo from the portfolio at her feet, then crossed the open area to hand it to Harrington. He asked Judge

Whitby that it be included as an exhibit, then positioned it onto an easel so that those in the courtroom could see.

The first picture showed a stack of bills, about an inch thick, with a twenty on top. The twenty featured a small blue X in the upper right corner. "Do you recognize these bills?"

"Yes, if it's the money that showed up at my place," Dani replied.

The attorney confirmed this. "Have you had any other experience with this marking?"

Dani said, "No. I mean, not until Jim Kelly started coming around."

"Please explain your answer."

"Jim has the same marking tattooed on the inside of his wrist."

"Oh, what the hell, now—" Jim's complaint was hushed from someone at the defense table. The judge asked for quiet, then directed Dani to continue.

"It was also painted on that deer, that dead deer, that someone hung in my front yard. And it was printed on a bunch of little baggies I found in Mr. Randolph's trailer. The drug trailer."

As Dani recited her list, the ADA pointed to various photos on the easel that confirmed her claims. "And another person in town— someone I know pretty well—got the same tattoo, after Jim came. Matthew White, the one we call "Tot", the one who attacked me in my barn? He has that same blue X." Dani cleared her throat. "He's not the same person anymore. He's using heroin. I'm sure of it."

Anderson appeared livid at her response, though Dani couldn't tell whether it was genuine emotion or a calculated attempt to derail her testimony.

"In what capacity does this witness offer this information?" he sputtered. "Is she a medical professional?" He looked like he was about to combust.

Judge Whitby asked him to approach the bench. Harrington strode up as well, and the two attorneys quickly cited cases to support their conflicting viewpoints. Apparently, Harrington's argument won out.

The judge dismissed them. "Ms. Holden? Please continue."

Anderson mumbled something about an appeal as he returned to his seat. But Harrington gave Dani a quick smile—a shot of courage to keep going.

"Ms. Holden, would you tell the court, please, what experience you have that would inform the opinion you've just shared?"

"I was engaged to a heroin addict," Dani revealed. "My fiancé changed—like, into a completely different person, I mean—when he started using it. All he cared about was finding his next hit. Every action, every interaction, was motivated by his need for that drug. Horse, he called it."

"So how does your neighbor, Tot White, remind you of your fiancé?" Harrington asked.

"He's been acting the same way—distracted from things that used to matter, oblivious to his dangerous behaviors and bad choices, so desperate for a fix that he'll hurt someone he cares about," Dani replied. "Like my fiancé." She looked at her hands, folded in her lap. "I've seen it." She closed her eyes. "It's what happens when you ride the wild horse."

The ADA's voice startled Dani back from her recollections. She asked him to repeat the question.

"Do you think Mr. Kelly knew there were drugs in the trailer?" he repeated. "That first one, on the trip you and Donna Lund Kelly took with him to Missouri?"

"Objection!" Anderson tried to salvage what he could.

The judge interceded. "Try again, Mr. Harrington."

The ADA nodded. "Sorry." He turned back to Dani. "What did you observe that would make you think that Mr. Kelly knew what he was hauling on that first trip?"

This is it, Dani told herself, recognizing where the line of questioning leads. *Here we go.*

Dani testified about the overpowering smells of the animals, including the odors they produced as they relieved themselves in the trailers, on the ramps, and on each other. She explained how it took three showers of scrubbing for the stench to fade away.

Just before Anderson began to object about relevance, Dani went for the gold: "I know from Mr. Randolph's trailer that heroin has a distinct smell—vinegary—and I think Jim used dirty stock trailers to mask the scent of the drugs he hauled."

Jim shouted this time, his words unintelligible.

Though equally apoplectic, Anderson tried to calm his client while simultaneously lodging a complaint to exclude Dani's opinion.

"Enough! Enough!" Judge Whitby knocked his empty coffee cup against his table in rhythm with his words. "I've heard enough for the morning."

He placed his cup to one side and trained his severe countenance first on those behind the public defender's table, then at those behind the prosecutors' table. "Be prepared to finish this portion this afternoon. I want to keep things moving in a good way, now, through the end of the day."

He didn't wait for his bailiff's traditional dismissal. Instead, he gathered his robes and escaped to his office outside the strained courtroom.

As they had the day before, Dani's team adjourned to the same conference room for lunch and for a quick realignment of their afternoon objectives.

The break passed in what felt like minutes. In the final moments, Dani detoured to the ladies' room. She was shocked to see how worn she appeared in the mirror. She pinched color back into her cheeks, tucked her blouse more neatly into her black slacks, and readjusted her necklace so that the clasp was hidden at the back of her neck.

A stall door opened, and Donna emerged.

The oxygen in Dani's chest escaped with a muted hiss.

Donna's heels clicked across the linoleum to the shared wash basin. She turned on a tap, pushed up her sleeves, and placed her hands into the water.

"I didn't think you'd say anything."

Frozen, Dani waited.

"About the trailer. Trailers, I guess; there was more than one."

Dani drew a shuddering breath. "He asked, Donna. I had to answer."

Donna straightened up from the sink and shook the water from her hands. She positioned herself slightly behind Dani, blocking her exit back to the hallway.

They stared at each other in the mirror.

"Couldn't you've let that go?" Donna's question was sharp.

"No. Not anymore. Can you let it go? With all that's happened?" Dani's words had pointed edges, too.

Donna's expression drew in. Her mouth pursed. "I don't know what you're talking about."

Dani bit her lip, which made her think about Scout and the pain her horse endured, all because of Tot's drug-induced attack. "Did you know what Jim was hauling? What you had me hauling, when the two of you sent me to Missouri?"

The energy around the two women drew tight.

"Would you have even told me?"

A smirk crept across Donna's demeanor. Her bearing reflected Jim Kelly, her husband, the shark-faced schemer.

"Wild horses couldn't drag it outta me."

This time, Dani couldn't form a reply.

Just then, another woman entered the restroom. The steely tension between Donna and Dani, taut as a piano wire, snapped as easily as a cobweb.

Donna eased out of the woman's path, and in doing so, cleared space for Dani to exit.

But Dani was frozen. Stunned. The other woman disappeared behind one of the stall doors.

"Poor Jim." Donna's voice was so low it was like she was talking to herself.

Dani struggled to make out her next words.

"Class 1 Narcotics. What's that, a minimum of ten years?" Her face regained its usual healthy glow. Her smile looked real again.

She winked at Dani.

A toilet flushed, and the other woman emerged.

Dani used the opportunity to escape. Her heart had resumed ticking, its frantic pace propelling her race back into the courtroom. She sat, quickly, up close near the prosecutor's table, as the adrenaline dissipating from her skin left her cold. Clammy.

Realization clicked into place. Or perhaps confirmation—confirmation of something her intuition had sensed but couldn't articulate.

Donna knew.

Harrington resumed questioning Dani after lunch. He was the only one in the entire courtroom who still looked fresh and energetic.

"Ms. Holden, let's go back to that first trip, the one you made with both Jim Kelly and Donna Lund." He hesitated. "Donna Lund Kelly."

Dani didn't know whether he forgot her married name naturally or by design; she suspected it was the latter.

"You stated that it's your opinion"—the attorney stressed this word to make a point—"that Jim Kelly knew that his trailers contained illegal drugs." Harrington hesitated, but when there was no response from Jim's team, he pushed on. "Would you share how you came to this conclusion?"

She nodded. "After he hooked up the second trailer, the one the man at the Subway wanted him to pick up, Jim unlocked it and went into it. He—"

Judge Whitby interrupted her explanation. "Excuse me, Ms. Holden, but I need some clarification here."

Anderson had been about to interrupt at this point as well, but when he realized that the judge had gotten there first, he retreated.

Dani waited for Judge Whitby's question.

"What did you observe, exactly, to make you think that Jim Kelly went inside the trailer?" he asked.

"After he pulled ahead a few feet, he told me he needed to relieve himself, so he went to the back. I couldn't see him in the side mirror or by looking behind me, but I heard things, like keys jingling and the door squealing, and then the trailer dipped and bounced like he stepped inside."

Harrington took the follow-up and continued to pursue this angle. "Did you see him enter the trailer?"

Dani faced forward again. "No, but I felt it when he hopped back down, and I heard the trailer door shut again."

"You testified yesterday that the container, the trailer, was locked. How was Mr. Kelly able to open a locked container?"

Dani swallowed. "He got the keys from that man at the Subway in Hannibal."

"She don't know that! What the—" This outburst came from Jim, his cocky composure vanished.

"You mentioned this man yesterday as well," Harrington said. "Can you describe now why you believe he provided the keys to unlock the trailer?"

"When he was talking to Jim, that man was mad—"

Dani stopped herself there. She tried for a more precise picture based on facts. "That is, he looked angry, and he poked Jim in the chest. Then he dropped some keys onto the ground, and I saw Jim pick them up. When Jim returned to the rig, he told me and Donna that this man wanted him to haul back the trailer for him."

Those behind the table on Jim's side huddled together. They paid no attention as she continued her explanation.

"Donna saw him, the other man at the Subway, too. When I asked her about it later, though, she—she said she didn't remember." Dani was aware that she'd probably said too much, but for once, it felt good to let out what she'd been trying to avoid admitting.

Judge Whitby looked for Jim's team's objection, but they were still doing damage control and evidently weren't keeping pace. "Let's just focus on the questions, Ms. Holden. No need for elaboration."

Harrington brought her back on track. "Did you see him again, this other man who confronted Jim and gave him the keys?"

"Yes, I did. I watched him follow us from Hannibal until we reached the stockyard exit." She allowed herself a smile. "He probably didn't know if he could trust Jim either."

The judge cleared his throat.

"Just one more area to clear up." The ADA checked the papers on his table. "Are you okay to continue?"

Dani nodded. "I am. I'm okay."

Eager to set his snare, Harrington left his notes and placed himself in the open area in front of the center aisle. "Did you know that the trailer you helped drive back to Iowa, the first time, contained heroin?"

It was almost time for Dani to turn over the last card she'd been holding. "I did not."

Jim's defense team ceased their whispered conference.

Jim shot a leering wink her way.

Harrington went on. "Did you know that the trailer you drove out of the stockyard on your second trip, the solo trip, contained heroin?"

Dani's pulse beat faster. She didn't dare to look away from Harrington's face, desperate to glean any extra strength she could from his nod and his smile.

"I did."

Jim cursed. Anderson grabbed his upper arm and whispered at him.

"Does your client need a break, Mr. Anderson?" Judge Whitby's steely voice held no warmth and little patience.

Jim glared; his knee pumped up and down, under his table. Anderson shook his head. "No, no thanks," he muttered.

"How did you know that trailer contained heroin?" Harrington's voice was calm.

"Agent Wahlquist told me, when he asked me to make the second trip as part of the BCA's sting against Jim Kelly."

This time, Jim couldn't help himself. He leapt up, flipping his chair over behind him, and shot his outburst directly at Dani.

"She said ya didn't know! Said ya wouldn't have the guts to question it!"

The defense attorneys encased their client in a huddle, but they couldn't quiet his diatribe.

"You had one job! Easy money!" Jim's face dramatically reddened; the veins on his temples were angry scarlet welts.

His team realized that the fabric they'd woven to support Jim's stance had ripped, and that a body, Jim's body, was about to fall through the gash.

"Bitch!" he screamed.

The bailiff inserted himself into the knot of people. He cuffed Jim's wrists. Under the group's combined force, Jim sat. Spittle he'd cast off with his last ejection clung to one side of his round chin.

Dani squeezed the front of the witness stand; she was ready to run if she needed to. But she didn't want to.

She wanted to see this through.

A strange calm settled over her. She wanted this man to learn a lesson—or at the minimum, to pay for his mistakes. For the sake of Tot and the many other faceless addicts infected by the poison Jim carried, those who now carried the mark, whether etched in ink or hidden inside, of the "easy money" that the selfish, greedy man in front of her worshipped.

"Ms. Holden?" The judge's voice was kind as he claimed Dani's attention. "You're dismissed. Thank you."

In truth, there was nothing left inside Dani to form an appropriate response. Over the last two days, every word she'd uttered had been selected with gravity. Each word's importance had been evaluated and discerned at record speeds before she dared share it out loud.

Dani waited for the bailiff to accompany her before she stepped down from the witness box. She wanted the man beside her in case Jim erupted again.

Though free to leave, once they exited the courtroom, Dani asked for another moment. The bailiff left her on a bench just outside the double doors. "You going to be all right?"

She nodded. She just needed her heart to keep beating and her legs to keep her moving until she was safely back home.

Again, Jim's outburst echoed through the wisps of the facts she tried to connect.

Donna knew what he was hauling, she decided.

Donna used the fruits of that knowledge for her own reward—the diner. And from what Donna whispered in the restroom, she wasn't one bit concerned about her Jimmy's fate when the law caught up to him.

Dani wasn't as shocked as she probably would have been weeks or months before. The realization confirmed what had been twining through her subconscious, poking out a sharp thorn here or there to keep her questions flowing.

Dani needed rest and time to allow her hurt to settle and dissolve, of course. A friendship she'd deemed genuine and valuable had been wrenched from her, leaving a raw, gaping hole inside. And there'd still be struggle ahead: she would have to find a way to rebuild her confidence and reset her place in her community—a community consisting of people who were likely standing outside this very courthouse, talking sideways about what they'd never really know.

More than anything else, more than the scars the lies and greed had caused, Dani felt disappointed. Disappointed and exhausted.

But not beaten.

Just then, the bailiff reappeared. Surprised to see Dani still sitting there, he detoured to the bench to check on her.

"Can I get you anything, miss? You okay?" He glanced over his shoulder. "You know, there's a back exit. Would you like me to show you?"

Dani got to her feet.

"No, I'll be fine. I think I'll head out the front." She paused. "Like everyone else."

22

THE WOODEN FRAME AROUND THE FRONT WINDOW needed resealing. Wind clawing through the cracks smelled tinny, pricking Dani's face like scratchy lace.

A sudden temperature drop formed quarter-sized tufts of snow that skidded slantwise out of the taut gray clouds clipping by. Glossy black ravens clung to the pines' heaving branches, jeering each other as they rode the wind's waves.

Cody needed to go out. When she inched the front door open, the chilled air entered Dani's throat like a needled icicle. She wrapped her arms around herself and advised the dog to hurry his business and get back inside, pronto.

It was too cold to wait for him, though. She let the coiled spring pull the screen door shut before she firmly closed the heavy oak door. She locked it.

Grabbing her hooded sweatshirt, she padded back to the kitchen for a second cup of hot coffee. Now properly attired, with her hands around her steaming mug, she returned to the window and watched for the dog.

Right after the trial, Dani moved into this farmhouse, a different one owned by Mr. Randolph. It was one of the properties she used to check for him every month. It wasn't as nice as her former home.

At night, stumbling in the dark for the bathroom, she had to remind herself of the new floorplan so that she wouldn't barge into a wall or crack her knee on a table. Everything was in a new position.

Over by the outbuilding she was using as a barn, Cody was exploring. He wasn't in any hurry to come back in. He nosed around the perimeter of the mare's pen, the wind blowing his tail like a flag. He didn't mind the cold.

Scout must be camped inside her shelter, Dani decided. The small structure was mostly enclosed, but she hadn't yet organized much except water and a feed bucket for Scout. She wondered how long she could wait before going outside to throw hay. It was already after nine, but she convinced herself that she'd be more ready to tackle the temperature after she finished her second cup of "anti-freeze."

This time of year, the locals drank it all day long. Granted, winter days in the Midwest were brief, with the thin light dissolving each afternoon before 4:00 p.m., so "all day long" didn't end up being that many hours all together. Sometimes folks added a little splash of whiskey or schnapps to their cup to strengthen their resolve.

Dani sighed. She shuffled into the bedroom for her flannel-lined jeans and a warm turtleneck to layer under the hoodie, insulation against the cold fingers that tickled the back of her neck. Perched on the bed's edge, she slipped on the denims, then hopped to her feet to fasten the zipper and button.

Partially emptied cardboard boxes mocked her from the bathroom and the corner of her new bedroom, waiting for her to find the energy to continue unpacking. She told herself she needed to figure out where things should go before she finished this task.

In truth, she was still feeling stunned from the demands of the trial and its aftermath.

Jim Kelly's new home was the Potosi Correctional Center, where he'd be staying for the next sixty months, the minimum sentence for a first offense. She wondered if he'd get out early for good behavior but doubted he had the self-control or the humility required for that gift to be bestowed upon him.

Donna was gone, too. Word got around that she'd bought the diner with Jim's illegal funds. The regulars who'd eaten breakfast there every morning for years upon years began going to the coffee counter at the Stop-N-Save instead. When only a handful of diners, all out-of-towners, showed up for her next Theme Night, Donna got the message.

The café closed for good the next day. The windows were boarded up, the parking lot closed off by traffic cones and long yellow tape. A large white "For Sale" sign was planted firmly into the snow in front of the property a week later.

She never said goodbye.

Pete talked to Donna at Christmas. She told Pete she was hunting for a little restaurant or diner someplace else to start again, maybe southwestern Minnesota or somewhere in the Dakotas, once she sold Susie's Café and the house she'd been left by their parents. She claimed that she didn't want to come back to Crestview, didn't want to "stir things up again", but most folks said it was more to do with the authorities wanting to question her and her involvement in Jim's activities than simply avoiding her hometown.

The trial also left its ruinous mark on the White family. Dani hadn't returned to the courtroom that afternoon to hear Tot's testimony, but Pete did. Enduring the first throes of detox, young Tot didn't have the ability to concentrate. He could barely sit still, much less follow the trains of thought required to address the questions. His answers swam somewhere beyond his mental grasp.

It was so sad, Pete said, to see Tot like that. And watching Bud and Missy witness their son's testimony was enough to break the most loyal heart. To make things worse, someone saw Tot panhandling in Decorah soon after, so it seemed he checked himself out of rehab.

Dani remembered Tater, the Whites' other son, who died in an ATV accident. Bud and Missy must have felt like they'd lost not one but both sons now.

Then there was the man Dani had seen talking to Jim at the rest stop. The one with the Mercedes. After Jim's trial, he was located, charged, and sentenced to twenty years for his role in the trafficking. The heavy sentence was due mostly to the large amount of heroin being transported, but it was also due to his prior convictions.

The man refused to give up those he worked for, despite offers of a reduced sentence and transfer to a facility near his children in Chicago. She knew that there were people above this man in the cartel. For that matter, she knew there were people below him, too, including some people still living in the Crestview area. This fact completely unsettled Dani.

Wahlquist told Dani there wasn't anything to worry about. Their names had been struck from all affidavits and documents, and the trial itself had been closed.

Dani didn't believe him.

She decided for herself that it was time to leave her leased quarter-section. The process of packing and schlepping her possessions to the new place took all of two days. She didn't remember any of it.

Her mail was redirected to the post office, which would help keep her physical address out of public record. She was thinking about getting some of those security alarms, too—the kind that hung from a doorknob or window frame, more affordable than a wired system.

Dani sighed again. The weather outside her window hadn't improved. Little snowdrifts collected like mounds of white ashes under the low-hanging tree branches next to Scout's shelter.

She trudged to the front closet, bundled herself into her boots and parka, and went out. The wind had carved the irregular terrain around each fence post to a pristine, level smoothness. Chilled air rimed her mare's nostrils and the base of her tail. Scout stamped one front foot, impatient for her grain.

Reaching through the bars to touch the horse's shoulder, Dani checked for heat or possible infection. The horse didn't run from her, but since the night she'd been cut by Tot's knife, she'd lost a good amount of the trust she'd begun to develop.

"Good enough, girl," Dani murmured, pushing up her knit cap to see the area more clearly. "We'll both be better by spring."

She wondered if the mare believed her. She wondered how long it would take for her own scars, the ones inside her, to heal as well.

The winter months finally passed. Tender green shoots poked out from every field as Dani set out for the place where that strange old double-headed tree once stood. The tree she'd helped cut down almost three years ago.

But she wasn't farming this spring. Instead, she was enrolled in the first level of training for the dispatcher position John told her about. Although she'd been too late to fill the temporary slot, she hoped to be one of three new dispatchers to be hired in June by the department, part of a new federally funded initiative to get more responders out into the rural areas.

The instruction schedule filled her days and gave her purpose and a means of moving past the trial. And it left her weekends free for hiking and helping Scout.

Regaining the horse's trust was a process that took more time and courage than Dani imagined she possessed. They had to backtrack to regain what they'd learned before Scout's attack. Through hours of patient and slow repetitions, Dani and Scout reviewed each task and skill with a concentrated awareness, one at a time. Case in point, they'd just resumed their former daily routine of brushing and hoof work. Dani chose to see it as a victory.

Scout's laceration healed to a long, raised scar. Breathing in the animal's warm scent and being present in each moment helped Dani to heal and gain strength as well.

Lilly died after Christmas, just one week after Jamie and April flew to California to spend a bittersweet holiday with her. They knew then that their time together was limited. It seemed to Dani that Lilly willed herself to live long enough to welcome her family to her home, before agreeing to pass into her new adventure.

Lilly's will bequeathed her estate to Jamie, with gifts marked for April's college fund, a nest egg for Gene, and a little cash for Dani.

Dani didn't hear anything from Donna. She didn't try to contact her, though, either.

To her thinking, it was on Donna to make the first move. Donna knew what was in those trailers. Donna was willing to sacrifice their relationship, to misuse their friendship and put Dani in danger, to get what she wanted.

Yet Dani realized that the fracture of their friendship didn't sting as much as it once had. The sharp edges of her anger and confusion had begun to smooth out. As spring settled in, Dani remembered more of the good than the bad.

Much of her resentment seeped away with the snowfall. She figured she was given another opportunity to practice what it meant to be herself in the midst of things she could not control.

Dani, Jamie, and April brought Lilly back to rest where her tree once stood: the tree that sheltered a younger Lilly as she dreamed and loved; the tree where her son's father had been hung.

Dani was the first to arrive, surprised to find a bench made of looped and weathered metal at the base of the massive circular scar left behind when the tree had been cut down and carted away. She had no idea who brought it to this place, an unremarkable area in the center of two adjacent fields. Someone who knew Lilly, she surmised. Someone who knew more than they'd allowed the rest of Crestview to figure out.

Regardless of the bench's origin, there was peace, as Dani sat. From this place, she saw that a new neighbor had put up white fencing across the hill. Two horses grazed, side by side. A green tractor pulling a disc growled from her right, a farmer eager to get things growing again.

Birds dipped and spun overhead, intoxicated by warmer weather and the promises this turn of the cycle brought with it. The sky was unblemished, washed in cornflower blue.

She shuffled her feet across the rough grooves on the slab of the trunk and tried to count the rings. Some loops looked tightly bound, while others stretched and lazed wide apart, an apt illustration of the prosperity and want of variety of seasons.

Dust advanced from the east along the gravel road. A small car skidded to a stop behind Dani's truck. Lilly's son and granddaughter got out and crossed through the cornfield's tented furrows to the bench, their heads bent together.

April placed a brown ceramic urn, nothing gilded or fancy, onto the bench beside Dani. "What do you think we should say?" she asked her father.

His dark sunglasses hid what he couldn't bear to convey.

Dani rose. She lifted the urn, holding it close in her arms. "This is your place, Lilly," she said, before reaching out to include April in a hug, sharing comfort for this last goodbye. "You wanted to return here, but it's so hard"—she swallowed—"so hard to let you go."

Lilly's son reached for his mother's urn. He gently removed the top, but he could go no further.

His daughter took the container from his hands. She tipped it so that plumes of silt and spirit spilled into the breeze and onto the trunk's flat surface, glittering and sparkling in the sun.

Dani returned to the bench. Jamie and April joined her, sitting knee to knee. Together, the three shared the noise and sunlight and energy of the growing things around them.

No one spoke, but words weren't needed. The gentle forces of this holy place began to stir, its magic working to purify the misunderstandings, the unfair judgments, the anger that cleaved friend from friend, mother from son, lover from lover.

For the next tender moments, it served them best to sit here together, close to the place that Lilly loved the most.

23

She slides the silver bit between my teeth. She takes her time, her voice soft. I can tell she doesn't want to rush me. She's different than the ones before.

She eases her ribcage up against mine. I can feel her heartbeat. Fast. Her hand smooths my spine in long strokes, slow, careful not to rub my hair the wrong way. She breathes, taking slow, long swallows of the sunshine and the birdsong and grass poking up from the pasture.

She grasps the reins and a hank of my mane, down low by my shoulder. She balances her other palm on my hip. She's perched on an overturned bucket to climb onto my back, but she hasn't done that yet.

The little four-legger, the nosy one that makes such a racket, whistles out from the barn and startles her. She says words to him, but she's not mad. His plumy tail whips back and forth, and he smiles at her.

He trots to me and sniffs at my leg. No smile now. All business.

I get his warning: he's watching me. He doesn't want me to hurt her.

I won't. I wouldn't. She's the only one who's ever cared for me. Even when I ran away, when that blade cut me, she wasn't angry. Instead of beating me, she sang to me. I think she thought it was her fault that I got hurt.

But that pain is gone now. I feel whole and healthy—young, even. I have a new shelter and a new pasture. But she's the same. My food, my water, her visits are the touchstones of every new day.

But now her pulse quickens. I wait and listen for her to loosen her breath. She's on her toes. She gathers herself, then springs onto my broad back.

She makes a happy sound when she lands. I think she's surprised. Her words come out again, this time from behind my ears.

I turn to see her fist still clenching the ropes and my mane with both hands, but her face is shining. She holds her body proudly.

She's light. Her bones rest on either side of my spine; her legs twine around my heart. I wish she would let herself settle onto me. I will take care of her. I'll make sure I stay beneath her.

We make a circle together, the four-legger alongside. She loosens. Her seat, her hands on my lines, her breathing, all her stiffness and strain let go.

We circle again, and another time, before she pulls on the reins. She wants me to stop.

She slides off and wraps her arms around my neck. I feel moisture seep into my coat, and I reach around to touch her, to let her know that she doesn't have to be afraid anymore.

She leaves me so she can free the gate that separates us from the open. We walk through together.

There's a fallen branch ahead. It's thick, so she steps onto it, gathers my lines and my mane, and hoists herself onto my back again.

Her heart thuds. I can feel the blood pulse through her body as her shivering legs cradle my ribs. We move toward the trees. She tries to match her movement and balance with my steps. At the windbreak, she slides off again.

I don't expect this, and I look to comfort her, but she isn't afraid.

Resting one hand on my flank, she turns back to the open field, the endless rolling hills and the rolling creek and the growing spaces where no fence or lines can hold us in.

We're going to be okay.

NOTE FROM THE AUTHOR:

Many OTTBs (Off the Track Thoroughbreds) are often overlooked for a second career like dressage or eventing or trail riding when their racing careers come to an end. Currently, there are no federal animal welfare laws regulating the treatment of these animals while they're on the farm or being transported. While we hope they're treated humanely as they transition, many come to a sad end.

My first horse was a chestnut OTTB gelding named Prince. He taught me what it meant to move softly, speak quietly, and have intention—every ride was a training opportunity! Scout from "Wild Horses" is based on another OTTB we knew who also went on after racing to become a broodmare.

I became aware of the Retired Racehorse Project (RRP) before I wrote "The Witness Tree" in 2018. A portion of every sale of that book has been donated to RRP, and I'll continue this practice with "Wild Horses".

The mission statement of RRP is as follows:

> The RRP exists to facilitate placement of Thoroughbred ex-racehorses in second careers by increasing demand for them in equestrian sports and serving the farms, trainers, and organizations that transition them.

If you're interested, please go to www.therrp.org . I'm so glad that more people are getting involved in preventing the premature deaths of these glorious animals.

ACKNOWLEDGEMENTS:

I've enjoyed meeting many readers through various Book Clubs, and I'd like to thank you all for your thoughts, interpretations, and ideas for Dani and Lilly. I hope you enjoy "Wild Horses" and that you'll invite me to visit your group again soon! Please contact me at amyp5204@gmail.com and we'll set a date.

Thanks to Angie Wiechmann, who is infinitely more than an editor: a co-conspirator? Teacher? Definitely now a friend.

To Mom, Janelle, Ellie, Marcia, Sanna, Mike, and Lorna, thank you for being my beta readers. Your time, suggestions, and support mean the world to me.

Thank you to Kati, my proofreader, who is also an amazing daughter and human.

Lastly, thanks to Dmytri for the time, space, and patience required to live with a writer. Love you!

ABOUT THE AUTHOR:

Amy Pendino, a Minnesota native, lives on a small horse farm. She also wrote the award-winning novel "The Witness Tree" which explores rural life and small-town crime.

She taught middle school English for a number of years, played keyboards for a local band, waitressed, worked as a secretary, sang backup (once) for an international star, and helped over thirty baby horses make their way into the world.

A frequent book club visitor, she's a member of the Twin Cities chapter of Sisters in Crime. Her other writing has been published in regional anthologies, magazines, and reviews. You can find more information at www.amypendino.com .